SECRETS
OF THE
MIDWIFE

ANN ORMSBY

Helping talented writers publish exceptional books

Secrets of the Midwife

Printed in the United States of America.
For information, address
Acorn Publishing, LLC
3943 Irvine Blvd. Ste. 218, Irvine, CA 92602

www.acornpublishingllc.com

Interior design by Kat Ross
Cover design by Damonza

ISBN-13: 979-8-88528-158-4 (paperback)
Library of Congress Control Number: 2026900730

For Lois
My best friend for life.
Thanks for always supporting me.

1

ANABEL

I am sitting in the little park situated between the town clerk's office where happy couples come rushing down the steps, laughing and kissing after tying the knot, and the family court where some of them will end up, when things go badly. As I eat my lunch, I chuckle to myself at the irony of these two tall, brick buildings facing each other like powerful gods who already know our fate, providing what we need when we need it.

The thick scent of the candied hazelnuts cooking in a nearby vendor cart wafts over me in the cool April breeze. I pull the collar of my trench coat up around my neck and tighten the knot in my silk scarf. Collecting the wrapper from my sandwich, I put it back in the brown paper bag as my eyes catch a stooped old woman pushing a double stroller with two girls in it.

The one closest to me is a baby with golden blonde hair. Maybe a little more than a year old. I can't take my eyes off her. The other girl has thick brown hair and looks to be about four years old. They make their way down the path to me, and then, without warning, the older girl unbuckles herself, jumps out of the stroller, and runs into the crowd.

The woman yells at her to stop, but the girl keeps running, weaving between the people walking through the park. After unbuckling the smaller child, the woman picks her up and thrusts her into my lap.

"Hold her," is all she says before she runs after the other girl, leaving the stroller behind.

I look down at the small face staring up at me. The child does not seem afraid, relaxed even. She explores my face as a growing tension rises in my chest. Groaning in frustration, I stand up, holding the baby in my arms, shifting her weight to my hip, and desperately search the crowd for the woman or the other little girl. They're gone. My first inclination is to go after them, but after a few steps I stop. What am I doing? I'm holding a child who isn't mine in the middle of a public New York City park. My armpits grow wet with sweat, and I loosen the scarf around my neck.

Wondering what to do, I go back to the bench and sit down. Without thinking, I smooth the girl's wavy blonde hair, tucking a piece behind her tiny ear. Time passes and the woman does not return. Panicking, I'm afraid to leave the bench because I want the woman to know where to find me. Assuming she's coming back. The baby rests her head on my shoulder, and her beautiful blue eyes study me. Without disturbing her, I raise my arm, pull up the sleeve of my coat, and look at my watch. It's getting late. I have to go back to work.

Twenty minutes pass. Without hope, I stand up again and look for the woman. The lunchtime crowd is starting to grow thin, and I am beginning to feel desperate. After pulling my cell phone out of my bag, I call 911 and the operator says she will send a patrol car.

The minutes tick by slowly. The wait is agonizing. Finally, a squad car pulls up, and I watch as two officers get out, walk to the gate, and scour the park. A man and a woman. They look so young, fresh-faced with heavy equipment hanging off their belts. They see me, and I stand up with the girl who is starting to feel heavy in my arms.

When they reach me, the male officer asks, "Did you call 911?"

"Yes. I was just sitting here, and a woman wearing a scarf and a long skirt gave me this baby." I stammer knowing how incredulous it sounds.

The officers stare at me, then at the baby.

Finally, the female officer takes a pad out of a box on her belt. "What's your name?"

"Anabel Leigh."

"Where do you work?"

I tip my chin in the direction of my building. "Right there."

"No. What's the name of your employer?" she asks with annoyance.

"Oh, sorry. C&W Communications."

"Okay. So, what did the woman look like? Where did she go?" She continues to question me.

Turning in the direction the woman ran, I point down the path lined with benches. "There was an older girl who got out of the stroller and disappeared into the crowd and the woman went after her. But before she ran away, she put this baby right in my lap and told me to hold her."

"Another girl . . ."

"Yes, I need to go back to work. Will you take her?" I try to peel the baby away from my shoulder.

The cops observe me. Four brown eyes looking for lies. "I think you need to come down to the station and give a complete statement. We'll send another patrol car to search the area," the male cop says.

"I can't. I have a meeting. I . . ."

"You'll have to call your office. C'mon," says the male cop pointing to the squad car.

The woman officer reaches out to take the baby so I can

make the call, but the girl locks her arms around my neck. I say it's okay and take out my cell phone, leaving a message for my secretary. I tell her I have something to take care of and that I will get back as soon as I can.

The officers lead me out of the park and put me and the baby in the back of the squad car. The stroller goes in the trunk. The little girl holds onto me tight, and I try to comfort her on the short drive to the police station. Once we get there, she clings to me like a koala bear as I struggle to get out of the car and follow the cops into the station.

This is my first time inside a police station and the sound of the door closing behind me sends a shiver down my spine. I know my story sounds crazy.

Once inside, they usher me and the baby into a room with a beat-up old table and four chairs. I sit down and wonder if I should call a lawyer. My musing is interrupted by a large man in a tired brown suit entering the room. The female officer says that she is going to call Child Services. She leaves the room, closing the door behind her.

I start to feel dizzy. Part of me wants to hand the baby over and go back to work, but another part of me wonders who will take care of her? Where will she go?

"I'm Detective Andrew Harris," the large man says as he takes a card out of his wallet and slides it across the table to me. He sits. "This is a first. Thirty years on the job, and I've never caught a case that involved a baby being thrust into the arms of a woman in a park. In Manhattan." He stops talking and stares at me, never breaking eye contact.

I stare back at him as my bottom lip starts to quiver. Detective Andrew Harris is tall and obese with fleshy features and tired eyes. He does not seem sympathetic or caring. His suit is the same brown color as the table and carpet. He asks me what happened, and I tell him what I've already told the officers.

He closes his eyes and rubs them before giving me another penetrating stare.

I can tell he is sizing me up. An attractive woman in her early thirties, nicely dressed in a fashionable trench coat and pearl earrings, who seems rational but may be a psychopath.

Trying to avoid his intense stare, I turn my focus to the baby. "What's your name, sweetheart?"

"Name," the baby says.

"What?" I ask.

"Name," she repeats.

Detective Harris watches me. "So, you were just sitting in the park, and a lady puts the girl in your lap and runs off."

"Yes."

"What did she look like? The woman."

"She was old. She wore a scarf on her head and a long skirt."

"What color scarf?"

I close my eyes to see the woman in my mind. "Kind of dark orange and the skirt was patchwork with a lot of different colors."

The detective studies me over his glasses. "How old?"

"Maybe sixty-five."

"And there was another girl? What did she look like?"

"She had dark brown hair. About four years old. Wearing a red sweatshirt."

The detective makes a note. I feel uncomfortable as he studies me. He seems to have run out of questions to ask.

"Well, I gotta hand it to you," he finally says. "This is a one-of-a-kind case. Babies left in front of the church. Babies left at the station house, the fire station, hospitals, schools, but I don't remember a case where a baby was actually put into the hands of a stranger in a park. Why you? Why did this woman leave the baby with you?"

I hesitate. He looks at me like he doesn't believe me and I

can't blame him. Who leaves a baby with a random woman sitting on a park bench? His eyes are boring into me now. There is a long silence before he says, "This baby seems attached to you."

"Babies like me. Always have," I say. "Listen, I really need to go back to work."

"Do you have kids? Are you married?" He shows no signs of dismissing me.

"No, I have no children. I'm divorced."

There is something in the detective's demeanor that I don't like. Fear starts to form in my stomach, sending bile up my throat. My claustrophobia kicks in and I'm afraid that he won't let me leave. I want to go back to work, but the baby feels so good in my arms. Warm and soft. She smells like cinnamon. I watch her play with my pearls.

"When did you leave work? What time?" The detective's question brings me back to the interrogation.

"Twelve-thirty. I remember looking at my watch as Peg, my secretary, reminded me that I have—*had*—a three o'clock meeting." I glance at my watch. It's three-thirty. "I really have to go." But I can't help but ask, "Who will take her? Where will she go?"

I absent-mindedly brush a strand of hair from the baby's soft cheek.

"Child Services will take her," the detective says. "Before you go you'll need to sit with our sketch artist so that we can start looking for the woman and the other girl."

"How long will that take?"

Detective Harris cocks a brow in my direction. "As long as it takes."

Resigned to the fact that I'm stuck here, I look down at the baby. A pang of sadness squeezes my chest. "Will I be able to call tomorrow and see how she is?"

The detective squints his beady eyes at me. "Sure. Let's keep in touch. My number's on the card."

I pick it up and slip it in my coat pocket. "Okay, let's do

the sketch. I really must get back to the office. Who should I give her to? You?"

He shakes his head, putting up his hands and looking alarmed. "No, the officer who brought you in. I'll get her." He heaves himself up and goes to the door. Looking back, he says, "Cute kid."

I smile weakly.

The officer comes into the interrogation room, but when she reaches out for the baby, the girl tightens her little arms around my neck.

"*No,*" she cries.

I feel terrible as I close my eyes and try to pry the girl's little hands from my coat. The officer reaches for her, grabbing the baby's little wrists, and wrenches her away from me.

"Never saw her before, huh?" the officer asks with a smirk and leaves with the baby.

"Toby, our artist, will be in shortly," says Detective Harris as he closes the door behind him.

I fall back into the chair feeling exhausted and realize I am crying.

2

ANABEL

Going home on the subway that night, I think about the baby. About how good she felt in my arms, how soft she was, her cinnamon smell and bright blue eyes. I start to daydream about taking care of her, feeding her, buying sweet dresses and stuffed animals. As always when I think about babies, I think about Sam.

Sam Flynn and I were married for five years. We met in graduate school at NYU where I was studying communications and he was getting an MBA. We couldn't wait to get married and start a family. So a month after graduation we were married. I was twenty-four. He was twenty-five. I got pregnant on the honeymoon and had a miscarriage six weeks later. We were devastated.

The doctor assured me that I would be fine and would have a healthy baby in the future. However, the next year I miscarried again. And the year after that I miscarried at six months.

After three miscarriages, we decided to take a break. No more pregnancies until the doctors could figure out what was wrong. After a few years of tests and procedures, the doctors couldn't come up with an explanation. They suggested we try to focus on other things. Just relax, they said. Maybe it would happen if we weren't so nervous about it.

We talked about adoption, but Sam didn't think he could bond with a child who wasn't his biologically. I thought I could but didn't push it. We poured ourselves into our work and tried to get used to a life where we would be childless forever. We traveled to exotic locations; bought a two-bedroom apartment and entertained family, friends, and business associates; slept late on Sunday mornings and read *The New York Times* in bed. But, over the years, our friends and siblings started to have families. They stayed in on weekend evenings, traveled to theme parks, and talked only of diapers, temper tantrums, and tutors.

Most of my friends quit their jobs after the second baby and looked at me with sad eyes when I asked to hold their newborns. Little by little, my friends and I had nothing to talk about and little in common. My career was on the fast track and I had worked my way up from assistant director to senior vice president at the communications firm where I worked.

When feelings of emptiness would creep into my chest, I would start planning the next get-away or order an expensive purse. Sam and I rarely talked about the family we both had wanted so much.

Then, I came home one night, and Sam was sitting on the couch in the living room. He hadn't put the light on and was still wearing his coat. I could tell that he had been crying—his blue eyes were red and bloodshot. Something told me that his tears were about us. That the crisis wasn't a death in the family. Or work related.

No, I knew instantly that this was about us. That he was leaving me.

"Sam . . ." I walked slowly toward him, dread filling my chest.

"I'm sorry." He sobbed, hanging his head.

I sat down on the couch, not next to him to console him,

but a few feet away, to demand an explanation. "Are you leaving me?" When he nodded, I asked, "Why?"

"I thought I could do it. I thought it wouldn't matter." He held his face in his hands, careful not to meet my gaze.

He was leaving me because we couldn't have a family. He didn't have to say it, but I wanted him to. I wanted him to feel as bad as he possibly could.

"We haven't even tried some of the things we could try," I said.

He jumped off the couch and started to pace. "I want it to be easy. I'm sick of doctors. I just want a family." Now he sounded angry.

I stood up to defend myself. "The doctors never confirmed that it's my problem," I shouted. "Maybe you're the problem."

His face turned red, a tortured cry rose in his throat as he said, "I'm going to be a father so it's not my problem."

As I sank to the floor under the full weight of what he said, he went to the closet in the hallway. He pulled a heavy suitcase out, marched to the apartment door, took one more look in my direction, and left.

The sound of the door closing made me double over in pain.

3

SAVANNAH

My big red barn with the pointed roof is situated about two hundred yards from the main house. After dinner, I always take Charlie, my Collie, for a long walk. My grandpa, Robert Maas, had built the barn and run his breeding stable for fifty years before my father took over and ran it into the ground. When my ma and pa died in a car accident a few years ago, I inherited ten acres of land, a dilapidated old farmhouse, and the barn all in Dubois, Georgia. An investor came and took all the horses as payment for the money he had given Pa.

Even though the horses are gone, I love the way the barn looks and have great memories of my grandpa teaching me how to ride and how to take care of the horses. I love the dusky, fragrant, slightly stale smell of the hay up in the hayloft that hasn't been cleaned out since my parents ran off the road. Sometimes I come out here and read, lying in the pile of hay under the loft with my feet perched on the ladder leading up to the second floor. On the outside, one wall is covered with ivy and the other with moss. I know I should hire someone to clean it out, or do it myself, but I just haven't gotten around to it. Tonight, Charlie is very animated, running to and fro, and sniffing the ground.

"What's up, boy?" I ask him, but then I hear it. A moan coming from the barn. Maybe some animal is trapped in one of the stalls. It's a big barn with twelve stalls, six on each side of the central hall. I know that feral cats live in the nooks and crannies of the storage room, but as I pull open the weather-beaten door and take a step into the entrance, I hear it again, louder this time, and I can tell it's a human sound. Because I'm a midwife, I know that a woman is in labor in one of the stalls. Teenagers sneak in here to fornicate and now one of them has probably come back at the other end of the process. A lot of girls could avoid this type of trouble if Georgia didn't have such strict abortion laws. Six weeks isn't long enough for most of them to figure out they're pregnant, let alone make a decision and then a plan.

After putting Charlie outside, I call out to the woman—my voice is deep and raspy. "Hello? Don't worry. I can help you."

Walking slowly down the center hall, I peer into each stall, listening for the moaning that will start with the next contraction.

"Where are you? I can help you. I'm a midwife," I call again. I'm about halfway down the hall when I hear an urgent cry. Transition. It won't be long. In the last stall on the left, I see a girl—maybe sixteen—squatting down, breathing hard. Her instincts must have told her that is the best position to deliver her baby. It's so unnatural for women to labor and give birth lying down. Obviously done for the ease of the male physicians, not for the birthing mother.

She looks up at me with fearful eyes.

I want to calm her. "What's your name? I'm Savannah."

"Kelly," she says as the contraction is done. She plops down to a sitting position to rest and looks at me with wild, scared eyes. Sweat mixed with dirt runs in rivulets down her soft cheeks.

"How long have you been at it?" I try to sound nonchalant so she won't bolt.

"Nearly five hours."

I smile. "That's pretty good, because I think you're about ready to give birth. Can I check you? To see how dilated you are?"

She gives me a quizzical look.

"To see if the baby is ready to come out?" I explain.

She nods. Her thick brown hair is matted and pieces of hay are tangled in it.

"I'm going to go wash my hands." I notice that she has placed a towel on the floor between her legs. "Brought your own equipment, I see."

I rush to the old sink in the back, tying my hair up in a scrunchie as I go, and wash my hands as thoroughly as I can. I don't think there's time to go and get my bag. Charlie is howling for me at the door to the barn.

When I get back to the girl, another contraction is starting, and she's squatting again. I squat down too, so we can look into each other's eyes as I help her through it. "Breathe, Kelly. Look at me and do what I do."

We stare into each other's eyes and do the breathing exercises that expectant mothers learn in Lamaze class.

I can tell that Kelly never went to a Lamaze class, but she watches me and mimics what I do. I start with a deep breath in through my nose and exhale in two short pants. *Pant-pant-blow*. Repeat. She picks up the rhythm quickly and makes it through the contraction.

When it's over, I examine her and feel that she is fully dilated. "Kelly, I want you to push with your next contraction. It will come naturally to you." I look around for something for her to bite down on and see a piece of soft rope. I shake the dust off and tell her to push and bite down.

I'm not going to describe what happened over the next hour because it wasn't pretty, but I will say that at the end of the hour, we had a very loud baby boy swaddled in the dirty towel.

Kelly had been torn up pretty bad and needed a stitch or two, and I wanted to clean the baby up, so I suggested that we go into the house. As I stood there holding the baby I watched as the girl reached for her underwear and pants and started to pull them on.

I let out a chuckle. "Darlin', there ain't nobody but you and me for ten acres so spare yourself the trouble of getting dressed. Let's go up to the house and get you and the baby cleaned up."

"Thank you, Miss Savannah. I really appreciate your help, but I gotta get going. I am very late for dinner, and my daddy is probably tearing the house apart right now demanding to know where I am."

I look at the girl, and she defiantly looks back at me as the baby cries. "Girl, this baby is hungry, and I don't have anything to feed him. What's your daddy going to say when you walk into the house holding this bloody baby? How's that going to go?" I demand. "I suggest you call your house and make up some story of where you are and then you let me sew you up. And you feed this baby. Then, if you want, I'll take you and the baby to your house."

The girl looks down at her sneakers. "I don't want that baby. Can you bring it to the church for me? Can you get rid of it?" Her big brown eyes still have a wild look in them. Straw is still sticking out of her matted hair and her T-shirt and legs are covered with blood and dirt.

I startle the girl by laughing out loud. "And how do I explain where I got the baby? What if the priest sees me leaving the baby and calls the cops? What do I say then? A girl had the baby in my barn and asked me to drop it off? I don't think so." My voice is getting louder and louder as my anger increases. Does she really think she's dumping this baby on me?

The girl's head drops to her chest and her arms hang down at her sides in defeat.

"C'mon. Let's get you cleaned up and feed this boy, and then we'll figure it out. What'a you say?"

Kelly looks down at her dirty shirt and bloody legs and heaves out a sigh. "Have a washing machine?" she asks.

"Yes, and I even have a diaper and a onesie for the baby."

4

SAVANNAH

Kelly was the first. Turned out she wasn't even sixteen when she gave birth in my barn. A minor who could cause all sorts of trouble for me. I know I should have called her parents myself and then brought Kelly and the baby home, but she confided in me that her father would probably kill her and the baby, so I relented and let her stay with me. My heart went out to the girl and she seemed to be genuinely afraid of going home with the baby.

So, we made a deal: I agreed to keep the baby at my house and try to find him a home, and she agreed to cut school and take care of him during the day when I was at work until I could figure out what to do with him.

But after two weeks of sending out feelers to women I knew through the clinic and getting no takers, I started to feel desperate. Usually, through my work as a midwife, I would meet women who wanted to have a baby and couldn't for various reasons, but the timing just wasn't good. I definitely didn't want to raise the baby myself. Then, Thomas Moore popped into my head. An old boyfriend who was now a doctor in New York City. When I googled him, it turned out that he was a partner at a fertility clinic. Bingo! He must know a few couples who were in the market for a baby.

I wasn't sure that Tom would take my call. We have a complicated past, but he picked up after the second ring.

"Savannah?"

"Hi, Tom." I made sure to emphasize the natural rasp in my voice. Tom had always loved my low, deep voice.

"Long time. How are you?"

"I'm good. You?"

"Good. I'm good. Still living in Dubois?" Tom pronounced the town's name like a true southerner. *Du-boys.*

"Yeah. Still living in my parents' place. You heard about their accident. Right?" Always good to play the sympathy card.

"I did. I'm sorry."

"It was years ago now, thanks. How are you? Southern boy living in the big city up north?"

"I like it up here. Lots to do . . ."

"Not like Dubois." I gave him a throaty laugh. "Listen, the reason I'm calling is that my cousin had a baby—a boy—that she is looking to put up for private adoption, and I was wondering, since you work in the baby business, if you might be able to hook us up with a family."

There was a pause before he answered. "Why doesn't she give it to the Christian Sisters in Dubois? Maybe they can place it."

"Well, she went through a lot to have the baby. She had to quit her job, and she needs to be compensated. Also, I don't think she wants to give it to a local family. She wants a clean break. She'll sign away her rights."

Another long pause on the other end of the line. "I can't help you, Savannah. It's been good talking to you, but I have to go."

I could tell that warning bells had gone off in Tom's head.

I decided not to push it. "Okay, Tom. It's been so great to hear your voice. Thanks anyway." I hung up and my palms were sweating. I wasn't sure of the laws back then, but I knew it was illegal to sell a baby.

Kelly and I went back to our shifts, but the school had contacted her parents and there was hell for her to pay at home. Kelly thought they were getting suspicious, and I felt like what started out as a helping hand was now taking over my entire life. I needed someone else to look after the baby, and I started to ask around for a sitter using the story about a cousin who was staying with me but needed help. No luck.

The next week, I took Monday and Tuesday off to stay with "boy" as we called him. He was gaining weight and was now a chubby, healthy two-week-old. I started to consider giving the baby to the Christian Sisters, but how would I explain where he came from? Maybe they wouldn't ask. Maybe I could leave him in a basket at their door. I thought about making Kelly bring the baby to the Sisters, but she had grown on me, and I couldn't make her do it.

On Wednesday morning, I had to go back to the clinic. Kelly had returned to school, so I was planning to bring "boy" with me when the phone rang. It was Tom.

"Tom! Hi."

His voice sounded thin, his words sticking in his throat. "Listen, I think . . . I might have a couple. Can you come to New York and bring the baby?"

And that's how it started. I came back from New York with ten thousand dollars in cash. In a duffel bag! Tom, the couple, and I all knew it was illegal, but the desperate couple didn't seem to care. They fell in love with "boy" instantly and would have paid a lot more.

In some absurd way, I felt cheated. It was like being on a job interview and you name your price and they snatch you up and you know you could have gotten more. Next time, I would ask for more. Next time. As I drank the champagne on the first-class flight back to Georgia, I knew there would be a next time. It was too easy. Besides, those people were so happy. Kelly was free. How wrong could it be?

5

———————

ANABEL

Thinking about it later, it might have been strange that I didn't mention the baby to anyone at work. What had happened was so surreal that I didn't think they would believe me, but by the time I trudged home from the subway and turned on the news, she was on every channel with her golden blonde hair and angelic face staring at me.

The police had obviously issued a press release because they were sharing my story. Sitting in the park. An old woman with two little girls in a stroller. Baby plopped in my lap by the woman who then ran away. The baby being turned over to social services.

Having started my career in media relations, I knew it was only a matter of time before some enterprising reporter found me at home or at work.

I was also worried about the baby. Where was she? Were they treating her okay? Was she hungry? When I closed my eyes, I could still feel her in my lap and smell the cinnamon in her hair. I longed to hold her again.

Enough. Stop.

I turned off the TV and decided to read my email on my phone, but there she was in my inbox. Offers to adopt her were pouring in according to *The Daily News. The Times* had set up a special hotline for the mother or father of the baby to call. Flipping over to Facebook, she was all over my feed. Instagram, same thing.

Needing to talk to someone, I thought about calling my sister, Sylvia, but she'd be in-between dinner, homework, and baths. She wouldn't have a minute until ten o'clock tonight to talk.

Why had I been singled out? Why had the woman chosen me? My eyes filled up with tears. Needing to talk to someone, I call my colleague, Dennis Wells, our chief operating officer at C&W Communications. Dennis is also single, so there wouldn't be a wife in the background wondering what the conversation was all about. I look through my contacts and press call.

"Hey, Anabel. What's up?"

I play with the ties of my soft cotton hoodie. "Hey, Dennis. So, this isn't about work. Do you have a minute?"

"For you, sure." He sounds genuinely concerned.

I picture him smoothing his mustache. "Have you been watching the news about the baby who was given to a woman in a park?"

"Yeah?"

"Well, guess who?" I laugh nervously.

"Oh my God! It was you? What happened?"

"Well, the news has it right. I was just sitting in the park, right across from the office, and this woman comes walking through pushing a double stroller with two little girls. The older girl unbuckled herself and ran into the crowd and the woman took the baby and practically threw her in my lap and then ran away after the other girl."

Dennis expels a breath. "Unbelievable. That's wild! Then what happened?"

It feels good to tell my story to someone other than the police. "So, I sat there waiting for the woman to come back, but when she didn't, I called the police who insisted that I go to the station to make a formal statement. That's why I missed the book tour meeting."

"Yeah, Sol was not happy about that," he said, referencing our boss.

"I heard. What did he say?"

"Oh, one of his usual curse-laden tirades."

"Yikes. I'll have to go in and genuflect tomorrow. Do you think I should tell him why I missed it?"

"Yeah. It wasn't your fault. Go see him. So, do you have to do anything else? With the baby I mean?"

"I don't think so. The cops didn't say not to leave the country or anything. I'm a little concerned that the media will get my address and start to hang out at my apartment."

"That could happen. Probably will. One of the cops will leak it."

"You think so?"

He hesitates. "Sadly, I do."

"I know you're right. Dennis, thanks. I needed to tell someone."

"Call me anytime. Let me know if you need anything."

"Thanks. I'll see you tomorrow." I hang up the phone and stretch my legs out on the couch. My mouth ticks up in a little smile. Talking to Dennis was nice. I never thought of him like that before. Hmm.

However, my good feelings shatter when I think about him agreeing with me that it's only a matter of time before the media finds me.

6

SAVANNAH

I didn't know it at the time, but the birth of Kelly's baby was the beginning of my business. My very lucrative business of supplying babies to rich couples. Kelly has a knack for finding girls who are pregnant and don't want their babies. I also suspect that some enterprising girls got pregnant and sought Kelly out because we give the girls a few thousand dollars to have a chance to start again. To maybe get out of an abusive home or get away from a boyfriend who doesn't treat her right. Maybe even go to community college or beauty school, possibly buy that ticket to LA or New York.

About three years ago, the operation got too big for just Kelly and me. So, now there are four of us—Kelly Parker, Vadoma Krivko, Hattie Jones, and myself. We all live at the house together and the work is divided up. Kelly recruits the girls and helps to take care of the babies. Vadoma is our main caretaker and Hattie and I are midwives. She helps me with the check-ups and the births. My main job is working with Tom to place the babies with rich couples in the tristate area.

From the beginning, I decided a few things: not to get attached to the babies, not to name them, to get rid of them quickly, to work only with girls eighteen or older, and not to get involved with the girls' personal lives outside of the immediate transaction.

I don't name the babies because I try not to think of them as individual people. They're really a commodity to us.

The barn is now the birthing center, and I have had state-of-the-art equipment installed behind the ramshackle walls of the barn. I could have built a whole new barn and house, but I like the cover of the old walls. They don't attract attention. In the main house there are four bedrooms upstairs for us and a large nursery. The house is so isolated that no one ever comes out here.

The business, which is run completely under the table, has been growing for the last five years. After Tom's initial reluctance, he came on board all in. Ever the Boy Scout, he still tries to help his patients carry their own babies but so many couples just can't. After two or three in vitro procedures, Tom tells the couple that he knows of a woman who might be able to help them. He sets up a meeting in a fancy hotel, and I go up to New York, always looking like a thousand bucks—thanks, Ma, for the good bone structure and thick blonde locks—and sweep them off their feet with a gush of my southern charm. I interview them, and if I feel that they are willing to play our game, I put them on our list for a baby.

When it is their turn, I meet them in the hotel in New York and give them the baby. While the woman bonds with the child, the husband and I handle the finances. They are usually willing to pay just about any amount for the baby and the documents that say they are the biological parents.

That part was a little tricky, but enough money and the right cleavage can get just about anything done. One of Kelly's first assignments when she started working for me full-time was to go into the Department of Vital Records office to see who she could seduce. It was almost too easy.

Kelly is one of those women who clean up nice, as they

say. Untended she's a six, but add mascara, lip gloss, a blowout, and the right low-cut blouse, and she is a knockout. Not by New York standards, but by Dubois standards. Calvin Banks didn't even see the turn his life was about to take when Kelly walked into the office and up to his desk. Her mouth is her best feature, and her smile is a combination of innocence and raw sexuality. She gave Calvin her dirtiest innocent smile, and he's been allowing us to put the adopting parents' signatures on birth certificates ever since. Of course, Kelly lucked out because Calvin is married and respects his vows, but he can't resist Kelly's dimples. A few thousand dollars at Christmas, Labor Day, and the Fourth of July helps to keep him dishonest.

But now the baby, who we refer to as the Golden One, is threatening my business operation with her adorable face and golden hair on every news channel out of New York City. It's uncanny that *The New York Times* has also dubbed her "The Golden One" on the front page of their paper. That baby did have something special about her, kind of an aura. She just got old too fast, and we couldn't find a family for her. When they're paying top dollar, the couples want an infant, usually less than a month old. Then they know that someone hasn't done anything to them that has damaged them permanently. Newborn shelf-life is fleeting.

Vadoma, who drew the short straw and had to go to New York to dump the baby, is on her way home from New York. When I hear car tires crunching the gravel in the driveway, my anger at her rises up in my chest. I push the heavy taffeta drapes in my dining room aside and watch as Vadoma gets out of her car. She is dressed ever-so-chic in a gray tailored suit and pink silk shirt. As she walks toward the house, she is dragging the dark-haired girl with her. I feel the blood rush to my cheeks, as I leave the dining room to go and confront Vadoma when she comes in.

"Hello?" I hear her call from the kitchen. "Savannah?"

I storm down the hall into the great room in the back of the house. "So, the media star returns. Run and play," I say to the girl who is all too happy to get away from me. "So, I saw your handy work on the news last night and this morning. What the hell happened?"

Vadoma starts talking a mile a minute, which tells me she's nervous. "The woman was the perfect mark. Just sitting in the park relaxing, and I can tell that she's not a screamer. Real refined with pearl earrings and a stylish trench. I tell the dark one to make a run for it when we are right in front of the lady and meet me around the corner. She's a good little actress. Unbuckles herself and heads into the crowd, bobbing and weaving, and then waits for me a block away. I deliver the package, so to speak, and take off into the crowd. I reach the dark one and drag her into an alley, whip off the scarf and the skirt, and "Voila!" I'm dressed like this. I peel off the kid's red sweatshirt and cover her hair with a hat and jump into a cab." Vadoma smooths her short dark hair as she tells me her story.

My nostrils flare as I confront her with sweeping hand gestures. "But now we're all over the news. The national news! The police are looking for you, Vadoma. Tom is going to have a stroke."

"We knew this might happen. Beautiful white baby. We knew the media would have a field day, but we both know the baby's parents are not going to step forward. End of story. This was a risk we chose to take. *We* discussed this." She stares at me defiantly, voice growing louder.

"Are you sure you can't be traced? You checked for cameras in the park?" I tuck my long hair behind my ears.

"No cameras that I could see. Especially near the bench that the lady was sitting on. It'll blow over. In a few days, no one will be looking for the old woman in the park." She goes over to the cupboard, grabs a glass, then to the sink to pour herself a drink of water.

I glare at her when I say, "You better be right."

"Look, the goal was to get rid of the girl before she could talk and that's what I did. She's gone, and she's not coming back. People are already lining up to take her home and make her their own."

"And what about the other one? What's the plan for her?" I walk over to the fridge and grab a can of Diet Coke. Taking a long pull, I consider our options. I don't want the responsibility of raising the girl, but she has started to talk. A lot. She's smart and knows too much. She knows our names.

"Well, the first thing we need to do is give her a name. It's just not right. I don't think she's going anywhere. It's time we accept that."

Staring out the window into the endless green fields, I know she's right. "Yeah. Okay. What do you want to name her?"

Vadoma smiles. Clearly, she has grown fond of the girl.

"Do you want her?" I ask.

"What's the difference? We all live here together. Yours. Mine. Ours. We're all in so deep that no one's going anywhere."

She's right. "Well, you can name her and as far as I'm concerned, she's yours." The girl is spoiled goods.

Vadoma frowns as we sit at the large kitchen island that has six tall chairs around it.

"What?" I ask.

"She said I was sixty-five," Vadoma whines, her mouth pulled down in a frown.

I smile for the first time since she walked in the door. "It was the gray wig peeking out from the scarf." I laugh and she smiles.

"Still, sixty-five? She could have said fifty-five."

"Yeah, but she didn't. She must have noticed the crow's feet."

"What?" Her hand flies up to the outside corner of her eye.

"Get over yourself," I say and give her a throaty laugh before I finish my soda.

7

———

ANABEL

I decided not to tell Sol the truth. Sol Moskowitz is one of the greatest old-school public relations guys who ever lived, so I could see that it would send his mind churning on how to get publicity for the firm out of my story. Instead, I tell him I had food poisoning and was holed up in the bathroom at the Chinese restaurant a few blocks away. I promise to call the client and apologize profusely. He acknowledges that it could happen, and I make a speedy exit from his office.

Back in the safety of my office I pull Detective Harris's card out of my purse and sit at my desk staring at it. What do I want to say to him? What do I really want to know?

Absentmindedly pulling on my strand of pearls, I try to convince myself that it is only natural to want to check up on a baby that is thrust into your lap in a city park. He did give me his card and told me to "keep in touch." If he didn't want to hear from me, why did he say that?

I straighten the piles of papers on my desk while I think of my opening line. *Hello, Detective, it's Anabel Leigh. I'm just calling to see how the baby is.*

You're overthinking this. Just dial the number, I say to myself.

I type in the number. My heart is thumping, and I am sweating. *Anabel, you are ridiculous.*

"Harris," he grumbles.

I can't find my voice.

"Harris," he says louder.

"Yes, Detective Harris. It's . . . it's . . . Anabel. Anabel Leigh. From the other day. With the baby."

"Yes."

"I'm just calling to . . . see how . . . she is. To see how the baby is. How is she?" I stammer.

"She's with Child Services."

"Do you have that number? A number for me to call to see how . . ."

"Sure. Hold on."

I hear music while I wait and decide to tell him what I remember. It's just a detail, but somehow, I think it might mean something.

"Here you go." I jot down the number. "Ask for Ms. Alvarez."

"Thanks. And, Detective Harris?"

"Yeah."

"So, obviously I've been going over what happened in my mind and there is a little detail that I remembered."

"Yeah?"

"The woman had a fresh manicure."

"A fresh manicure. What'd'ya mean?"

"It just looked fresh. The polish was shiny with no chips or anything. And I keep asking myself, would a poor, old woman have a fresh manicure?"

There's a pause on the other end of the phone.

I continue. "And she was wearing a sapphire and gold ring. A nice round stone. It all happened so fast that it could have been a fake stone, but in my mind's eye it looks real. So, maybe she wasn't poor or old like I first thought. Maybe she was wearing a disguise. Anyway, I thought I should tell you."

"Yes, I'm glad you did. If you remember anything else let us know. Thanks." The phone goes dead.

After hanging up, I feel nervous. He makes me feel guilty, which is so weird because I have nothing to feel guilty about. I should get back to work, but I want to call the social worker.

Ms. Alvarez picks up on the first ring.

"Alo?" she says with a cheery sound in her voice.

"Hello. Ms. Alvarez?"

"Yes, this is she."

"My name is Anabel Leigh. I wanted to inquire about the baby you picked up from the police yesterday."

"Yes, and who are you?"

"I'm the woman who was sitting in the park and found her. Well, not exactly *found* her but she was given to me in the park."

"Detective Harris told me you might call."

"He did?"

"Yes, he said that you were quite attached to her."

"Oh, well, I do want to know that she's okay. Is she? Okay?"

"Yes, she's fine. She's a celebrity! Have you seen the news? I was interviewed today! I couldn't say anything because of confidentiality laws, but the reporters were waiting for me at lunch."

"Ms. Alvarez, do you think that I could . . ."

"What?"

"Do you think that I could see her? Like visit her?"

"Ms. Leigh, are you related to this baby?"

"No, I just want to see her. For some reason I can't stop thinking about her. It's not every day that a baby is plopped into your lap in the middle of your lunch hour."

"Well, that's true," she says with a laugh. "I'll tell you what. I will discuss it with my supervisor. That's really the best I can do."

"That would be great! Let me give you my number. And, Ms. Alvarez, thank you."

8

SAVANNAH

"Tom, baby, slow down." I pick my head up from the pillow to see what time it is. Six in the morning. I grimace.

"She's the top of every news report. On the cover of *The Daily News* and *The Post*." Tom's voice grows louder with every word.

"Tom. Tom. So what? There's no connection to you. To us. Vadoma had a great disguise. Calm down."

"Do not tell me to calm down. We have to slow down. That's what we have to do. We have to slow down," Tom's voice is getting louder and louder.

My head is starting to spin. "Tom, can I call you back?"

"No, I'm already at the clinic. I have a procedure to administer in a few minutes." I picture Tom sitting at his desk, pulling on his curly brown hair, at the fertility clinic on Park Avenue in Manhattan where he is a partner. Whenever he's nervous he worries the soft curls right behind his ears.

I put the phone on speaker so that I can continue to listen to his rant while I put on my bathrobe and open the shades.

"Another beautiful day on the farm," I say to myself with a frown.

"What? What did you just say? Are you listening to me?" Tom yells.

"Nothing, baby. Listen, take a deep breath. I know it's scary to see the girl on the TV but now she'll be adopted and that's that. She's gone. Out of our lives. Poof. Of course, we didn't make a payday, but what can you do?"

"Are you seriously worried about not making bank on that kid? Savannah, we are both richer than we ever thought possible. We literally have made millions of dollars stashed away in offshore accounts. I cannot believe I have an offshore account. What have we become? It's insane. We're insane. This whole thing is insane."

"*Tom*. Stop it. Calm down for God's sake. It'll blow over in a few days. Let's take a vacay. Do you want to meet somewhere and we can fool around for a few days? What'a ya think?" I say in my sexiest voice.

Tom and I have also started seeing each other romantically. Well, maybe not exactly romantically, but we've started sleeping with each other when I'm in town. We've been attracted to each other since we were teenagers and it's been easy to start it all up again.

I can picture him looking out the window of his palatial office frowning and pulling his hair. Between the two of us, Tom is the worrier. He once told me that I had the biggest balls of any guy he knew. Ha! I loved that. He knows me so well. We were each other's first in high school and then I got pregnant in my junior year. Had the baby and my pa took it. Still don't know what he did with it. Maybe he drowned it in the lake. Don't even know if it was a girl or boy. Ma helped me through it and then it was gone. Never laid eyes on it. Poof. Like I shit a ham, and then nothing.

"Tom, are you still there?"

"Yes," he says. I can tell by his voice that he's pouting. He's so cute when he's mad. "How many are in production now?" he finally asks.

I hesitate knowing that he will blow his top. "Nine. One a month for the next nine months." I wait for the storm.

It doesn't come. "Starting when? When will the next one need placement?"

"In a week to ten days. She needs to gain a pound or two."

"Let's take a break after these. That's a few million more for each of us."

I watch my jaw clench in the mirror above the sink in my bathroom. My eyes look like gray steel, but I know when to assert myself and when to back off. "Yes, let's take a break then," I answer sweetly.

"Okay. I have to do this in vitro. I gotta go."

"Let me know if you change your mind about the vacay," I say in a light tone.

As soon as I hang up, I hear the baby start to screech. Another girl. Damn it! She was born two nights ago, and it's Kelly's turn to feed her. We put the babies on a bottle from day one. We do not promote mother-child bonding. Just the opposite. No skin-to-skin contact. The women stay in the barn which I've outfitted with two recovery rooms. The girls are so young and fit that they usually leave after the first night, but I allow two nights if they need it. The babies are taken up here to the nursery immediately after the birth.

As I hurry to the baby, I stop to rap loudly on Kelly's door. "Get up!"

Throwing open the door to the nursery, I can't help but admire how I've decorated it. In another life, I could be an interior decorator. It is a hassle, though, to move furniture into the house. I have it all delivered by private carrier so there are no nosy deliverymen.

The room is done in matching yellow fabrics—gingham, flowers, and stripes—with four cribs, two changing tables, two playpens, two bouncy chairs, two cots, and two rocking chairs. Hattie, Vadoma, and Kelly take turns being on call, and Kelly was supposed to be in here a half-hour ago.

She comes into the nursery slowly, rubbing her eyes as I finish changing the new one. Sometimes Kelly is just lazy.

"Don't oversleep again," I tell her. "We all have a job to do, and it's not so fucking hard to live in this palace and get up early a few mornings a week. Do you hear me?"

Looking at me sheepishly, she says, "I'm sorry. She was up twice in the night. Next time I'll sleep in here." Kelly takes the baby.

"Want coffee?" I ask her as I leave the nursery.

"Yes, I'll be down." She yawns.

I go down the central stairs and into the great room to make coffee. Flicking on the TV just in time for a breaking news alert on Channel 2.

"We interrupt this program to bring you the following breaking news alert."

My heart skips a beat. I know it has something to do with the Golden One and there she is—as big as life—on my screen. There's been a development.

Shit, I think. *What?*

"The police have discovered new evidence about the woman who had been described as old and poor. They were looking for a woman in her sixties, but now think she may be much younger and had been wearing a disguise," says the reporter.

Fuck.

I go to the bottom of the stairs and yell, "Vadoma! Come down here. You will want to see this!"

In a matter of minutes, the team has assembled in their robes around the kitchen island. Kelly has the baby, and Vadoma has the girl. I flip the channels to see if I can get a report of the new evidence in the case.

"Well, what did they say?" asks Vadoma before taking a sip of coffee and checking her manicure.

"You'll be happy to know that they think you are not as

old as first reported. They think you were wearing a disguise," I tell her. "Which, of course, you were."

"How would they know?" asks Hattie, the only one of us in gray sweatpants and a GAP football jersey instead of a silk robe. She is the newest member of our little cabal. I stole her from the clinic that I used to work at when my trips to New York became too frequent and did not always allow me to be here for the birthing mothers. A midwife with a lot of experience is hard to come by, and she has a good way with the breeders. Much better than my bedside manner.

We all look at Vadoma for an answer.

"Do you think there were cameras in the alley where you changed out of the disguise?" asks Kelly.

"I went there the day before and surveyed the walls and poles and windows to see if there were any cameras and it was clean. Maybe someone took a photo of me handing off the baby to that woman. I don't know." Vadoma bites her bottom lip and looks seriously distraught.

I frown.

"What?" asks Kelly.

"Tom has already called this morning. Think, Vadoma. How would new evidence be coming out now? What exactly did you say to the woman?" I ask.

Vadoma, usually very confident, clearly doesn't like the interrogation. "I just said, 'Hold her,' and put the kid in her lap. I even tried to walk hunched over like an old woman and kept my head down so she couldn't get a good look at me. I honestly don't know what new evidence there could possibly be."

"You told me you yelled after the girl. What did you yell?" I demand.

"'Girl.' I yelled, 'Girl. Come back,'" Vadoma says.

"But I didn't," says the girl.

Vadoma hugs the girl. "No, you didn't. You played your part just right and did exactly what I told you to do. You were great! By the way, everyone, this is Kayleigh. I've given her a name."

"Kayleigh. That's me," the girl says with a smile.

"Oh, I love that!" exclaims Kelly.

"Hey, Kayleigh," Hattie puts her hand up for a high five.

"Great," I say flatly. I look at the girl and wonder what we are going to do with her. Vadoma says we'll raise her up as one of us. Now that's an inspiration. Just like us. Sisters in crime. I use the remote to check the other stations.

Channel 4 has the latest from the NYPD police commissioner. I turn up the sound. "Originally, we were told that the woman handing off the girl was 'a poor, old woman,' but new details seem to suggest otherwise. According to an eye witness the woman had a fresh manicure and was wearing an expensive sapphire and gold ring."

The whole table turns to look at Vadoma's hand, confirming the "fresh" red manicure and the sapphire ring.

"Seriously?" I ask my voice rising. "You were supposed to make sure that there were no details linking this back to you, to us. A manicure? Are you fucking crazy? And an expensive ring? Did you buy that on the trip? They'll be reaching out to all the jewelry stores that sell rings that look just like that."

"No. No, I didn't buy it on this trip. I didn't think she'd notice it."

"That's the truth. You weren't thinking!" I yell waking the baby who has been sleeping soundly in Kelly's arms and now starts to wail.

"Kayleigh, go upstairs, honey," says Vadoma. "Kelly, take them upstairs."

"C'mon, Kayleigh," says Kelly, holding out her hand and moving quickly to escape the scene that we all know is about to take place.

Now, I'm off the stool and on my feet. "Of all the stupid mistakes you could have made. How could you be so irresponsible? Do you want to go to jail? Huh?"

"Of course not. I made a mistake."

"A mistake? Ordering the wrong Chinese food is a mistake. Showing up late is a mistake. But this? This is something more. This is incompetence, Vadoma. Incompetence that could have real negative consequences for all of us," I yell into her face.

"Well, the next fucking time you need to dispose of the spoiled goods, you do it yourself!" screams Vadoma. We're both on our feet now.

"Where and when did you buy that ring?" I shout.

"Last year. At a small jeweler in New York. Savannah, I seriously don't even remember the name."

Hattie's dark brown face looks ashen. I realize I have to keep it together for all our sakes. Taking a deep breath, I try to steady myself.

"I have to think. I'm going to take a shower." I storm out of the room with my silk bathrobe flying out behind me.

9

ANABEL

It's been four days, and the baby is still all over the news. Not always the lead story, but the second or third story now. I'm glad the coverage is slowing down a little because today I am going to see her, and I am nervous and excited at the same time. I would be lying if I said that I hadn't fantasized about adopting her. Just her and me living here in my two-bedroom apartment.

When Sam and I divorced, I got the apartment. A good-sized apartment by New York standards with an eat-in kitchen, living room, two baths, and two bedrooms at Seventy-Sixth Street and Second Avenue. I'm sure his decision to give me the apartment was born out of his guilt.

Whatever the reason, it means that I have adequate space for the baby. She's been placed in short-term foster care, and the foster care mom has agreed to bring her to the Child Services office so that I can spend an hour with her. I even look forward to seeing Ms. Alvarez who will supervise the visit. She has been a great help to me. During my lunch hour yesterday, I bought a pink baby bag and filled it with toys. I also bought a sippy cup, apple juice, and animal crackers. All kids like animal crackers. Right?

I have a nine o'clock appointment at child services and then I'm going into the office, so I have to dress for work. Choosing a plain blue suit, striped blue and white shirt, a chunky gold necklace and blue flats. In the back of my mind, I am also going on an interview of sorts. I want Ms. Alvarez to like me in the event that I decide to put my name on the list as a possible adoptive parent.

According to my research, single people can be adoptive parents, but I worry that a couple would be more likely to get the baby than a single woman.

I leave my apartment early, wanting to be on time for my appointment, but as I get off the elevator I can hear them. Like a brood of cackling hens, the reporters are jockeying for position in front of my building. They have found me. Oh, no! What to do? Jose, the doorman, confirms what I already know.

"Ms. Leigh, this is all for you. They all want to talk to you. They say it's about that baby. The one all over the news. I told them you didn't have the baby . . ." But now his eyes rest on the pink baby bag.

"I don't have the baby, Jose. Is there another way out of here?"

"C'mon. Through the garage," he says with a wave.

I follow him quickly through a door at the back of the lobby. "Jose, do you think you can hail me a cab?"

"For you? Of course," he says with a smile.

Once I'm safely in the cab, I breathe a temporary sigh of relief knowing that it's only a matter of time. They'll get me at the office or they'll get me when I come home tonight. But they will track me down and ask a thousand questions that I cannot answer. I'd discussed it with Dennis over lunch yesterday and we both thought that a polite, but firm, "no comment" was the best way to go.

Traffic is bad and now I'm going to be late. I hope that

Ms. Alvarez will understand and still let me see the baby. I leave her a message letting her know I'm running late.

The cab finally arrives at the grim-looking Child Services building and I jump out and jog into the lobby where I am met by four security guards and a metal detector. I guess I'm glad they screen people on their way in, but right now it is slowing me down. I look at my watch: it's nine-thirteen. Being late is rude and irresponsible. Ms. Alvarez needs to know I am taking this seriously.

"Take it easy, mama. Slow down," says the security guard on the other side of the metal detector as I quickly collect my purse, cell phone, sunglasses, and baby bag from the plastic bins.

I shoot him a nasty look and hurry over to the ancient elevators. The building is so old that the mustard-colored tiling around the elevator buttons has been worn down. All I can think about is taking the baby out of this place.

When the elevator doors open on the third floor, there she is in the arms of a nice-looking woman with a kind face who is talking to Ms. Alvarez.

I spill out of the elevator shaking my head. "I'm so sorry that I'm late." I smile at the baby. "Hello, sweetie," and then my attention moves back to Ms. Alvarez. "The press was waiting for me outside my building, and I had to sneak out the back and jump in a cab which took so much longer than the subway. I'm so sorry."

"No worries. I got your message," says Ms. Alvarez. "Ms. Leigh, I want you to meet Mrs. Carter."

"Hello," says Mrs. Carter with a wide grin.

"I'm so glad to meet you. Thank you so much for bringing her in," I say to the woman and then turn to the baby. "Hi honey!" The baby watches me. Her eyes glued to my face.

"Let's go in the meeting room," says Ms. Alvarez, leading us down a depressing hallway to a room at the far end of the hall. The smell of Clorox fills my nose. I'm happy to see that the room has been decorated with posters of brightly colored animals and there are toys in a crate with a little, child-sized table and chairs on a red, blue and yellow carpet.

Mrs. Carter hands the baby to Ms. Alvarez and prepares to leave. "I'll be back in an hour. I have a few errands to run."

"Thank you," I say.

Ms. Alvarez puts the baby down by the crate of toys and I go and take a seat at the tiny table next to her. She is more beautiful than I remember. Her silky soft blonde waves, big blue eyes and sweet little face melt my heart.

"Let's take off your coat, sweetie," I say as I help her slip off her jacket. "I brought you some presents. Would you like to see what I have in my bag?" She stares at me without answering. I grab the pink baby bag. "Look at this." I pull a soft, wooly lamb out of the bag and hand it to her. She takes it and looks at me. "This is a lamb. Can you say lamb? Lamb." She gives the lamb a little hug and throws him on the floor.

"Don't like him? Can I read you a book?" I pull a cloth book with A to Z in animals out of the bag and show her the cover. Pulling her into my lap, I say, "Look, this is an alligator. A is for alligator." I turn the page. "This is a bird. B is for bird. Have you ever seen a bird?" She watches me intently as I talk. "Birds fly. In the sky," I smile at my rhyme and turn the page. "C is for cat," when she sees the cat she gets very excited and points to the cat. "You've seen a cat."

"Cat," she says and smiles at me.

I look over at Ms. Alvarez who is watching us. Turning back to the baby, I say, "Do you have a cat at home?"

"Cat."

I continue, "D is for dog." Again, she gets very animated.

"Charlie," she points to the dog.

"Charlie? Is Charlie your dog?"

When she doesn't answer, I turn the page to see the next animal. "Elephant," I say. "E is for elephant. Elephant."

She stares so intently at my mouth that I laugh. "Do you

want some juice?" I take the sippy cup out of the side pocket of the bag and hand it to her. She takes the cup and snuggles into my lap. This feels so good that tears well up in my eyes and my chest feels tight. I give her a hug while Ms. Alvarez watches.

"She likes you," she says.

"And I like her."

"A couple is coming to meet her the day after tomorrow. They've been on a waiting list for some time now and we're still waiting to see if the baby's parents come forward. But if you want her, you should file your application."

"But they're a couple and I'm single. Won't they get her?"

Ms. Alvarez shrugs. "You never know."

"Has she said anything else? She called that dog in the book Charlie. So, no one has come forward saying that they are the parents?"

"No. No one has claimed her. No one has said they know who her parents are. It seems to me that someone was trying to get rid of her," she says with a frown.

The baby has finished the juice, and I take the cup. "Do you want an animal cracker? I can give her an animal cracker, right?"

Ms. Alvarez nods.

I open the package with the baby in my arms and I pull out an elephant. "Elephant," I say, showing her the cracker.

"El-fant," she says.

"Good girl! El-e-phant."

"El-e-phant."

"She wants to talk. She just needs someone to teach her," says Ms. Alvarez.

"Yes." I look at my watch. Ten more minutes. The time has gone so quickly. I want to give her the other presents. I pull a small baby doll out of the bag.

"Baby," she says.

"Yes. This is a baby. A girl baby. What do you want to name her?"

She looks at me. "Name."

"Do you want to name her Linda?" I ask saying the first name that comes into my head.

"No. Baby."

"What's your name?" I ask pointing to her chest. "What's your name?"

"Baby."

"Okay."

"So, what do I have to do if I want to adopt her?"

"I'll give you a packet on the way out."

I'm shaking as I hug her goodbye.

Ms. Alvarez looks at me and hands me the adoption application. "Get it in quick."

I smile and nod at her.

10

KELLY

I do love driving this car!

Let's see how fast you can go, little BMW, I think as I step hard on the gas pedal. Great pick-up. Woo-hoo! I bought myself this white sports BMW with red leather interior for my birthday. I went all the way to Atlanta to buy it.

This is one of the perks of my job with Savannah, and I know that I can't earn as much money as I do with her anywhere else being a high school dropout and all, but seriously, I have got to get the fuck out of here. I'm going to stay with Savannah through next year, and then my debt should be paid off. I'm so sick of her bossing all of us around.

Kelly, get the baby. Vadoma, mop the floor. Hattie, take out the garbage. Who the fuck does she think she is anyway? And, I'm gonna smoke in my car anytime I want to. I light up and take a deep drag. Oh yeah, that's good. Think I'll sprinkle the ashes all over my car, too. I purposely flick the cigarette on the passenger seat pretending that Savannah can see me.

She takes every opportunity to let us all know it's her house, her furniture, her floor, her bathroom, her carpet, everything is hers. We all love it when she goes up to New York or on one of her mystery "vacays" as she calls them and the three of us get to slack off. Put our feet up on her couch. With our shoes on! She would die if she saw the kitchen after one of our parties. Of course, we clean it all up before she gets home.

I know I owe her. Owe her a lot. Big time. No doubt about it. I had no way of getting rid of that baby and she helped me out of a jam, but I'm getting to the point where I think I've paid my debt. Sure, she pays me good for what I do. Christ, I'm twenty and have $200,000 in my savings account. Didn't even graduate high school, and she got me away from my father, that bastard, who beat the shit out of me once a week from the time I was little just for the heck of it. Yeah, I owe her, but I just wish she wasn't such a fucking bitch.

And now I have to see Calvin. So disgusting. His breath always smells like onions, so gross, and I have to act like I have a crush on him. Seriously, does he really believe that I would have a crush on him? Twenty years older than me, overweight, dirty fingernails. Geez. But obviously he does because I can make him do just about anything I want him to do. He puts the clerk's special seal on the birth certificates I bring him without any questions at all. I have the new baby's birth certificate with me now. He types in the names of the parents that Savannah finds up in New York and presto! Their adoptive baby is now their biological baby.

I always find it funny how some people go to great lengths to get rid of their babies and other people go to great lengths to get a baby. I guess in that way Savannah is just matching these people together. A public service she says. But to live it makes you feel like a criminal. We are sworn to secrecy about what goes on and none of us knows the whole of it. None of us has ever met Tom, the magic doctor. Vadoma sometimes gets to go to New York with Savannah to transport the babies and act as the nanny. Savannah hates to touch the babies. She won't even let us give them a name the poor things. We were never allowed to name the little girl all over the news and she was with us for a year and a half. The Golden One or Goldie. That's what we called her because of her beautiful golden hair, but to her face we called her "Baby."

Couldn't get rid of that one or Kayleigh. At least now Kayleigh has a name. We were trying to move too many girl babies at the same time when Goldie was born and when her scheduled adoption fell through, Savannah and Tom just couldn't place her. People with money will pay top dollar for a newborn. Under a month. They also want boys. They'll pay more for boys and choose a boy over a girl every time.

I don't really know how much Savannah gets for a baby, but she pays me fifty thousand dollars a year. I don't know anyone, outside of the farm, that makes that kind of money. And I don't have any expenses. I live at the farm and eat at the farm. If I get sick, Savannah and Hattie take care of me. I only buy clothes, jewelry, personal stuff. I did buy this car, which is awesome. My biggest purchase ever. But, besides that I just bank my money and wait to leave. Trying to figure out where I'm going.

I park the Bimmer in front of the Department of Vital Records and apply a new coat of lip gloss. As much as I hate Calvin it's good to get away for a while. And after this I'll see Lee. Even though Savannah frowns on us having boyfriends— they are strictly forbidden to come to the farm—I've been seeing Lee for a few months. He works at the local Exxon, and I met him when I got gas one day. I like the way he smiles all the time, and he has his own apartment so we have somewhere to go.

Calvin likes to stare at my boobs so I wore a tight, low-cut T-shirt for him to get a good look before he fills out the forms. Savannah is constantly on me about my weight, but I like my curves. Not everyone was blessed with a perfect Barbie-body like her. Big boobs, tiny waist, and firm butt. She could be a Victoria's Secret supermodel if she wanted to, but she would never do anything like that. Well, Hattie said I was "curvaceous" and that made me feel good.

Anyway, I reminded Savannah once that we had Calvin under our thumb because of my ample cleavage and that shut her up for a little while.

Today, I need Calvin to give me the embossed birth certificates for the new baby. The application for the birth certificate needs to be signed by the "biological parents," so I always tell Calvin that our clients pay me to get the forms, bring them back for signature, and then bring them back to him. In reality, we all take turns signing them so the signatures won't all look the same. We only had one lawyer who wanted to sign his own form but when he was gently reminded by Savannah that the whole operation was a fraud he didn't complain again.

I take a deep breath and head into the one-story government building. It's showtime!

"Hi, Calvin!" I say in my sweetest sing-song little girl voice as I saunter over to his desk swinging my hips.

"Kelly, hi," he says as he looks up at me. I see him start to sweat. Little beads of moisture on his top lip.

"Have a minute?"

"Yes, of course," he says trying to sound business-like.

I sit down in the chair next to Calvin's desk and press my arms into the sides of my boobs to puff up the girls. To make sure that he gets a good look. Giving him the innocent eye, I ask. "How've ya been, Calvin?" My voice is a slow, silky drawl and I look at him like he is the smartest, most important man that ever lived. "You look so busy."

"Well, I am busy. Very busy."

"This will only take a minute. I just need to have a seal put on these birth certificates."

"Yes, yes. Where's my embosser?" He starts to open drawers, all the time staring at my cleavage.

"It's warm in here," I say as I take off my jean jacket.

"Yes, warm." Beads of sweat drip down from his sideburns.

"Isn't that it?" I say pointing to the embosser right on his desk.

"Oh." He chuckles. "Yes, yes."

"I need six copies," I say sweetly. "You do such important work, Calvin. My gosh, how would anyone have a baby without you?" Then I laugh. "Well, I guess I know how to make a baby, I mean, that's so silly of me." I giggle as his eyes grow wide and he can't look at me anymore. He's in a complete sweat now, cheeks blazing red. I can smell his sweat. He's so pathetic I want to gag.

Calvin very quickly embosses the documents and hands them to me. "You can pay at the cashier," he says without looking at me.

"Thank you, Calvin. You're the best," I say as I get up and leave.

"Yes, yes." I hear him say behind me.

11

ANABEL

This is my recurring flashback. I'm sitting on the floor in the second bedroom of my apartment poring over fabric books. Sam had told me to go ahead and create the nursery of my dreams, and I am choosing beautiful pink and raspberry fabrics for the quilt and sham for the day bed and coordinating stripes for the pillow for the rocker.

I've already had the walls painted the lightest shade of pink and stenciled a garden scene with raspberry cats, light blue dogs, and yellow bunnies. On one wall is a white crib and under the window is a matching changing table.

The drawers in the dresser are already full of little undershirts, T-shirts, and socks. I know I should wait. All those wives' tales about bad luck, but things are going well, and I've waited my whole life to set up this room. The flashback ends when I miscarried at six months. After I lost her, Sam and I had just stopped going in this room. We shut the door and never opened it again.

But tonight, as the subway screeches to a stop and I am brought back to the present, I know it is time to open the door, to go into the nursery. If I am really considering adopting the baby, I will have to come to terms with this room. I will have to finish the room and get it ready for her. There will be a home study done and they will want to see the room where the baby will sleep.

I walk home, sneak into the back door of my building because I am still avoiding the press, let myself in the apartment, and immediately go and open the door to the nursery. But there's an invisible shield in the doorway, my legs will not cross the threshold into the room. I am frozen in the hallway. Trying to be positive, I congratulate myself for opening the door. The room is spotless. The cleaning lady vacuums and dusts every week but knows to close the door before I get home. As I stand there peering into the room, Dennis calls.

"Hi," I say, trying to disguise the sadness in my voice.

"Hi. I just wanted to see if you made it past the reporters on your way out of work. Are you okay?"

"Yes, I'm fine. I snuck out the service door and then into the back of my building. It's . . ."

"I know it's hard to be hounded by the press."

"No, it's not that. I mean, yes, it's that, but . . ."

"What's wrong?"

"If I told you, you'd think I was crazy."

"Try me."

So, I do. I tell him about the miscarriages and the room.

"So, you're standing in the hallway but can't go in?" he asks. I can hear the concern in his voice.

"Yes, I know it's nuts."

"Do you want me to come over and we can go in together? I'll bring Chinese and a bottle of wine and after we eat, we can go in. What do you think?"

I hesitate. I think of the decision I have to make about the adoption and how it would be nice to talk it over with someone.

"That would be great." I feel like I take a breath for the first time since I've been home.

"I'll be over in a bit. Just leave the door to the room open. Start to get used to the idea." Dennis hangs up.

I go into my bedroom and change into jeans and my NYU sweatshirt and go into the living room to wait for him. I can see the adoption packet that Ms. Alvarez gave me when I left Child Services sticking out of my briefcase, and I pull it out now. The first page is full of simple information: name, date of birth, gender, race, level of education, marital status—I think being divorced will work against me. Criminal history? No to that.

The next page starts with "If a child has been identified." Name. The child doesn't know her name. No one knows her name. She's obviously been well taken care of. She shows no signs of abuse. She doesn't hide in the corner like she's afraid. She knows Charlie is the name of her dog. But not her own name. It's a mystery. Why aren't her parents looking for her?

I hear the buzzer from the doorman and get up to answer it. I tell Jose to let Dennis up. A few minutes later, the doorbell rings. I can't resist looking in the hallway mirror on my way to the door. I fluff my hair.

Geez, what are you doing? He sees you every day.

I open the door and Dennis is standing there, hands full of food and drink. "Hi! Thanks for coming over. Oh my gosh, I love guests who bring dinner with them. That's pretty great. C'mon in." I hold the door open. Heat rushes to my cheeks. I know I'm rambling, but I can't control myself.

"It's only Chinese." He says lightly as he hands me the bottle of wine and looks around the tidy living room.

I head down the hall. "Take your coat off. Just throw it on the couch and come back into the kitchen."

I set the table for two and start to open the wine as he comes in. I notice he is wearing a tan cashmere sweater that fits him just right. "Thanks so much for coming over. I know I'm being neurotic, and I know it's late."

"It's not that late," he says. "I hope you're hungry."

"Starving," I say with a smile.

"Nice apartment. Eat-in kitchen. A luxury in New York."

"Yes. Here you go." I hand him a glass of wine.

"Chin. Chin," he says.

"Cheers."

We clink glasses and sit down. It feels good to have a person to sit down with.

"So, tell me what happened this morning with the baby."

I launch into the story and in my enthusiasm, I tell him every detail. He indulges me until I realize that I must be boring him out of his mind.

"I'm sorry," I say.

"About what?"

"Boring you with all of this. You should be home, on your couch, watching whatever it is you watch."

"Anabel, I'm not bored. I want to be here." He looks sincere.

I smile, feeling shy. He's so relaxed and easy to be with. Why haven't I noticed him before? He's very handsome. I guess I haven't been looking.

When we're done eating, I clear the plates, rinsing them and putting them in the dishwasher. Dennis comes over and watches me.

"Okay, okay. You've rinsed that plate four times. No need to put it in the dishwasher. Let's go to the nursery."

My heart starts to pound. "Maybe a little more wine."

He offers me his hand.

"Okay, yes, the nursery." I look up at him and take his hand. "I left the door open, as you suggested." I feel embarrassed. What's wrong with me? Why can't I go into a room in my own apartment?

"Good. Which way?"

I drop his hand, and he follows me down the hall, stopping in front of the nursery. The sun has gone down and now the room is dark.

"Does the light work?" he asks, feeling for the switch.

"I honestly don't know," I say with a nervous laugh.

He finds the switch and flicks it on. The room is awash in light. I'm sorry that it worked. I hang back.

"C'mon." He enters the room and holds out his hand. I take it and he gently pulls me into the room. I look around and see all the things I remember placing there so many years ago. Like I put them there yesterday.

"Are you an artist? Did you sketch these?" he asks.

I look down at my hands. "No, stencils. I never got to paint them in."

Dennis puts his hands on my upper arms and turns me to him. "Would you want to paint them or would you want to start over? With new colors? New sketches?"

I look into his eyes because I can't look at the walls anymore. The pain in my chest is growing too great. "I want to start over. I want to paint over all of this and start fresh. That's what I want to do. New colors. New things for the crib." I look at Dennis with enthusiasm. "Will you help me?"

"Are you talking about a new nursery?"

"Yes, I'm putting my application in to adopt the baby. I can't really explain it, but I really think she was meant to be with me. C'mon, who sits in a park and a baby gets plunked in your lap? Did that ever happen to you?"

"No, I can't say it ever did." He laughs.

"See? It doesn't happen."

We're very close to each other, and he's already holding my arms. So close, that when he pulls me into his arms for a kiss I am already there.

12

SAVANNAH

Hattie and I arrive in New York with the newborn the day before the meeting with the potential parents so that I can see Tom and calm him down. This is Hattie's first trip to New York so I told her that she can keep the suite for two extra days after I leave. She can't believe her good fortune. I didn't want Vadoma back in New York City so soon with the police still looking for her. The baby continues to be on the news but much farther down in the lineup.

Tom and I have agreed to meet at his apartment for dinner and a chat and whatever comes after that. I always look forward to seeing him. He's so familiar, like a comfy pair of slippers. I wonder why he never got married. He's a catch —good-looking, tall, smart, a doctor—every woman's dream. I like to think it's because of me. Because he loves me, not because I've ruined him which could be the case. Either way he's always there for me.

Hattie and I have a two-bedroom suite at the Erickson, a small boutique hotel in the West Village. If I ever live in New York City, which I doubt will happen, but if I do, I will live in the Village. There's something romantic about the little windy streets and the cobblestones. Tom, on the other hand, likes the structure of the grid of upper Manhattan. He lives and works uptown, so that's where I'm going tonight. I'll probably sleep there and leave Hattie to mind the baby.

Tomorrow I'll meet with the couple that Tom has introduced me to via email and Zoom. They have been trying to have a baby for five years and are tired of the ceaseless doctor appointments and procedures. They sound ready to meet the baby that we have brought for them. I like to share a cup of coffee with the couple to make sure they are desperate enough to skirt the strict adoption laws.

They told me that they tried to adopt a few years back and that the birth mother had changed her mind at the last possible minute, and they had had to return the baby after having it for six months. It had been a heart-breaking experience for them, and they do not want to go through that again.

I want to reassure them that the mother of this baby is long gone and that she has no desire to ever see the baby again. Part of my procedure is to not give any information about the birth mother to the couple. That was not part of the deal. They got to meet the baby and that was it. I told the couple that the baby was born to a young, healthy woman who wanted nothing to do with the baby. This was true and it was all the information they got.

But that was tomorrow. Tonight, I just want to have sex with Tom and make him feel better about our little business. I have no intention of stopping production because of the Golden One being in the news, so I need Tom to continue to supply me with couples. There must be other doctors I can seduce and work with, but none that I would trust the way I trust Tom.

I pull my little black dress out of the closet and grab the sleek black, patent leather high heels and sheer black stockings that I packed for tonight. Now, a shower and definitely a shave are called for. On the farm I wear only scrubs, jeans, or sweats, so this is a fun change of pace. Maybe I'll suggest we go out.

When I get to his apartment, with a little bit of prodding, Tom takes me to a nice French bistro around the corner, and we're seated in a private back corner. This gives me time to calm him down before the eventual fight about the baby and the continuing news story. It's hard for us to have a conversation because both of our jobs involve the farm and talk of the farm leads to discussing the continuing police investigation.

I try to get him to think about taking a vacation, but he's not buying it.

"Savannah, I'm not going off to Paris or Bali right now. The police are looking for Vadoma in real time. Probably scouring footage of every airport and every flight that left New York that day," he says.

"She flew out of Newark. Listen, I'll leave Vadoma in Georgia for the time being. I brought Hattie with me." I see him wince. "What?"

"I'm not so sure you should have brought in someone else."

"I couldn't handle all the births and all the placements alone. I need a midwife at the farm when it's someone's time, and I have to be in New York. She's fine."

Tom pulls on his hair. He looks so sexy when his big blue eyes are so serious. "I want to get out, Savannah. I don't want to live like a fugitive. One baby was fine. Two. Three. But now we are literally making and selling babies," he whisper-hisses at me.

I sit up tall, my cleavage on display, turn my head in a seductive way and, in my throaty voice, I say, "We can practice making babies, later, if you want." I look at him from under my eyelashes.

"Savannah, that's not going to work this time. We're not a couple. We're . . . I don't know what we are."

"Tom, darlin', they're never, ever gonna trace that baby to

you. You didn't even have anything to do with that baby and now she'll be adopted. Couples are coming out of the woodwork to adopt her. I saw it on the news. She's gone. Out of my life. Out of *our* lives." I reach my hand across the small table to take his hand but he pulls away.

"Let's order," he says, picking up the menu.

"Let's get lots of wine," I say with an edge.

We order our meals and the waiter brings a nice bottle of Chablis. He pours a little for Tom to taste but Tom waves him away and the waiter just puts the bottle down.

"Tom, let's just try and have a nice dinner. What do you say?"

"Okay. I'll try."

I raise my glass. "Cheers."

"Cheers."

The dinner is a downer. I can't get Tom to let it go, and frankly I stop trying. I didn't twist his arm to get into this business. I gave him an opportunity, and he joined me of his own accord. If he feels regret or fear now, he only has himself to blame.

After dinner, on the street I hail a cab. Tom's light blue eyes flicker with anger and then surprise when he realizes that I am going back to the hotel without him. He watches me as the cab pulls up, his jaw clenching and unclenching.

"Good night, Tom. We'll talk." As he turns away from me, I say, "Tom, you entered this partnership willingly. You always act like this is all my doing, but you know it's not. It's *our* doing."

At first, he looks like he's going to object, but then he shakes his head and walks away.

I get into the cab, give the driver the address of the hotel, and put my head back against the worn seat and watch the lights in the buildings go by as we drive down the FDR. A partnership is a very hard thing to dissolve. Tom and I have a business relationship, and a sexual and emotional relationship, but we also have the hardest partnership to dissolve. We are partners in crime. We've literally planned the procurement and distribution of human babies for great personal profit. We've worked outside every legal, and probably, every ethical boundary. I don't really feel that way about the ethical boundary. We are supplying risk-free adoptions for couples who want a family and helping low-income girls from Nowheresville get a start in life that they would never get otherwise.

That's how I see it as the cab zips by the Manhattan Bridge on the way downtown.

13

ANABEL

I'm so tired of running in and out of back doors to get away from the press, but when I take a look outside my building this morning the coast looks clear. The TV cameras are definitely gone. I don't see any stalkers with press badges hanging around holding little notebooks and talking on their cellphones.

"It's been quiet this morning, Ms. Leigh," says Jose, as I walk toward his desk in the lobby of my building.

"Good morning, Jose. Do you think they're gone?" I ask, peering out the glass in the front door. Purposely standing half-hidden behind a potted palm.

"Let me go out and check. You wait here."

I give him an appreciative smile.

He returns in a few minutes. "Obviously, one of them could be hiding somewhere and I just don't see them, but I think they're gone."

I breathe a sigh of relief. "Okay, Jose. Thank you! I'm going to try and go out the front door like a normal person. Have a great day!"

He opens the door for me, I give one last look around and venture out onto the sidewalk. No one confronts me. I start to walk the two blocks to the subway when a young man falls in step next to me. He has the reporter look—corduroy jacket, plaid shirt with mismatched tie, khakis. I wince.

"Good morning. Are you Anabel Leigh?" he asks.

I just keep walking, looking straight ahead.

"I'm Jeremy Nicholson from *The Times*. I know you're on your way to work and this is not a good time to talk, but maybe we can set up a more convenient time. I know we're all interested in finding the baby's parents," he says.

I stop in my tracks and realize that I haven't thought a lot about reaching the baby's parents. I've been so caught up in my desire to adopt her that I haven't focused on her mother's pain. What kind of terrible person am I?

"Listen, I have to go to work. Let me think about it. Give me your card, and I'll call you. Either way I'll call you. Okay?"

"Okay," says Jeremy and hands me his card. "Call me either way. And thanks."

I smile. "Thanks."

On the subway, I try to think of reasons not to talk to Jeremy Nicholson. First of all, I don't have much to add to the story. No one has contacted me. I haven't seen the woman from the park. There are no new details to share. Will Detective Harris be mad if I talk to the press? What will Ms. Alvarez think? And then there's Sol who will know that I lied to him that day. Shit. This is getting complicated.

When I get to the office, I see the line of cameras and I start to shake, my armpits feel sticky. They have found me at work. I have no choice. I call Sol from across the street.

"Where are you?" he bellows into the phone.

"Across the street."

"Are you holding a press conference?"

"No! No! Sol, let me explain. I was sitting in the park—"

"I know the story, but why didn't you come to me? Let's try to control this. Can you get in the back?"

"I'll go around," I say, but he has already hung up.

I decide to go two blocks west and then turn north to go behind my building, making a large circle around the gaggle of reporters. I enter through the loading dock and have to explain to the building manager why I am sneaking into the building. After checking my ID, he begrudgingly lets me in.

Sol, Dennis, and Tanya Talbot, our media relations director, are huddled in Sol's office when I enter. It irks me a little that Tanya is already involved seeing that she reports to me. Sol must have reached out to her directly. He seems cheerier than when I spoke to him on the phone.

We offer hellos all around and I sink into an empty chair rubbing the back of my neck. They get right down to business.

"So, Tanya is suggesting two to three well-chosen interviews instead of a press conference," says Sol. "That'll be easier for you and allow you to control the story instead of the herd throwing questions at you." At this point he looks at Tanya to elaborate on the plan.

Everything about Tanya is shiny—her hair, her skin, her nails. Like she is laminated every morning. "I'm thinking *The Times*, *The New Yorker*, and one other. You'll agree to the interviews because you want to help find the parents of the girl. A Good Samaritan who didn't choose this and now wants to do the right thing," says Tanya.

"What do you think, Anabel?" Dennis asks. "Is this something you even want to consider?"

I look from Dennis to Sol to Tanya and try to focus on the fact that this situation has nothing to do with C&W Communications. This is my decision to make. "Well, before this morning I didn't want to speak to the press, but then a *Times* reporter, Jeremy Nicholson, found me on my way to work and he got me thinking about the parents of the child, and I do want to help find them if they're out there. I think I want to speak with him, but I don't really have anything new to say."

"It doesn't matter. It'll be the first time the case will be reported from your point of view. The only eyewitness," says Tanya, her teeth gleaming. "I can help to prep you."

"Be sure to mention that you work here, at C&W Communications," instructs Sol, pointing at me and raising his bushy eyebrows. "It'll be good for business. What's good for business is good for you. Now, I need to get back to work. Take the day to figure it out. Thanks, everybody," he says, dismissing us.

We all collect our things and move out into the hall.

"You okay?" asks Dennis.

"I guess. What do you think? Should I talk to them?"

He hesitates a minute, thinking it through. "If you think it will help to give the baby's parents the opportunity to know where she is then I think you should do it. Maybe when they realize you don't have any other information the press will leave you alone."

"Yes. That would be nice." I turn to Tanya. "I'm going to talk to social services and then I'll let you know what I want to do."

Dennis and I head toward my office and he puts his arm around my shoulders. I lean into him and he smells so good, like sandalwood.

"Are you okay?" he asks.

"It's just a lot, but I'm okay. Thanks for being there for me," I say as we turn into my office.

He plants a quick kiss on the top of my head. "I gotta go. I have a meeting. Dinner tonight?" he asks as he walks out of the office.

"Yes, I'd like that," I smile.

Plopping down at my desk, I check my calendar. I have time now to call Ms. Alvarez. I find her contact in my phone and hit the button.

"Good morning, Anabel. I thought I might hear from you," she says.

"Good morning, yes, I wanted to touch base with you and let you know that I will be dropping my application off later today. I had such a great visit with the baby, and I just feel that we are destined to be together. I really feel that way," I tell her.

"I saw the connection, Anabel, and I'm glad that you are moving forward."

"Ms. Alvarez, *The Times* has approached me. Actually, every paper in town has approached me for an interview, and I've literally been running away from reporters for days, but I think I should tell my story and try to reach the girl's parents if they are out there somewhere now before the adoption goes forward. For me or any other adoptive parents. And I just wanted to let you know before I do. Talk to them, I mean. Is that okay?"

There's a pause on the other end of the phone. I hold my breath. "Yes, I think that's okay. Obviously, you can't say where the baby is or who she's with."

"No. Definitely not. Can I say that I've seen her?"

"No. Just say that you have been advised by Child Services that there are confidentiality laws and that you can't answer questions specific to the girl. Only about what happened in the park. Also, I'll text you a number to run with the story in case anyone has any information."

"Okay. Got it. I'm glad we talked. I'll see you later to drop off the application. Thanks."

"Thank you, Anabel."

I get out a pad of paper and a pen to write out key points that I want to make when I talk to the reporters. Halfway through, I stop to think. Should I be doing this? Does it help the baby? Does it help me get the baby? I realize there are no definitive answers to these questions, but it seems like the right thing to do.

After I've written out my key talking points, I call Tanya and ask her to come into my office.

As she steps into the office, she says, "I've already booked a conference room."

My nostrils flare and my cheeks get hot. "I haven't even

told you that I agree to the interviews yet. That was presumptuous of you to book a conference room."

Tanya runs her hand through her perfect hair. "Are you doing the interviews?"

"Well, yes. I have decided to do the interviews."

"Well, now we have a conference room."

Our gazes lock. God, why did I hire her? She constantly challenges me and never shows me the respect I feel I deserve. "Fine, call Jeremy and get him up here this afternoon. Reach out to Sarah at *The New Yorker* and see if we can do them at the same time."

Tanya makes a note and then looks over at me. "Okay. Let me see what you're wearing." She gives me the once-over, frowning slightly at my tan suit, cream silk shirt, pumps, and pearls. "Nice. Respectable, but fairly fashionable."

I ignore the insult.

Tanya and I prep for an hour. I tell her that I am going to try and adopt the baby and she is adamant that I not share this with the reporters.

"Stick to the day in the park. It's none of their business how you feel about the baby or your future plans. I can tell that you have feelings for her. Try not to go there. The reporters will smell blood if you do. A random woman chooses you in the park and now you want the baby. That can be misconstrued. They will go in for the kill—they'll think you know more about the baby than you're telling them. We don't want you to be put on the defensive. Okay? You got this. You started in media. And try to mention C&W at least once so Sol doesn't bite our heads off." She rolls her eyes. "Okay. I'll invite them both in at two p.m. Does that work?" she asks.

I nod. "Tell me again, why am I doing this?"

"They're going to follow you around until you do. Let's do one and done," she says.

"Okay."

After she leaves, I try to clear my mind and think like a

media specialist. I dial Tanya's number. "Get *USA Today* also. They have a huge circulation."

"Thinking like a pro," she says and hangs up on me.

Once this is over I really have to think about Tanya's future in my department.

14

SAVANNAH

Hattie and I are sitting in the living room of the suite drinking a second cup of coffee when my phone dings. I see it's a text from the couple. "Hattie, they're here. Take the baby and go in the bedroom and keep her quiet."

"C'mon, baby." Hattie puts the baby in the infant seat and carries her into the smaller bedroom in the suite.

"I'll come and get you if they want to meet her. Make sure she's clean," I say as she retreats into the bedroom.

"My babies are always clean," says Hattie without looking back.

I smooth my hair and check my lipstick as I wait for the couple to come up in the elevator. I count to five after hearing the knock, then open the door and let them take me in. This is important because I look legitimate, smart, perfectly coiffed and tailored; I look like someone who knows what she is doing and this first impression is what will make them trust me. While they are judging me, I am sizing them up.

Mr. Synder is smart but nerdy. Probably a tech titan. Totally in love with his wife who is the definition of a walking broken heart. Her tired, worried eyes tell me how nervous she is. She's obviously been up all night trying to decide if this is a good idea. All of this is helpful. I can allay her fears and make her feel hopeful by telling her what she wants to hear. That she will have a perfect little baby that will never be taken away. That she can have her today. That the mother of the baby is long gone and will never know where the baby has been placed. There's no waiting period. This baby will belong to her forever.

While I am winning over the wife, I have to keep the husband in line. Sometimes the hard questions come from the men. Legal questions. Money questions. We will get to these questions, but first, I need to completely get the mother on board. Get her to believe everything will work out with this child. After I lock her in, she'll help me work on him.

"Please sit down." I gesture toward the loveseat in the sitting room. "Can I get you something to drink? Coffee? Seltzer?"

The man looks nervous as he sits.

"How about you, Mr. Snyder? A glass of water? Might be a Coke in the mini-fridge."

"I'll just have some water, thank you," he says.

I smile. A kind smile and his shoulders relax a bit. "And you, Mrs. Snyder?"

They sit very close to each other on the loveseat holding hands. "Yes. Water would be nice."

When we're all settled in, I start by bringing up the painful experience they have been through. "I'm so glad you decided to meet with me. The services I offer are different from the adoption path that you followed last time. I know how difficult it must have been to give your baby up after being with her for six months. After you had become a family."

Mrs. Snyder starts crying and Mr. Snyder puts his arm protectively around his wife's shoulders.

"The uncertainty that you felt for six months and then the wrenching ending will not happen with me. I can see that you love each other and that is the most important gift you can give a child." They're both crying as I continue. "The baby in the other room, her mother was young. Too young to raise her. She made a mistake and had nowhere to turn. She was a college student with a bright future. I helped her and now she's getting her life back on track. I want to help you put your life back on track, and, most importantly, I want to put the baby in a loving home. One that I know you will provide for her."

Damn, I'm good if I do say so myself. I pause to let the story sink in. Smart girl. Young. Has a bright future that would be ruined by the baby.

"The baby is here. She's in the other room." I point to the door across the room like Vanna White. "Do you want to meet her? Do you want to take her home today?"

Mrs. Snyder looks up at her husband, her face full of fear and longing.

"Yes, yes, we want to see her," says Mr. Snyder.

"Okay." I get up and go into the bedroom where Hattie is changing the baby. I look down at the child on the bed and she looks perfect. All pink and warm in her little white sweater suit with pink flowers. I swaddle her in a light pink flannel receiving blanket and grab the pre-filled baby bag.

"It won't be long," I say to Hattie. This is Hattie's first time at the sale, and she is a little nervous. She is usually so loud, always quick with the one-liners, but today she is quiet.

"It's going well," I say to calm her.

Going back into the sitting room, I present the child to Mrs. Snyder. There is more crying as I check Mr. Snyder to see how he's doing. Completely enraptured with the vision of his wife and child. Placing the baby bag at Mrs. Snyder's feet, I give them a minute to bond and go and get myself a glass of water. I never leave the child alone with the couple. There's nothing stopping them from walking out of here without making the payment, but they don't realize that.

Five minutes later, I go back over to the sitting area. "How's it going? Do you like her?"

"She's beautiful," says Mrs. Snyder, looking up at me with pure love on her face.

Mr. Snyder asks, "What about the documents?"

"You will get the documents when we complete the transaction."

"I'll call my broker. He said the transfer would be quick." He takes out his phone.

I get up and go back to the kitchen area and pretend to make coffee. He makes the call.

"He says within the half-hour."

"I'll get the baby a bottle. It's almost her feeding time. She's a good eater," I volunteer.

"How old is she?" asks Mrs. Snyder.

"Ten days old." I go to get the bottle. While I'm in the kitchen, I take out my phone to check if the wire transfer went through. I've had enough of these two crying sacks.

Nothing yet.

I go back to Mrs. Snyder and hand her the bottle. She feeds the baby and the baby stares into her eyes. I think that this baby will have a good home, but that's not really my concern. I just need to move the product so Tom doesn't have a coronary.

I check my phone and there it is. Five hundred thousand dollars has been deposited in my account in the Cayman Islands. I look over at the little nativity scene and want to break up the party. The baby's almost done. I'm one burp away from sending the Snyders on their way.

"I see that the transaction is complete. I'll get your documents." I go over to the desk and get an envelope filled with six birth certificates complete with Mr. and Mrs. Snyder's names. I hand the envelope to Mr. Snyder. "Please review the documents. We won't be seeing each other again."

He takes the birth certificates out of the envelope and

checks them. "Let's go," he says to his wife grabbing the baby bag.

"Enjoy her," I say. "Give her a good life."

"We will. We will. Thank you," said Mrs. Snyder.

"Thank you," said Mr. Snyder.

I close the door behind them and smile to myself. A very lucrative morning, indeed.

15

ANABEL

"I had to pull you away from the slippery slope you were teetering on." Tanya admonished me after she dismissed the reporters.

Rubbing my forehead, I try to remember every word I had said during the interview. Why did I bring up the picture of the dog? Who walks around with a children's picture book in their purse?

I've always had a need to fill up silences, and reporters know many of us do. They sniffed me out and knew I couldn't keep my side of the silence. They wanted to give me the space to fill the void with new details, and I delivered.

"One more minute, and you would have told them all about your visit with the girl. We had agreed that we didn't want to go down that road." Tanya sits judging me as only she can do. As I look at her, I notice that there is a stray hair that is caught on her high cheekbone. I've never seen a hair out of place on her and I stare at it. She clicks and clicks her pen. She looks distraught that she has not delivered a perfect interview. Her subject has made an error. She's making me sweat.

"I know. I know. It's just like they were waiting for me to

say something. It was uncomfortable. You should have jumped in earlier." I pull on my pearls.

"I honestly can't believe that you used to do this for a living." The perfect skin on her cheeks starts to redden.

Anger flares in my chest. "You can't believe I used to do this for a living? You're right. SVP's don't usually give interviews. We leave that to the media director and the program heads. And, besides, this is personal. It's different," I say with an edge. I stand up to go, determined to get away from her.

"Yes, well at least Sol will be happy. They'll all be using your title in their stories," declares Tanya.

"Which is the most important thing to you," I shoot back at her.

She stands up and as she turns to confront me, her perfect veil of hair flies out around her face. "I'm not your personal hack. I did you a favor."

"Sol told you to do it but thank you." I head back to my office to lick my wounds. Dennis is waiting for me, sitting in one of the chairs in front of my desk.

Slamming the door to my office behind me, I throw my notepad on the desk and take a deep breath. "Dennis, I am so glad you're here."

"I was going to ask how it went but I can see from your face that it didn't go well." He gets up and gives me a hug.

I allow a quick embrace, breathing in his familiar scent of soap, clean laundry, and something spicy, but then pull away from him, too wound up to enjoy the warmth of his embrace. "First, I made a mistake and gave more information than I should have to the reporters, and then Tanya was kind of bitch."

"She can be sometimes. What happened?"

"Well, I was telling them the story of the park and the police station and when I was done, they all just stared at me. I started to feel uncomfortable, and I just started talking. I told them that the girl had pointed to a picture of a dog and called him Charlie which of course happened at my meeting and not at the park. Ms. Alvarez didn't want me to talk about the meeting, so Tanya had to shut it down and then she said that she couldn't believe that I had ever done this for a living . . ." My voice is getting more high-pitched as I go along. "Who says that to their boss?"

"Wow. I think that's called insubordination. She's not allowed to talk to you that way. But that aside, the interview is over. It's over and you're not going to talk to the reporters or the cops any time soon."

Just at that moment, my phone starts ringing. I look to see who it is. Detective Harris's name comes up on the screen. I show Dennis and he motions for me to pick it up, silently mouthing, "put it on speaker."

I breathe in through my nose and answer the phone. "Detective Harris, hello."

"Hello, Ms. Leigh. How are you doing?"

"I'm fine. What can I do for you?"

"Well, I just got a call from Jeremy Nicholson at *The Times* and he was asking me what I know about Charlie the dog."

"I thought that Ms. Alvarez would have told you about that."

"About what? Ms. Leigh, I am trying to conduct an investigation and if I don't have all the facts, how can I do that?"

"I didn't know it was my responsibility to report to you everything that happens. Is that the case?"

"Ms. Leigh, do you want the baby to be returned to her parents?"

"I do, if she has parents. That's why I did the interviews."

"*Interviews?* Who else did you talk to?" His voice is stern.

I look desperately at Dennis who mouths, "tell him."

"I spoke to *USA Today* and the *New Yorker*."

Detective Harris clears his throat. "Okay, now tell me about the dog, Charlie."

I tell him about my visit with the girl and the picture book.

"So, the baby said the name Charlie when shown a picture of a Collie?"

"Yes."

"Another piece in the puzzle. Are you seeing the baby again?"

"I don't know. I want to."

"You want to."

I can feel the detective's suspicion which makes me feel guilty. Guilty of what I don't know, but guilty all the same. "Is there a problem with my seeing her?"

Silence. And then, "If you see her again and she volunteers any information, please call me and not *The New York Times*. Okay?"

"Okay." I hang up and to Dennis I say, "Why does that guy make me feel guilty?"

"That's probably just his way. He wants you to feel intimidated."

"Well, he has accomplished his goal."

"Listen, you haven't done anything wrong."

I look up at Dennis, taking in his concerned, sad face, and wonder if I was falling for him for real or only because he was there for me now. I study his bright brown eyes and his full lips and think that maybe, just maybe, this is the real deal.

16

TOM

"Holy fucking shit!" I exclaim as I bring in *The Times* from outside my apartment door. "I cannot fucking believe this!"

I spread the paper out on the kitchen table to take a good look at the lead story. There she is on the front page, the woman who Vadoma accosted in the park by thrusting the baby in her lap. Anabel Leigh's nice face stares out at me, mocks me. I can't read the story. I feel like I might throw up and start to head to the bathroom, but the nausea fades and I head back to the table.

The headline says it all: "Woman Who Received Baby in Park Wants Parents to Come Forward." The story retells the drop in the park and then quotes the woman. "She didn't seem afraid at all. She just curled up in my arms. I asked her what her name was, and she just repeated the question saying name but later I showed her a picture of a dog and she said Charlie."

Oh, wonderful. Savannah's dog, Charlie. The details are adding up.

My chest hurts. I am not made for this life. I moved to New York City after med school instead of going back to Georgia to stay away from Savannah. She has been throwing me off my game since high school. She was the bombshell from the wrong side of the tracks. Gorgeous. Buxom. Confident. We were the epitome of the Ken and Barbie prom king and queen. But in her junior year, my senior year, she got pregnant, and we were just kids. By the time we told her mother she was five months gone. Too late for an abortion, so when she gave birth, her father took the baby and got rid of it. I still shudder to this day when I think about what happened to that baby. My baby. We never asked what he did with it. My flesh and blood. I had confided in my mother, but she told me that my future was bright and that I should go to college and not look back.

I went off to Dartmouth that August, but Savannah was always with me. I dated other girls, but I couldn't commit to them. She was in every conversation, every flirtation, on every date, in every bed. And still is. We are more married than any married couple has ever been. We're married from the inside out, not like most couples who are married on the outside. Marriage certificates, mortgages, joint checking accounts. Mean nothing next to what we have. We are under each other's skin. We've never talked about it, but it's true. I know she feels it too.

People always say that Savannah looks like Stevie Nicks and she does, but only better. I've never heard Savannah sing, but she has the same husky, gravelly voice. A voice so low and throaty that it reminds me of a big cat purring. Like a lioness or a jaguar might sound. In addition to being a knockout, she's also cunning and smart and manipulative.

We share a lot. We share the experience that makes us who we are. The pregnancy and the fear and shame that went along with it and the dark secret of what happened to our baby. A secret that died with her parents. Her mother might have been the only other person who knew what he did to our baby, who he gave it to, but that secret died with the car crash that took both their lives. I felt sorry for her loss and relief that the secret died with them. I could breathe easier after they were gone.

When I heard that Savannah was studying to be a midwife, I understood her need to be near birth. I became a fertility doctor for the same reason. A vain attempt to erase the birth of our own child. To make amends for our child's botched beginning.

I'm mad now and say I want to stop our business, our relationship, our partnership. But what I really want is to end this madness and live a normal life. She could shut down the farm, move up to New York, be a midwife here. God knows we have more money than we'll ever spend. We've had to open offshore accounts just to park all the money we have. The operation is getting too big. Any one of the women involved could go straight to the police and tell their story. A raid on the farm would produce the evidence. How would Savannah explain the birthing rooms in the barn?

I suddenly wonder if it's only *The Times* that has the story. A quick google search brings up the cover of *USA Today* as well. I scan the story for any more nuggets of information but Charlie seems to be the news of the day. How did that happen? Anabel Leigh just happened to have a photo of a Collie in her pocket? The story doesn't say.

I call Savannah's number and wake her up. "Savannah, the story is on the front page of *The New York* fucking *Times* and *USA* fucking *Today* with a nice photo of the woman in the park and a new tidbit about Charlie—your fucking dog!"

"What? How does the woman know about Charlie?" Savannah's voice is even deeper in the morning when she first wakes up.

"The girl saw a picture of a dog and called him Charlie." My voice gets louder and louder as I speak.

"Shit. Let me get a paper and call you back."

I disconnect and throw the phone down and decide to take a shower while I wait. Glancing at the alarm clock beside my bed, I realize that I'm going to be late for work, and I have an early morning consult.

As I soap up in the shower I think about getting caught. There's no good story to tell about the Golden One or the Dark One as Savannah calls them. They were both born when we had a lot of babies to place and they were the leftovers. When the Dark One was born, we had just started this whole ill-conceived plan. We had two girls and a boy come due, and I couldn't find a third couple. After that, Savannah really tried to space the babies out, but shit happens. When the Golden One was coming, I thought I had found a couple for her but they got spooked at the last minute and didn't show up for the meeting with Savannah. It was my policy to never go after a couple who changed their minds.

The Dark One is now too old and knows all the women's names, so the women are keeping her. And then they hatched this plan to get rid of the Golden One before she knew too much. As soon as I heard the scheme, I was against it, but Savannah does what Savannah wants to do. No one can convince her if she thinks something will work.

I get out of the shower and can't remember if I've washed my hair or my feet. I'm pretty sure I washed everything in between. Wrapping a towel around my waist, I go to make the coffee that I had wanted to make before I saw the paper. I take another look at Anabel Leigh in the photo and feel guilty that this poor woman's life has been turned upside down.

The coffee maker beeps. I pour a cup and go back to the bedroom to get dressed. By the time I'm ready to leave, Savannah has not called me back.

"Typical," I mutter as I grab my coat and rush to the clinic.

17

SAVANNAH

Recruiting the girls started naturally enough. Working at the clinic as a midwife I met many young women who were unintentionally pregnant, as they say. A few months after I placed Kelly's baby, a girl showed up at the clinic one afternoon in the early stages of labor. The doctor at the clinic didn't want us to take walk-ins like this. She wanted us to have a relationship with our clients and start working with them early on in their pregnancy, but here's a girl, scared and crying, standing in front of me, and I didn't have the heart to tell her I couldn't help her. That was back in the day when I still had a heart.

"What's your name?" I asked her.

"Shannon," she said. Her long honey-colored hair was braided down her back and she wore a loose-fitting cotton top, shorts, and flip flops.

"Anyone with you, Shannon? Husband? Boyfriend? Momma?"

Shannon's eyes grew round with fear at the mention of her momma and her hand moved instinctively to her belly. "No. I'm all alone."

"How old are you?"

"Eighteen."

I assumed she was lying.

"C'mon back. Let me see what's going on." She followed me down the narrow hallway back to the small examination room and I handed her a gown. "Take off everything from the waist down. I'll be back in a few minutes."

She took the gown, looking up at me with large, scared eyes and quivering lips.

I put my hand on her shoulder. "It's okay. I'm here to help you."

I gave her a few minutes and then went back to examine her. I learn that she is in the early stages of labor. I look up at the big clock on the wall and see that the clinic is closing in fifteen minutes. "Okay, Shannon, sit up, here's the deal. The clinic's closing in fifteen minutes, and you are going into labor. You have lost your mucus plug, and your cervix has started to efface. That means that you will start to have contractions soon. Listen, I'm a midwife. I can bring you back to my house where you can give birth, or I can bring you to the county hospital. Your baby's coming tonight either way."

The girl starts to cry. "I can't go to the hospital. My pa works there."

"Well, then it looks like you'll have to come home with me. No one will be there but me. How does that sound?" I ask, making direct eye contact. Willing her to trust me.

Shannon nodded her head and agreed to come home with me.

"Okay, get dressed and wait here for me to close up the clinic." I leave her knowing that it will be hours before the baby comes. When we get to my house, Charlie greets us at the back door with yips and licks and overall excitement.

"You okay with dogs?" I ask her.

"Love dogs," she says as she leans down to pet her new friend.

"So, we probably have a long night ahead of us. I think we should eat something. You hungry?"

She looks at me gratefully. "Yes!"

She sat down at the old farmhouse table in my kitchen, and I cooked scrambled eggs and toast for us. While I stirred the eggs around the pan, I talked to her about what to expect.

"Shannon, I don't have any drugs to give you, so this will be a natural birth. It's gonna hurt like hell, but you'll be okay. Feel free to scream all you want. No one's gonna hear you out here. It's just me and Charlie."

By the time the sky started to turn gray with dawn's first light, the baby took its first breath. Shannon collapsed onto the bed in my parent's old room, exhausted, and was instantly asleep. I looked down at the baby. A girl. I hadn't asked Shannon what her plans were, but I was pretty sure she didn't want to raise her.

I set up the port-a-crib that I bought from the Salvation Army when Kelly had her baby, place it next to the bed and get some shut-eye myself. A few hours later, I wake to the baby crying and Shannon nowhere to be found. Now that's gratitude. Fuck! I grind my back teeth together as I look down at the crying infant and can't believe the girl just skipped out on me. Ungrateful little bitch!

I have no choice but to go to the supermarket and buy a supply of Similac and diapers. Remembering the box of left-over things from Kelly's baby, I go and get it and dress the baby in a little hat and sweatshirt and wrap her in a blanket and head to Walmart. I think about maybe getting a car seat.

Avoiding the stares of the women throughout the store as I run to the baby section with my crying baby, I open a bottle of Similac, put a nipple on the bottle and feed the baby. A Walmart employee, a young pimply boy, is stocking the shelves across the aisle. He watches me and I can tell he is trying to decide whether or not to confront me. I purposely narrow my eyes and glare at him, challenging him to confront me.

"I'm going to pay for it," I hiss.

"Uh-huh," he says and goes back to stocking the shelf.

I load the cart with formula, diapers, wipes, three onesies, two sleepers and a car seat. I'd rather go and get one from the Salvation Army, but I just want to go home and take a shower and figure out what to do.

By the time I get back to the house, the baby is out cold from an overload of calories, so I think things through as I clean up the mess from last night. If I'm going to do this again, I need supplies: extra sheets, towels, gloves, something for them to give birth in besides their T-shirt. And right then it happened. I knew I would do this again. Now, I needed Tom to come on board.

My first call was to Kelly who I saw once in a while in town but usually ignored. She had told me that she wanted to move on with her life, but now I need a favor. I want her to babysit while I go up to New York to see Tom. After I placed Kelly's baby, I gave her a thousand dollars to get herself together, and I'm about to offer her a nice paycheck for three days and two nights of babysitting.

"Hey," she picks up the call.

"Hey, how are ya?"

"Hangin'."

"I'll get right to the point. I need a favor. Can you watch a baby for me for a few days?"

"You got another baby?" Surprise filled her voice.

"Yeah, just helping out another girl like you."

"When you need me?" She asked, quick as a bird.

"I'm flexible. I need three days and two nights."

"Have to take time off work."

"I'll make it worth your while."

That's how Kelly came to work for me. She moved in and came on the payroll so to speak that Friday when she came to take care of the baby. I put her in the spare bedroom and gave her some chores to do as well.

After Kelly agreed to watch the baby, my next call was to Tom. I hadn't spoken to him since we placed Kelly's baby. I told him I was going to be up in New York and asked him to have brunch on Saturday. We met at a little bistro on Madison and Sixty-Third Street. Very close to Tom's apartment. I was hoping that he would suggest going back there after brunch.

I wore a lilac Lily Pulitzer sheath dress with strappy white sandals and carried a new green purse. My long hair was pulled back in a low chignon, and I knew my large silver hoops caught the light as I walked. I could tell by the way Tom smiled as he came toward me that he liked what he saw. I did too. He looked very handsome in pressed khakis, loafers— no socks—and a light blue UNTUCKit button down.

After we sat down, I suggested we order a pitcher of mimosas, but Tom said that he was on call and couldn't drink. I didn't know why a fertility doctor was on call, but I let it go. Although Tom was pleasant, I sensed that he was suspicious of my visit. Trying to put him at ease, I started to reminisce about our high school days. He laughed when I asked if he remembered the time we got caught skinny dipping in the pond out behind old Doc Johnson's house, and he brought up how beautiful he thought I looked when he picked me up for his cousin's wedding. Our first serious date. He looked at me then the same way he was looking at me now, and I thought I might have a chance of convincing him to be my partner.

After the meal, I suggested we take a walk in Central Park and so we headed to Fifth Avenue where there was an entrance on Sixty-Fifth Street. Once in the park, we walked until we found a short trail off the main path away from the tourists and dog walkers and lovers taking a stroll. The trees and bushes were thick and overgrown, forming a canopy of greenery making me feel safe and protected. At the end was one lone bench. Most of the people were walking on the main path, so I thought this was a good place for us to talk. It was a warm sunny day, and I was happy that we had found this shaded spot. As soon as we sat down, Tom relaxed putting his arm on the bench behind me and stretching his long legs out before him. I decided to jump right into why I was in New York.

I straightened my posture and began. "I have another baby."

As soon as I said the word *baby*, he sat up straight. "Oh God. Savannah." He put his head in his hands and shook it from side to side.

"Just let me say what I want to say and then you can think about it. Okay?" I gave him my most charming smile.

"What? What do you have to say?" He looked at me as if he was afraid of my words.

"Tom, there are so many girls in Dubois and the surrounding other small towns who get themselves in trouble and need to find good homes for their babies. You work with couples every day who can't have a baby of their own. It just seems to me that there is a perfect pairing here. I can work with the girls and bring the babies to New York, and you can help me place them. Supply and demand. I think I can produce a baby a month."

"A baby a month!"

"Shh. Keep your voice down and let me finish. I also think I can provide documents, birth certificates, with the couple's names on them."

"How? How are you going to do that?" Tom had started to pull on his curls right behind his ear.

"Let me work out my side, and you work out your side," I reached down and put my hand on his thigh.

Tom looked at my hand and then up at my face. As soon as his eyes met mine I held his gaze. I knew the effect I had on him, that I'd always had on him, and I could feel his resolve start to lessen. He looked down at my lips and I knew things were going my way.

"Let's go back to my apartment," he said.

"I'd like nothing better," I whispered as I placed a gentle kiss on his lips.

From that day forward, we produced a baby a month and placed them in wealthy homes in the tristate area. There seemed to be no dearth of rich people who desperately wanted a baby. Were we technically drawing outside the lines? I guess so, but it just felt so right that I never gave it much thought.

And Tom and I were back on, picking up just where we left off in high school.

18

KELLY

With no babies in the house and Savannah in New York City, Vadoma and I relax. Like two teenagers with our parents out of town we eat pizza, drink margaritas, and leave dishes in the sink overnight. When Savannah is home, dishes must go right from the table to the dishwasher. She even takes the plates off the table when we're still eating sometimes. But she's coming home tonight so the party's almost over and we're enjoying one more stress-free morning.

Vadoma is fixing Kayleigh pancakes as I turn on the TV to find some cartoons for the girl to watch, but as soon as the picture comes on there's the Golden One as big as life on the screen and the reporter is talking about the woman who Vadoma gave her to in the park.

"There's a new piece of evidence in the story of the baby who was left with a stranger in a park two weeks ago. The baby has used the name Charlie in connection with a dog that she saw in a picture shown to her by Anabel Leigh the woman who she was left with in the park. Authorities believe that the girl's family must have a collie named Charlie."

The segment ends with a split screen of Anabel Leigh and the girl.

Vadoma and I look at Charlie sleeping peacefully in his bed by the backdoor, and then at each other. It is one of Savannah's rules that we don't teach the girls our names, including Charlie's name for this exact reason.

"Did you ever hear her say Charlie?" Vadoma asks me.

"I don't think so." I shrug.

"Kayleigh, did the baby know Charlie's name?" Vadoma asks the girl as she puts a plate of chocolate chip pancakes in front of her.

Kayleigh nods her head and turns her attention to her pancakes. Kayleigh is quiet, but smart.

"Did you teach her how to say Charlie?" Vadoma asks taking a step toward the girl.

I get up and put myself between Vadoma and Kayleigh as I pretend to go to the fridge for more milk. "Even if she did, how are the police going to trace the name back to this dog?" I don't think Vadoma has ever hit the girl, but I can see a darkness in her eyes that I don't like.

Vadoma goes over to the sink and starts doing the dishes. "She's comin' back tonight, and she is gonna be livid. She doesn't like loose ends." Vadoma is throwing the dishes in the dishwasher and soapsuds are flying all around her.

I watch her and can feel the panic she is radiating. "Aren't you tired of her?" I ask in almost a whisper. Like Savannah might hear me if I speak in a normal voice.

"Where I come from, you don't mess with the hand that feeds you," Vadoma says without turning around. "She took me in when I was hungry. I was hungry for a year before she hired me, and I don't want to ever be hungry again. Sure, she's gruff, but our stomachs are full—our bank accounts too —and that's 'cause of her, so let's clean this place up and get ready for the storm."

"I guess," I say reluctantly. Although Vadoma is right, I don't want to admit it. Savannah treats us like we're not as good as she is and that makes me angry. I know she's done a lot for me and was there when I needed her, but does that entitle her to treat me this way?

After we clean up the kitchen, I go upstairs to take a shower and get ready to meet Lee. We have a date to go horseback riding and then back to his apartment. When I'm with Lee, I turn into this giggly girl that I don't even recognize. I pretend that I live with my strict parents in a loving home and that I go to the community college in Evertstown. I try not to say too much about myself because I'm not good at remembering the lies.

I've been riding since I was little, just like everybody else that grows up in these parts, so when he says he wants to go to the stables and ride, I agree. All I really want to do is go back to his place and ride him, but if he wants to take me on a real date I'll play along.

I have a lot of clothes, which he has remarked about a few times, so I purposely wear the same yellow shirt that I wore when I saw him two weeks ago. The clothes and the BMW mark me as a rich bitch, and I don't want Lee asking a lot of questions that I can't answer. Like, what does your father do? Can we go to your house? What are you studying at school? I told him that I am an au pair for a rich woman in Dubois. That's not too far from the truth. I do work for a rich woman and take care of babies.

The first time I saw Lee, he was working at the Exxon. He had a car up on the lift, fixing some unseen part. His biceps were expanding and contracting as he wound the wrench around and tightened a nut. His broad back slimmed like a funnel to his waist and then his thighs puffed out again. I was waiting to ask him to put air in my tires, but I became mesmerized by watching him work. He had his baseball cap on backward, thick blond hair peeking out. When he realized that I was there leaning on my BMW, I couldn't remember what I wanted him to do.

After that day we met at least once a week to fuck ourselves into a coma. He's the first man I've been with since the baby, and I feel like I have a lot of catching up to do. But today we're going on a real date. Our first. Conversation is going to be tricky, but I can use Kayleigh and the baby as the kids I take care of. Savannah can be their mother. I laugh at the thought of that. Savannah as a mother. I'm sure that the only thing she can give birth to is a dollar bill.

When I pull up to his apartment, he's standing outside waiting for me. I glance at the clock in the dashboard and realize that I am fifteen minutes late. Annoyance and relief flash across his face. I run over to him and give him a long smooch before he can scold me.

"I'm sorry. I lost track of time." I giggle and feel him melt in my arms.

"I thought you weren't coming," he pouts.

"But here I am. Got my cowboy boots on and everything."

He smiles, a sexy lopsided grin. "Let's take the truck. We don't want to get mud in your fancy car."

On the way to the stable, I can't decide whether or not to let him pay for the horse rental. I know I have so much more money than he does, but I don't want to insult him by paying. As I mull this over, I stare out the window at the endless fields of peach trees just starting to bloom.

"We'll be able to get peaches soon," I say just to break the silence.

"Not a big fan."

"Lee, is there something wrong?"

"I'm just a little nervous. Never been on a date before."

I look over at him and I realize that he has on a new shirt and that his hair is combed.

"Well, I'll tell you a secret. Neither have I."

He looks over at me to see if I'm serious. "Never?"

"Nope, never. Not till now. With you. You're my first."

He looks over at me and raises an eyebrow. "Really?"

"Well, not the first at that, but my first date."

"Well, I guess the pressure's off then." He says with a playful chuckle.

"Yeah, no pressure," I say.

We go to the stable and Lee rents two horses for an hour. I let him pay. I jump up on Rusty and Lee gets up on Sue, and we canter off across the field to a wooded area about a mile from the ranch.

"You ride like a pro." He gives me a grin as we slow the horses down to enter the forest. "You have a nice seat."

I wink at him. "I've been told that before." I take my feet out of the stirrups and stretch my legs. "These woods are pretty deserted."

He comes up beside me and reaches over and runs his hand up my thigh starting at my knee. I arch my back and bring myself up to his hand.

"C'mere," he says.

He helps me jump from my horse to his horse, facing him, squeezing in between the horn on the saddle and Lee. My horse bends his head and starts to eat the new vegetation. Lee kisses me so deep I think I'm going to faint. His hands are on my breasts, and I knock his hat off to run my fingers through his hair.

"My hat." We both jump down to get it.

He looks around at the forest bed, the light is dappled from the thick leaves on the tree overhead, looking for some place soft. At the foot of a big oak tree is a bed of leaves. He grabs my hand and leads me over. Pushing me up against the tree he kisses me with such urgency that I rip his belt open and reach inside. He lays down and I straddle him. The pine needles digging into my knees somehow only add to the pleasure. The horses watch us with placid brown eyes.

When we're done, I look down at him and say, "So, how's your first date?"

"Pretty great!" he says. "You?"

"Yeah. Pretty great!" I plant a big kiss on his lips.

We lie under the tree, still half dressed, looking up into the green leaves over our heads. Savannah and the farm and the Golden One seem very far away.

19

ANABEL

It's Saturday morning and I am getting dressed to meet Dennis. Considering my new celebrity status, I wonder if I should wear all black? Hide my hair under a hat? Don large sunglasses? My face has been on the cover of almost all newspapers and news shows in New York City and requests for interviews are still coming in. The story is being covered on national news programs. It's hard to get used to all the attention. Random people telling me they saw me on the news, asking me if the story of the baby just getting thrown into my lap is true.

The parents of the baby have still not come forward, and Ms. Alvarez doesn't think they will. How do I feel about the baby's parents? Conflicted. Guilty because I feel conflicted. Sure, I want the baby's mom and dad to be reunited with her. But, if they've been killed in a plane crash or car accident, isn't it out of my hands? Still, wouldn't the police have connected a dead couple to the baby? Wouldn't there be other relatives? Grandparents? Aunts? Uncles? So many questions. Where did she come from?

If they come forward, I'll deal with it then. I'm meeting Dennis at the store to buy new paint for the nursery. I want the baby's room to be ready for the home visit by Child Services. I'm keeping all the furniture but changing the color scheme. I haven't decided what color yet. Yellow? Green? Lavender?

All of a sudden, my life is so full. Sitting in the park that day I was feeling alone, and now I'm painting this room for a baby I might adopt. And Dennis. Sweet Dennis. Why didn't I see him before? We were always friends but now we're . . . I'm not sure exactly what we are. Are we dating? We've shared one kiss. I don't usually wear any make-up on Saturdays but since I'm spending the day with Dennis, I want to look nice. Not too much, just a little mascara and blush.

Sherwin Williams is between my apartment and his townhouse, so we decided to meet there. When I get out of the cab, he's standing in front of the store, off to the side, waiting. I catch my breath like a schoolgirl. Dennis greets me with a hug. Unexpected but welcome. I love the way he smells, mostly like the dryer and clean clothes. He keeps his arm around my shoulders as we walk over to the front door and it feels like heaven.

Dennis, who is always dressed in beautifully tailored clothes, is wearing old jeans and a Nantucket-red crewneck sweatshirt.

"Are you sure you want to get paint on your Nantucket sweatshirt?" I ask.

He looks down at his sweatshirt. "Well, I can always get another one. Have you been?"

"No, never. You obviously have or, sadly, you just bought the shirt online," I grin.

He laughs. "I'm not that much of a loser. I go up as often as I can. Maybe I'll take you up there sometime." All of a sudden Dennis sounds unsure.

My heart starts to pound. "That sounds great, but today, we paint!"

"Yes, today is all about paint!" He sounds happy to be on firmer ground.

As we get to the door, two women both look at me at the same time and say "Baby Lady." That's what *The Post* has been calling me. Dennis and I stop in our tracks and stare at them.

The older one shrieks, "Oh my God! It's you. The lady in the park with the baby. You're the Baby Lady!" She's pointing at me. "Did they find the parents? It's so sad." She frowns and shakes her head.

Other pedestrians turn and stare at me and wait for a reply. A man with a dog actually tells the dog to "sit" so he can hear my answer. Other people stop and form a circle around me, around us.

Dennis pulls me closer and simply says, "No luck yet," as he hurries me through the door and into the safety of Sherwin Williams.

"This is getting really old, really fast. Let's get the paint before anyone else recognizes me," I say.

We make our way over to the display of paint colors. Hundreds of little cards with every imaginable color. The number of choices is overwhelming.

"Let's just focus on the paint. What are you thinking?" Dennis stands beside me studying the various shades. I can't tell if he's really interested or just wants me to make a quick selection. After a few minutes, he simply asks. "Yellow?"

Drawn out of myself, I try to focus. "Mmm. Yellow or lavender."

Dennis screws up his nose at lavender.

I look up at him. Was he always this tall? "No? Don't like lavender?"

"Not really. It's so Easter."

Laughing, I repeat, "It's so Easter? What does that even mean?" We're both laughing. "Now I can't make it lavender even if I wanted to. Is green too Christmas?"

"A certain green is, but not pastel green."

"And what about yellow? Is that connected to a holiday?"

"No, I like yellow. It's sunny, happy, cheerful."

I am just about to agree to yellow when I notice a young couple staring at us. No filters, no boundaries, just standing there gaping at me, like I'm famous or maybe infamous.

"Oh no," I whisper.

"What?" Dennis looks around and sees them. "Do you mind?" He growls at them. They walk off. "Wow, this is crazy. Pick a color, and let's get out of here."

I pull the color stick for a nice yellow called "Scrambled Eggs" and a pastel green for the trim. We head to the counter to get the paint mixed. Dennis grabs two paint brushes, two tarps, and a roller with a tray, and I grab blue tape and extra rollers.

For the checkout, I put on my dark glasses and pull my hair around my face. We exit the store and run to the curb for a cab. Safely inside the car, Dennis turns to me. "I feel like Bonnie and frigging Clyde."

"Well, Clyde, do you think you can take being with such an infamous woman?"

"I don't like the way they're hounding you," he says seriously.

"It'll blow over. It has to. Right?"

"Right." He gives me an encouraging smile.

We get to my building and haul the supplies through the lobby, into the elevator and into my apartment. We start to prepare the room to be painted, pulling all the furniture into the middle of the room and covering it with old sheets. We protect the floor with the tarps that we bought. The work goes quickly, it's not a large room, and the walls are done before we know it.

"Break for lunch?" I ask.

"I am kinda hungry. Want me to go get a pizza?"

"No, I can make a salad."

Dennis has a stripe of yellow paint drawn across his cheek like a whisker. Without thinking, I reach out and draw a line on the other side of his face to match.

"Really?" he says with eyes twinkling and grabs me and holds me close while he paints the tip of my nose.

"Okay. Okay." I laugh but he doesn't let go. We kiss and like a match being lit, we feel the heat between us and start shedding clothes, trying not to step in the paint trays. When I'm down to my underwear I run into my bedroom with Dennis close behind me.

I guess we're technically more than friends now.

20

SAVANNAH

How can that be? Charlie, my favorite being, is now a problem. I wait to call Tom until I am pretty sure that he will be with a patient. Straight to voicemail. Awesome! I leave a convoluted message about planes and cars and how I have to get back to Georgia. There's really nothing to talk about. The baby said the dog's name was Charlie. So what? Yeah, I wish she hadn't because for some reason it seems to give the police something else to look for, but, really, how would they connect my unlicensed dog to the baby?

Still, Vadoma and Kelly have a lot of explaining to do. They were under strict orders not to teach the two girls any names. Give them any information about where they are, who we are, when they were born, who they are. Kelly didn't seem to care one way or the other, but I knew that Vadoma had a weak spot for the older girl. Kayleigh, as she has now been named. What else could the Golden One say? She does have ears and it's not like we kept her locked up in the nursery, so yeah, she could have heard any of us calling the dog. Damn!

I also hope that Miss Anabel Leigh with her snooty nose, expensive haircut, and pearls is done talking to the press. Hopefully she's had her fifteen minutes of fame and now will sink back into obscurity. Taking one last look at her before I toss the paper, I chuckle. Can you imagine sitting in the park and someone dumps a kid in your lap and runs away? That was a great plan on Vadoma's part and she chose this woman well. Miss Leigh would never make a scene or dump the kid on the bench and leave.

I start to pack my Louis Vuitton bags and think about how happy the Snyders must be with their new little daughter. I guess that's what people want. What they are willing to pay hundreds of thousands of dollars for. And as I wipe a stray thread from the carry-on case that retails for thirty-eight hundred dollars, I am so happy that they are willing to pay that kind of money for a baby.

I'm leaving Hattie in the suite—I'm sure Tom would add that to his growing list of grievances—but I promised her, and she's already invited her cousin in from Chicago, so it's done. I want to get home and see Kelly. She's been on my mind. Something is a little off about her. I know sometimes I'm a little rough with her, but she is so sloppy and lazy. Always late. Has to be reminded about her chores. We've discussed this, and Kelly wants to hire a cleaning lady, but I don't want anyone snooping around. We all have to do our part. Christ, I clean my own fucking bathroom. I made well in excess of two million dollars last year, and I clean my own toilet. I stop packing. Seriously? I made two million dollars! I do need to hire a cleaning woman. I'll have to think about that on the plane.

No, Kelly seems uppity. I know she has a new boyfriend, and I don't want him at the house. She just smiles when I ask her who he is but maybe he's filling her mind with all sorts of ideas. Like she should have a bigger cut. She's got gobs of money though. I don't charge her rent or money for food. The Bimmer must have set her back, but still, she's rolling in dough. I guess I can give her a raise. Maybe.

Kelly has recruited a lot of our girls. It's true. It's easy to like Kelly. The girls feel comfortable with her. They meet me and they are tongue-tied and shy, intimidated by the way I look and act. But she's one of them, and she tells them the story of how I took care of her problem. How I didn't go to work for three weeks and risked my job to help her, which is all true.

After Kelly came to work for me, we hatched a plan for her to hang out at the coffee shop near the high school. She was still only sixteen, although she had dropped out of school, and she would sniff out the young girls who were pregnant. At the right time, she would tell them about me, no names or anything, and ask if they wanted help. Tell them what a midwife does and how they wouldn't have to go to the public hospital. You could see how grateful they were when she brought them to meet me.

As the years went by, I only wanted to work with girls who were eighteen and older to minimize the risk of any pesky parents getting involved, so Kelly started to hang out in local bars that didn't card and the coffee shop. We have never had a shortage of girls. That's why we have Kayleigh and the Golden One in the first place. A glut on the market.

I take a last look around my room in the suite and call the front desk for a porter. In the living room, Hattie is making herself comfortable, sitting on the couch and painting her toenails. The bright blue of the polish pops next to her dark brown skin.

"Going out on the town tonight?" I ask, lifting an eyebrow.

"Yes, we're going to dinner and a show. Thank you so much for letting me use the suite. I feel like Cinderella going to a ball!"

"Enjoy it! It's one of the perks of the job! Don't forget to tell your cousin that you won the weekend at a silent auction."

"Already told her. She's so excited. It's like Christmas!"

I smile. "Hey, Hattie, how's Kelly? She okay?" I feign caring about the girl, try to look concerned.

Hattie concentrates on polishing her big toe. "I think she's okay." She doesn't sound convincing.

"What is it?" I go and stand right in front of her, hands on my slender hips. "What's her problem?"

Hattie looks up at me, hand in mid-stroke, polish dripping off the brush. "She said something about wanting more money."

I feel my face tense up. That little bitch. The doorbell rings. "There's my porter," I say, walking toward the door. "Listen, you have a great weekend, and we'll see you in a few days." As I walk out the door, I glance at Hattie who looks worried. I can tell she feels terrible about ratting Kelly out. I give her a cheery smile as the porter takes my bags.

"Hattie, have a great time! You deserve it," I say as I smile and see her shoulders relax. "See you in a few days."

21

ANABEL

I'm not one of those people who sit in a meeting reading their email or their texts. I actually like to listen to the conversation and participate. Call me a nerd. I'm not cool like Tanya who can do both at the same time as she is doing right now in the Monday morning staff meeting. She can be scrolling on her phone, but if the conversation in the room lands on her, she seems to know exactly what's been said. She never misses a beat.

Monday morning and everyone looks a little tired except Tanya. Her black hair falls like swatches of heavy silk down the sides of her face. Her suit looks new, and the blue of her pumps matches it exactly. She looks like she was up at six, ran ten or twenty miles, went to a salon, and was at her desk by eight.

"Tanya, your report?" growls Sol.

She gives him a tight-lipped smile. "C&W was mentioned sixty-two times in the press last week."

"Thanks to Anabel," says Sol. "How's that going? Have the parents shown up yet?" Looking at me for an answer.

"No, not that I know of, but I have become a reluctant

celebrity. I can't even go to the paint store without people staring at me and asking me questions. It's really unnerving." I volunteer, more than I should, purposely not looking at Dennis at the other end of the table. Until we figure out what we are, a couple or not, we've decided to keep our relationship secret.

"Just keep walking. Don't engage," instructs Tanya. "I do have a pile of requests for you to do morning talk shows. Interested?" She asks, looking at Sol.

I wince. "No, not interested. I want the story to wind down. I don't want to stir it up." My eyes flit to Dennis and I nervously straighten the papers I have in front of me.

"Think about it," commands Sol and I know that means he wants me to do them. "What else, Tanya?"

Tanya finishes her report and the meeting ends. I hear Sol instruct Dennis to stay behind to discuss an urgent matter.

Going out into the hall, I turn my attention to my phone and see that I have three missed calls from Detective Harris. Damn, is he calling to tell me the parents have shown up to claim the girl? I swear under my breath. I hope they haven't, hating myself for feeling this way. Finally, at my office, I press redial.

"Harris," the sound of his voice like gravel under a tire.

"Hi, it's Anabel. You called?"

"Yeah, yeah, I did. I wanted to know if the woman in the park tried to contact you."

I gather my thoughts, even though I know she hasn't. All of a sudden, I'm not sure. He makes me so nervous. "No, she hasn't," I finally stammer.

"Okay and the parents? Has anyone contacted you about the girl?"

"No, have they come forward? The parents, I mean."

Harris clears his throat. "No one has come forward. Ms. Leigh . . ."

"Yes?"

"We found video footage of the woman entering the park with the two girls, so your story checks out. Thought you should know."

Finding courage from his statement that my story checked out, I ask him, "Why? Did you think I made it all up?"

"Ms. Leigh, in my business, you never know."

I hang up with Detective Harris but the phone rings again. It's my sister, Sylvia. We've been playing phone tag for a few days now.

"Well, thank you for taking my call!" she says. "I've been trying to get you for days! Ms. Celebrity!"

"I've been a little busy," I say with a smile.

"You look great on television, in *The Times*, and *USA Today*, and . . ."

"It's so weird to be all over the media like this."

"Tell me about the baby. What happened?"

"Well, it's pretty much as they reported it, but, Sylvia?"

"Yeah?"

"I want to adopt the baby."

"What? Wow! She is beautiful! But, are you sure you want to do this alone?"

I want to tell her about Dennis. Not that Dennis has agreed to help me raise the baby, but he is a part of my life now. It feels like we are going to have a long-term relationship, and he knows about the baby and that I want to adopt her and he hasn't run away. Actually, we've been spending almost all of our time together.

"Anabel? I didn't mean you couldn't do it alone."

"I've met someone."

"Wow! There's a lot going on in your life. Who is he?"

I think of Dennis's sweet face. "His name is Dennis, and I work with him. He's the COO." I can hear the gush in my voice.

"I feel like we're teenagers again and you have a crush on the quarterback of the football team. Is he cute?"

Sylvia is two years older than me, almost to the day, and we've had one of those rare sister relationships where we've always been best friends. We're so different that there was little competition between us. She was the captain of the cheerleading squad, and I was captain of the debate team. We never crossed over into each other's lane, except that one crush I temporarily had on the quarterback.

I giggle. "He is cute and smart and just a really nice guy."

"You're giggling."

"I know. Anyway, he's been helping me get the nursery ready for the home visit. We painted it yellow." I'm not giggling anymore.

Sylvia has been after me for years to sell the baby furniture and make the nursery into an office. She said it wasn't healthy to shut off one room in a two-bedroom apartment. "You went into the room? And repainted it? They're doing a home visit? This is serious."

"You should see her, Sylvia. When the woman threw her into my lap she didn't cry or seem scared. She just sat with me like she belonged in my lap. It was amazing. And then I went to see her at Child Services, and she wanted to be with me. I know it sounds crazy, but it was meant to be."

"What about her parents?"

"Not a word."

I look up and Dennis is standing outside my office. "Syl, I have to go. I *am* at work."

"I'm coming over to see the room and to meet Dennis!"

"Okay, bye!"

"Bel, good luck. I hope it all works out. Love you."

"Thanks, love you, too."

Dennis hears me say, "love you, too," and his face changes. His bright eyes go flat.

I point to my phone and say, "My sister. Sylvia. She wants to meet you."

His eyes light up again. "I'd like to meet her, too," he says, the corners of his mouth tipping up, then he looks serious. "I have bad news and worse news. Which do you want first?"

"Gee, how do I choose?"

Dennis comes into my office, closes the door, and takes a seat in one of the leather chairs facing my desk. "Sol knows about us. He says he can sniff it out when two of his employees are having an affair. That's not exactly what he said, but the cleaned-up version."

An affair. The word hangs in the air over my cluttered desk. Is that what this is? An affair? The phrase "torrid affair" comes to mind. I feel like Dennis just punched me in the chest.

I put my hand over my eyes. I can just imagine what Sol really said. Probably something about two of his employees screwing. I look up at Dennis and ask, "How did he know?"

"Something about how you looked at me when he asked you if you wanted to do the morning shows. Like you valued my opinion more than anyone else at the table." Dennis's lips are turned down in a frown. Somehow Sol knowing about us makes our relationship less special.

"And the worse news?" I sit up straight waiting for the bullet.

"He wants you to do the morning shows."

Dennis and I sit staring at each other. "Look at my desk." I run my hand over the piles of papers. The stacks of files containing the ad campaigns that I have been neglecting for the last week. "I have so much work to do. How am I supposed to get my work done if I have to give these interviews?"

Both of our phones ring. He looks down to see who it is. "I have to take this. Think about it. Delegate. We'll work late and get Thai take-out." Speaking into his phone, he says, "Yeah, I'm here. Can you hold for a minute?"

Letting my call go to voicemail, I eye Dennis over the files. He reaches down, touches my cheek and then leaves my office. I exhale loudly. He clearly thinks I should do the interviews. I know it's crazy, but I feel that he's on Sol's side. Tanya's side. I get up and take off my jacket, push my hair off my face, and open the top file on my desk.

22

SAVANNAH

I wasn't always like this. In high school, before I got pregnant with Tom's baby, I was happy, carefree, and filled with hope. Maybe a little conceited, because I looked like a full-grown woman by the time I turned sixteen. Everyone said I was beautiful, breathtaking, even. The compliments made me feel special, better than the other girls. I was the light in my father's eyes, my mom's best friend, and Tom's willing girlfriend.

Then I got pregnant and became—overnight—scared and alone. When Pa took the baby and did whatever he did with it a part of me died. I remember running into the yard after him, screaming at him to give me the baby back, but he just kept walking toward his car and Ma held me back. Told me it was for the best. I can still see the dust kicked up from his tires as he quickly drove down the long, windy driveway that leads to the highway from the house and how I finally broke away from Ma and ran after the car in my bare feet. Twigs and rough pebbles digging into the soft soles of my feet. But he had already turned onto the highway and sped off.

Luckily, it was near the end of the school year. It was June and the school allowed me to take my exams at home. The summer was a blur and then I went back in September to finish high school. Tom had graduated and gone off to college. I spent most of the year in the library and was accepted to Georgia State University's nursing program in Atlanta for college the next year. Once I was out of Dubois, I felt better but I never recaptured the person I had been before that night.

I decided I wanted to be a midwife to give other women a positive birth experience. It was almost like I wanted to be there at the moment of birth to make sure that the baby was given to the mother and that they would never feel the emptiness that I felt as Pa charged out of the room. I wanted women to control their bodies and their lives in a way that I hadn't been allowed to do.

As a midwife I learned how to deliver babies and how to administer prenatal and post-pregnancy care. The first birth I attended as a trainee was a homebirth. It was the woman's first child, and she had decided she wanted a natural birth at home surrounded by her husband, her sister, and her husband's mother. Instead of my situation, where I had both my parents just waiting to spirit my baby away, this woman was surrounded by love and encouragement.

My teacher at Georgia State, Marney Addams, who was also a practicing midwife, and I arrived at the young couple's home when the woman had been in labor for two hours. The contractions were still erratic, but Marney wanted to see how the woman, Sonia, and her husband Marc, were doing. She wanted to head off any panic they may be feeling, but when we arrived Sonia was comfortable in a loose, flowing dress, her long hair tied back in a low ponytail, and she and Marc were doing the breathing techniques that Marney had taught them.

Sonia's sister was also taking a turn here and there as a breathing coach or making sure that Sonia had ice chips to suck on. There was a lot of positive energy in the room. As the hours wore on, the contractions started to come more regularly and with greater intensity. I had to keep my mind from wandering back to the night in my childhood room as the pain reached unbearable levels and Ma held my hand and stared into my eyes as the contractions intensified. The next morning, I saw the bruises and scratches on her forearms from my desperate attempts to fight the pain.

Sonia's birth turned out to be easy for a first-time mother. After eight hours, she welcomed a son into the world. The joy I felt as I watched Marney place the baby on Sonia's chest healed a little piece of me. As we left the house, I felt a euphoria that I had never felt before. I remember smiling and giving a little skip and a little jump. Marney looked at me and laughed.

"When's your next birth?" I asked her, gushing with enthusiasm. My long blonde hair flying behind me as I twirled around.

"Wow! I haven't seen a high like this since my first birth. It's amazing, isn't it?" Marney grinned.

"I feel . . . powerful. Like we did something important. Like . . . I don't know." My cheeks hurt from smiling so hard.

"I know. Birth is powerful. It's awe-inspiring."

"Yes, it is."

That was thirteen years ago. Between college, graduate school, working at the clinic, and the births at the farm, I have lost count of all the babies I have seen come into the world. Must be hundreds by this point and each one I experience with a little less enthusiasm. Somewhere along the way, after we started matching the babies with parents and receiving large payments, I became more focused on the money than the miracle of birth. I now worry about timelines, traveling to New York with the babies, work schedules, and document procurement much more than birth experience. Most of my mothers are so young and healthy that the birth is uneventful.

Money makes life so easy and so nice. Maybe money can't buy happiness, but it can buy so many things that make you happy. Greed creeps up on you. It makes you feel invincible. The power that comes from knowing that you can take care of yourself no matter what happens makes you fearless. With each five-hundred-thousand-dollar payment, I could feel myself up on a ledge, taking the next step toward my destruction, but that's the thing. Once you're on the ledge, it's impossible to turn back. To give back the money. To eviscerate the transaction.

No, once greed has felt its victory over you, there's no turning back.

23

ANABEL

Dennis and I have fallen into a routine without having a clarifying conversation about our relationship. I just assume that I will be spending my weekends with him. He no longer asks me if I have any plans. He says things like *this weekend we should try the new restaurant on Second Avenue after we baby proof the apartment* or *I have to save time to read the Atlantic Healthcare creative brief on Sunday afternoon.* Statements that imply we have to fit these things into our life.

Our life. I haven't had to take anyone else's needs or desires into account in a few years, and it feels good. I love the fact that he wants to help me in my quest to adopt the baby. She is still mentioned once in a while in the news, but since no one has come forward to claim her there's no news to report. Ms. Alvarez has confided to me that there are a stack of applications to adopt her and that her agency will have to consider them all in order to make the final decision. Because there is no one to surrender their parental rights, a judge will have to rule on the adoption.

On Saturday, after a nice brunch at The Penrose where we order the Cinnamon Bun French Toast Sticks, we head down to Little Folks on Twenty-Third Street to buy baby proofing items and a highchair. We don't know exactly how old the baby is but Ms. Alvarez says the city's pediatrician guesses she's about a year and a half.

As I'm putting the safety latch on the last cabinet in my kitchen, I'm thinking about Dennis's townhouse. "Dennis, how come we never go to your place?" I ask out of the blue.

Dennis owns a townhouse on Eightieth Street between Fifth and Madison, but I've only been there once, on a Saturday afternoon when we'd decided to rent a rowboat in Central Park, so that he could change his clothes. He left me in the foyer with the black-and-white tiled floor while he ran upstairs to find his topsiders and jeans. I wanted to ask him to give me a tour, but he came flying down the stairs and ushered me out the door so fast that I didn't get a chance to say anything.

Dennis looks up from the instructions to the highchair, holding the tray in one hand and the footrest in the other, leans back in the chair at the kitchen table, and looks at me like he is trying to decide how to answer.

"I mean it's fine for us to stay here. I was just wondering, like, do you have a wife hidden upstairs in the attic?" I say with a little chuckle to fill the awkward silence.

"Very funny. No, I do not have an old wife or two locked upstairs. It's just that I want to clean some things out of the house before I give you a tour," he says cryptically.

"Like the dead bodies?" I laugh.

He gets up and comes over to me. I'm sitting on the floor with a screwdriver in my hand. He slides down next to me. "I bought the townhouse ten years ago with my last girlfriend, Mala. My fiancé actually. We had been together for five years at the time and we were happy, or so I thought. Anyway, we bought the townhouse, and she just kept putting off setting a date for the wedding. Finally, she went home to Hyderabad."

"In India?"

"Yes, and I got a beautifully worded email a few weeks later telling me that she had met her soulmate and that she wasn't coming back. That she was starting over. That she was giving me the townhouse and all its contents." Dennis is studying the knuckles on his hands, but he looks up at me for my reaction.

I manage a weak smile.

"I'm so sorry. That must have been awful." I put my hand on his thigh and give him a squeeze. "At least Sam had the courage to tell me he was leaving in person."

Dennis leans his head back against the cabinets. "That was right before I was offered the position at C&W and it couldn't have come at a better time. No one there knew about Mala and so I didn't have to explain what happened."

"So, the house reminds you of her? That's why you don't want to take me there?"

"No. Well, yes. I just never cleaned out her stuff, and I didn't want you to think I was married or that I was living with someone. It's kind of like you and the nursery."

I get a kind of sick feeling in my stomach. "What do you think that says about us? That we're procrastinators? That we can't deal with bad things? That we can't move on?"

Dennis puts his hand on my cheek and urges me to look at him. "Maybe it says that we need each other."

"I can help you. Like you helped me with the nursery."

"Hmm. I think it's a little different. Painting over the nursery is different than throwing away pictures of my ex. This week, one night, I'll go home and purge. It's not that I want any of it, it's just that I haven't had a reason to get rid of it. I know I have to deal with it, and I will now that we're a thing." He looks at me and continues, "We are a thing. Right?"

I stand up on my knees with my hands on my hips, "Dennis Wells. We are definitely a thing. I might even say that you were my boyfriend. Do you want to go steady?"

He pulls me into his arms and kisses me tenderly. "Should I dig out my old high school ring and you can wear it on a chain around your neck?"

"Sure, I'd love that," I say with a grin as I snuggle into his lap.

24

SAVANNAH

The blow-up between me and Kelly and Vadoma was fierce and cyclical and prolonged. It was one of those twisted arguments that had extensions, tangents, and segues. At times we were yelling at the same time and no one was listening. We went around and around about the dog. We agreed that no one else knew he was here or knew his name. We tore into salaries and bonuses. Chores, job descriptions, and responsibilities became a hot topic. Boyfriends and lovers got a thorough going-over. We were tired and spent afterward, but it cleared the air.

We had started out in the kitchen but ended up in the office, a large room that has two desks, a built-in filing cabinet that runs the length of the back wall, and a sitting area with two brown leather chairs and a glass-top coffee table. A large picture window looks out at the barn.

It was a good thing there were no newborns in the house because we were all screaming at the top of our lungs, letting off steam. Vadoma had sent Kayleigh upstairs, telling her to stay in the nursery. Charlie was hiding in the mudroom. I realized halfway through that I had lost control of the situation, so while I kept yelling into the middle of the room I was also figuring out how to handle the situation. It seemed like there were three issues. Money, management, and Kelly's bad attitude that I figured I could control by negotiating a deal. She would try harder to be punctual and do her chores, and I would back off. I would also give them all, including Hattie, who was still in New York, a hefty raise.

I knew I needed to keep my little sorority of sisters together.

"Okay, okay, okay," I shouted over their voices. "Let's all calm down. Now that we've had our chance to let it all out, I want to propose the following." I took a minute here to look each of them in the eye. We were all sweating, our faces flushed, hair mussed, eyes bulging. I leaned back against one of the desks.

Vadoma took a chair, and Kelly went to sit on the built-in cabinet arms folded across her chest.

"First of all, each of you will get a raise. I'll just double what I'm giving you now. Kelly, for your part, you need to do what you're supposed to do in a timely fashion. Don't wait for me to remind you. Vadoma, you will pay more attention to details. Not that we are dumping anymore babies in the park, but whatever has to be done has to be done without loose ends. For my part, I will try to be less critical even though you all make it hard." I realize that the baby being all over the news has put us all on edge and I know I need to be the one to get us through this rough patch. "Okay? How does that sound?"

But Kelly smells weakness like a bloodhound. She pushes her long wavy hair away from her face, ties it back with a scrunchie. "Why can't we get a maid? We have nine babies coming due in as many months and when we're up all night with a crying newborn we're tired. We have bags of money. I think we should hire someone to clean the house."

"Well, you're welcome for the raise," I say, my voice sharp.

"Thank you," says Vadoma.

"Thanks," says Kelly reluctantly. "Look, I'll just tell you I don't want to clean the bathroom anymore. We could hire a whole team of cleaning people."

I jump up off the desk. "Sure. Let's do that and how do we explain that we have girls coming here and giving birth in the barn? Hiring someone else is a risk. Do you think I like cleaning the bathroom?"

Kelly jumps up and we start in again. "The barn will be off limits. We can regulate when the maid comes, or we can find a live-in who will become one of us."

"The more of us the harder it is to control the operation. Let me think about it. Why are you so quiet?" I ask, looking at Vadoma.

Vadoma takes her time answering. "I can see both sides of this argument. I am richer than I ever dreamed of being, but I still mop the floor. It would be nice to have help. However, it is hard to find people to trust. Trust is precious."

"Yes, trust is precious. We're all banded together because if one of us goes down we all go down, but a person who just cleans and isn't part of the business, they have nothing to lose by turning us in," I tell Kelly.

"Well, I'm just telling you now, I don't want to clean the toilet anymore." Kelly stands up, puts her shoulders back, and looks me right in the eye. "You think about it, but those days are numbered."

I meet her gaze and take a step toward her. "You little bitch. I remember the night you were squatting in my barn with hay stuck in your hair."

But, before I can continue, her phone starts to ring. She looks down, "Caroline," she says and takes the call. "How far apart? Yeah, come over now." She hangs up. "Caroline's in labor. She'll be here in ten minutes."

I realize with Hattie still in New York, I'll be Caroline's midwife tonight. "Vadoma, you're up. You can assist me tonight. Kelly, we'll continue this conversation later." And with that I walk out of the office to go put on my scrubs.

25

ANABEL

Ms. Alvarez has told me that it could take between six and eighteen months to adopt the baby and that there are a few other families being considered.

All week I have had an empty feeling in the pit of my stomach. Sol has asked me if I had a problem twice in meetings when I haven't been able to answer direct questions about my accounts. I can't think of anything else but the home study. I've collected my tax returns and my bank statements, mortgage statements, 401K, and IRA documents. I have spent a lot of time thinking about my parenting plan. It seems unfair somehow that I have to have a detailed parenting plan for the next twenty years when people get pregnant every day without a thought about how they will parent on day one.

I've looked online at some of the questions I should be prepared for: Can you provide unconditional love? Do you have the patience to wait for her to show you love? Will you be an advocate for her in the school system?

I have carefully written out answers to all these questions as if I were prepping for the SATs of parenting. My main concern is that I will be a single parent. I know that if I had to choose between giving the girl to me or to a couple, I would choose the couple. Well, there's nothing I can do about that. Ms. Alvarez is on her way over and I have already changed my outfit three times. I've gone from a lavender sweater set to a coral-colored popover to a light blue linen blazer with a silk tee. I keep thinking about the new pink and green silk blouse I bought last week. Would Ms. Alvarez like that better than the blazer? I wish she would hurry so that I don't have time to change again.

Dennis put together the car seat/stroller, swing, and infant seat with hanging primary-colored toys and they are lined up in a row in the living room so that Ms. Alvarez can inspect them. The nursery turned out lovely with its yellow walls, hand woven rug, and matching yellow and white gingham spread for the day bed and pillow in the rocker. A large toy chest sits in one corner, a play table under the window, and a bookshelf filled with all the classics, including *Goodnight Moon*, *Angelina Ballerina*, and *The Very Hungry Caterpillar*.

I think about the baby with her sweet and innocent wide blue eyes and wonder who in their right mind would give her up. If I am lucky enough to get her how will I explain to her where she came from? As I ponder that and take one last look around the apartment to make sure everything is in place the doorman buzzes me.

I pick up the phone to the lobby, and Jose says brightly, "Good evening, Ms. Leigh, Ms. Alvarez is here to see you."

I take a deep breath and say, "Hi, Jose. Send her up. Thanks."

When I got home from work, I baked chocolate chip cookies so that the apartment would smell wonderful when she walked in. I take one more look at myself in the hall mirror and the doorbell rings.

I smile as I open the door. "Hello, Ms. Alvarez. Please come in." I step back and let her in.

"Hello, Anabel. How are you?" She smiles and I feel a little better. "It smells great in here!"

I lead her into the living room. "I thought you might like some coffee and cookies while we talk." We stand there awkwardly with the display of baby equipment taking up half of the room. "Would you rather sit in the kitchen at the table?"

"Yes, that would be good." As I lead her down the hall, she says, "It's so funny that we need so many places to put a baby while we go about our daily life. It looks like you are fully outfitted. She might be a little big for the swing."

"I'm not sure how much she weighs. Most of the items have weight and height restrictions." I feel my back start to tense up. Why did I buy that swing? I feel my pulse start to race.

We move into the kitchen, and I point to a chair for her to sit. She puts down the canvas bag she's been holding and takes a seat. "Let's talk first and then you can show me around."

"Would you like coffee?"

"Please."

I get each of us a cup of coffee and put a plate of cookies in the middle of the table between us. I have a round wooden table and have positioned her so that she can see my well-appointed counters with the standing mixer, coffee maker, blender, and toaster all gleaming from a good polishing.

Ms. Alvarez interviews me for an hour. I have answers ready for each question. At first, I feel my throat closing up, and I repeatedly try to clear it. I get up to get a glass of water. "Sorry, I think I'm a little nervous."

"That's natural, but Anabel, I've seen you with the baby and I felt the natural connection that you have with her, so don't worry." She offers me a gentle smile.

"It's so strange, but as soon as the woman put her in my arms it was like she belonged there. She didn't cry. She didn't struggle. She didn't look after the woman. She just kind of settled in and nestled into my lap. When can I see her again?"

I blurt out. I was going to ask at the end of the night, but I can't help myself.

Ms. Alvarez looks down at her papers. "Anabel, I want to be perfectly clear that there was a lot of interest in adopting the baby. We have narrowed it down to a number of applicants, and I am meeting with each of them. This is going to take some time, but I will try to set up a meeting. Okay?"

I nod. "Okay, I think about her all the time. Have you given her a name?"

"No, we've decided to let the parents or parent name her. It would be too confusing to give her one name now and then change it. So, Anabel, you live here alone. Who else comes over on a regular basis?"

I gather my thoughts. "My sister, Sylvia, and her family. She has three children, so the baby would have cousins. I'm seeing a really wonderful man, Dennis Wells. He's here on a regular basis. And right now, I throw dinner parties for friends and business associates, but I'm sure that those will be put on hold for a while when the baby comes."

"Does Dennis sleep here?"

"Yes, sometimes."

"I think I should meet him, too."

"Okay, that would be fine. He's very nice and gentle. He helped me paint the nursery and buy all the baby stuff. It took him an hour to put together the highchair!" I give a little laugh, trying to ease the tension.

We talk for another twenty minutes and then we start the tour. I point out the safety locks, plug protectors, and window guards throughout the apartment. We walk through the gates guarding the entrance to the kitchen and the two bathrooms. Ms. Alvarez smiles with approval as we enter the nursery that I have outfitted with all of the things I might need to bring the baby home. I have diapers, wipes, PJs in various sizes, beautiful dresses, leggings, T-shirts, sweatshirts, socks, and shoes in a variety of sizes.

"She'll go right to the best-dressed baby list!" comments Ms. Alvarez. "This is a very beautiful room."

"I hope so!" I laugh as we head back to the kitchen for Ms. Alvarez to collect her things.

"I just want to say how much I want this baby, Ms. Alvarez. I'm not a terribly spiritual person, but I really believe we were meant to be together."

As she looks up from her papers, we lock eyes. "Some things are just meant to be," she says.

I am bursting inside as I show her out. As soon as we say goodbye, and I close the door behind Ms. Alvarez, I skip over to my phone and call Dennis.

"Hi!" I say cheerily. "I think it went really well. I think she feels the connection that the baby and I have, and she liked the apartment and everything we bought."

"Anabel, honey, that's great! I'm so happy it went well. Did she like our line-up of baby equipment?"

"She said the baby might be too big for the swing," I say. "But, Dennis, at the end, she said 'some things are just meant to be.' I hate to read anything into her words but that sounds promising, doesn't it?"

"It does. Anabel, I think you'll make an amazing mother."

Tears catch in my throat, and it takes me a minute to answer. "Dennis, thank you. That means a lot. She also said that she would like to meet you because I said that you were here sometimes. I mean, she asked me who comes over a lot, and I said you did. Is that okay? Will you meet her?"

"Of course. I'd love to and I'll tell her what a great mom you'll be. You said I have to talk to her as one of your references anyway."

"Yes. Dennis, thank you. You are so good to me. How did it go on your end?"

Dennis exhales a deep breath. "Twenty-seven black bags of trash. It went fast. The place looks great. Now, I have to dust. And fire my cleaning lady for never moving anything to dust. It's clear surfaces from now on out. Honestly, it feels good. I'm also getting rid of a few pieces of furniture, and I will need your expert opinion on replacements. Your apartment is so nicely decorated. I need your advice."

"We'll go this weekend, if you want to."

"First, I'd like you to see the place. Friday night? I'm cooking!"

"That sounds wonderful." We hang up, and I miss him. It hasn't been that long but I'm getting used to him being here. I wish he were here with me right now. I do want to see his house, but honestly, I'm thinking he should move in with me.

26

SAVANNAH

After Caroline's call, I leave the office and enter the kitchen. Opening the fridge to get a Diet Coke, I hear Vadoma say to Kelly, "You have to take care of Kayleigh tonight, okay? I'll have to assist Savannah with the birth."

And Kelly's sulky reply. "I was meeting Lee."

Leaving them to figure it out, I hurry upstairs to put on my scrubs. About two years ago, I decided that we should wear scrubs when we meet with the girls, either for check-ups or when they give birth. It kind of goes against the relaxed atmosphere that midwives are supposed to create for a home-birth, but I want the girls to have less details to remember about us, so I bought us all lavender scrubs.

I start to think about the task at hand. Closing my eyes, I take a deep breath, hold, repeat. My adrenaline is still pumping from the free-for-all with Kelly and Vadoma, but I think we've dealt with a lot of the problems. They are so ungrateful. Both of them would be slinging hash or cleaning toilets full-time if it wasn't for me. Of course, their raises will have to come out of my cut. I can't go to Tom with any more problems, or can I? Costs are going up. Without my staff we wouldn't be in business. Problems for another day. I need to focus on today's problem.

Caroline is nineteen with stringy, mousey brown hair and freckles across her tiny pug nose. She's very small, probably weighed about ninety pounds when Kelly met her at a coffee-house downtown. Kelly did a lot to help her throughout the pregnancy. New clothes, money for healthy food, a kind ear when things got rough.

The only thing Kelly's not allowed to do is offer the girls a place to stay for the endurance of their pregnancies. I don't want to start running a ward for wayward girls. They have to get themselves through it living at home or wherever they live and then we help with the birth and take the baby off their hands.

The last time I saw Caroline, which was about a month ago, she had gained fifteen pounds throughout her pregnancy. In her Walmart tunic, no one could tell she was pregnant. I was a little bit afraid of how slim her hips were. I usually insist on medication-free, natural births—they go more quickly and there is less recuperation time. Most of our young women are up and about in two or three hours, but with Caroline I thought she would need some pain medication to get her through.

Dressed in my lavender scrubs, my long wavy hair tied back in a neat bun, I make my way out to the barn. From the outside, the barn still looks shabby and dilapidated, and I've left a small vestibule filled with old wood and strategically placed hay when you first walk in, but after you open the first inside door you walk through to a state-of-the-art medical clinic. We have two exam rooms with brand new ultrasound equipment, two birthing rooms each with a comfortable bed, a birthing chair, a comfy rocking chair and a birthing ball, and two recovery rooms. While it is our practice to space out the births, it has happened on a number of occasions that two girls are here at the same time.

I go quickly to the stockroom to make sure I have enough Demerol to help Caroline with the pain that I have no doubt is going to be excruciating for her. Tom gives me a limited supply of the drug to use when one of the girls needs it. I think of Hattie and her cousin drinking champagne and taking a car to the theatre up in New York as I prepare for a long night of breathing and coaxing Caroline through the birthing process. It's unfortunate because Hattie has been the one seeing Caroline for her check-ups. I've only met her once before and we really haven't had time to bond.

Kelly texts me to let me know that Caroline has arrived and she's bringing her in. I'm glad Kelly is meeting her because I've changed my mind about having Vadoma assist. I think the girl will be more comfortable with Kelly by her side.

Waiting in the center hallway as they come in, I'm ready to show Caroline to the birthing room. Kelly opens the door, and I see this hesitant, shy, pitiful girl enter the hallway as if she's on her way to her execution.

"Hi, Caroline!" I say cheerfully. "How are you feeling, sweetheart?" I walk toward her, smiling.

The girl starts to cry and looks to Kelly who envelops her in a bear hug. "You remember Susan, don't you?" Kelly asks Caroline. We never use our real names with the girls. Kelly goes by Casey when she's working. I'm Susan.

"Oh Caroline," I say. "It's going to be fine. Casey and I will be right here with you." Kelly eyes me over Caroline's head and makes a face like *what?*

"Casey, bring Caroline to the blue room and help her get settled. Will you?"

Kelly leads Caroline to the first room, and I hear the girl cry out as the next contraction starts. I go back to the stockroom to get towels, a cloth to wipe the girl's face with cool water, and a plastic bag to put her clothes in. Kelly will have helped her change into a flowing gown to labor in.

On my way back, Kelly is waiting for me in the hall

outside the room. "I thought you said Vadoma was assisting. I have plans tonight." She hisses at me.

"Well, cancel them. The girl is scared out of her mind and you're the only one she knows," I hiss back. "For a hundred K a year, you can reschedule your plans with Mr. Gas Station."

Kelly glares at me but I know that she will do it. She actually cares about the girls, and this one is like a pup who's been beat up by her owner. She turns and heads to the house to tell Vadoma and to get into her scrubs.

Pursing my lips, I hope to God we can move this baby. It's bound to be scrawny. All I need is another Golden One to deal with. Exhaling a loud sigh, I head into the blue room—we have the blue room and the green room, soothing colors to relax the women—and Caroline is doubled over in pain holding her breath.

Hurrying over to her, I kneel down and take her by the forearms. "Look at me. You have to breathe, Caroline. You can't keep the pain locked inside. Think of each breath as exhaling a little bit of the pain. Try it with me," and I take her through a series of breathing exercises.

When the contraction ends, she sinks back into the overstuffed chair. Her hair is stuck to her forehead with sweat and her cheeks are flushed. I bring her a cup of ice chips and she starts to relax a little.

"What will happen to my baby?" she asks.

I am surprised by the question, most of the girls don't want to know. "It'll be placed with a nice family. Out west," I say. "Don't you worry about that. How are you feeling?"

"How much are you selling it for?" she asks.

I wonder if Kelly has put her up to this line of questioning to get back at me.

"Caroline. Caroline, look at me and listen to what I say. Do you want my help right now? Because if you want to keep your baby, I will drive you to your parents' house right now and let your mother spend the night elbow deep in shit and blood. Or to the public hospital. Is that what you want? Because, I gotta tell you, girl, I don't care one way or the other. I'm trying to help you, but if that's not what you want that's fine with me. You think about it, and I'll be back in a few minutes."

I decide to let her muddle through the next contraction on her own, and I hope it's a doozy. The air is balmy as I walk out of the barn to wait for Kelly to come back from the house. A few minutes later, moving slow, with a sulky look on her face, she starts to walk past me without a word.

"That little bitch in there just asked me how much we're selling the baby for. Has she asked this before?"

"No. She's usually just hungry, and I take her out to a big lunch. She eats and eats like she hasn't eaten in a few days."

"Why am I just hearing this now? We need healthy babies. What are we going to do if we can't move the baby?"

"We'll fatten him up."

"I have a bad feeling about this. I want to know from now on if you think there are problems with the breeders. Do you hear me?"

"Loud and clear," she says, holding my gaze.

We head back into the barn and find Caroline curled up in the fetal position on the bed, crying. When she sees Kelly, she breaks into loud sobbing. "I don't think I can do this. The pain is bad," her thin body is racked with sobs.

Kelly moves over to the bed and starts rubbing the girl's back. "Where's the pain? Is it in your back or in your belly?"

"It's everywhere," she wails.

Kelly looks over at me, and I walk over to the bed. "Okay, Caroline, I'm going to give you some Demerol for the pain. It will slow down the labor, but you'll feel better. Okay?"

"Yes! Yes! Make it stop!" she sobs.

I go to get a shot of the drug and when I come back she's in the middle of a contraction. Kelly is trying to get her to do the breathing, but the girl is writhing and twisting, and she starts to scream.

"Get up!" I say. "Lying down is the worst way to labor." I grab Caroline's arm and motion to Kelly to grab the other one. "Let's get her up. Let's put her in the birthing chair."

We struggle to pull her to her feet. The pain is making her stronger than she looks. She is wild-eyed and cursing at us to get away from her. I know I need to check and see how dilated she is, but I have to wait until the end of the contraction. We get her into the chair and that's when I notice the bright red stain spreading out on the dress she is wearing. I know that Kelly has seen it too because her smug face has gone white. I think back to school and try to sort out why this might be happening.

The contraction starts to wane, and I say to Kelly, "Go and get the ultrasound machine."

She stares at me with big eyes.

"Go and get the ultrasound!" I say louder and more forcefully.

She gets up and jogs out of the room and comes back in a matter of minutes pushing an ultrasound on a cart.

"Okay, sweetie," I say to Caroline. "We need you to lie down on the bed. We're going to look at the baby and see how it's doing."

We help Caroline up and she flops onto the bed and closes her eyes. Kelly and I quickly set up the machine and pull up the blood-stained dress so that Caroline's belly is exposed. I pull on blue rubber gloves and squirt lubricating gel on her belly and start to look for the baby's heartbeat before the next contraction. As I suspected, I can't find it.

Kelly and I exchange a look over the monitor. I give her a stern eye willing her to be quiet.

"Okay, Caroline. Everything looks good. Now, I'm just going to take a peek and see where you are." I ease two fingers into her and feel that she is about eight centimeters dilated.

Think! Think! What should we do?

I decide to knock her out and use forceps to birth the baby. "Caroline? I'm going to give you a little bit of pain killer to numb the pain because the next part is going to be pretty intense. Okay?"

"Yes, yes, please," she whispers.

I fill the syringe with enough Demerol to knock out a horse and tell her to count backward from ten as I administer the shot.

"She's out," I say and take a deep breath.

"The baby's dead," Kelly states flatly.

I look at her and try to determine how she's holding up. Her big brown eyes are wide and still. "Kelly, listen to me, we didn't kill the baby. It was going to be stillborn whether it was born here or in the charity ward and that's the truth. The only question is how to handle it."

"What'a'ya mean? How to handle it?" Kelly is shaking and her eyes are wild with panic.

"Well, to be frank, Kelly, what are we going to do with a dead baby? Let me think on it while we birth this baby. Okay?"

Her bottom lip is trembling now, and I wish that Vadoma was here instead. She would realize that these things happen. I think about telling Kelly to go inside and send Vadoma out but I'm afraid that Kelly will run off to Mr. Gas Station and tell him everything.

For the next two hours we watch Caroline's seemingly lifeless body go through the birth process and at the end, I use the forceps to give birth to the lifeless baby boy. After two hours, I have decided to bury the baby somewhere on the property and tell Caroline that the adoption has gone as planned. The girls never see the babies anyway, so it won't be any different than our usual process I try to tell myself. Except for the tiny baby and the digging of the grave that is.

27

TOM

I get up and start my day by taking my run in Central Park. By the time I get back to my apartment, my automatic coffee maker has my coffee ready and the paper has been delivered. I am a man of habit and this has been my routine since I moved to New York. I'm not good with all of this drama about the baby, the woman, the news coverage, the girls in DuBois, Savannah and her women. All of it seems to exist in another universe. When I really think about it, what do I have to do with any of this?

I do love Savannah. That's real. Not in a Hallmark sort of way, but with a love that is based on history and on moments that define both of us as people. I can't deny it.

I scan the front page of *The Times*, and I am grateful to see no mention of the baby or the old woman or Anabel Leigh or any of it. Breathing in deeply through my nose, I realize that I have been holding my breath. Thank God! I don't see how the police can connect Charlie to Savannah. I've thought about that for hours. At three in the morning, I was afraid that a dog I've never met would expose our entire operation. Definitely surreal. Savannah has assured me that the dog is unlicensed and that she picked him out of a litter for sale at a state fair years ago. He was unnamed at the time, and she hasn't reported his existence to any government authority. I really don't see how a connection can be made.

Now, I'm starting to sweat just thinking about the dog. Irrational or not, every detail gives the police another piece of the puzzle. I go and quickly take a shower, get dressed and head out the door. I want to get to the clinic and start working to keep my mind off things.

My first appointment of the day is with the Blakes who are on their third IVF. Mrs. Blake, a high-powered attorney who just turned forty, waited to make partner before she had a baby. She told me she felt that she would have more power over her life as a working mother if she was a partner at the law firm. She lost the last two pregnancies very early and now this is week seven. The longest she has held onto any fetus so we're optimistic.

When I go into the exam room I can immediately see from the look on both of their faces that something is wrong.

"I started spotting last night," says Mrs. Blake as I close the door behind me.

Mr. Blake gives me a nod hello.

"Well, let's see what's going on. A lot of women spot during the first trimester. I'll do an ultrasound." As I wash my hands, Savannah's babies pop into my mind. The Blakes would be a perfect couple to adopt one. Three IVF procedures are many times the breaking point for couples. The emotional stress, the pain of harvesting the eggs, the waiting to see if it worked all become too much.

Going back to Mrs. Blake, who is now lying down on the exam table, I apply lubricating gel to her belly and start to move the wand up and down, looking for the heartbeat. After a minute of trying, I know the truth, but to be thorough, I say, "Let's try the internal wand." When I look up at her face, she is crying.

The internal wand does not find a heartbeat. I apologize

to both of them, tell Mrs. Blake to get dressed and for them to meet me in my office. As I look back at them on my way out the door, Mr. Blake has taken his wife in his arms, and they are both crying. This is the hardest part of my job and one of the reasons that I work with Savannah.

In a few minutes, they meet me in my office, and I ask them to sit down. "I'm so sorry for your loss," I start. "We'll have to do a D&C later this week. How are you both doing?"

"We're through. We're not going through this again," says Mr. Blake shaking his head.

Mrs. Blake just puts her face in her hands and cries.

"I know this has been a lot for both of you. We just don't know why some fetuses can't implant. I wanted to mention another path. I know we've talked about adoption in the past, and I know you have been hesitant because of not wanting to be involved with the birth mother, but what if I knew a way for you to adopt a newborn—ten days old at the oldest—and the birth mother would never be known?"

Mrs. Blake has stopped crying, and they are both staring at me like I am a miracle worker.

After a minute, Mr. Blake says, "Tell us more."

28

SAVANNAH

Hattie arrives home the next morning, and I fill her in on Caroline's delivery. A pall hangs over the house. Kayleigh can sense the tension, and she refuses to come into the kitchen as we drink our morning coffee. Kelly is out in the barn with Caroline who I am keeping a little doped up until we figure out what to do.

I washed and wrapped the baby in a simple white receiving blanket and put him in a boot box. Caroline is pretty beat up. She will have to stay at the barn for a few days to recover.

"The girl will never know the truth," I state. "She wasn't expecting to see the baby. Most of them just want to get out of here as fast as they can."

Vadoma and Hattie look bleak. Their mouths are turned down, and I can smell their sweat. Vadoma's neck is so taut the tendons are straining under the skin, and Hattie is shaking.

"It wasn't our fault. It's not like we murdered the baby. It happens. You both know it happens," I say, realizing that I am yelling. I'm the leader of this motley crew and I can't take the time to analyze what went wrong. Right now I need to control what happens next.

Vadoma is the first to speak. "What's the plan?"

I take a deep breath. "Tonight, after dark, we go out to the far end of the pasture and bury him." I see Hattie take a gulp of air.

Vadoma knows this is the only solution. I see her straighten her shoulders and stiffen her back. "And the girl? What do we tell the girl?"

"We tell her that the adoption went through, that her baby has been placed and that the family is very happy. It's going to take her a few days to recuperate, and we'll have to take care of her until she's strong enough to resume her normal life."

"What about her parents?" asks Hattie.

"I think she lives with an aunt. Hopefully one who is occupied with her own life. I'll have to talk to Kelly about that." I look from Vadoma to Hattie and nod my head. "It's important that we do this together. All four of us."

They nod their heads in agreement.

"I'll talk to Kelly," I say. And with that I head out to the barn to see how Caroline and Kelly are doing. The gravel on the path between the house and barn crunches under my sneakers.

When I get to the blue room, they are both fast asleep. Caroline in the bed and Kelly in the rocking chair, exhausted from the night we've had. I look down at Kelly who looks like a child sleeping in the chair. Sometimes I forget how young she is. I wonder if I should let her go, release her from this business, but, honestly, where would she go? Besides her rough upbringing and abusive father, I am the only role model she has ever had. Talk about drawing the short straw. No. Better to keep her under my wing.

I nudge her shoulder. "Casey." I say just in case Caroline is awake and can hear me. Kelly opens her eyes, looking dazed.

She cringes, and I know images of the birth are surfacing in her brain. "Let's go outside."

She follows me out of the barn. She's still in her bloody scrubs. "You need to get cleaned up."

She nods, eyes glazing over with tears.

I take her shoulders and make her look at me. "Kelly, we haven't done anything wrong. The baby was going to die. There was nothing we could do to stop it."

"I know that," she growls at me. She pushes me away. "He was so little." The tears start to flow.

"I know. It's okay to cry. We'll take care of him tonight."

The blood flows to her cheeks. "What does that mean?" She looks at me in terror.

"We'll bury him in the pasture. All four of us. Hattie's back. It's important that we all do it together."

"Important for you!" She yells at me.

I narrow my eyes at her. "No, Kelly, important for each and every one of us. We are all in this together and we all need to understand that. We'll head out as soon as it's dark. And don't breathe a word of this to Mr. Gas Station. Do you hear me?"

"His name is Lee."

I consider her as smart comebacks swirl in my head. "Lee," I finally say.

We head back to the house, and I send Hattie down to the barn to sit with Caroline. She is under strict instructions: If the girl wakes up, she is to text me, and I will come and talk to her. It's a stressful day to say the least, but somehow the hours slip by. I need to keep Caroline on a low dose of tranquilizer so that we can bury the baby with no interruptions.

Finally, it is nine-thirty at night and the moon is shining low in the sky. Vadoma has found two old shovels in the barn. Kayleigh and Caroline are sound asleep.

Like a coven of witches, we head out into the night. We're all wearing dark shirts, jeans, and boots. As the leader, I go first, carrying the boot box, Kelly and Vadoma each carry a shovel, and Hattie brings up the rear, praying under her breath. Her constant singsong chanting is getting on my last nerve.

"Quit your praying, Hattie!" I scold her.

"Praise Jesus," she says with trembling lips.

I roll my eyes. "We'll head to the back near the old oak." We head out past the barn through a thicket of trees and come out the other side into a clearing that stretches as far as we can see. The full moon hangs heavy in the sky, and we can hear the horned owls calling to each other. The pasture spreads out before us, and I point to the great oak tree about a quarter mile in and off to the side of the pasture.

I know Vadoma is my strongest link. She's had a tough life, and it has given her thick skin and an accommodating outlook. She knows that you have to do awful things sometimes just to keep going. I also know that she is loyal to me, having taken her off the street a few years back.

Kelly is the weakest link. She's young and she's missing that gene that allows the heart to harden. She can be silly and girlish at times when she needs to have a level head. She doesn't truly understand the legal consequences of what we're doing. Of what she's been doing when she recruits the girls. She just knows these are girls with few choices. She's been in their shoes. If they don't figure out how to get the money to have an abortion in a few short weeks their only option is to have a baby they don't want and can't take care of. Traveling to another state is too expensive for them to consider.

I've known Hattie the least amount of time, but she was quick to understand the ramifications of our operation when I recruited her from the clinic where we both had worked. I didn't have to spell it out for her. She didn't ask about the legality of what we were doing, and she was thrilled by the money and the house she would live in. If she would just stop her praying, I would feel more comfortable.

The box is getting heavy in my arms as we approach the oak and I'm happy to place it on the ground. I start to look for a place where the gnarled roots from the oak will allow us to dig a deep enough hole.

"I think we should bury him away from the tree, away from these roots," says Vadoma. "Why not in the middle of the pasture where the earth will be soft?"

"Sometimes the pasture floods, and I'm afraid the grave will wash away," I say.

Kelly tries to dig near the tree, but the roots are too thick. She and Vadoma work away at the ground under the tree but it's tough going. We move about twelve feet away from the tree and the digging is easier. Taking turns, we dig and dig, moving the rich brown soil from the hole and creating a pile of dirt around the hole. We toil for an hour, and the hole is about three feet deep.

"Keep going, Google says we need to go down at least four feet. We don't want the vultures to smell the body and dig him up," I say pushing the hair back from my face.

"Praise Jesus," says Hattie as she spills a shovelful of dirt on the side of the grave.

"Thank God for Google," Kelly says sarcastically. "Let's just get this done," she grabs the shovel out of Vadoma's hands and attacks the dirt with a vengeance.

"Praise be to the Lord," says Hattie.

"Hattie, if you praise the Lord again, I will hit you with the shovel! Keep your voice down. It travels on the wind," I declare.

At last, the hole is deep enough, and I take the tiny corpse out of the box and start to place it in the grave.

"You're not leaving it in the box?" Kelly cries.

"No, I don't want any clues left with him," I say.

She starts to walk away.

"The Lord is my shepherd; I shall not want," says Hattie.

We look at each other. We feel the solemnness of what we

are doing. I nod for Hattie to continue. Kelly comes back to the grave.

"He maketh me to lie down in green pastures: he leadeth me beside the still waters. He restoreth my soul: he leadeth me in the path of righteousness for his name's sake. Yea, though I walk through the valley of the shadow of death, I will fear no evil: for thou art with me; thy rod and thy staff they comfort me."

It's strange how the words of the Bible can comfort even us sinners in hard times. "That was beautiful, Hattie," I say, meaning it, as I throw the first shovelful of dirt.

"Beautiful," echoes Vadoma as she reaches out and squeezes Hattie's arm.

We finish filling the grave, smoothing the earth over the area, knowing that after the first rain it will be hard to tell where he is. We steady our tired selves for the walk back to the house, collect the shovels and the boot box, and start back through the pasture. The moon has dipped very low in the sky, and it lights our way.

29

ANABEL

Detective Harris called yesterday and asked me to come in at one o'clock today. He opened the conversation with something about catching a case that kept him up at night. He needs to solve this case so he can retire at peace. I feel the stress in my shoulders when I think about going back to the police station. Detective Harris makes me a nervous wreck. I had a client breakfast this morning followed by back-to-back meetings, but now it's late and I just have time to rush over to the police station. I'm wearing the typical New York City working woman uniform—black suit from BOSS, white silk blouse, Cole Haan flats, and pearls. Lots of pearls. Pearl earrings, pearl necklace, and pearl bracelet. It's my signature look.

Going to the police station is still intimidating. It's like entering another world. There are bars and barricades and worn wood and broken tiles and uniforms. There's an officer standing behind a counter that has bars and a sliding bullet-proof window. He picks his head up from the papers on the desk and looks at me like he's sizing me up, wondering what I am doing here. "Yes, can I help you?" No smile.

"I have a meeting with Detective Harris," I say, gravely.

"Name."

"Anabel Leigh. The appointment's for one o'clock." I look up at the large clock behind his station. It's one-fifteen.

He picks up the phone and lets Harris know I'm here. "Take a seat," he says and points to two old, wooden chairs in the corner.

I'm walking over to sit down when Detective Harris appears, holding a bulky file, and swings the gate open for me. "Hello, Ms. Leigh. Come with me."

"Hi, Detective Harris. How are you?"

"Can't complain. You?"

I follow him into the same interrogation room where I met him the first time and he pulls out a chair for me. He lumbers over to the other side of the table, plunks the thick file down, and pulls out his tape recorder. "I'm going to record this, so I don't have to take so many notes."

I nod my head in agreement, but I feel my pulse rate pick up and I start to perspire.

"So, Ms. Leigh, I called you in today because I've been going over the facts of this case and I can't understand why a woman would abandon a child in this way. She could just put the child up for adoption, but because she chose to leave the child in a park with a stranger, I can't help but think that something criminal is going on here. Where did she get the baby? Where are the baby's rightful parents? I do not think the woman that you describe is the baby's mother so where did the baby come from? And, why you? Why did she choose you to leave the baby with?" Detective Harris pauses, puts his elbows on the table and narrows his bloodshot eyes at me.

I feel, and probably look, very frightened at this point. I should have let Dennis come with me. He told me this morning that he wanted to come with me to the police station and I should have taken him up on his offer. I feel like I'm about to be arrested. I feel my bottom lip quivering.

"I don't know," I blurt out at him. "It is the honest truth that I was sitting in the park, after I ate my lunch, and the woman gave her to me. I don't have any additional information to give you. I've never seen her again."

Detective Harris takes a deep breath. "I want to talk about the sapphire ring. You seem to remember the ring. How big do you think the stone was? Close your eyes and try to envision her hand. Was it old and wrinkled or younger?"

I close my eyes and replay the scene in my head. The woman pushing the stroller down the path. The other girl unbuckling herself from the stroller. The woman bending over to unbuckle the baby. The ring on her hand. Soft skin. I see the manicure.

Opening my eyes, I say, "Her hand looked soft, unwrinkled. I'm not an expert on jewelry, but if I compare the stone in my head with my sister's engagement ring, which I know is one carat, the sapphire was more like two carats with a fairly thick gold band. My impression is that the woman was older. I saw gray hair peeking out of the scarf, but it could have been a wig. It all happened so fast."

"If I showed you a catalogue of rings, could you pick it out?"

"I can try."

He reaches into his file and pulls a catalogue of sapphire rings out of the stack of papers and opens it before me. There are hundreds of sapphire rings. Some with diamonds, some plain, some with other gems. Small, medium and large. I start at the top of the page and inspect each ring. On the third page there is a selection of plain sapphires with gold bands. The way I remember the ring was that it was very elegant, very classic. And there it is, a two-carat round sapphire with a thick gold band.

"There it is!" I smile and point to the ring in the middle of the page. "That's what I remember! It looked just like that."

Detective Harris eyes me from under hooded lids. I think he wants me to admit that I killed the mother of the baby and paid the woman to make it seem like an abandonment. Why is he so suspicious of me? Or, is that just his way of interrogating a witness?

I smile at him and look at my watch. It's getting late. I involuntarily stand up. "I have to get back to the office," I tell him as I collect my bag.

"That's the one. Huh?" is all he says.

I point again to the ring and turn to leave the room. As I'm walking out, I turn to him and I say, "You might specialize in making innocent people feel guilty, but why don't you do your job and find this woman?" I turn on my heel and head down the hall and out the door.

30

KELLY

I, Kelly Parker, now earn one hundred thousand dollars per year! And I am only twenty years old! Don't get me wrong, I have a hard job. How many twenty-year-olds have buried a baby in a pasture in the middle of the night? I have to deal with things that most people never deal with in their entire lives, and I have a lot of responsibility. Finding our girls and offering them a chance to easily find a home for their babies. I know they don't want them, but still, it takes skill to get them to trust me. And all the documents that seal the deal in New York. I get them through playing Calvin. Savannah couldn't even do that. He would be so intimidated by her that he might wet himself.

I'm rich! Maybe, in a few years, I'll go to college. Of course, I'll have to get my GED first, but I can do that. Why not? Lots of people who aren't as smart as me have a high school diploma. I should start on that now so there'll be nothing stopping me when the time comes.

Driving this car feels so good, and I'm wearing my new red cowboy boots and I'm on my way to see Lee after eight days. I feel alive for the first time in days. I've been taking care of Caroline, and it's been hard to not tell her the truth about her baby. Savannah says she's better off not knowing and I get that, but I feel like I'm mourning the poor little boy all by myself. So tiny. I've never seen a baby so small. He looked like a little doll.

After I visit Lee, Savannah wants me to start recruiting a new girl to make up for the baby we lost. That means I have to find a girl who's newly pregnant and will be due eight months from now. I'll head down to The Bean after I see Lee, or maybe the laundromat or the diner.

I turn into the Exxon and see Lee talking to two guys I don't know. I know I look hot in my white crop top, jean shorts, and red cowboy boots, so I park and start to walk across the lot. All three of them are looking at me, mesmerized, as I walk toward Lee with a big grin on my face, my hair blowing out around my face. One of the guys whistles as I put my arms around Lee's neck and pull him in for a smooch.

When I push away, he looks a little sheepish.

"How ya been, Lee?" I ask, in a singsong voice.

"How ya been, Lee," one of the guys mimics and the other guy punches Lee in the bicep.

"Kelly, meet my brothers, Jed and JimBob," Lee says.

"Your brothers? You didn't tell me you had good-looking brothers! You should'a told me that, Lee." At that point, I look at each of his brothers and then I turn back to Lee. "But you're the handsomest, so I guess I made the right choice." I smile and loop my arm through Lee's arm. One of the brothers actually looks a little sketchy, but I'm just flirting.

"Give me a second, guys," he says to his brothers and puts his arm around my shoulders and leads me to the side of the building. I can hear them laughing as we walk away.

"Why didn't you text me that you were coming?" he says as he moves in for a kiss. "I've missed you."

"I know. I've missed you too. When can we be alone?" I ask as I rub my breasts across his chest.

He closes his eyes. "You are killin' me. I get off at six. Can you meet me then?"

"Sure, let's meet at six. Should I pick you up?"

"No, I have my car. Meet me at my place. I'll need to take a shower, though." He looks at me with big blue eyes and a lopsided smile.

"I will think about that all day," I say as I walk back to my car. "Bye, bros!" I call to his brothers.

"Bye, Kelly," they answer in unison.

I get back in the Bimmer and head to The Bean.

31

ANABEL

"How'd it go?" Dennis asks as he comes into my office at the end of the day and sits down in one of the chairs facing my desk.

I sigh and lean back in my chair. "It's so weird. That detective always makes me feel like I've done something wrong. Like I know more than I'm telling him. He's homing in on the sapphire ring, but the way he talks to me and looks at me. He puts me on edge. Today, I had to go through a catalogue and look for the ring."

"Did you find it?"

"I think so, but I only saw it for a few seconds." I get up and walk around my desk to Dennis. The office has cleared out for the weekend. I lean down and put my arms around him, and he pulls me into his lap for a hug.

"Well, let's forget about Detective Harris and the baby and the woman and have ourselves a nice weekend. How's that sound?"

"Mmm." I've buried my face in his shoulder and don't want to move.

"Nice!" Tanya's voice cuts into the blissful moment, and I quickly jump up, out of Dennis's lap. Tanya still looks fresh after a long day. Not one wrinkle in her orange Max Mara suit or coordinating floral silk shirt.

"Tanya," I stammer.

"The story's live again," she says with frown. "The police put out a press release looking for the jeweler who sold the sapphire ring to come forward."

My eyes grow wide. "Wow, you would think he might mention to me that he's putting out a press release," I say to Dennis.

"Who's he?" asks Tanya.

"Detective Harris, the detective on the case. He had me come in today to look at rings."

"Keep your phone on this weekend in case we have to comment," and she's gone.

Dennis stands up and pulls a hand through his hair. "C'mon. Let's get out of here before Sol calls a meeting."

I grab my jacket and my purse, and we head down to the street and try to hail a cab. It's hard on a Friday night. No luck, so we head to the subway and take the number six train uptown.

We decided earlier in the week that we would spend the weekend at Dennis's townhouse. But now that we're on our way there, I have a fluttery, nervous feeling in my stomach and my mouth is dry. I hear Dennis telling me a story, but I can't concentrate on anything he's saying. For the last few days, I've kept telling myself that I was married before so what if Dennis lived in this house with his fiancé? We're not young kids, but still, I feel Mala's presence as we walk west on Eightieth Street.

"Anabel, are you listening to me?"

"What?"

Dennis looks at me and gives me a hug. "It was a long time ago. Now, I only think of you." He smiles and gives me a kiss on the cheek. "C'mon, I want you to see where I live."

The townhouse is four stories tall and wider than the other houses on the street. The exterior is red brick with white trim and beautifully carved banisters. I stand at the bottom of the stairs and feel small looking up at the impressive building.

"You own this entire building?" I ask, sounding incredulous. "That time we stopped in I didn't understand that you owned the whole building."

Dennis is fishing in his pocket for his keys. "Yep. This is my home."

"Oh my God, you must feel like you're slumming it when you come to my little apartment."

Dennis looks at me quizzically. "Anabel, I do not feel like I'm slumming it when I go to your place. You live in a very nice building. I love your apartment."

I raise my eyebrows as if to say *really*?

He pulls me up the steps and opens the door and waits for me to enter. I step into the foyer with the black and white tiles. The air smells like lemon floor wax. "Let's get the tour out of the way so we can relax and have a nice dinner. We're grilling! I bought steaks! Here, put your purse down." Dennis points to a wooden bench with black leather cushions that sits under a large mirror on the right side of the foyer.

"So, back here is a guest bedroom and bath. Nothing special really, but it's nice for guests. They have some privacy down here." We walk through a medium-sized bedroom with a wooden bed, an armoire and an overstuffed chair. "It's really for a guest who might have trouble negotiating three sets of stairs up to the other guest room," says Dennis.

"Very considerate, very comfy," I add, taking in the expensive linens and window treatments.

We go back into the foyer and up the stairs with a beautiful wooden banister to the next floor. "This is the main floor —living room, dining room, kitchen, and powder room." As we walk through the rooms, I notice the clear surfaces on all the tables and many of the shelves and I imagine that Dennis has thrown out all of the photos, souvenirs, and trinkets acquired when he was with Mala. The floors in the living room and the dining room are bare, but I can see where carpets used to be. As I look at the beautiful living room tastefully done in cream, tan, and taupe my eyes spend an extra beat looking at the hardwood floor. "We can buy new rugs," Dennis offers.

I give him a little smile.

The kitchen is something out of a showroom. Marble floors and countertops. Stainless steel Viking appliances, I note the eight burners on the stovetop. The back wall of the room is all windows and sliding glass doors that looks out on a private garden.

"Dennis, are you secretly a millionaire? I know you earn more than I do at C&W, but this house is amazing! It should be featured in *Architectural Digest* or something," I exclaim as I look out to the back.

"I'm glad you like it. Let's see the rest of the house. I'm hungry and I bought a special bottle of wine that I think you'll like," he grins.

I follow him up another flight where there is the master suite, another bedroom and an office, and up to the final floor that has an additional bedroom and two undefined rooms.

We head back down to the kitchen and Dennis takes a bottle of Cloudy Bay Sauvignon Blanc out of the refrigerator along with a few different cheeses. "Let's have a drink and some cheese and crackers out in the yard," Dennis says as he arranges a slice of Brie and a block of cheddar on a platter with some crackers, and gets two wine glasses out of the cupboard. He pours the wine, hands me a glass, and holds his up to toast. "Here's to you," he says.

"And you," I say. We clink glasses and take a sip of the crisp wine. "Mmm. This is delicious!"

"I thought you would like it. C'mon, let's sit." He leads me out to the yard.

The evening is warm, and the yard is lovely. There's a flagstone patio and a wrought iron table and chairs. There's a tightness in my chest and an awkwardness between us that I haven't felt before. I'm realizing how little I really know about Dennis.

"Anabel? Are you okay?"

"Yes, of course. Your home is beautiful." I feel that the unspoken part of the sentence is "your home with Mala."

"So, what do you want to know? Maybe if we talk about it, you'll feel better."

I consider his earnest face. "Where did you and Mala meet?"

"We met at the hospital. She's a surgeon, a resident at the time, and I was in a biking accident and was taken to the ER at NYU. I was banged up pretty bad, and I needed twenty-five stitches in my head. She sewed me up. It's funny, she went to medical school here, but she never really felt comfortable in the US. I think that's why she would never agree to a date for the wedding. She didn't really want to be here, and I wasn't going to live in Hyderabad, so for more than a year, before she left, we were at a standstill." Dennis takes a break to see how I'm doing.

For some reason, hearing that she didn't like it here makes me feel better. I start to relax. "And I know this sounds gauche, but are you a secret millionaire?"

"It's not a secret, but I don't introduce myself as a millionaire," he chuckles. "That would be weird. I do have family money, and so did she, and that's why we have this house. Why *I* have this house."

I flinch. "Does she still own part of this house?"

"No, she signed it over to me. The man she fell in love with has so much money this house is nothing to them. It's all mine. I'm sorry that you don't like it." Dennis cuts the hard cheese with a swift action.

"No, Dennis, it's not that I don't like it. It's gorgeous. It's just that I'm learning a lot about you in a very short time.

You're someone different than I thought you were this morning. It might just take me a minute to adjust."

"I'm a different person because I live in a townhouse and I have some money in the bank? I'm still the same person. The same person that loves spending time with you. Who wants to be a part of your life. Who loves the way your nose crinkles up before you smile. Who wants to support you in your quest for the baby you want so desperately."

I feel tears welling up in my eyes. "I'm being stupid. I'm sorry." My throat catches.

"Most women would love the fact that I have money." He says with a mischievous grin. "But, because you feel differently, I won't give you any of it."

I look at him and he is smiling. We both start laughing.

"C'mere," he says, getting up and pulling me to my feet and putting his arms around me. "We can redecorate the house. We can buy a new house. This house. Your apartment. They both have memories in them. But let's not focus on the place we're in. Let's just focus on how we feel when we're together. Okay?"

"Okay." I reach up to kiss him and I feel the strain slipping away. What's wrong with me? How hard can it be to love a millionaire? Dennis is right, most women would be thrilled.

32

VADOMA

Lying has always made me itch and now my back and shoulders are raw from me scratching them with a small branch. I couldn't reach the spot right in the middle, so I went outside after cleaning the barn and found a foot-long skinny branch that feels so good when I get underneath my shirt and scratch away.

I've always liked jewelry. Of course, for most of my forty years I never had any money for jewelry. After my parents died in Hungary, me and my aunt were living outside Budapest. Her major occupation was begging, and she would use me to attract the tourists. They would give us—me really —a coin or two. But then she got a chance to move to America with a man, and she took me with her. I don't really know what the deal was between them, but he was as mean as a hornet and as soon as we could we left him and traveled south to Georgia.

My aunt started working in a house as a cook and I spent my days peeling carrots, shucking corn, and picking beans from the garden in the backyard. I tried to be helpful, but as soon as I was fourteen, my aunt told me I had to leave the house so I struck out on my own. I went to work in a restaurant washing dishes and the owner let me sleep in the back-storage closet. She paid me next to nothing, but she fed me and wasn't too mean to me. I stayed with her for five years.

When I was nineteen, I met a boy and moved to Florida, but as with most relationships that happen quickly at nineteen, we soon found that we didn't really like each other and went our separate ways. I ended up at a resort in Boca Raton where I worked as a dishwasher but then moved up to busgirl near the pool and that's where my fascination with jewels began.

The women would go down to the pool with their hair done, make-up on, and their jewelry. They would sit under umbrellas, never going near the pool, and read or have lunch with each other. Most of them had large diamond engagement rings, but it was the other gems that caught my eye. The rubies, sapphires, emeralds, opals, and stones I couldn't name in shades of yellow, purple, turquoise, deep blue. I would slowly take away the dirty plates and glasses so that I could get a look at the rings, necklaces, and bracelets. It made the time go faster. Dreaming of wearing these beautiful baubles.

They were the stuff of dreams and certainly out of my reach until years later when I met Savannah. I had fallen on hard times, lost my job at the resort, and made my way back to Georgia where I got a job cleaning the clinic where Savannah worked. After she left the clinic, I would see her around town and she recruited me to work with her. She told me that all I had to do was watch babies, travel with her to New York sometimes to deliver the babies, and help around the house. I wanted to know what the catch was but she just said I needed to keep everything I did strictly confidential.

At first, I didn't realize that everything we were doing was illegal and by the time I figured it out I was in real deep. Not that it bothered me. I slept in a room the likes of which I didn't even know to dream of. I was paid more money than I knew what to do with and, after a time, I started to buy myself a few beautiful pieces of jewelry.

Now, I had told Savannah that I bought that sapphire ring the year before, but that was a lie. I had bought it the day before the drop in a small jewelry store in Midtown. I was walking the girls back to the hotel after getting pizza for lunch, and I saw it in the window. It called to me. Why shouldn't I buy it? I pushed the double-stroller through the doors of the store and tried it on. It fit perfectly and I bought it on the spot for four thousand dollars. I bought it with a credit card that I got under a fake name and address. A Florida address since I got the card when I was in Boca.

The thought never entered my mind that the woman in the park would see the ring and be able to describe it to the police, but there it was on the front page of *The New York Times*. The exact ring. That woman must have a photographic memory. How long did she have to study the ring? Fifteen seconds? It is a simple ring. That's the problem. One sapphire and a gold band.

Now, the police are asking the jeweler who sold the ring to come forward. The itch has spread to my legs and palms. Savannah is going to kill me.

33

ANABEL

Dennis and I have started to spend more and more time at his townhouse. It's just so beautiful and spacious that my apartment seems small in comparison. But, as amazing as it is, every morning when I wake up, all I can think about is the baby and the adoption. This week, Ms. Alvarez called my sister, Sylvia, and spoke to her for a half-hour and her husband, Walter, for ten minutes. Now, she wants to set up a face-to-face meeting with Dennis. She wants to talk to Dennis alone and then both of us together. She says that she and her supervisor have narrowed their search for the adoption down to me and a couple from Queens.

I feel her rooting for me, but I don't want to take anything for granted. The baby is still with the foster care family and when I think of that woman holding the baby and soothing her when she cries and feeding her Cheerios, my chest hurts. I want to be that woman. I've asked Ms. Alvarez if we can set up a date and time for me to visit with the baby again, but she hasn't gotten back to me. I'd love for Dennis to meet her. I fantasize about the three of us sitting together on the couch in my living room and we're all smiling. The baby is cuddled up in my lap, and Dennis is holding up a pink bear for her to see and she reaches for the stuffed animal. Then, I stop myself and try to think of work, but my mind keeps going back to the baby and then to the ring.

Detective Harris caught me off-guard when he issued the press release about the ring, jumpstarting coverage of the baby again. Now, the papers and TV news lead with the story of "The Golden One" along with my photo and hers and the sapphire ring. I wonder if the jeweler who sold the ring to the woman will come forward.

I feel that I am so close to adopting the baby that I actually don't want the parents to be found. Guilty feelings over wanting to deprive the baby of a life with her biological parents surface, but I quickly justify my position. If they wanted their baby, wouldn't they have come forward by now? What if they find the parents and give the baby back to people who don't really want her?

I'm so full of fear. I'm afraid the parents will be found, and the baby will be returned to people who will hurt her. I'm afraid that Dennis and I will get married and we won't be able to have a baby. I'll have another miscarriage. And another and another. I'll be forty and he'll leave me. Spiraling now, I burrow my head deeper into the covers and try to clear my mind when I hear the squeak of the door opening.

"Here we go, madam, breakfast in bed for a queen." Dennis is wearing striped boxer shorts and a faded brown Nirvana T-shirt.

I open my bloodshot eyes and when he sees my pale face he stops mid-step. "What's wrong?"

We've moved into the second bedroom on the third floor. Dennis was quick to realize that I didn't want to sleep in the bed that he and Mala bought together, and so that first night he took me to the second bedroom without a word.

I look up at him, the sunlight pouring in from the window. "Nothing," I say.

"Liar. What happened?" He sets down the bed tray next to

me, and l look at the beautiful breakfast he has brought me. Coffee, juice, scrambled eggs, English muffin, butter and jam for two.

I prop myself up and lean on my elbows. "Nothing's wrong. I'm just afraid the parents will come forward, and I'm afraid even if we're together I'll have another miscarriage, and another, and you'll . . ."

"Whoa! Whoa! Anabel, I am not going to leave you. I'm not." He picks up the tray, places it on the nightstand, and crawls into bed beside me. "I want us to be together. I'm not leaving. Ever." He says wrapping his arm and his leg around me and burying his face in my neck. "I know that Sam left, but I'm not leaving. I'm forty, and I've lived this long without kids. Sure, I want them, but I want you more."

I'm swaddled in the blankets with his arm and leg holding me tight, and I start to cry. His words are exactly the words I want to hear.

"Please don't cry," he begs me. "I hate it when you cry."

"I'm crying because I'm happy. I don't want you to ever leave me, and I'll never leave you. I promise I'll never leave you. Let me have my arms back so I can hug you." I start to laugh.

When he realizes I'm laughing, he starts laughing too, and lifts his arm so I can come out from under the blanket. I hug him and give him a kiss.

"Even if we don't have kids, we can be happy together," he says. "But I really feel that we will have kids. Worst case scenario, things don't work out with this baby, there are hundreds, probably thousands of other babies who need a good mother like you."

I look at Dennis and my heart bursts with happiness. "Why did it take us so long to see each other? How is it that we worked side by side for two years and didn't get together sooner?"

Dennis looks serious. "I'll tell you a secret. I've had a crush on you for a long time and when you called me that night out of the blue, I couldn't believe it. It was like a miracle had happened. Anabel, I think, I really think, I love you." He looks at me with the biggest, most beautiful brown eyes I've ever seen.

My heart skips a beat. "Dennis, I really think I love you, too."

34

SAVANNAH

I wake up early to work on the birth timelines. Throwing on my navy silk robe with the green dragons, I shake out my hair and head into my bathroom for my morning routine. Weight, 118. I inspect my roots, could do with new highlights. I like to take care of all my beauty needs in New York. I make a mental note to make a few appointments for when I go up there, hopefully, next week or early the week after. Kelly checked in with the next girl, Mackenzie, and she is feeling tired and bloated. Won't be long now until we have our next baby.

Mackenzie is a much heartier girl and a few years older than Caroline, so I'm not expecting any problems. She's taller, wider, bigger than Caroline in every way. Peasant stock with rosy cheeks and bright blue eyes. I imagine that her baby will be big and blonde and beautiful.

Worth every cent the Ackermans will pay us for him. I am really hoping for a boy. The Ackermans want a son but are willing to take any healthy baby. Kelly says she's having a hard time finding a new girl who can replace Caroline's baby. I have to drill down on that with her today.

The house is quiet as I head down the upstairs hallway

and take the stairs to the first floor. I love my foyer! It makes me happy every morning. It's painted a buttery yellow and the carpet on the stairs is green with small yellow flowers. A small Warhol of Marilyn, which Tom and I bought together in SoHo, is on the opposite wall over a marble cabinet. She has a very come hither look on her face and I blow her a kiss as I walk by. Charlie meets me at the foot of the stairs, and I bend down to give him a good morning scratch. He follows me into the kitchen where I let him out the back door.

No one's up. Hattie and Kelly usually sleep in when we don't have a baby to take care of, but Kayleigh gets up with the crack of dawn. I briefly wonder why she and Vadoma aren't up yet while I head over to the coffee pot and set it to brewing. I notice some spilled juice on the counter which is weird, because I always check the kitchen before I go to bed. I frown and wipe it up.

Grabbing my laptop from the office, I head back to the kitchen to read the news and have my coffee at the island. Filling my favorite red mug with steaming hot coffee, I tie back my hair with a scrunchie, and wait for my browser to open, mentally noting to get an upgrade on my server for faster service.

My Gmail opens and the first email is the online *New York Times*. Yawning, I click the email, and it opens to the front page where the Golden One's photo is front and center alongside Anabel Leigh and Vadoma's ring. I feel my heart begin to jump while I read the article which quotes a Detective Harris asking for the jeweler who sold the ring to come forward. The photo of the ring is an exact duplicate of the one on Vadoma's finger when she returned from New York.

Anger is a funny thing. It starts slow. You're not always sure if it will swell or fizzle. I can feel the set of my mouth, my back teeth are clamped together, and I can't regain the sense of calm I felt just a few minutes ago. Where is Vadoma? Why was there juice on the counter?

I feel my cheeks reddening, and I slam my fists on the marble island which releases some of my frustration. I feel claustrophobic in my robe, so I fling it off my shoulders and it flutters to the floor. I stomp out of the kitchen wearing only a thin white T-shirt and my bikini underwear, fly up the stairs, and throw open the door to Vadoma's room. Her perfectly made bed and clear vanity top tell me she is gone. I make a mad dash down to the nursery where Kayleigh usually sleeps, her bed is empty.

I stand in the middle of the nursery, legs planted wide, fists clenched and scream her name, "Vadoma!" Swiftly moving to the hallway, I throw open Kelly's door and then Hattie's, "Get up. Now!" I scream and head back downstairs.

A few minutes later, I hear them on the stairs.

"What's going on?" asks Hattie.

No response from Kelly. They enter the kitchen clutching their robes around them, groggy from sleep.

"What is it?" asks Kelly. "What happened?"

"Do either of you know anything about this?" I scream.

They both look at me, eyes wide. Hattie has her back against the wall just inside the room and Kelly is hugging her robe as if it can protect her from my anger.

They both shake their heads.

"What are you talking about?" Hattie whispers.

"The police have released a photo of the sapphire ring and it's now on the front page of *The New York Times*, and probably the other papers and TV stations, with a photo of the baby and that Leigh woman. They're asking for the jeweler who sold the ring to come forward. And Vadoma and Kayleigh are gone." I take a deep breath. "Do either of you know where they went? Did she tell you she was leaving?" I take a menacing step toward Kelly.

She comes alive as I do. "I don't know anything about any of this," she yells at me. "I said good night to Vadoma last night on my way to bed. That's the last time I saw her. I was sleeping until all the yelling woke me up." She heads over to the coffee pot.

I turn my attention to Hattie. "And you? What do you know?"

Hattie shrugs. "I don't know anything. The only thing she told me was that she was itching. Thought she had a rash. Maybe she went to the pharmacy." She goes to the cupboard for a mug.

I step out the back door, Charlie runs out, and I check to see that Vadoma's Toyota is gone. The place she always parks is empty. "Fucking mother of God," I swear under my breath and go back into the house. "She's gone. I can't fucking believe it!" I scream.

"At least she took the girl," says Kelly who is now sitting at the island hunched over her coffee.

I pick up my robe from the floor and slip it back on. I give Kelly a glare, but I don't say anything. I stomp into the office and grab my cellphone from the desk and call Vadoma. Straight to voicemail. Of course, why would she leave in the middle of the night and then pick up for a chat?

When I get back, Hattie has joined Kelly at the island. I take one of the seats across from them in order to watch the conversation. I don't want to miss any telling looks that might transpire between them. Right this minute, I don't trust anyone.

"Okay, where do you think she might have gone? Kelly? You've known her longer. Any ideas?"

"You've known her just as long as I have. Do *you* have any ideas?" she avoids meeting my eyes.

"Kelly," I jump off the stool. "What do you know?"

Kelly continues to stare into her coffee. "She might have lied to you about when she bought that ring."

As I open my mouth to ask Kelly more, Hattie says, "She told me once that when she lies, she starts to itch and that would explain her itchin' yesterday and her supposed rash."

I turn back to Kelly. "When did she buy the ring?"

Kelly closes her eyes and presses her lips together in a grimace. She opens her mouth, but nothing comes out. She takes a deep breath, slowly releases it and spits out, "The day before the drop."

I hear a pounding in my ears and feel a surge of adrenaline. "The day before the fucking drop?" I take a step toward Kelly, and she jumps out of the seat to face me. "And, when did she tell you that? How long have you known this?"

"It didn't seem important!" Kelly wails.

I grab her arm and stick my face in hers. I start to squeeze into the soft flesh above her elbow. "Well, let me tell you something, now it's important."

Now Hattie is up and pushes my shoulder. "Let her go! We have to be smart about this. We can't go beating the shit out of each other. Let's think about the various scenarios. One, maybe the jeweler won't come forward. Two, let's think through how the police could trace the purchase back to us. How do you think she would have made the purchase?"

I give Kelly's arm one last squeeze and drop it. Hattie's right, we have to keep our wits about us. We have to stick together.

I go back and sit at the island. Hattie joins me, but Kelly is pissed, refusing to sit down. "Kelly, I'm sorry."

She jerks her head in my direction. I'm not prone to apologies.

"Hattie's right. Please sit down and let's talk this through. I've repeatedly told you guys that you have to make all big purchases with cash, but I can't imagine that Vadoma was walking around with thousands of dollars in the baby bag. In addition, we all have our P.O. boxes for anything that needs to be sent to us. This address should be clean. Nothing should come here with any of your names on it." I look from Kelly to Hattie, but neither of them says anything.

Finally, Kelly says, "I use my ma's address for the Bimmer.

Since Pa died, I've been helping her out, and it's easier for me to just go and pick up my mail there."

I can see that my tight ship is full of holes. "Hattie?"

"I have a P.O. box two towns over in Howarth. I also deposit small amounts of cash in my checking account, so I can use my debit card," she says.

"Okay, go through Vadoma's room today and see if you can find any clues as to where she went. Now, let me see what the other papers are saying." I get up, grab my laptop, and start to walk to the office, but as I pass the Sub-Zero refrigerator my eyes land on a drawing that Kayleigh and Vadoma were working on earlier in the week. It's a picture of Charlie and the barn. I tear it down and rip it furiously into small pieces letting them flutter to the floor.

35

ANABEL

I can tell as soon as I see Ms. Alvarez's face that something is wrong. Dennis and I had been sitting quietly in my living room waiting for her when the doorman called up. My pulse started to race when I heard the doorbell ring, excitement coursing through my veins, but when I open the door and see her face I know that there is a problem.

"Hello, Anabel," she says with apologetic eyes, there's no other way to describe them.

Dennis has followed me to the door and steps in to save the situation when my shoulders droop. "Ms. Alvarez, I'm so happy to meet you. Dennis Wells." He holds out his hand, gently moving me to the side so she can step in.

Ms. Alvarez comes in and shakes Dennis's hand, and we usher her into the living room.

I can't stop myself. "What's wrong?" I ask her quietly.

"Let's sit down," says Dennis.

"Yes, let's sit down." Ms. Alvarez takes the chair at the head of the glass coffee table and Dennis and I go to sit on the couch. "Anabel, you know that I see the connection between you and the baby, I do, but my supervisor, Ms. Marino, is taking the position that the other family would be a better placement for her."

I collapse into Dennis as he pulls me close.

"Why?" I ask.

"Well, one thing is the constant publicity around you and the baby. She feels that a quieter, less newsworthy adoption might be better for the baby. We have no idea how this will all turn out."

"But I had nothing to do with the way she was found. I did the right thing. I called the authorities. And I have no control over what the police say to the press. It's out of my hands. It's not fair." The tears start to flow, and I cover my face. Dennis holds me tight.

"Is this decision final?" asks Dennis.

Ms. Alvarez smooths her skirt as I sit up, away from Dennis. "No, but I wanted to come here tonight and suggest that you get an adoption attorney. You're going to need one anyway, if the adoption were to go forward. I have a list of names." She reaches into the canvas bag that she has put on the floor by her feet and pulls out a piece of paper.

Dennis leans forward to receive it. "We'll talk to a few tomorrow and choose one by the end of the week or should we move faster?"

"I think we should go forward with my interview of you tonight, Mr. Wells. Tomorrow you should try to choose an attorney." She holds Dennis's eye to impress that we should move quickly. "Anabel, I know you're upset and I'm sorry. Ms. Marino is just trying to do the best by the baby."

Wiping the tears from my cheeks, I ask, "How is she? How's the baby?"

Ms. Alvarez smiles. "She's doing fine. Talking. Picking up new words every day. We think that wherever she was they weren't talking to her a lot. When she first was placed at the foster home, she hardly said a word, but now she's chatting and laughing. Why don't I speak to Mr. Wells for a short time and then we can chat more?"

"Of course." I get up to go in the other room and Dennis reaches up and gives my hand a squeeze. "Let me know when you're done." I take a step but then turn back. "I'm sorry, I completely forgot my manners. Can I get you a cold drink or a cup of tea?"

"No, I'm fine. Thank you." She gives me a tender smile and I go into my bedroom and close the door.

My feet feel like they each weigh a hundred pounds as I stumble over to the bed and try to get ahold of myself. I was so certain that I would be the one to get her. Cursing myself for feeling confident, I vow that I will never talk with Detective Harris again. Let him get out on the street and do his job. They will have to subpoena me before I speak to anyone at One Police Plaza again.

She did say that it wasn't over yet. I can continue to hope that I will be chosen over the other family, but they probably have a house since they live in Queens and I'm sure there's a mother and a father. How can I compete? If only Dennis and I had gotten together sooner. Maybe we would be married by now.

I study my nails. Change into more comfortable shoes. Sort the earrings in the top drawer of my jewelry box and arrange them in pairs. What are they talking about? Flicking the light on in the adjoining bathroom, I check my make-up and wipe off a smudge of mascara. Dennis will say nice things about me, I know he will, but we've never talked about a parenting plan. What if he says something she doesn't like?

Flopping down on the bed, I cross and uncross my ankles. My palms are sweating, and I wipe them on the comforter. Suddenly, the door opens, and Dennis is standing there, beckoning me to come out into the living room. He's smiling, which is encouraging.

Ms. Alvarez is taking notes in her notebook, but she looks

up when I come back into the room. "Join us, Anabel. How are you doing?" She looks genuinely concerned.

"I'm okay. I just want to be with her so bad. I've told you this before. I just think it's meant to be," I say, retaking my place on the couch.

"Let's see what happens. I haven't finished your home study or the other family's study. I just thought you should know about my supervisor's feelings. Dennis says he'll help you find an attorney tomorrow, and we'll see what they can do. I wanted to know if you reviewed your company's maternity policy and if it includes adoptive parents."

"Yes, I reviewed it, and I'll be able to take twelve weeks. I'm also thinking about taking a leave of absence—if I get her—to be with her for the first six months."

"I think that would be lovely, Anabel. That was really the only question I had for you tonight. Do you have any questions for me?"

I tuck my hair behind my ear. "I guess, just, what happens next?"

Ms. Alvarez smooths her shiny black hair. "We will proceed with the home studies and take it from there. My advice to you is to let your lawyer talk to the police if they call again. Don't talk to them yourself."

My mouth goes dry and I feel light-headed. Somehow, her last comment comes across as critical. Is this my fault? Have I lost the baby because I cooperated with Detective Harris?

Dennis leaps in to save the conversation. "We're going to find the best attorney first thing in the morning, and we'll let you know who we hire."

Ms. Alvarez starts to collect her things.

A bit of panic sets in. I don't want her to think I'm ungrateful for the advice. "Thank you for being so honest and upfront with me. I know you want the best for her. What are they doing about a name? It's so strange to keep calling her the baby."

Ms. Alvarez laughs. "We've taken to calling her Goldie."

36

KELLY

Hattie and I tore Vadoma's room apart, but we didn't find any clues about her plans. When I went downstairs, I told Savannah I thought Vadoma had left for good and that I think it's better for us this way. If the cops do come nosing around, she's not here. We just have to decide if we lie and say we never knew her or if we pin the whole drop on her alone. Savannah says she's thinking that one through. Part of me is happy she's gone because now maybe Savannah will take me to New York with her. I've never been on a plane, and I'd like to see the Empire State Building.

Savannah sent me to town to find another girl, but my heart is just not in it, and my gut is telling me not to do it. Too many bad things have happened. The Golden One on the news, the stillborn baby, and now Vadoma running off. My ma always says that bad things happen in threes, so maybe we're in the clear now, but I just don't know.

Feeling like I've lost my sparkle this morning, I can't even muster the enthusiasm to go and flirt with Lee. I also didn't bother getting gussied up for him like I usually do, so I'm on my way to The Bean. The plan is to just sit in the back and drink some coffee until I feel better.

Fortunately, the parking lot is only half full, so I pull the Bimmer into a space in the shade. I plan on staying here a while so I can have a break from Savannah and her rage and her planning and her high energy. She has Hattie on stand-by if Mackenzie goes into labor. Muttering a little prayer that Mackenzie hangs on a few days, I head into The Bean.

The smell of hazelnuts and fresh baked bread surrounds me as Mitch, the barista, starts making my Chai Latte as soon as I walk in. It feels good to have someone take care of me a little. It's slow in The Bean today, and I breathe a sigh of relief. Hopefully, no one talks to me and then I can go home and tell Savannah there were no prospects today.

"G'mornin' gorgeous," Mitch says, as he puts my steaming hot beverage on the counter.

"How ya doin', Mitch?" I smile as much as I can.

"Not your perky self this morning. What's a matter?"

"This and that. This and that," I say as I hand him a five, pick up the latte, and start heading to the back of the coffeehouse. "Keep the change!"

"Thanks, Kelly!"

I choose a table in the back, get out my phone, and start watching YouTube videos. Bruno Mars always cheers me up, so I search "Uptown Funk" and watch as Bruno dances down the street with his drinking buddies. Between the soothing hot latte and Bruno's cool dance moves, I start to relax as a girl with strawberry blonde hair slides into the chair across from me.

"Hi?" I ask.

"She told me your name was Casey," she says, staring at me with intense light blue eyes. "The barista just called you Kelly."

My stomach drops as I stare at the girl. Beads of sweat sprout on my forehead. "Who told you my name was Casey?"

"Caroline."

"You must have the wrong girl. My name's Kelly."

The girl's eyes grow hard. "She pointed you out to me. She says that there's a barn out by the Old Post Road and a bunch of midwives live out there. She says they help girls out."

I study her and try to decide how old she is. Could be sixteen, or she could be twenty. Sometimes it's hard to tell. "Why? Do you need help?"

She sits back in her chair and looks down at her lap. She's wearing a tight striped tank top and white shorts with a ketchup stain on the fly. If she's pregnant, it's too early to tell. I want to fill the silence, but something tells me to wait her out. I see her lower lip start to quiver and I know she needs our help.

"How far along are you?"

She shrugs.

"Are you with the father? Is he your boyfriend or just a casual fling?"

She looks down and studies her chipped, dirty nails.

"Can I buy you a cup of coffee? Are you hungry?"

She nods, and I go up to the counter and ask Mitch for a coffee and two egg, ham, and cheese sandwiches. He says he'll bring them over, so I go back to the table.

The hair on the back of my neck is standing up as I sit down. There's something about this girl that I don't trust. "How do you know Caroline?"

"From around the neighborhood. We went to school together."

"In the same grade?" I ask, still trying to figure out how old she is.

"She's a year ahead of me."

"So, you're still in school?"

Mitch arrives with our breakfast. "Another latte?"

"Please." I try to smile at him, but those muscles are just not flexing this morning.

We start working on our egg sandwiches and I can tell by the way she eats that she is ravenous. I take a small bite as I watch her wolf hers down in huge bites. A little yellow stream of egg-goo slithers down onto her chin, and I hand her a napkin to wipe it off.

I decide not to bring her back to the barn to meet Savannah. My stomach is telling me not to, and I am a thorough believer in following my gut. When she's done, and Mitch has brought me another latte, I ask her if she wants half of my sandwich, and she eagerly accepts.

"What's your name?" I ask.

"They call me Berry, 'cause of my hair. Straw-*berry*-blonde." The color has come into her face and the intense look in her eyes has faded away. I realize now that she was starving.

"Okay, Berry, here's what I'm gonna do. I have some appointments, and I need to talk to some people, but if you think you need a friend, meet me back here day after tomorrow at ten o'clock in the morning. Okay?"

She nods and I get up to go. On my way out, I pay Mitch and tell him to take her a chocolate cookie.

37

SAVANNAH

Tom hasn't called me about the new development with the sapphire ring, which at first made me happy, but now his silence is making me nervous. It's been twenty-four hours since the first story hit the news, and he hasn't called to yell at me and whine about shutting down the operation. I hope he hasn't done anything stupid like going to the police with a guilty conscience. That would be crazy, but I could actually see him doing it.

To ease my mind, I dial his number. Straight to voicemail. I decide to go for a jog; the physical activity will do me good. I'm already wearing sweatpants, sneakers, and a T-shirt. I'm pulling my hair back into a ponytail as I go out the back door, but when I get to the side of the house, I see Kelly's Bimmer coming up the drive. I wonder if she has been able to secure another girl.

She comes and parks next to me, and I have to say she does look cute sitting in that red leather seat. She can do so much better than Mr. Gas Station but I know she'll get pissed if I tell her that. She jumps out of the car and comes toward me with a sour look on her face.

"How'd it go?" I ask her.

I notice the dark circles under her eyes, and she looks up at me, biting her lower lip. "We gotta talk. Let's go in," she says.

I follow her back around the house and into the terra cotta tiled mud room which has cubbies for our boots, crocs, and sneakers, and a bench to sit on while we tie our laces. Across from the bench is a large utility sink and a dozen hooks on the wall for our barn coats, rain jackets, hooded sweatshirts, and a shelf overhead for hats.

I still want to take my run. "What?" I ask with annoyance.

"A girl came up to me in The Bean and said that Caroline told her there was a barn with a bunch of midwives who help girls out. She said that Caroline said my name was Casey, but Mitch, the barista at The Bean, called me Kelly."

"That little bitch!" I explode. "After we waited on her hand and foot. Making her tea and boiled chicken. She goes around talking about us! Is the girl pregnant?"

Kelly sits down on the bench. "Listen, Savannah. I think we need to lay low. Too many bad things are happening, and I don't want to spend years in the slammer. This girl gave me the shakes. There was just something about her."

Everyone around me is spineless. Tom, Vadoma, now Kelly. A bunch of cowards. I stand over Kelly with my hands firmly on my hips. "What did you tell her?"

"I told her that I needed to talk to some people, and that if she needs help, she should meet me day after tomorrow at The Bean. But I gotta tell you, I have a bad feeling about this girl. The hair on the back of my neck was standing up when I was talking to her." Kelly's bent over, leaning her arms on her knees. She shakes her head, and her hair falls in front of her face.

"Look, Kelly, go take a nap. You're right. There's a lot going on, and you've been with me since the beginning. You deserve a rest. Take the day off," I tell her.

She looks up at me with suspicion in her eyes. "What's the catch?" she asks.

"No catch. Go see Mr. Gas Station tonight. Have a little fun." I give her an encouraging smile. "Go! Nap, shower, Mr. Gas Station! Forget about all this for the day. I need time to think anyway."

Kelly stands up and I see her relax a bit. She offers me a small smile. "Really? Because, honestly, Savannah, I could use a break."

I let my arms drop to my sides and then put one hand on her shoulder. "I can see that. Go. We'll talk tomorrow." I point down the hall, dismissing her.

She walks quickly out of the mud room and as soon as she turns the corner, I can feel my chin jut out from my neck. I think I need to cut these partners loose and start over with a different crew.

I am self-aware enough to know that it might be better to shut down the barn at this point and simply pick up and move to the island of my choice and never look back. Problem is, I can't give it up. Like a gambler whose fingers itch to roll the dice, I live for the thrill of the successful exchange. Changing people's fates gives me a high that champagne or great sex can't rival. I give a new life to the girls who think there's no way out and I grant a family to the hopeless couples with too much money and too little progesterone to maintain their pregnancies. I alone can make all this happen. Only me.

It's funny, once you start living outside the law and getting away with it, it's like the law doesn't exist. Everyone spends hours each day justifying their actions, their words. We work on justifying like whittlers work on a piece of wood. Carving, smoothing, manipulating, drilling down on a little piece that doesn't fit right, until everything works. Until everything fits into place. I know that we are working outside the law. Intellectually, I know we are, but I do feel we're doing a lot of good and that's the thought I'm hanging onto.

I make my way through the kitchen and into the office, deciding I'm too distracted to jog, and stand in front of my new white board. The board tracks the births and the exchanges. I had to rearrange everything after Caroline's baby died, and I spend the rest of the morning making sure the flowchart works. I decide to get Kelly to give me all the contact information for all the girls in case I have to take over recruitment and development.

Kelly is just running scared. She's young and that's both good and bad. Sure, she had a rough start with her abusive father, but she's been away from him for years now and this life, the life at the farm, is all she knows. A night off will be good for her. She'll spend it in the sack with that loser, but every girl needs a release now and then.

38

TOM

When I saw the baby and the woman featured again on Channel 2, I made the call. Savannah has always been stronger willed than me, and I know I'll never be able to make her stop. I can't reason with her. She's not rational. I think she believes that we are serving a higher purpose. Like God, we're giving the girls a second chance and the couples a baby. In reality, we are breaking a long list of federal and state laws. Not to mention transporting minors over state lines in order to sell them.

Mr. Harry Meyer is the best criminal lawyer in New York City. Meyer handled the infamous Hunt case in which Lionel Hunt was accused of murdering not one, not two, but three wives, and Meyer got him off. I met with Meyer and confessed everything. Everything we've done up to this point. I had lost track of the exact number of babies we had placed, but I knew it was over fifty.

I could tell that the story fascinated him, especially in light of all the publicity with the baby and this poor woman, Anabel Leigh. I told him about Savannah and her team of helpers. I told him as much as I know about the clinic in the barn and the girls. I didn't really know a lot about how

Savannah recruited the girls. She had told me that recruitment was Kelly's job. I've never met Kelly or Vadoma or Hattie. I had decided early on that it wasn't in my best interest to know all the details.

After I spilled my guts, Meyer looked at me with his small, hard brown eyes and took me in. He pushed his reading glasses down on his long thin nose to study me. I knew he was sizing me up to see how I would do in front of a jury. His eyes paused on my curly brown hair and gentle blue eyes. In my business, dealing with couples who are sad and desperate for a baby, I had mastered a way of looking at them that tells them they are safe in my hands. I looked at Meyer this way and he smiled. He knew I had what it took to make a jury feel sympathetic toward me.

But what I really want Meyer to work out for me is a deal. I want immunity from prosecution by both the Feds and the state in return for handing them Savannah and her gang. I want to walk away scot-free. I have had five nail-biting, hair-pulling, sleepless years and I want out. I tried to reason with Savannah, but reasoning with Savannah was a difficult proposition. She was a manipulative liar who used me like a pawn. Sure, I had enjoyed our first-class trips and the advantages that came with having infinite money, but it just wasn't worth having to look over my shoulder every minute. Wake up every day in a sweat.

Savannah had always been the stronger one. I was putty in her hands when we were teens, and later, when she approached me with this scheme of hers. I just couldn't resist her seduction. Her complete control of every situation, her complete control over me. Her confidence and arrogance are bewitching. I remember once, back in high school, she wanted me to borrow my brother's motorcycle, even though I was just learning to ride, and go out to the lake. We'd been drinking and I knew it was too dangerous, but this was why she wanted to do it. She always loved beating danger. I wanted to wait until Chad, my brother, had given me a few more lessons, but Savannah couldn't wait. She made me take the key when Chad wasn't home and steal the bike. This was just one of so many instances where she made me do what she wanted me to do against my better judgment.

Chad got home early, called the cops, and told them that the bike had been stolen. When I pulled up two hours later, my father, mother, and Chad had been waiting. I had already dropped off Savannah, so she was safely asleep in bed, while I endured the wrath of Chad and a two-week grounding by my father. But still, I went back to her. She was and still is every man's fantasy. Blonde, bold, beautiful. Ready, willing, and able to fulfill my every dream. I've always been her lapdog.

But now I am on the verge of losing everything. My medical license, my practice, my freedom. I can't see her again. She's called me so many times, and I've just let it go to voicemail. We're waiting on the baby for the Ackermans that could be born any day now and then she'll come to New York. Meyer told me I might have to wear a wire and get her on tape and the thought of that scares me to death. We'll have to stay in public places because when we're alone the clothes usually come off.

39

KELLY

When I text Lee that I want to see him tonight he hits me back right away.

> Lee: *Good. Something I want to talk to you about.*
> Kelly: *6:30 at your place?*
> Lee: *K*

My first thought is, now what? I am really beginning to feel that I am in over my head. I try to count my blessings—I have boxes and bags of money, I have beautiful clothes but nowhere to wear them, I have the Bimmer which I love, I have Lee—and he's cute, but is he worth it if he is going to cause me any stress? Quite frankly, he is my stress relief and if that changes, he has to go. Something inside my gut is telling me to run.

Run, Kelly, run, keeps coursing through my thoughts like a news ticker crawling along the bottom of my brain. *Get out now*, it screams.

But where would I go? They would find me if I went back home to Ma. She and Savannah are the only adults in my life. I wonder sometimes where Vadoma ended up. I've tried to call her and text her, but nothing. I think she got rid of the phone she had with us. I can go anywhere I want, but there's nowhere I want to go. That's my problem.

I head into my bathroom that adjoins my room. All the tiles are bright white except for a rim of turquoise at the top, about eye height. I look at the soft, white towels, the expensive shampoo, the soap in the shape of a butterfly that I saw in a gift shop downtown, and bought for myself and I feel that I'm not good enough to have this bathroom. What have I done to deserve this bathroom?

Maybe a bath will help. Sitting on the side of the tub, I watch as it fills up with hot water and bubbles and I realize I'm tired of this life, weary to the core. Suddenly, I am so sad about the lives of the miserable girls that we help. We are solving their problem but at what cost to ourselves? What is the cost to me?

Throwing my clothes on the floor, I sink into the suds to clear my mind and relax in the hot water. I try to picture myself on a beach, but I've never been to the beach, so I only have pictures of beaches in my mind, not actual beaches. Savannah runs off to the islands all the time. Maybe I should book a flight and head to Aruba, Jamaica, or Bermuda. Savannah said I could have the night off. I decide that after Mackenzie delivers her baby I'm going to the beach for a week. I won't ask Savannah's permission. I'll just tell her I'm going. Maybe I won't even tell her. Just go. Maybe I'll bring Lee with me or maybe I'll just meet a guy on the beach.

When the water starts turning cold, I get out and get dressed. I put on my new white lace bra and thong set, a feminine white cotton shirt with lace on the collar and a short jean skirt. I leave my hair free and curly and put on an extra coat of black mascara. My red cowboy boots finish the outfit. I want to lose myself and my troubles in Lee's bed.

I sneak out of the house. I'm not giving Savannah the opportunity to go back on her offer of the night off. I slip into the Bimmer. Once I am out on the Post Road, I feel free and crank up Sabrina Carpenter on the radio and smile for the first time today. Pulling into the Dubois Liquor Mart, I decide to splurge and buy a bottle of Moet and two plastic champagne flutes. The man behind the counter looks me up and down and then asks to see ID, and I give him the fake driver's license that Savannah gave me.

Back in the car, my heart starts pumping like a jackhammer when I think of Lee lying on his bed all naked and excited. After I pull to a stop in the apartment parking lot, I check myself out in the mirror on the visor and open another button on my shirt. I skip with anticipation up the stairs to his apartment, but when Lee opens the door, I see Berry, the girl from The Bean, and Lee's brother, Jed, standing there, staring at me with blank expressions. I take a step back before Lee reaches out, pulls me into the apartment, and closes the door.

I lean back against the door and feel the blood rush to my cheeks, my knees wobble. "Berry, what——"

"Berry's been telling us all about your breakfast," says Lee real slow. "Says you offered to meet her again if she needs help. You told me you were a babysitter. She says you help this illegal midwife birth babies and then sell them. Did you lie to me?" I've never seen Lee mad before and it's not a good look. His eyes are slightly bulging, and his chest is pumped up in a menacing fashion.

I go to Lee and put my arms around his neck. "Lee, baby, calm down. I do watch the kids. I never lied to you." I turn my attention to Berry. "Is this the father?" I point to Jed.

She smirks. "I'm not pregnant, but my sister Caroline was, and Jed was the father of her baby. Caroline says she almost died giving birth at your place, in your barn, and she never saw her baby. You took it. She thinks it died. Did it?" Berry's fair skin is mottled with red splotches.

"Listen, I don't know what all these questions are all

about." My voice is louder than I expected. "We helped her. She came to me and said she wanted to get rid of the baby."

Berry takes two steps and points her finger in my face. "Did you sell it?"

"No, we gave it to a good family up North," I say as I turn around to leave but Lee moves between me and the door. I look up into his eyes. "Baby, what does all of this have to do with us? Can't we talk just you and me?"

A frown darts across Lee's face and he looks over at his brother. "Jed has a right to know where his baby is. What did you do with it?"

I feel a large strong hand wrap around my forearm and twist me around and now I am face-to-face with Jed. The bag with the champagne drops to the floor. "You paid Caroline, the baby's mother, and now you have to pay me, the baby's father. I want ten thousand dollars on Friday. In cash. Do you hear me?" His face is right in mine. His breath smells like whiskey and onions. I would have to be deaf not to hear him. "Or else I'm going to the police." He squeezes my arm until it throbs and gives me a shove backward. Lee catches me and helps me find my footing.

I look from Jed to Berry. My arm aches as I turn to leave and push Lee out of the way.

As I reach out to open the door I look at Lee. "You know what my boss calls you? Mr. Gas Station. That's what. That's all you'll ever be. A gas station attendant. Enjoy the champagne." I spit on the floor and walk out into the dusk.

When I get in the car my whole body is shaking. I have to talk to Savannah. This has got to be her problem, not mine. I decide right there and then that I am getting the fuck out of town. California or the south of France sounds really good right now.

I start the car and haul ass out of there. And I thought Lee was so sweet and dumb. Fuck him! As I drive down the road my phone pings. It's Mackenzie.

40

TOM

Meyer has set up a meeting with the FBI for me to give them our whole operation on a silver platter. Meyer says I'll be "Queen for a Day" which means I will be able to walk into 26 Federal Plaza, tell them all the laws we've broken, and they won't be able to use what I say against me in the criminal proceeding.

"Queen for a Day. That's a strange thing to call it," I say, and he tells me it's named after an old TV show of the same name in which contestants would tell their sob stories and the audience would vote on which contestant got to be Queen for the Day. The winner would go home with the help they needed which could be a new refrigerator, silver-plated flatware, or care for a sick child. Basically, in exchange for handing over Savannah, I get to be the Queen and go free.

I agree to meet with the US Attorney and the two agents who have been assigned to my case—Special Agent Nigel Thacker and Special Agent Jack Entenmann. Meyer says that when they realize that the Golden One is part of the case they will be ecstatic. The Feds love to solve high profile cases. And let's be honest, when photographs of Savannah are splashed on the front page of the papers the case will heat up to a fever pitch.

There's a rundown Korean deli across the street from 26 Federal Plaza on Worth Street and Meyer and I agree to meet there an hour before the meeting with the Feds to go over our strategy. We grab coffee and a muffin and head to one of the small tables in the back.

I feel eyes on me as we sit down, and my knee begins to bounce. The tables are so close together that I could reach out and take a sausage off the plate of the guy next to me if I wanted to. My two-thousand-dollar custom-made suit, my Rolex, and Gucci loafers scream Uptown in this deli full of government workers in khakis, button-downs, and tie-no-jacket. Meyer notices my discomfort. "I should have warned you to dress down a bit," he gives me a half-smile.

"Should I go home and change?"

"Don't have time. I doubt there are any polyester suits in your closet anyway."

I scowl.

When we're settled, he asks me if I brought the records and I produce a list of the names of the couples who we gave babies to and the approximate dates.

After he looks over the list, he says, "The couples will be seen as sympathetic victims. What the Feds will be interested in is the money. Where is the money? Have you paid taxes on the money? Did you launder the money? What did you buy with the money?" Meyer lays this out in between large bites of his blueberry muffin. Crumbs are stuck on his mustache.

My muffin remains untouched in its plastic wrap. "I thought they would be more interested in the babies. Where are the babies? Who vetted the parents? How were the documents forged? To be honest, I don't even know how much money I got in total. I guess I could do a rough calculation. Some of it is in bags and boxes in my closets. In cash. It took us a while to set up the offshore accounts. I didn't do it for the money, Harry," I tell him.

"Why did you do it?" His glasses are on the tip of his nose.

"I did it for her. For Savannah. Unfortunately, I'd do anything for her." I know how ridiculous I sound, but I also know that I am not the first man to get in over his head because of a woman. It's a common malady with no known cure.

Meyer's small brown eyes are looking at me like I am pathetic, and I know I deserve that, but still it hurts. He is not building up my confidence right before I go up against the Feds.

He points a finger at my face. "Here's what we're gonna do. We're gonna lead with Savannah. Tell them how she called you out of the blue. You hadn't seen her in years. How you said no, at first, but then you gave in. How she ran the operation. Tell them she's a midwife and how she recruits the girls and that the births are her responsibility. She's the one who transports the babies across state lines. That point is important. How she's the one who physically hands the babies over to the couples. She's the one who accepts the money. Keep the focus on her side of the operation. You've never even been to the barn, have you?"

"Not since we were teenagers."

"What did you do in the barn when you were teenagers?"

I hesitate. "We screwed. We have a long history together. We met when we were in high school."

"Okay, let's say you were friends in high school. Don't bring up the fact that you used to get laid in the barn. Let's keep you out of the barn if we can."

"Honestly, all I do is connect her with couples who have given up on trying to get pregnant but they still want a baby. Desperate couples."

"Don't say desperate couples. It sounds like you're preying

on them. Keep it factual. They've had a number of procedures. They're out of options. That kind of thing. Okay?"

I nod.

"Good. Now back to the money. Have you bought any houses? With the money, I mean?"

"No."

"Any cars?"

"No."

"Artwork?"

"No. Yes. We have bought artwork."

Meyer squints at me like he's trying to see into my mind. "They'll take the artwork. What else have you done with the money?"

"Savannah and I have traveled. There are a few islands she really loves, and we go to them together. We went to Europe, to Paris, Barcelona, Lisbon."

"What did you do on these trips?"

I start to pull on the curls near my ears.

"Did you recruit girls on these trips?" Meyer's voice gets louder but when he remembers where he is he readjusts to a whisper.

"No! We went to . . ."

"What?"

"Screw."

Meyer takes off his glasses and rubs his eyes. "Okay, you can't be so blunt. Just say that you went on vacation. Listen, Tom, you're a smart guy, and I can tell that you are loaded with guilt, but you've got to take the fucking high road. You weren't screwing, you were taking a few days to unwind. Do you get it? Your job is very stressful. It's all in the spin. You gotta spin it. I'll step in if you're sinking yourself but try to get in a mindset. Okay? And, you are going to have to count the money and hand it over. You know that, right?"

"Yes. I can't wait to get rid of it. I can't stand to look at it,"

I'm totally drenched in sweat now. I pull at the knot in my tie, trying to loosen it a bit.

Meyer looks at me and his eyes soften. "Listen, Tom, there's one woman in each man's life who makes him crazy, and this lady, she's your crazy. Hopefully, she's the only one. Now let's go in there and do this."

41

SAVANNAH

C'mon, Savannah, I chide myself. This is what you're good at. Keeping it all together when everyone else is falling apart and pulling their hair out. Tom is definitely pulling his hair by now. I texted him about Mackenzie right after Kelly texted me. Her text said, *Mackenzie in labor. Coming home with situation.* I just need to get everyone through this birth and the exchange, and then, maybe, we can all calm down.

Damn, I had a quiet night planned after Kelly went out. I look at my bed longingly with Emily Henry's new novel and my glass of wine sitting on the nightstand. I long to curl up with Charlie and my cashmere throw, read a good book, and drink the bottle of Chardonnay, but it will have to wait. Birth waits for no woman.

I pull off my jeans and Georgia State sweatshirt and put on my lavender scrubs and sweat socks. My thick hair has a life of its own from the humidity and so I braid it in a long plait down my back.

When I open my bedroom door Kelly is standing there looking as if someone has died. She startles me and I jump back. "Jesus Christ, Kelly, what are you doing lurking in the hallway? You didn't have to come back. Hattie is going to assist me."

Kelly walks brusquely past me back into my room. "I told you there was a situation. C'mere," she says ominously.

"Now what? Honestly, what is wrong now?" I say as I follow her back into my room where she has plopped down on the side of my bed.

"So, I go to Lee's and guess who's there waiting for me?"

"Lee?"

"Yeah, Lee, but he's with Berry, that girl from The Bean, and his brother Jed."

"Okay?" I ask looking at my phone for the time. Mackenzie is supposed to be here by now.

"Well, it turns out that Berry is Caroline's sister and Jed is the father of Caroline's baby. The dead baby that we buried in the pasture. You do remember the dead baby, right?" Kelly is back on her feet now, pacing, her red cowboy boots stomping on the hardwood floor. "And that's not the worst of it. The worst of it is that Jed wants ten thousand dollars, in cash, on Friday and if he doesn't get it he's going to the police. Savannah, I . . ." Kelly starts to cry.

Anger rises so quickly in my chest that I cut her off. "He's going to blackmail us for taking care of his problem? That fucker! And where was he when Caroline was pregnant? He certainly wasn't taking care of her. I cannot believe this!"

Kelly stops pacing. "And that's not all, Caroline is suspicious that the baby died. They asked me if the baby died!" Kelly's face is white.

"What did you say?" I reach out and grab her arm and she winces and pulls her arm away.

Kelly is on the verge of hysteria now. Her eyes are bulging out of their sockets as she screams at me, "I said it didn't die. I said that we gave it to a couple, but I could see in Berry's eyes that she didn't believe me."

I notice that Kelly is rubbing her arm. "What happened to

your arm?" There are purple marks, small beads, like purple grapes in a ring around her bicep.

"It doesn't matter. What matters is that you . . . we need to deal with this," she stammers.

I sit down on the tufted bench at the end of my bed and stare straight ahead. Kelly sits down on the side of the bed. "We do have a situation. Let's think on it. Let's focus on Mackenzie's baby tonight and we'll come up with a plan."

"Savannah, I'm getting scared. Too many things are going wrong. We've got to figure a way out. This is the last baby."

I look into the mirror over the bureau which is directly in front of me and see Kelly staring back at me.

"Figure a way out," she growls.

I meet her eyes. "We will," I tell her.

42

TOM

There are probably a hundred conference rooms at 26 Federal Plaza, which all look alike, but room 429 will always be etched in my brain. Plain brown paneling, scratched wooden table with eight chairs, dirty windows that looked south toward City Hall making the sunny day look cloudy, faded tan carpet with coffee stains. A room designed to make you feel uncomfortable.

My palms are slick with sweat as Meyer and I wait for the Feds. Meyer looks calm, in his element. He gives me an encouraging smirk when I look over at him. All I can think about are handcuffs being slapped on my wrists and a beefy guard giving me a push from the back when I'm on my way to prison. Meyer assured me that this was not going to happen, but after we went through the metal detectors downstairs, I wasn't so sure. They had me now. I felt trapped.

They're ten minutes late. Meyer said they would do this to make me nervous and it's working. Finally, the door opens and three men with short haircuts and dark suits walk into the room. We shake hands and introduce ourselves. US Attorney Phil Ravens sits at the head of the table like a king indulging his subjects. His broad shoulders fill the space above the end of the table and I notice that one of his front teeth is chipped when he gives a big possessive grin letting us all know that this is his house and we should all bow accordingly. His face is familiar from the nightly news.

Special Agents Thacker and Entenmann sit across from me and Meyer. The air is oppressive, and I wonder if they purposely lower the air conditioning or if I can thank budget cuts for the warm room.

"So, thanks for coming in today," says Ravens looking in my direction. "Mr. Meyer says you have some information you'd like to share with us. The session is being recorded. Mr. Meyer, would you like to make an opening statement?"

All eyes turn to Meyer. "Yes, good morning and thank you for agreeing to meet with me and my client Dr. Thomas Moore. Dr. Moore has information about a midwife, Savannah Maas, in Dubois, Georgia who works with young mothers who do not want to keep their babies and then sells the babies to childless couples in the tristate area. Savannah runs a clinic for the girls out of her farm. Each couple pays Ms. Maas up to five hundred thousand dollars for a child and false documents stating that the couple are the birth parents. One of the children born in her clinic is the baby that has been dubbed "the Golden One" by the New York press."

As soon as Meyer says "the Golden One" both special agents lean into the table. Eyes glowing, Thacker actually licks his lips. They share a quick look.

US Attorney Ravens clears his throat. "What is Dr. Moore's involvement with this process?"

"Dr. Moore is a fertility specialist, and the adopting couples were his clients. After many unsuccessful procedures to get the couple pregnant, Dr. Moore arranges for a meeting between Ms. Maas and the couple where the baby changes hands."

"Tell us about the baby in the park," says Special Agent

Thacker. His mouth hangs open and I'm afraid his saliva will spill out on the table.

Meyer nods at me to comply. "On two occasions Savannah couldn't place a baby. It gets harder to find a home as the child gets older. Savannah knew that one of the girls was too old to place and her employee had taken a liking to that girl so that girl was given to the employee, but the younger one, the baby in the news, well, I know it sounds crazy, but Savannah and her team decided to just put her in that woman's lap in the park."

All of the eyebrows belonging to the Feds jump up on their faces. Special Agent Entenmann is the first to recover. "Where are the parents of that baby?" he asks.

"The mother is dead," I say.

"And the other child who couldn't be placed, where is she?" Entenmann follows up.

"She's living on the farm."

"So, what exactly are you offering us, Dr. Moore?" asks US Attorney Ravens, folding his large hands on the table in front of him.

"I have a list of the couples who bought the babies. Their names and the dates of the exchanges. Savannah's information, name, address, what I know about her operation, her employees. And my share of the money."

"How much money are we talking about?" asks Thacker.

"Roughly twenty-four million dollars between us. I have approximately twelve million dollars."

The eyebrows salute again.

"Where's the money now?" asks Thacker.

I rub my forehead with my fingers. "Well, some of my share is in my apartment. In cash. The rest is in an offshore account."

"So, you split the money with Ms. Maas?" asks Ravens.

"Savannah handled the money. She paid the other women who work for her, the birth mothers, the expenses that come with the clinic she has in her barn, and then we split what was left. I never cared about the money. I want to give you the money. I've only spent maybe a hundred thousand of it," I feel the sweat dripping down my armpits and my back.

For the next three hours, I take the Feds through our black-market baby adoption operation. I tell them everything I know about how the mothers are recruited, their prenatal care, the births, how the documents are forged, the little I know about Kelly, Vadoma, and Hattie, I answer all their questions and volunteer any information that I think is important.

Finally, Ravens calls the meeting. I am so drained that I feel a little dizzy when I stand up. Meyer puts his hand on my shoulder to steady me, and I give him a weak smile. My skin, under my suit, is wet and clammy.

"Just one more question, Dr. Moore," said Ravens. "If you didn't do it for the money, why did you do it?"

I hang my head, ashamed. "Because she asked me to."

As we wait for the elevator, I overhear Thacker say to Entenmann as they walk down the hall, "*Cherchez la femme.*" They both laugh and shake their heads.

43

ANABEL

A week goes by, and I don't hear anything from Ms. Alvarez. I try to pour myself into my work. Client meetings all start with questions about what happened in the park, if the woman has been found, what's going on with the baby, and my nerves are getting frayed. I keep wondering if the jeweler ever came forward to the police. Have they found the woman? Who is this baby really? Where did she come from?

The baby I want so badly that I feel lost, who I think about all the time. I've closed the door to the nursery in my apartment again and I know this is a bad sign. Slipping back into a state of grief. Each miscarriage I suffered felt like a hollow death. Grieving someone who I never even met. Like I was grieving the promise of a person, not an actual person. Part of me feels this way now. The difference is that I know Goldie is out there. She's real. When I close my eyes, I can smell the cinnamon in her hair and feel the weight of her small body in my lap.

I give myself credit for actually showing up at work every day. Dennis has been very helpful in this regard, waking me up each morning by bringing me coffee in bed. Bellowing "rise and shine" as he heads into the shower. How did I ever live without him? He is the ultimate glass half-full person and between the coffee in the morning and the wine at night he is always filling my glass.

Between loving him and longing for the baby, my heart, which had been stagnant for years, on hold, having a time out, is now working on overdrive. Sometimes I feel bad that I'm not a hundred percent focused on Dennis now—at the beginning of our relationship—but I also feel that the baby played a role in bringing us together. If I hadn't needed someone to confide in that night, would we even be together? However, if there was no baby, I could just relax and bask in the glow of being in love.

I open my eyes and force myself to turn my attention to my email. There must be some ad campaign that can excite me, some memo to write, to make me forget about her until tonight. Nothing in my email. I open Outlook to check my afternoon schedule, and I feel my face wrinkle up when I see that I have my one-on-one with Tanya. Technically, I'm Tanya's boss, but lately, these meetings feel the other way around. I only have fifteen minutes to throw together an agenda.

At precisely two o'clock, Tanya and her perfect haircut arrive in my doorway. As always, she is impeccably dressed in a suit I've never seen before. I, myself, have a lot of clothes, but, still, I am always jealous of her seemingly endless supply of feminine suits, coordinating silk shirts, and pumps.

"Tanya!" I try to take control of the meeting by greeting her first. "C'mon in. Take the hot seat."

She looks at me like I have lost my mind and says flatly, "I only have fifteen minutes. Sol wants to see me."

I glare at her. "What does Sol want?"

"It's about the new client."

"What client?" I hear my voice sounding aggressive.

She sits back in the chair and crosses her legs. "It's only media. I don't think you have a role."

"I'm the senior vice president of communications! How can I not have a role?"

She picks an imaginary piece of string off her skirt but remains mute.

"I'll discuss that with Sol," I say changing tactics. "Tell me about the articles you're pitching this week. Where are we?"

I realize, when she starts to speak, that she has come to the meeting without a notebook or pen. Nothing to write down my directions and comments on. I listen to her report, take no notes myself, politely thank her when she's done, and watch as she pops out of the chair, spins around on her kitten heel, and leaves me in a heap in my chair.

Clearly, I have to get my head back in the game or Tanya will be my boss.

44

SAVANNAH

By the time I get down to the barn, Hattie has everything set up in the green birthing room for Mackenzie. The place has a heavy smell of Lysol and Mr. Clean. I decide not to tell Hattie about the new development with Jed until later. Why have all of us as nervous as a pack of rats trapped with the neighborhood tomcat during Mackenzie's delivery?

"Hey," I say, taking out the patchouli oil and spraying a few puffs into the air.

"Hey, I washed everything down," she says.

"Smells clean, but maybe a little overbearing."

Hattie shrugs.

Kelly is still at the house suiting up and then meeting Mackenzie at the door. I hope she can keep it together for the birth. I do a mental calculation of when I might be able to bring the baby up to New York. I figure ten days is a safe bet. Kelly always says that she wants to go with me to New York and I think maybe now is the time to do it. Don't want to leave her here with Mr. Gas Station and his brother. After the birth I'll figure out what to do about Jed's demands. There's no fucking way I'm giving him a penny.

The door to the barn creaks and I hear Kelly and Mackenzie laughing. A good sign.

"And here we go," says Hattie, raising her eyebrows. "I've been praying all week that this one is easier than the last."

"It will be," I assure her with a smile, but my throat feels so tight I think I might choke. As Kelly and Mackenzie step into the green room, I start to feel the ground steady. This is where I feel prepared. My training kicks in as I greet the girl and try to make her feel comfortable.

"Mackenzie, look at you! The picture of health! When did the contractions start?" I ask cheerily.

"Hi, Susan, about three hours ago."

I'm always shocked when they call me Susan, my clinic name, but I recover seamlessly. "And how far apart are they now?"

"They're still coming erratically, but they're getting stronger. The last one nearly knocked me to my knees," Mackenzie says, her cheeks are bright red, and her blue eyes are bright.

"Well, I'm glad you came in early. Hazel, why don't you help Mackenzie into a birthing dress. Casey and I will be right back." I nod my head toward the door and Kelly follows me into the hall.

Keeping my voice low, I say, "Let's keep the little blackmail request to ourselves until after the baby comes. I don't want to do anything to jeopardize this baby. Then we'll have a team meeting. Okay?"

"Go team," Kelly says giving me an exaggerated sarcastic grin.

"And I want you to stay down here at the barn. I think we all need to stick together."

Kelly rolls her eyes.

For the next six hours, we take turns encouraging Mackenzie to breathe, rubbing her back, and feeding her ice chips. By the time she's ready to push, we are all exhausted. She has the perfect breeder's body with her wide hips and physical strength, and it only takes her an hour to birth a nine-pound baby boy. Just as I predicted, big and healthy and beautiful.

Kelly takes the baby and starts to walk out of the room, and Hattie and I watch Mackenzie's eyes follow her.

"Let me see it," she whispers. "Is it a girl or boy?"

Kelly stops halfway out the door and looks at me.

I go quickly up to the top of bed and sit down next to Mackenzie, waving Kelly off behind my back. Kelly takes the baby out of the room. "Casey needs to clean the baby up, Mackenzie," I take her hand. "Remember? We talked about this. It's gonna be harder for you if you see it. I don't think you should."

She closes her eyes and starts to cry.

Usually, at this juncture, I give the girls one last opportunity to leave here with their baby, but the Ackermans are waiting. This baby has got to go up to New York.

"Mackenzie, you don't have a job. You have nowhere to go with this baby. You told me yourself that your parents wouldn't take care of it. It's best for the baby if you give it to a couple who can care for it. That's what you wanted. That's what you said. You're just feeling scared now, but don't you want to do what's right for the baby?"

"I just want to see it. That's all." She tries to get up, but I gently hold her down.

"You can't get up yet, Mackenzie. I had to give you an episiotomy and now I have to sew you up. Relax. The baby's not going anywhere." I get up and move back to the bottom of the bed. Hattie is staring at me with her big eyes, and I tell her to go and help Casey attend to the baby.

"Tell me about your parents, Mackenzie," I say, as I start to sew her up. "What's your dad like?"

"He's real strict. I haven't been home in a month 'cause I couldn't let him see my belly. I've been sleeping on my friend's couch, but she said that her husband's coming back to town, and I can't go back there."

"See, Mackenzie, you can't go back to your friend, and you can't show up at your father's doorstep with a baby, screaming in the middle of the night, needing to go to the doctor, needing new clothes and diapers. Babies are expensive, Mackenzie."

She's sobbing now, her head turned into the pillow.

"You're tired, honey. Close your eyes," I say. "I'm almost done here."

I know from experience that after they sleep and feel a little better, they just want to hightail it out of here. That's what I'm banking on as I sew the final stitch.

45

TOM

Meyer told me not to talk directly to Savannah. The woman is a master of manipulation, and I have confided in Meyer that it is hard for me to resist her. He gave me one of his condescending over-the-glasses looks and I said, "Wait until you meet her. You'll see."

He squinted at me like I was a weakling.

Just listening to her voice makes me feel weak in the knees. I had to put the phone down on the kitchen table and put it on speaker to listen to her last message.

"Tom, honey." Her voice is so husky, so sexy. "I don't understand why you're not picking up my calls. I know things have gotten a little stressed, but, baby, we have to stick together. Our work makes people happy. Try to focus on that. The baby for the Ackermans has been born. Kelly and I will be in New York soon."

After I listened to that call, I was lightheaded. I thought I might need to go to the toilet. Even though she sounded sweet as pie, I have seen the other side. The ruthless, cold, calculating side of Savannah Maas, and I will not be able to stand up to her. Somehow, after the call, I stumbled around the apartment, trying to get ready for work, but I was consumed by thoughts of Savannah finding out that I have set her up.

I have no recollection of getting on or off the subway, but somehow, I made it to work. Now, sitting at my desk, I start to weep. Images of her, the sound of her voice, the curves of her body are all I see when I close my eyes. I try to count to clear my mind, but I only make it to four when my mind reverts back to images of her face. Her beautiful face. Her silky hair. I jump up and start to pace around my office. I feel the floor beneath my feet start to buckle as my eyes catch on my diplomas, mounted in gold frames, mocking me. Asking me why I think I might be worthy of the power they give me to create life. How did I get here?

After that horrible senior year of high school with Savannah and our baby, I took the full ride that Dartmouth offered me and moved to New Hampshire. I never looked back. From Dartmouth I went to Yale Medical School followed by an internship through the University of California and then my residency at Columbia Presbyterian. After twelve years of studying, I became a reproductive endocrinologist helping couples get pregnant and I joined the premiere fertility clinic in New York City.

All of that work for nothing. The deal that Meyer crafted with the Feds and the DA stipulated that I have to return all the money, give up my license in New York, turn Savannah and her women in, and testify against them. The money is easy. I haven't used much of it. My license is harder, although I don't want to do this anymore. I don't want a profession that is so emotionally charged. Where my clients cry on a regular basis and I see their desperation and their pain. And, of course, hardest of all is knowing that I will be the one who puts Savannah in prison. My mind can't even think of her in an orange jumpsuit behind bars.

After I gave my affidavit admitting everything we'd done, I'd handed over the names of the couples, Savannah's address in Dubois, and as much as I know about her operation. Meyer told me that the Feds will get a judge to issue an order for a wiretap, and they will put cameras and microphones in the hotel suite to get Savannah giving the baby to the Ackermans in exchange for transferring the money to her offshore account. Savannah, Kelly, and the Ackermans will be arrested at the hotel. The baby will be taken to social services, and the other women will be arrested in Dubois at the same time.

And for handing over all of this information, I will be granted full immunity. I will walk away free and clear.

If only she had agreed to stop.

Damn it! Savannah! I know you're not doing it purely for the money. I know, at first, you thought you were helping the girls, helping the child-less couples. I also know we both are making amends for our baby. Our baby who is an adult now if they're alive. But, Savannah, we went too far. We're selling babies as if they were commodities, things. Not living, breathing babies. Why did we take it this far?

46

SAVANNAH

Mr. Gas Station and his brother might think that they can intimidate Kelly, but they're no match for me. Jed better buckle up. A quick background check proves what a low life he is. He's a high school drop-out with a number of priors for assault, a few outstanding warrants, and a wife in Kentucky who is after him for child support. I know that he only wants the money. He doesn't give a shit about Caroline or about what happened to the baby.

It's the night after Mackenzie delivered, and I can't sleep. Thoughts of Jed, Mackenzie, the baby, and Tom haunt me. When the light in the room turns to gray, I call Tom. When he doesn't pick up, I feel a tightness in my throat and chest. Why is he avoiding me? What is he doing? I throw a red cashmere wrap around my shoulders and make my way downstairs, Charlie dancing around my feet. Flicking the lights on in the kitchen, I put on the coffee and check my email as I wait.

Hattie had the night watch, sleeping in the barn with Mackenzie, so I text her to see if the girl is up yet. No response. I grab a thermos and fill it with black coffee, dump the cashmere throw on the bench in the mudroom, pull an Athleta sweatshirt over the T-shirt I slept in, and head out to the barn. The sun is just coming up and the air smells clean and fresh. The sky is pink and gray over the pasture, but I don't have time to reflect on nature's beauty. I stride purposely over to the barn and pull open the door and an eerie silence greets me.

I hurry over to the green room where I left Mackenzie sleeping but the room is empty.

"Hattie?" I call. I hear rustling from the blue room and rush across the hall.

Hattie is sitting on the side of the bed rubbing her eyes. "Savannah?"

"Where's the girl? Where's Mackenzie?" I demand.

"Sleeping?"

"No. She's not sleeping. She's gone."

Hattie stretches and gives a big yawn. "She's a runner. Maybe she left."

All my senses are on high alert now. "Check every room in the barn. I'm going to check the nursery." Hattie is wide awake now, and she jumps up and hurries down the hall as I spin around and head out the door and back up to the house.

I throw open the back door, run through the mudroom and the kitchen, and take the stairs two at a time to the top floor. I sprint down the hall to the nursery. Has she taken the baby? I pound on Kelly's door as I fly by and fling open the door to the nursery. My heart pounding, trying to catch my breath.

In the corner of the large room, near the window sits Mackenzie in one of the rocking chairs. Her shirt is open, and the baby suckles peacefully. She looks up at me and smiles.

Kelly comes into the nursery behind me with Hattie right behind her. The three of us stand in a semicircle in front of Mackenzie, staring at her in all her Madonna-like glory. She has taken to breast feeding without a hitch and the baby is going to town on his breakfast as we stand gawking at them.

I break the silence. "How did you get up here?" My hands are on my hips, chin jutted out toward her.

"Came in the back door," she states.

I turn an accusatory eye to Hattie who presses her lips together.

"So, what's it gonna be?" I ask her straight out. "Where are you going to go? Where are you going to live?"

The baby has fallen asleep, but still Mackenzie sits there with her huge breast exposed and makes no sign of covering herself up. "I'm thinking . . ." She stops here and looks from me to Hattie to Kelly. Then, keeping her eyes on Kelly, says, "I'm thinking I'll stay here for a while. You've got this nice nursery, and it doesn't look like you're using all the cribs."

I laugh out loud at her audacity. "Well, that's not going to happen," I say with a sneer. "If you're leaving with the baby, I want you out of here in an hour. Take a baby bag full of diapers and good luck."

I point to Hattie and then the closet and Hattie goes and gets one of our pre-made baby bags and puts it on the floor in front of Mackenzie.

"And Mackenzie," I say. "You won't be getting the money we talked about. That's for your trouble for our client. If the client isn't getting a baby, then you're not owed a thing. Now, what's it going to be?"

She looks at me defiantly with her bright blue eyes. The room is flooded in sunlight now, the light coming in the window behind her makes her blonde hair shine. Finally, she pulls her shirt over her breast and buttons up.

I take a step toward her. "Listen to me, girl. We had a deal. What's it going to be? Are you going to live up to your side of the bargain or not?" My hands are clenched into fists, and my gravelly voice sounds angry, getting louder with every word.

Her eyebrows pull together, causing deep lines to form in between them and her mouth gapes open before she wails, "What if I want my baby? I don't even know where you're taking him or who you're giving him to." She instinctively puts a hand on the top of the baby's head.

"That was the deal, Mackenzie!" I yell.

"Well, I don't know if I can keep my end of the bargain. This is my baby we're talking about." She gets up and puts the sleeping infant in one of the cribs. "Can we go somewhere else? To let him sleep?"

Mackenzie and I stand in the middle of the room facing each other like two prize fighters waiting for the bell.

Hattie breaks the silence. "Let's go downstairs. Let's all cool off and get something to eat."

Flabbergasted by this turn of events, I turn on my heel and motion them all to follow me. Once we get down to the kitchen, Hattie takes charge.

"Okay, I'll make us all a good breakfast so we can think straight. It's not good to argue or make decisions on an empty stomach. That's what my grandma Jones always taught me." Hattie goes over to the refrigerator and gets out the eggs, bacon, and sausages. Then she gets out three frying pans and starts to cook the bacon and sausages. "Casey, please crack me eight eggs and scramble 'em."

Kelly looks happy to have something to do and gets to work on the eggs, leaving me and Mackenzie to stare at each other across the island.

"That bacon smells so good," Mackenzie says to Hattie's back. "I haven't had a good home cooked meal in a long time." She looks down at her nails and I notice that they are dirty and broken.

Hattie turns and gives her a tentative smile. I give Hattie a dirty look. Hattie scowls at me and turns back to her frying.

Kelly sets the island up for us to eat and when Hattie serves everything up they all dig in. I feel that I am losing control of this situation. If she takes her baby, I don't have a baby for the Ackermans and Tom will be upset. On the other hand, besides threatening her, how can I get her to give up the baby? I think of letting her stay here and taking the baby in the middle of the night. I'm trying to formulate a plan before she eats her last sausage. If she stays, I have options.

Before I can tell her my decision, she stands up and puts her plate in the sink. Then, she turns and walks back to stand by my side. "Now I'm really tired. I'm going upstairs to take a shower and a nap. When I'm feeling better, in a few days, I can clean for you. I can also cook." She looks me straight in the eye as she talks. It's not posed as a question.

I feel the blood rush to my cheeks, but my voice is calm. "Sure, go get some rest." She walks out of the kitchen, and we hear her climbing the stairs.

I motion to Hattie and Kelly to come to the office, and I close the door behind us. They both have the same look of fear on their faces. Eyes wide open, mouths drawn, watching my every move. I sit on my desk, and they both pull over chairs.

"Kelly, bring Hattie up to speed on our other problem first before we discuss what to do with Mackenzie."

Kelly recounts her visit with Lee, Jed, and Berry. I watch Hattie tense up as Kelly tells about Jed's demand for ten thousand dollars by Friday which is tomorrow.

When Kelly is done telling Hattie what happened, I get up from my desk, take off my sweatshirt, smooth back my hair and put my hands on my waist, elbows akimbo. I'm wearing a tight white T-shirt which makes my large breasts look huge, and I tower over them as they look up at me.

I give each of them a stern look before I say, "We're not giving that piece of white trash a cent." Venom drips off each word. "He wasn't around when Caroline needed him, and he's not entitled to a dime. We also have to get to Caroline and tell her to shut the fuck up." Each word delivered like a hammer driving a nail.

Kelly looks pale as she says, "He said he's going to the police."

"To say what? To say that his girlfriend sold her baby and now he wants a cut?"

"Maybe he'll just say we took her baby. Don't you think the police might come and investigate?" Hattie asks.

"No, he won't go to the police," I say with authority. "Pieces of shit like him don't want to go to the cops. I looked him up, he's got a long rap sheet. He's on probation, for God's sake. He's wanted for child support! Ha! He's just threatening us. And I don't scare easy." I give a steely look to Kelly and then Hattie.

I see Kelly's bottom lip start to quiver and a tear wells up in her eye. "Savannah, I'm scared. I don't want to do this anymore." She's crying deep sobs now, and Hattie reaches over and pats her shoulder.

"We're just going to ignore him, but we've got to keep all the doors locked from now on. I'm having a locksmith come by to put bolt locks on all the doors in the barn and the house. He's coming this morning." I start to pace around the room.

"What about the girl upstairs?" asks Hattie. "What are we doing with her? I think we should just tell her to go. To keep her baby and go."

I pivot from my pacing and turn to face Hattie. "I need a baby for the Ackermans, Hattie," I say with a hard edge filled with exasperation. "Where am I going to get a baby by next week to bring to New York?"

"They'll just have to wait," she says flatly. "When you're trying to illegally adopt a baby you might just have to wait." She purses her lips tightly together and rolls her eyes.

Kelly's phone dings, and Hattie and I watch her as she takes the phone slowly out of her sweatshirt pocket. She reads the message and her eyes grow wide. "It's Jed," she looks up at us. We're both standing directly in front of her now. "He wants to meet here tomorrow at noon. He wants the money in cash in a plain duffel bag."

My hands fly up to my hair and I smooth it back.

"Meeting here is impossible. Tell him we want to meet in a public place."

Kelly types in the message and hits send.

We hear a knock on the front door and for a minute we all freeze. I walk out to the front hall and can see the locksmith's truck outside. I breathe a sigh of relief.

Kelly follows me when her phone dings again. She reads the text and then looks up at me. "He says it's non-negotiable. He's comin' here."

47

ANABEL

Detective Harris's gruff voice barks at me from voicemail saying he needs to talk to me. What now? I'm not returning his call because my new lawyer, Selma Stevens, told me not to. We don't want my photograph in the news right now because this is the week that Ms. Alvarez will give her report to her supervisor. The final determination on Goldie's placement will be made shortly thereafter.

I've asked Ms. Alvarez repeatedly if I can visit with the baby, but she has been evasive. She doesn't say I can't, she just never sets it up. The pressure to know what will happen is making me crazy. My mind is a sieve. Facts come in but they don't stick. I used to pride myself on my ability to remember dates, appointments, client preferences, ad campaign analytics, but now it's like the storage part of my brain is on strike. Retrieval impossible.

And Tanya is nipping at my heels. She has sensed my weakness and, like a cat who spies a wounded bird, she is watching me. Waiting for me to make a huge mistake and she'll be there to save the day and finish me off. She's already started going around me and directly to Sol for approval on press releases. While it upsets me that this is happening, I just can't muster the motivation to care enough to fight for my rightful place at the company. Dennis has even gone so far as to suggest that I take a short leave of absence while the adoption is decided.

When he suggested it, my first reaction was to be adamantly opposed. What would stand in Tanya's way to replace me? If I was gone, she would be elevated and how could I ever return as her supervisor? But, as the days go by and I feel myself slipping deeper and deeper into this funk, I'm beginning to think that a few weeks off might just be the thing I need.

Dennis has also started to talk about us not needing two residences. Like last night, when we were having dinner in his backyard the conversation went something like this: "It's nice back here, don't you think?" he asked, pushing himself back from the table, a Yuengling in his hand, and stretching his long legs out.

"It's beautiful," I said, looking around at the brightly colored petunias that we planted in a variety of ceramic indigo blue pots. "We have some deadheading to do."

Dennis looked at me with soulful eyes. "I was thinking…"

I felt my eyebrows go up. "Thinking? That again?"

He smiled. "Do we really need a house and an apartment?"

My mind went immediately to the nursery with its yellow walls and the new rug I'd bought featuring little ducks with orange bills.

"We can recreate the nursery here," Dennis said reading my mind.

"Am I that transparent?" I frowned and sipped my white wine.

He looked at me and gave me a little smile. "I think we should renovate the third floor here. Reimagine the primary suite and turn the second bedroom into a nursery."

"Dennis, I . . . we . . . don't even have a baby. I think we're getting ahead of ourselves. Aren't we?"

"Are we? Goldie's not the only baby in the world."

His words had hit me like a smack in the face. He didn't think I was getting the baby. I had gotten up from the table and started to stack our dishes.

"Anabel, I didn't mean . . ."

"You don't think I'm going to get the baby."

"We don't know." Dennis stood up to face me. "I'm only saying that if, for some reason, we don't get that particular baby. There are other babies. We could, maybe, have one of our own."

"I've had three miscarriages. I might never . . ."

"You don't know that. We don't know that."

At that point I had given into my fears and started to cry. Dennis wrapped his strong arms around me and pulled me close. The cotton of his T-shirt was so soft and smelled like Snuggle. I buried my nose in it and drank him in.

He kissed me and then he said, "With or without a baby, I still want to be with you. To live with you."

I looked up into his big, brown eyes. My chest felt tight. "Can I think about it for a few days? There's just so much going on right now."

"Of course, but you do realize you spend almost every night here."

My mouth felt dry. The last thing I wanted to do was push Dennis away. "I know, but making it official is a big step. Just let me wrap my head around it."

"Okay, let's go to bed. You have a big day with Sol," he said as he reached down to grab the stack of dishes. I took the rest of the serving bowls and glasses from dinner, and we headed inside.

The next morning at work I ask Sol for a leave of absence for one month. He approves my request a little too quickly for my comfort and assures me that Tanya will keep things going in my absence. Great! Just what I wanted to hear. But, the next day, my first day of rest and relaxation, I am back in the news. A jeweler has come forward and the police have combed through the shop videotape and have found footage of a woman with a double stroller buying a sapphire and gold ring. The woman that they show on the news is not old or poor. Sans disguise she is a glamorous woman, maybe forty, with beautiful, shiny black hair and lovely clothes. I watch her buy the very ring that I pointed out in the catalogue. The stroller is captured from the back so there is no image of the girls. This development leads into a recap of the whole story with my photo and the baby's photo sitting on the screen as the voice-over goes into the details.

As the weekend approaches, Dennis suggests that to get away from the madness, we go out of the city for a few days. He books us a suite at the Mohonk Mountain House in New Paltz which is in the Hudson Valley for a few days of hiking, kayaking, and swimming.

I've never been to the famed resort, and I am eager to spend time with nothing to look at but the lake and the trees. The police have launched a national "woman hunt" for the woman and set up a hotline for the public to call if they see her. I spent last night at my apartment to give myself a chance to think about Dennis and our relationship, and I think I'm ready to live with him. It feels right. Pushing off the couch where I've been having my morning coffee, I weave my way around the baby equipment in the living room and go into my bedroom to pack. Opening my closet, I start to take out shirts, slacks, dresses, sweaters, shawls, and shoes and put them all out on my bed. I am the ultimate packer. If packing for vacation was an Olympic sport, I would come home with the gold every time.

Dennis is picking me up in an hour, so I jump in the shower and then quickly pack all my toiletries. This is the first time we are going away together, and I can imagine his face when he sees my large suitcase, small case for toiletries, my laptop bag, and a bag full of snacks and water for the car. I pull on a pair of light blue linen capris and a crisp white linen shirt and I smile at myself in the mirror. *Forget your job. Forget the baby. Forget the woman hunt. Forget Tanya nipping at your heels. This weekend is about Dennis and only Dennis.*

Thinking of the devil, I hear the buzz of the doorman and rush over to the intercom and tell Jose to let him up. When I open the door, I have to catch my breath because Dennis looks so handsome. His hair has gotten longer and curls up around his ears. He's wearing a light blue Hawaiian shirt with pink flowers and navy shorts and he's sporting the happiest grin.

"Good morning." He greets me with a kiss.

"Good morning! I'm all ready to go," I say moving aside so he can come in.

When he sees my pile of suitcases and bags he laughs. "You warned me. You said you couldn't pack light, and you were right."

I frown. It does seem like a lot of stuff for three days. "I'm sorry. I just want to have everything I need."

"Well, if we get stuck at Mohonk for the next month at least you'll be well-dressed."

"I will be!"

He looks at me and his eyebrows go up.

"It's important. I need all this stuff," I whine.

He feigns trying to pick up my suitcase but can't because it's too heavy.

"Oh, come on. You're so strong." I go over and squeeze his forearm.

He makes a muscle, and I feel how hard his bicep is. "Very impressive," I say wiggling my eyebrows suggestively.

He reaches down and gives me a quick kiss. "Okay, let's get going." He grabs both my suitcases, I scoop up my purse, laptop bag, and bag of treats, and we head out the door.

Two hours later, we arrive at the Mohonk Mountain House which is situated on Lake Mohonk. When we get out of Dennis's Audi Q8 SUV the fresh mountain air surrounds us. I take a deep, refreshing breath. The grand old resort is decorated with dark wood and overstuffed furniture, but the best feature is a wide porch with Adirondack chairs.

We settle into our suite with a sitting room that has a fireplace, a large window that looks out on the lake, and a small terrace. The bedroom also has a fireplace and a large four-poster bed. In the sitting room is a long leather couch in front of the fireplace, two coordinating leather chairs, and a small table and chairs with a complimentary bottle of champagne which Dennis puts in the mini fridge for later.

It's still early enough in the afternoon to go rowing on the lake so we put on our bathing suits, shorts, and flip-flops and head down to see if we can get a boat. The lake is small, only about a half-mile long, and it only takes us a short time to travel to the south end where Sky Top Mountain, one of the highest peaks in the Shawangunk Ridge, towers over us. After being in the city for months and looking only at concrete mountains, the switch to the lush green trees, deep blue lake and puffy white clouds clears my mind. Surely, I've imagined the media circus, the baby, and the woman with the sapphire ring.

Dennis is rowing, and I'm lazing in the bow of the boat watching the hawks fly and listening to the steady splash of the oars as they hit the water.

"Oh, sweet Aphrodite, where shall I take thee, my queen?" Dennis wakes me from my reverie.

"Stroke on, mighty warrior. Take me to Sky Top Mountain," I command him.

"As you wish, my queen."

I look up at him and we both laugh. "Isn't this heavenly? The city so far, far away. Thank you for bringing me here," I say.

"It is beautiful, isn't it?" Dennis stops rowing and we take in the majesty of the mountains. The only sound is the dripping of the water from the oars. Dennis puts the oars in the boat and comes to lie next to me. The lake is calm around us. Our bodies are squeezed into the curve of the bow. He kisses me lightly. "Anabel, you know that I am head over heels in love with you."

Tears come to my eyes because I know it's true. I know he's in love with me and I feel the same way.

"I love you, too." He kisses me passionately, and I move my hand down his side in a caress where I feel something hard in his pocket.

He pulls away from me. "Well, I wasn't sure when I was going to do this but since you found it on your own." He pulls a small red velvet box out of his trunks pocket.

"Anabel Leigh, will you marry me?" He whispers in my ear as he lies back down next to me. He hands me the box.

"I will," I say simply, looking into his eyes.

"Look at the ring, but don't drop it overboard," he says with a smile.

I open the box, and my heart skips a beat. A two-carat, square-cut diamond surrounded by small melee diamonds set in platinum.

"Oh my God! Dennis, it is the most beautiful ring I've ever seen!" I grab him and kiss him.

"Try it on."

"Put it on me," I tell him.

He takes the ring out of the box and slips it onto my finger.

"It's perfect," I say holding it up so that it sparkles in the light.

"You're perfect," he says.

The boat has drifted to the side of the lake where two egrets stand, each on one leg, staring at us like witnesses to our union.

48

KELLY

We strategized all afternoon about what to do with Jed, how to get rid of Mackenzie, and how to keep the baby. Personally, I had little opinion because I have my own plan. I am getting out of here. Tonight. Hitting the road in my little roadster and heading out to California. I've had enough, and I feel that five years of indentured servitude with Savannah is more than enough payment for her help when I needed her.

I have a lot of strategizing of my own to do, and I am tired of going around and around about Jed and Mackenzie. How to move my bags of cash and clothes from my bedroom to my car is the problem that I need to solve. The most important thing is that Savannah not find out what I am planning. Mulling it over in my mind, I toy with the idea of asking Hattie to help me, but my running will leave her alone with Savannah and I'm not sure how she will feel about that. She might even want to come with me. Or, worse yet, tell Savannah my plan. Rat me out.

No, this is something I have to do by myself. I have to leave before Jed gets here tomorrow because I don't want to be a part of whatever plan Savannah and Hattie settle on.

Both of them have a fighting streak that I don't have. If things get ugly and violent I want to be far away.

I start to yawn and close my eyes, not because I am tired, but because I want to go up to my room and start to pack.

"Are we keeping you awake?" Savannah snaps.

Trying to look as tired as possible, I frown and say, "I'm sorry, Savannah, it's been a hard morning and now it's midafternoon, and yes, I'm tired. I want to take a shower and a nap. Can we take a break?"

Savannah closes her eyes and hangs her head, before she looks up and says. "Sure. Why not? Our blackmailer will be here tomorrow, but why should that interfere with your beauty rest? Go ahead. You don't seem to have any good ideas anyway."

As soon as she stops speaking, I fly out of the room. My chest bursting with adrenaline. I have to somehow move my things from my room into my car. I have to be ready to go in case Savannah goes down to the barn and I get an opportunity to run. All the bags of cash in my room have to make their way down to the Bimmer. Thank God I have a car to get myself across country and start a new life and I need the cash to get me there. I don't want to touch my bank account just in case Savannah can track where I am. My statements go to my ma's house, but I can see Savannah going over there and demanding them.

I run upstairs and lock my door. Under my bed I have four wheeled duffel bags filled with cash. There's so much money in my room that I have actually stopped counting it. I want to try and take all four bags if possible. Besides the duffels, I don't really own a suitcase since I never went anywhere, but I do have two canvas tote bags that will just have to do for my clothes. My beautiful clothes! I run my hand down the shirts and jackets and pants and skirts. And shoes! When I was little, I never dreamed that I would own a wardrobe like this.

Pack light, I tell myself. *You can always go shopping in San Diego.*

I had decided that would be my destination. As I fill the two canvas bags, my heart is thumping against my rib cage. I almost can't breathe. I go into the bathroom and take a quick shower. When I get out, I pack my phone charger and my laptop. I look out the back window but don't see Savannah.

My eye travels to the pasture where Caroline's little baby is buried, and I know I have to find the strength to get out of here. To get away from Savannah. To try and forget the girls and the schemes and Calvin Banks and Vadoma and Kayleigh and the Golden One and Lee and Jed and on and on.

As I stand there with my hand on the flowered curtains, I suddenly see Savannah purposefully striding over to the barn. This is my chance. I pull two duffel bags out from under the bed, pull up their retractable handles, and put the two canvas bags one on each shoulder. Dizzy with fear, I quietly open my door and see that Hattie's door is closed. Trying not to bang the suitcases on the wall, I head for the stairs. I know they will thump on every stair, but I have no choice. Down I go.

Through the kitchen and out the back door to the Bimmer. Open the trunk and throw all the bags in. My heart is racing so bad that I have to lean on the car for a minute. I try to listen for Savannah or Hattie, but all I can hear is the blood rushing in my ears. I decide to go back for the other two duffel bags.

When I get to the upstairs landing, Hattie is just opening her door. I try to catch my breath.

"What's going on?" she asks, eyeing me suspiciously.

For a minute I want to tell her the truth, but my gut is telling me to just keep going. Telling her I'm leaving could complicate my plan. "Nothing. Just ran up the stairs too fast," I say walking past her to get back to my room. "Have to get more exercise. I'm out of shape." I need to get the two other duffels.

"Kelly. Wait a minute. What do you really think we should do about Jed?" Hattie asks as she follows me toward my room.

All I can think about is scooping up the other two duffels and heading back out to my car. "We both know Savannah is going to do whatever she wants and right now she doesn't want to give Jed the money. I'm just going to wait and see what she wants to do. You know, Hattie, she calls us a team, but we're not. You and me, we work for her." I reach out for the doorknob to my room and start to turn it.

"Be careful, Kelly," she says as she turns and starts to walk back toward the stairs.

I go quickly into my room and straight to the window and look out. Savannah is walking swiftly back to the house, her long blonde hair billowing out behind her, Charlie at her heel. I sink down into the window seat. Well, at least I got most of my stuff in the car. I can bring the other two duffels with me when I leave. Now, I'll wait for the dark to protect me. As I stare out at the pasture and try to calm down, I decide to make one quick stop tonight on my way out of town. Even though Lee kind of set me up by having Jed and Berry at his apartment the other night, I want to say goodbye to him. It might be a bad idea but he'll still always be my first real boyfriend.

49

TOM

According to Meyer, the Feds and the DA are all very excited. They will take the credit for solving the case. A case with national prominence and emotional appeal because of the babies. Everyone will take a side. Is it wrong to take babies who are unwanted by their biological parents and give them to couples who will devote themselves to them? Are the legal adoption procedures too cumbersome? Are the abortion restrictions to blame? I can hear Whoopi and Joy Behar on *The View* arguing pros and cons.

Meyer has changed his tune about me talking to Savannah, probably because I haven't heard from her again. After ignoring her for a week and only answering texts, now they want me to talk to her. The thought of talking to Savannah makes me dizzy. Pools of sweat ooze out of my armpits and stain my cotton shirt when I pick up my phone. It's hard for me to lie to her. What do I say? Do I still say I want to stop all of this?

I have to talk to Meyer before I call her. She's very intuitive and will pick up on a shift in my tone. She can see right through me. I hit Meyer's number on his contact page.

"Meyer."

"Hi. It's me. Tom."

"Tom, you sound terrible. Is everything all right?"

"Yes. No. I mean I got your text about talking to Savannah and, it's just that, she'll know something's up. By the tone of my voice."

"She hasn't contacted you?"

"No, she hasn't called or texted me at all. Maybe she found out about what we're doing."

"No, no, Tom, there's no way she would have found out. There are no leaks when it comes to raids like this. Call her. We've got to know the date. We've got to go to the judge for the wiretap."

"She would call me if she had a date. She'll know." My voice cracks.

"Tom," Meyer sounds stern now. "Tom, you've got to get it together, man. We've got to deliver for the Feds and the DA. Get it done. Do you want to do it from here? From my office?"

"No, I'll do it."

"Good. Call me after." He hangs up.

I sit with my phone in my hand, staring at it. I have to plot out exactly what I am going to say to Savannah. Luckily, I have farmed out all of my appointments to my associates so I have time to think. My hands are shaking by the time I finally press her number.

Straight to voicemail. I shut my eyes and feel relief.

After clearing my throat, I say, "Savannah, when are you coming to New York? Let me know." I end the call.

I throw my phone on the desk as if it were burning my hand and take a deep breath. Thank God she didn't pick up.

50

SAVANNAH

Kelly was acting so strange last night that Hattie and I decided to hatch a plan to deal with Jed without her. The plan is very simple. I'll meet him as he drives up to the house and tell him the money's in the barn. Once he comes into the barn, I'll tell him that he's not getting a cent from us and when he makes a fuss I'll take out my Glock, walk him back to his car and send him home.

I've been shooting since I was a little girl, and I am an excellent shot. Never miss my mark. I have no intention of shooting him, but I will if he won't leave without the money.

Hattie is putting a call into his probation officer and it's our hope that if the officer reaches out to Jed that he might not show up.

I decide to take a long shower to try and calm my nerves. My body feels tight and brittle, like I might shatter if someone poked me on the shoulder. I let the water get good and hot. The steam starts to cloud the mirror when my phone chimes. The caller ID says *Tom*. I let the call go to voicemail. I can't deal with him right now. Not until after Jed comes and hopefully leaves.

The water burns my skin as I get into the shower, and I

block out all thoughts of everything except what will happen in the barn. I'll be waiting for him outside and lead him to the barn. Once inside, I'll give him the bad news. That he's not getting the cash. I'll play it by ear, only using the gun if I need to, but if I need to it's better to shoot him inside the barn, not in the open.

Hattie will be in the first examination room, only to come out if somehow, he overwhelms me and gets the gun. Hattie's telling Kelly and Mackenzie to stay inside. Not to come out no matter what they hear. I don't want to see either of them this morning. Their jitters might make me lose my focus.

After I shower, I put on a short sleeve black T-shirt, black jeans, and black boots. I smooth back my long hair in a pony-tail and pull the Glock out of the bedside table. I check the magazine, buckle my holster around my slim waist, and put the gun in it. The silencer makes it heavy. I throw on my black leather jacket and go downstairs to wait for Jed.

In the kitchen, I call for Charlie and put him in his crate. I don't want any distractions. Hattie comes into the kitchen as I stand by the sink and sip a cup of water. She's also dressed in a black T-shirt and jeans, but with a jean jacket.

I look at the digital clock over the microwave. 11:22. "Ready?"

"Ready."

"You told the girls to stay put?"

Hattie nods. "Told 'em last night not to come down this morning."

We stare deep into each other's eyes. I can see that what-ever happens in the next hour, Hattie will be by my side. She has turned out to be my truest partner. Is that because we are both trained midwives? That we've been present for so many births and many deaths. That we understand life in a different way than other people who only witness birth and death when a family member or a friend is involved. When they have an emotional connection to the birth or death.

"Let's wait outside," I say, moving toward the door. We go around to the front of the house, and I signal for Hattie to go into the barn and take her position.

At the front of the house is a wraparound porch with four old rocking chairs that my pa put there years ago. I climb the steps leading up to the door and sit down in the first chair to wait. I have a good view of the driveway leading up to the house.

Right at the stroke of noon, I see the truck, a gray Ford, turn off from the road and drive slowly up the gravel drive. I see that there are two heads in the front seat, but I can't make out who he's got with him until the truck is right in front of me. Kelly's tear-stained face stares out of the passenger side window when the truck pulls to a stop. I start to sweat, and I feel my lips curling into a tight knot.

Jed gets out of the truck and comes around to the passenger door, opens it, and pulls Kelly roughly out of the truck. Her hands are tied behind her back. She looks up at me and starts to cry.

"Let her go," I say as I come down the porch stairs.

He looks at me and laughs. His dark blue eyes crinkle at the corners. "Howdy, Miss Savannah. Aren't you a fine-looking woman?" His smile is wide, and I can see his thick tongue.

The look of him disgusts me and I try not to retch. "I said, let her go, asshole. After she's in the house we'll talk about why you're here."

"She told me you were tough, but how tough are you really? No, she's staying with me until I see the cash."

I give him a hard look and Kelly mouths *I'm sorry*, but I don't pay her any mind. "C'mon, it's in the barn." I wait for him to take a few steps toward the barn because I don't trust having him behind my back. As he walks, he pushes Kelly in front of him, and I fall in place beside him.

As we cross the gravel driveway, I quickly create a contingency plan and try to imagine how this will go down now that Kelly will be between me and him. I'm a good shot, but I won't be able to pick him off with a shot to the heart. I'll have to go for the head.

When we get to the barn, I come around and open the door, which gives a tired creak, alerting Hattie that we're coming in. I point to the interior of the barn with a nod of my head. He grabs Kelly around the neck and puts her like a shield in front of him, between us, facing me, and walks backward into the barn. He never takes his gaze off me. He's a tall man with wide shoulders, and I note that Kelly only comes up to his chest. Hopefully I'll have a clean shot to his head. As we enter the dusky foyer, the smell of hay and Lysol causes him to wrinkle his nose.

He waits for me to come in, shutting the door behind me.

"Where's the bag?" he growls.

"So Jeb," I start.

"The name's Jed," he says real slow.

I note that this pisses him off, and I decide to use it as a distraction. "Whatever. Here's the thing, Jeb. You're not getting a fucking cent from me." My hand goes to the side of my jacket over the gun.

"I said my name is Jed, you bitch." He tightens his arm on Kelly's neck. "I'll kill her," he says real low, a gruff whisper. He stares at me with narrowed eyes, sweat dripping down his forehead.

Kelly whimpers.

Quick as a snake I pull out the Glock and aim at his face. "I don't think so," I say and pull the trigger hitting him straight on the nose.

He takes a step back as his head explodes. Kelly sinks to the floor as Hattie rushes in with a pitchfork raised like a javelin.

Jed's body gives one last quiver standing up before he goes

limp, his body falling backward, landing with a thud against the wall and sinking to the dusty floor.

I close my eyes and breathe for the first time in several minutes. My lungs burn. Kelly screams and starts to crawl forward. The Glock grows heavy in my hand as I turn to look at Hattie. We exchange a loaded look.

We've crossed the line of no return.

51

ANABEL

Floating. I don't walk anymore. I float, my feet hardly touching the ground. My cheeks ache from smiling so much. I'm going to marry Dennis Wells. I'll be Mrs. Wells. Mrs. Dennis Wells. I hadn't changed my name when I married Sam and he didn't care, but this time I'm thinking about it. This one is forever.

We're throwing a dinner party at Dennis's house for our siblings to announce our engagement and that is what I have been focusing on since we got back from Mohonk. It will be a sophisticated party, just adults, so that our announcement won't be interrupted by fighting siblings or tired toddlers.

We're hiring caterers, waiters, and bar staff. Right now, I have time and money to make our evening one that we will all remember. Money and time. Time and money. They say that money can't buy happiness, and that may be true, but when you are happy already and you have time and money, then you are truly blessed. With time from my leave of absence and Dennis's credit card, I hired one of the best caterers I know, ordered a case of expensive champagne, and started to redecorate Dennis's house. Our house.

Dennis has given me the go-ahead to get rid of any furniture, rugs, or paintings that I don't like. He says he wants the house to feel like it's mine. Somehow, without much conversation, we have agreed that we will live in the townhouse and not my apartment.

To start, I hire an interior decorator to remake the living room. I change the palette of the room from cream, tan, and taupe to indigo and ivory with touches of gold. Gold frames, gold lamps, and gold silk throw pillows pop against the deep, deep blue.

I've ordered a new couch and loveseat, two Queen Anne chairs, a glass coffee table, end tables, and an assortment of gold-framed paintings of the ocean. I've rushed everything so that it will be here for the party. I only have three more weeks off and I want to announce our big news as soon as possible. I'm bursting inside to tell Sylvia, and I just hope I can hold out until Saturday night, especially because we are going shopping this afternoon. Dennis said that he didn't care if I told her as long as she acts surprised on Saturday night. We're meeting in front of Saks on Fifth Avenue, and I have to stop myself from skipping up the stairs of the subway.

Looking glamorous as usual, she is standing in front of the large display windows wearing a long Boho wrap dress and tan suede sandals. She looks like one of the mannequins on display in the window. I go and stand in front of her and without greeting I pretend to sneeze, putting my left hand over my mouth but holding it there until she spies the ring.

Her face lights up. "Oh my God! It's beautiful." She grabs my hand for a closer look. "It's bigger than mine," she says with a fake frown. "I will have to talk to Walter, but I am so happy for you! Congratulations! C'mere!" She pulls me in for a tight hug. "And you, you are actually glowing. Your eyes are actually emitting light! When did this happen? How long have you been hiding this from me? Spill all the details."

"Thank you! I'm so happy. He proposed at Mohonk. I was supposed to wait to tell you, but I couldn't. I didn't want to take the ring off, and I just wanted to tell you, but you have to act surprised on Saturday night."

She links her arm through mine and pulls me toward the entrance to Saks. "I will put on an Academy Award-winning performance. I will channel Meryl Streep. Your secret is safe with me. Bel, I'm so happy for you."

"I'm so excited." But then I turn serious. "I never thought this would happen for me, Syl. I didn't think I'd have another chance."

We've entered the store and stand in the middle of the perfume section. She turns toward me, looks me straight in the eye and places her hands on my arms. "No one deserves this more than you. You are such a good person. This is your time. Everything's going to work out for you and Dennis."

I look up at her and her smile is bright, and I know she wants the best for me. "Thank you. I am so in love with him. I honestly didn't think it was possible to be this happy."

A woman in a white lab coat approaches us. "Eau de Chanel, ladies? Would you like to try Chanel?"

We both laugh and take one of the sticks she hands us after misting them with perfume.

Sylvia takes a whiff of the stick and closes her eyes. "Wow, that smells as beautiful as the shine of your ring. We've got to get you a bottle!"

"Yes, it smells like heaven." I smile.

"Let's buy whatever we want!" says Sylvia.

And we both say, "Because we're worth it!"

"That's the other thing I have to tell you, Syl. Dennis is a millionaire. Wait until you see his house!"

Sylvia grabs my arm and pulls me around to face her. "What? Are you kidding? I should have known from that ring. You're like Cinderella at the ball!" She grins.

After buying a bottle of Coco Mademoiselle by Chanel we make our way up to the fifth floor to try on dresses. Every time

I reach out to take a dress off the rack I take a moment to stare at my ring. I can't believe it's mine.

For an hour and a half, we try on dresses of every description. Sylvia decides on a black off-the-shoulder dress with a flowered skirt, and I find the most beautiful pink lace illusion tea-length dress that makes me feel like waltzing.

We move onto the shoe department, and it feels good to sit while we wait for the salesman to bring us the shoes to try on. I am so relaxed that I am just happy to watch the other women in the department browse while Sylvia checks in with her nanny. I am thinking about how to do my hair on Saturday night when my phone rings.

My pulse quickens when I see Ms. Alvarez's name on my phone. I look toward Sylvia, but she is deep in conversation with her nanny, so I pick up the call.

"Ms. Alvarez, how are you?" I say, sounding very upbeat.

I sense a moment of hesitation. "I'm good. I'm good, Anabel. How are you?"

I can hear the pain in her voice, and I know what she is about to say. I panic. I want to freeze the frame. I want to stop her from saying it. "Don't tell me, Ms. Alvarez."

"I'm so sorry, Anabel. My supervisor went with the other family. I know how—"

"But I'm engaged now, Ms. Alvarez. Dennis and I are getting married. The baby will have two parents with me and Dennis. Please, Ms. Alvarez, let us come in and meet with your supervisor."

Sylvia is off the phone now and by my side with her hand on my shoulder. I look into her eyes and shake my head. All of the happiness I've been feeling all day is gone and in its place is a numbness that starts in my chest and spreads outward until I can hardly hold the phone up to my ear.

52

SAVANNAH

Note to self: Don't shoot anyone else in the head. It's such a mess to clean up. As soon as Jed's head explodes it's like the world has gone into slow-mo. All of my movements seem to take forever to complete. I throw the Glock into a pile of hay, and it seems to linger in the air and then lands with a *thap*. I watch as Hattie drops the pitchfork and runs to Kelly. Thank God that Jed's body was blown backward away from Kelly who has now crawled to the center of the foyer and curled herself into a ball, head to knee, arms still bound behind her back. She is screaming, loud desperate wails.

When I come back into the moment, I want her to shut up, so I can think. "It's over. You're fine. Stop screaming," I tell her. "Hush your crying!"

Hattie falls to the ground, trying to comfort her and unties her hands. "Kelly, you're fine. Get up, baby, get up."

All of my muscles are tight, and I can't take Kelly's whimpering. I'm having a hard time catching my breath. "Take her out of here. Take her up to the house and check on Mackenzie. See what she's up to. When everyone's settled, come back to help me clean up this mess," I snap at Hattie as I look around and try to assess the situation. I turn on my heel and go into the clinic to get cleaning supplies, rubber gloves, and black garbage bags.

When I come back into the foyer, Hattie and Kelly are gone. I breathe in deeply through my nose and exhale loudly through my mouth. I can smell the sickly-sweet scent of Jed's blood. I gag. My leather jacket feels heavy, so I slug it off and throw it over the Glock. Pulling on a pair of rubber gloves, I notice Jed's phone has fallen out of his pocket. I pick it up and look at the display. Two unanswered calls from Lee. I think about Lee coming to look for his brother, and I start to formulate a plan to ward him off. The parts of Jed's head are a grisly sight, so I throw towels over them and onto the pool of blood that is gathering where the old floorboards buckle.

Grabbing a large broom that we keep in the corner of the foyer, I start to sweep up the hay that is spotted with Jed's brain until Hattie comes down. Without a word she starts to help me. We scrub, bag, wash, and sweep until most of the mess is gone.

"Where did you leave Kelly? Is she okay alone?"

Hattie is still on the ground working on Jed, but she looks up at me as if she is torn about telling me something. "She was leaving, you know. I don't know how Jed got her, but she had packed up her money and some clothes and—"

"And you knew about this and didn't tell me?" As we've been cleaning, Jed's blood has gotten all over my face and I feel it start to crust over making my skin feel tight. A shower will be my prize when we're done.

Hattie stands up slowly, at her full height she's got maybe six inches and probably fifty pounds on me. "We all gotta make our own choices. I felt it was her choice to make."

I feel my nostrils flare. "We can all make choices?" I ask incredulously. I start to argue with her and then cut myself off. I shake my head in order to prioritize what needs to be done. "Lee is calling Jed's phone. I'm gonna text him. We don't need him showing up here." I pull Jed's phone out of my back pocket. There's no password protection. This guy was really an idiot. I text: *Got the money. I'm hitting the road for a time.* I read Hattie what I wrote before I send it. "What do you think?"

"Should we ask Kelly?"

"I don't trust her anymore." I press *send.* "Hopefully, Lee thinks his brother has just left town with the money."

"What are we going to do with him?" Hattie kicks Jed's boot.

"Bury him in the pasture with his son," I say.

Hattie's big brown eyes grow round. "Burying a full-grown man is different from burying a baby that fit in a boot box."

"You don't think I know that? We need a tarp and duct tape to wrap him in. I think I have both in the back. I'm going to check." I turn and open the door to the clinic. "And Hattie, we've already made choices that affect how this all turns out. I want to talk to Kelly and convince her to stay."

"And Mackenzie?" she asks.

"Mackenzie has to prove her loyalty by helping to bury Jed."

Hattie swallows and nods her head. "We're gonna need 'em both. Go get the tarp."

When I get back with the tarp, Hattie and I wrap Jed up like a shrouded mummy and duct tape the package closed. We mop and scrub the floorboards, but the old wood has been stained and it's not coming clean.

"We're going to have to replace the boards," I say, "but not today. Let's go up to the house."

We take off our rubber gloves and toss them in a black bag. We'll have to make a run to the dump. I bend over to grab my jacket and my Glock, tucking it back into the holster. As we exit the barn, Jed's truck sits in front of the house, and I gasp. I had forgotten all about it.

"Shit! Check and see if the keys are inside and drive it round back," I tell Hattie.

She goes over to the truck, looks inside, and gives me a

thumbs up. A huge sigh of relief escapes from my throat. If the key wasn't in the truck, it was still in Jed's pocket. I start around the back of the house practicing my conversation with Kelly in my head. She and Mackenzie are both a part of this little operation and they are going to prove it by helping to bury Jed tonight. That's what I'm going to tell them.

We all need to understand that we have crossed over to the dark side and there's no going back.

53

ANABEL

Sylvia calls us an Uber, and we make it back to Dennis's townhouse. Another surprise ruined as Sylvia was supposed to see the townhouse for the first time at the party. We maneuver somberly into the foyer dropping our bags on the floor and hanging our new dresses in the coat closet.

"Wow! Bel, this place is amazing!" says Sylvia, as she takes in the woodwork, the staircase, and the black and white tiles on the floor.

"I know," I say flatly, heading up the stairs to the kitchen. "I wish I had the enthusiasm to show you around. Why don't you wander around while I call Dennis?" I take my phone out of my purse and head out to the backyard.

"Hey! How was shopping?" Dennis picks up sounding chipper.

I burst into tears.

"What happened?" Dennis voice is soft with concern.

"I didn't . . . *we* didn't . . . get her. We didn't get Goldie. They're giving her to the other family," I cry, my voice breaking.

"Oh, honey, I am so sorry. I'll come home. I'll be there in a half-hour."

"Are you sure?"

"Of course, I want to be there with you."

"Okay. Dennis, I love you."

"I love you, too. See you soon."

I feel a little better after hearing his voice and I go back into the house and call for Sylvia.

"I'm up here. Third floor. Maybe it's the fourth. I lost track," she shouts over the handrail.

I meet her on the third floor with the master suite. "Dennis is on his way home."

Sylvia smiles at me and puts her arms around me. "Listen to me, Mrs. Wells, you are going to have your own baby. Once you and Dennis are married, you'll get pregnant and, yes, you'll think about Goldie, but you'll have your family."

My lips twitch, but I can't form a smile.

I watch Sylvia look up and down the hallway. "The decorations are a little sparse, you definitely need some runners in these hallways and a few paintings on the walls, but you have such a great eye. You can do great things with this space. I wish I had all these rooms. Our au pair could have her own floor! She's as messy as the kids," Sylvia sighs.

"The place looks bare because Dennis bought it with his former fiancé and then, before he brought me here, he threw out everything they bought together except the big pieces like beds and couches. We're redoing the master suite and making this room, here, into a nursery." I look into the room and close the door. "Not like we need a nursery."

Sylvia pulls me into a hug. "But you will. You'll be pregnant before you know it."

I look at her and try to believe what she's saying, but in my heart, I don't. "Syl, I've had three miscarriages. No matter what the doctors say, I'm not sure I can ever have a baby."

"But with Dennis, the chemistry might be different."

I look at her skeptically. "And I'm thirty-six."

"That is ancient," she says sarcastically.

"Is it too early for wine?"

"Sweetheart, it's never too early for wine."

Moving back downstairs to the kitchen, I open up a bottle of Rombauer Chardonnay.

Sylvia looks at the bottle and raises her eyebrows. "Nice!"

I pour two glasses and hand her one. "Let's sit in the backyard." I open the sliding doors to a little piece of paradise, a little haven in the middle of Manhattan, hidden from view.

Sylvia steps out onto the patio and grins. "Gorgeous! Just fabulous! You are going to be so happy here, Bel. I know you will. I'm gonna be so happy here! I'll be here all the time. The kids penned in back here. This is going to be great."

I lay down on one of the comfortable lounge chairs with the canary yellow and white striped cushions and motion for her to take the other. "I don't feel like cheering."

Sylvia stretches out in the chair beside me. "We can drink to your engagement. That's huge, Bel."

I tent my eyes with my left hand and look at her. "I know. Yes, let's drink to my engagement."

"You should see the light bouncing off that ring! Congratulations to you and Dennis!" she says, holding out her glass for a toast.

We clink and drink.

My ear is primed to hear Dennis opening the door. An hour passes, and Sylvia has to go to relieve her au pair. I walk her to the door and help her collect her shopping bags.

"Everything's going to be fine. You'll see. I'll see you Saturday." She gives me a long, tight hug.

"Thanks. Say hi to Walter and the kids."

"Tell Dennis I'm sorry I missed him."

"I wonder where he is?"

"He'll be here any minute, I'm sure." Sylvia gives me a quick kiss on the cheek and leaves the townhouse. A cab is just pulling up. Dennis jumps out, sees me and Sylvia coming down the stairs. I hurriedly introduce them, and Sylvia takes the cab saying she will see us on Saturday. After we wave goodbye, Dennis takes me in his arms, and I start to sob.

54

KELLY

As scary as it was for Savannah to blow Jed's head off while he was holding onto me, I'm happy he's dead. He caught me outside of Lee's apartment last night when I went—I admit, foolishly—to say goodbye to him. I never got into the apartment because Jed arrived at the same time and grabbed me, threw me in his truck, and dragged me back to his house. Told me he was going to use me for leverage when he went to get the money from Savannah.

When we got to his house, more like a shack, he tied my hands behind my back. I tried to fight him off, but he's built like a tank, and I didn't have a chance. Then he tied me to a chair and stuck a dirty rag in my mouth. The chair faced his couch, and he sat there drinking beer and staring at me.

At one point, he came and unbuttoned my shirt and fondled my breasts but then he went back to the couch and just drank more beer. I wasn't sure if he was working up his courage to rape me or what, but I will say that the two hours he sat there staring at me were the scariest two hours of my life. Finally, he just passed out, and I tried to wriggle my hands free but I couldn't. I was able to spit the rag out of my mouth, leaving my tongue covered with dirt. After a few hours, I think I passed out because when I opened my eyes again, he was in the bathroom, and it was morning.

I looked around the filthy room, pizza boxes and beer cans everywhere, and tried to think of a way to get free. After a few minutes, he came back into the room, looked at me and smirked.

"You do have nice tits, but I don't like having women after Lee's had 'em. You're lucky. Almost time to head over and get my money," he said running a hand through his greasy hair. "Think she'll give it to me?"

I quickly debated the better answer and then said, "Sure. I think she has to. You have her in a tight spot." My voice quavered as I spoke.

"Good, let's go." He went behind me and untied me from the chair. "I'm gonna trust you not to run." He pulled up his shirt and showed me the gun sticking out of his pants. "Even hungover, I'm a good shot."

"Just take me back to the farm," I said.

"That's where we're going." He put his hand around my upper arm and pulled me up out of the chair. He was squeezing my arm so tight that I winced.

When we got to the door he turned and started buttoning my shirt. "We don't want you flashing my neighbors." There was a spark in his eyes, and I thought he might have changed his mind about sharing me with Lee, but he just grabbed my arm again and dragged me outside to his truck.

We drove to Savannah's farm in silence, went into the barn with her, and then Savannah blew his head off. It all happened so fast, and was so terrifying, that all I know is that I have to get Mackenzie and the baby and get the fuck out of here. I saw Savannah murder Jed in cold blood like she was shooting a dog. I looked into her eyes while she took aim and without wavering shot him in the head. No hesitation or indecision. Never mind that his head was very close to mine. I take a shower, trying not to think of the pieces of Jed's brain that might still be in my hair, and quickly get dressed, putting on my running shoes.

Peering out the back window, I see the barn door is closed. I go back to my closet and look for clothes that might fit Mackenzie. She's bigger than me so I grab my biggest sweatshirt, a pair of sweats and a pair of Keds and go tentatively into the hallway. The light is coming in from the huge window at the end of the hall. Hearing nothing, I jog to the nursery. Mackenzie is sitting in the rocker by the window nursing the baby and I put my finger up to my lips. I cross the room and kneel down in front of her.

"Shhh. Listen to me. You've got to trust me, and we've got to take the baby and get out of here right now. This is our last chance."

"Why? What's going on? I thought I heard a gunshot." Her hand goes protectively to the baby's head.

"Mackenzie, there are things happening that I don't think you want to know. Please, just get dressed and get the baby ready. We're going to have to walk to my car which is in town." She can tell by the sound of my voice that I'm serious.

I drop the Keds on the floor and put the sweats and sweatshirt on the top of the dresser.

"What size are those sneakers?" she asks.

"Eight."

"My size." She smiles and gets up to put the baby in the crib while she dresses.

While she gets ready, I go over to the dresser and throw onesies, sleepers, T-shirts, leggings, and tiny socks into a baby bag. I go over to the crib and pick up the baby and bring him to the changing table. He looks up at me with wide blue eyes and coos. I change him and dress him in a clean terry jumper and matching hat. I put him back in the crib and go into the closet to look for a baby carrier that Mackenzie can attach to her chest.

Pushing the curtain aside, I check to see if there's any movement at the barn. Nothing. I know we don't have much time. My palms are sweating, and I can hear my pulse racing in my ears. I think of Savannah holding that gun and how the bullet that killed Jed whizzed right over my head.

"Let's go." I walk over to Mackenzie and strap the carrier onto her chest. "We have to get out of the yard quickly. Okay?"

I can see the panic in her eyes, but she nods her head. I carefully pick up the baby and place him in the carrier, grab the baby bag, and motion for her to follow me. We silently slip down the stairs, out the back door, and I lead her across the driveway and start down the gravel path toward the road. I pray and pray that the baby doesn't start to cry.

The sun is high in the sky, and the mockingbirds sing in the oak trees. Drenched with sweat, I turn around to check on Mackenzie. She has one hand cradling the baby's head, and she's breathing heavy. I look forward and can see the road up ahead. We can't take a break now. We have to keep going. It's hard to catch my breath and my mouth is full of dust from the gravel. I keep imagining that Savannah is coming up behind us like in one of those dreams when you're being chased, but this is real life.

I see a truck go by on the road up ahead and I decide that we will try and hitch a ride into town. Who's going to pass a woman with an infant and not pick her up? We reach the road and take a right toward town. The road is a two-lane highway with no shoulder, so we have to be careful if a truck comes up behind us. The houses out here are about five acres apart and are mostly hidden by sugar maples and tall white oak trees. You can go for hours without a car going by.

I turn around to wait for Mackenzie to catch up to me.

Her cheeks are red, and her face is covered in sweat. She has slowed down now that we are on the road.

"How ya doing? Want me to take him?"

"No, I'm okay. Kelly, where are we going? I mean, after we get the car?"

I can tell she's having a hard time breathing by the way the words stick in her throat. "San Diego."

"California?"

"I'm getting as far away from here as I can. You can come with me if you want. I have money. Bags of it in my car. Or I can drop you somewhere, but you have to make up your mind by the time we get to town because I am hitting the road immediately." We're walking side by side now because we haven't seen a car go by yet. She doesn't answer me, and I know she's weighing her options.

I hear a vehicle coming up behind us, and I turn quickly to make sure it's not Savannah. It's not, so I breathe a sigh of relief. I haven't hitched a ride in years, but I stick out my thumb and smile when the truck slows down.

"Where ya headed?" asks the man in the truck good-naturedly. I can tell he's a farmer by his leathery skin, gnarled hands and overalls.

"Center of town," I answer with a big grin.

"Climb in."

I open the door, eager to take cover inside the truck. I help Mackenzie in first and then jump in myself. My head falls back against the seat, and I close my eyes for a minute as the truck takes off down the road.

"That's a little one you got there," says the farmer.

Mackenzie smiles proudly. "Yeah, he's just born."

"Well, ain't that something," says the farmer.

"We're bringing him to meet his grandparents," I say to fill the awkward silence.

The farmer smiles. I can't help but keep looking in the sideview mirror to make sure Savannah isn't coming up behind us. A slow smile appears on my face as I see the big red sign for Bacon's Hardware come into view, the first business on the outskirts of town.

"We can just get out at the corner of Main Street," I say. Lee lives two blocks off Main. The farmer pulls over and lets us out. He has no idea that he has probably saved our lives. We thank him, and he drives away. Now that we're out of the truck, I feel vulnerable. Someone we know might see us.

I steer Mackenzie into a small alley behind The Bean. "What's it gonna be, Mackenzie? Are you coming with me or not? I gotta know right now." My voice is husky with fear. I want to kiss Dubois goodbye.

"I'm coming." I see her swallow and blow out a long breath.

I smile at her and realize just how much I wanted her to say that. San Diego is all the way across the country, and it will be good to have company. "Great. Stay right here. Don't leave the alley. Stay out of sight. Turn around and pull your hood up. I'll be back as fast as I can with the car. Don't talk to anyone or go anywhere. Okay?"

She nods, and I start jogging to Lee's apartment. I turn the corner onto his street and survey the road. I can see my car in front of his apartment building just where I parked it when Jed grabbed me.

No one's on the street, so I start moving toward my car, hugging the trees on the side of the road for cover. There's a truck parked behind the BMW so I take cover there to make sure I can get into my car without being discovered. Just as I'm about to make my move, the door to Lee's apartment building opens and Berry steps out. She looks all clean and fresh like she just stepped out of the shower, dressed in a blue sundress with wet hair. When she gets down two steps the door opens again and Lee comes out shirtless, just wearing his jeans. Berry turns and skips back up the stairs and into Lee's arms for a long passionate kiss.

That bastard! I have to bite my tongue to not scream out at them. I hear them say goodbye and I hide behind the truck as Berry comes down the steps and walks across the street to her car and Lee goes back inside. Hunched over, I go to my car and get in. I can't believe how stupid I am worrying about not saying goodbye to that asshole. He's obviously already moved on.

55

SAVANNAH

Hattie and I look like something out of a Halloween fright-night freak show with blood and dirt and God knows what else on our clothes and in our hair as I open the back door. We go into the mudroom to pull off our boots. I hang my black leather jacket on one of the hooks and Hattie starts to wash her hands in the big sink. Earlier I had locked Charlie in his crate, and I can hear him start to howl.

"You go ahead and hit the shower, and I'll talk to the girls," I tell her.

She nods, stepping out of her boots and heads upstairs. My throat is parched so I get a glass of water in the kitchen and drink it down. Walking into the foyer, the house has that eerie, empty feeling when the air feels heavy like it hasn't been stirred up in some time. I assume that Kelly and Mackenzie are still upstairs, so I go to check. I know that I am going to have to threaten them to get them to help me bury Jed.

I hear the water running in Hattie's bathroom as I pass her room and continue down the hall to Kelly's room and slowly turn the doorknob. Empty. I notice her closet is open and clothes are spilled out on the floor. She must be with Mackenzie in the nursery.

Suddenly, it hits me. They're not here. The door to the nursery is open but I don't hear voices or sense any movement. The stillness in the air surrounds me as I stand in the doorway and survey the room. Dresser drawers are open with baby shirts and jumpers tumbling out. Mackenzie's nightgown is in a pile on the floor in front of the rocking chair, a yellow throw blanket flows over its arm and the closet is open with the light on. My blood boils over as I realize they have packed up and left.

"Hattie!" I scream. "Hattie!"

She comes running down the hall. "What's the matter?" She says as she enters the room in her robe. Wet hair in a towel on her head.

"They're gone. Kelly, Mackenzie, and the baby."

"Maybe they're downstairs."

"After everything I did for that little bitch. Kelly and her kid would be suffering the abuse of her drunken father if it wasn't for me. She'd be collecting food stamps and welfare if it wasn't for me. So ungrateful and now we don't have a baby to bring to New York," I say.

"I'm going to get dressed." Hattie says as she takes the towel off her head and starts rubbing her hair dry.

"We were in the barn for hours cleaning up that asshole's brains. Gave her time to leave. We're going to have to take care of the body by ourselves. We'll have to put him in the truck and drive out into the pasture. Probably good that it's been so dry, the land will be firm."

Hattie stands up tall and straightens her broad shoulders. "Just matter'a fact like that? You just think you can make a plan, and I'll fall in place? It's just you and me now, Savannah. This is a full partnership now. We sell any more babies, and you and me are fifty-fifty. Your little band has gone AWOL, and this soldier is now a sergeant. Understand? You killed that guy, not me."

"Under the law, you were an accessory to murder, so calm

down, and I want to remind you that last year you were making a pittance at the clinic."

She narrows her eyes. "Last year I had half the problems I do now. Last year I wasn't cleaning up the brains of some guy that was trying to blackmail us. Last year I was on the good side of the law with a clear conscience. So, listen to me good, Savannah, when I tell you that we are equal partners now. Fifty-fifty. And, right now, I'm bone tired. We'll have to wait till tomorrow night to bury him."

The blood on my face is making me itch. My shoulders and arms ache. I can't lose Hattie now. I know I need her. "Okay, partner. Fifty-fifty going forward."

56

TOM

Special Agent Nigel Thacker always sits in the same position when we meet. He leans into the table with his right elbow resting next to his notepad, with his index finger under his nose like a fake mustache, his left hand on the other side gripping the arm of the chair like he is ready to lunge at me. Periodically he takes his hand down from the perch on his upper lip to jot down a note. Sometimes Special Agent Jack Entenmann is also there, but today, it's just Meyer, Thacker, and me.

The air is thick with Thacker's growing anxiety. He is itching to set up the surveillance of the hotel room, but now Savannah is being coy and not returning my calls. I have a sinking feeling that I don't share with Thacker, that the baby has fallen through. Savannah is always eager to make the arrangements for her trip to NYC and to plan a romantic dinner for us, which I was dreading, but now that she's ignoring me I'm worried. Even though I'm turning her in, I'm still under her spell. I still want her to want me. She turns me inside out and upside down in ways that are both excruciating and seductive.

My reverie abruptly ends when I realize that Meyer and Thacker are staring at me, seemingly waiting for me to answer a question that Thacker has posed. Thacker's sharp blue eyes are looking at me with a mixture of pity, frustration, and disgust.

"I'm sorry. What did you say?"

"I asked if you had any insight into why the date hasn't been set." A hint of annoyance in his voice.

"Right, well, for one thing I was the one who started ignoring her calls." I look at Meyer when I say this and he shrugs. "So maybe, now she's just pissed and she's making me wait. That's a definite possibility. Listen, I've never played games with Savannah. Our relationship has always been on her terms. From high school to today."

Thacker takes his finger from under his nose and picks up his pen, but instead of writing a note he starts to click the point of it in and out, staring at me the whole time.

"We'll just have to wait," I say.

We discuss the Erickson Hotel, the small, high-end boutique hotel that Savannah likes to stay at in the West Village on Greenwich Street, and Thacker says that he and Special Agent Entenmann will scope out the hotel, but they can't go to a judge for the wiretap until we have a date. Since I've never actually been to the hotel, I don't have a lot of details about how Savannah conducts the exchange of the baby for the money. Because we have started demanding wire transfers, the couples no longer arrive with a suitcase of cash. I've shared my overseas account numbers with the Feds, but I don't have the information on Savannah's accounts.

I can tell that Thacker's mind is spinning, searching for the question he hasn't asked me. He slowly runs his finger back and forth under his nose, staring at me with slightly bloodshot eyes. I wonder if he had too many drinks last night.

Meyer takes Thacker's silence as his cue and stands up, looking at me to do the same. "We'll be in touch," says Meyer, collecting his papers and his phone. "You'll be our first call. Should be any day now."

Meyer and I are now on our feet, but Thacker has gone back to clicking his pen. Finally, he looks up at me. "Would she run?"

My knees start to wobble, and I fall back into my chair. Savannah disappearing has been on my mind. Visions of her thick mane of hair cascading down her back as she boards a private jet dance around in my brain. Of course she might run.

Meyer looks shaken as he stands and waits for me to answer. He can see from my face that this is exactly what I am afraid of, but I say, "No, I don't think she would."

57

KELLY

I drive around the block and pull over in front of the alley where I left Mackenzie. She's leaning against the wall, looking scared. I tap the horn, she looks over, and comes running to the car, the baby bouncing against her chest, and jumps in. The seat belt just about fits as she stretches it across her body and the baby and secures it in the latch.

"Are you hungry?" I ask.

"Starving."

"As soon as we get on the highway, we'll pull over at the first service station. Right now, I just want to get out of town and this car is unmistakable. If Savannah or Hattie is looking for us, we're easy to spot." I pull away from the curb and start heading to the turnpike. We're not far from the Tennessee border, and I want to put Georgia in my rearview mirror. I don't plan on ever coming back.

The baby is getting fussy now. He's been so good, and Mackenzie is trying to comfort him. "Kelly?" she says looking over at me.

"Yeah."

"Can we buy a car seat at some point?"

I smile for the first time that day. A problem I can solve.

"Yes, and a pacifier, but probably not until tomorrow. I want to put as much road between us and Dubois as I can first. Do you know how to drive?"

Mackenzie's face lights up. "Got my license on me!"

"Awesome!" I say, and for a minute I feel like just two girls on a road trip heading to sunny California to start a new life. I turn on the radio and my favorite singer, Harry Styles, comes on singing "Watermelon Sugar." I sing along and pretend that I'm just one of the pretty young girls in the song's video, wearing a bikini and playing on the beach.

58

ANABEL

My attorney, Selma Stevens, told Dennis and me that there wasn't much we could do to appeal Child Services' decision to place the baby with the other family. They've been waiting longer, they are a married couple with a three-year-old, so Goldie will have an instant family, and none of them have been in the news repeatedly.

Although I'm heartbroken, we've decided to go ahead and have our engagement party on Saturday. Dennis is very excited about it, and I'm trying to put my disappointment about the baby to the side and focus on our happiness. Sylvia and Walter are looking forward to getting out of the house for the evening, and I am excited to meet Dennis's brothers and their wives. This will be my new extended family.

Dennis has convinced me to invite the top executives from C&W, and we've both added a few good friends, so the guest list is now up to twenty. On Saturday morning, the caterers and the bartenders show up early to transform the townhouse into an event space for the evening. I've planned dozens of events for work so I throw on my event planner hat and help them reimagine the space for the cocktail party, which will be outside and the dinner party that will be in the dining and living rooms.

We've hired the Liquid Lab to do the drinks and the wine for the event. They are famous for their artisanal/Prohibition-era cocktails like the "Mary Pickford," named after the silent film star, which is a mixture of white rum, pineapple juice, maraschino liqueur, and grenadine syrup, and is a beautiful shade of pink served in a martini glass; and the "French 75" named after a World War I artillery piece made from gin, champagne, lemon juice, and sugar. It's always good to have something original at your event. Guests who don't know each other can start a conversation by talking about their drinks. An old party planner secret.

Dennis has run out to get a haircut, but I suspect he just wants to get away from all the hustle and bustle for an hour or so. I'm glad he's gone because all week I've been trying to be bubbly and happy when I'm with him when I really feel empty and sad. It's just bad timing. Hearing about not getting the baby and the engagement party coming in the same week. One minute I can feel the sparkle in my eye when I think of marrying Dennis and the next minute tears are welling up over Goldie.

On top of all these emotions, I have to be the perfect hostess for the night. Dennis told me that he will make the announcement and that I don't have to say anything. For that I am grateful. Even though I am in the communications business, I am not a skillful public speaker. Give me a PowerPoint and a set of talking points and I can sell a campaign or land a client, but I'm not good about speaking from the heart. If I had to say a few words tonight I would probably start crying.

The caterers have suggested making two long tables of ten that form a right angle—one in the living room and one in the dining room—and Dennis and I will be seated in the middle where the tables meet. We've covered the tables with indigo tablecloths with bright white napkins and gold accents to match the décor. The low centerpieces are white and blue with delphiniums, hydrangeas, and roses. By four o'clock, the tables are set.

Red umbrellas have been added to the backyard with a large bar off to one side in front of the apple trees that have cooperated by bursting into bloom yesterday. Small groups of chairs with small rounds have been set up throughout the yard. By the time Dennis comes home, smelling like talcum powder and aftershave, the house has been transformed. He finds me in the kitchen putting roses into bud vases for the bathrooms.

"Didn't we hire people to do that?" he asks taking my hands and pulling me gently into his arms.

"They always forget the bathrooms." I give him a tender kiss. "Aren't you looking handsome with your hair all neat?" I say with a smile.

"I have to say you look like one of the caterers right now, with leaves in your hair and whatever this is on your cheek?" he laughs.

"What?" I say feeling my cheek where there is definitely dried food of some description.

"Well, I know you clean up nice, so I'm not worrying."

"You're not worried?" I tease him.

"No, you will be the most beautiful woman in the room. As you are in every room." I feel tears start to surface as I stare into his soft brown eyes. "You are, you know. Always the most beautiful woman to me."

"You are so sweet."

"So, what's left to do?"

"Music? We haven't talked about music."

"I can handle the music." He gives me a little peck and goes into the living room. Two seconds later, he peeks his head back into the kitchen. "And, Anabel?"

"Yeah?"

"Sol and Tanya are coming together."

My eyes go wide. "Like together, together? What happened to Sol's wife?"

Dennis shrugs and holds out his hands. "Didn't work out."

"Wow! Thanks for burying the lead on that!"

I head upstairs to take a shower and wash the mysterious goo off my face. As I climb slowly up the stairs, I look over into the living room and smile. The place looks gorgeous! My phone dings, but it's just a text from Sylvia saying how excited she is for me.

The guests are invited for six o'clock and it is going on five when I get out of the shower. After I blow dry my hair, I pull it back into a low messy bun and put on my signature pearl earrings and necklace. Before I start on my makeup, I take a minute to admire my engagement ring. It is twice the size of the one that Sam gave me when he proposed, but we were so young. Dennis and I are mature and, frankly, Dennis has more money than Sam did. Somehow the size of the diamond makes me feel safe.

I put my makeup on with a little more mascara and eyeliner than I usually wear and choose a light pink lipstick to go with my pink dress. Nude heels finish the outfit, and I smile when I think about Dennis seeing me come slowly down the stairs. I hope he's in the living room or the foyer. When I get to the top of the stairs he is just about to come up, but he stops and stares at me and just says, "Wow." It's almost a whisper.

"You look stunning! That dress is perfect!"

"Well, thank you, Mr. Wells," I say in a southern accent. "You are surely making me blush."

He laughs and comes up the stairs. "I'd kiss you, but I don't want to ruin anything."

I laugh. "Your turn. Go and get beautiful," I say as I carefully walk down the stairs in my heels.

"I'll try."

Everything looks perfect. As I glance out to the backyard, I note that the bartenders are in their stations already to take orders and that bottles of red and white wine have been opened to breathe. All of the liquors and liqueurs stand ready and pitchers of mixers and cut fruit have been set out to make the fancy Prohibition-era drinks. I decide I will have a "Mary Pickford" after I greet everyone.

Tables of hors d'oeuvres have been set up across the back-yard and waiters dressed in black and white are waiting in the kitchen to start serving the passed appetizers. I see trays of pigs in a blanket, scallops wrapped in bacon, and tiny quiches being popped in the double oven. I feel like I'm working an event instead of the guest of honor, and I spend a few minutes rearranging napkins and silverware to be more accessible.

At five fifty-five, Dennis bounds into the kitchen looking so handsome in a dark gray suit and he waves the photographer over to take a few photos of us before the guests arrive. Antici-pation is in the air. I have to remind myself to breathe.

The doorbell rings and the guests start to arrive. Sylvia and Walter arrive at the same time as Dennis's brother Ben and his wife Briana. Introductions all around and we lead them into the backyard, letting a waiter answer the door for the rest of the folks. Dennis's other brother Gerard and his wife, Lacey, arrive and it's so nice for our siblings to have a minute to say hello before the C&W crowd arrives. I haven't seen any of my colleagues since I started my leave of absence.

The cocktail part of the evening is in full swing when Sol and Tanya arrive. I see her entering the backyard in a short sheath of brilliant bright red with spaghetti straps and four-inch heels. She's hanging onto Sol's arm and grinning. My stomach drops, and I feel my cheeks grow hot. I know that next to her, I look dowdy in my tea-length dress.

Summoning all of my good manners, I take Dennis's arm, and we go to greet them. He is our boss, and she's probably mine by now.

"Sol, Tanya, it's so nice to see you both," I say, reaching

up to air-kiss Sol. As I turn to Tanya it seems like all eyes are on us.

In a voice that's way too loud, she greets me by saying, "Oh, Anabel, I'm so sorry you didn't get the baby! Do you think you might want to give an exclusive to *The Times*? Maybe we can also get the couple who got her. What do you think?"

I feel Dennis's hand grip my arm as my knees grow weak. The need to get out of the backyard is overpowering. Everyone turns and stares at me, and I feel the fight-or-flight response kick in. Flight wins, and I start to walk blindly to the sliding doors. I can hear Dennis calling my name, but his voice is distant, like I am under water. A protective hand on my arm tells me that Sylvia is helping me into the kitchen as the tears start to flow, washing down my cheeks like a tidal wave.

59

SAVANNAH

It took me three shots of tequila to calm my nerves and fall asleep last night. Trying to convince myself that killing Jed was some sort of self-defense got easier with each shot. It erased the image of his head exploding like gray fireworks and the pools of thick red blood that spilled out onto the porous floorboards. After I agreed to an equal partnership with Hattie, and we had the first shot together, she told me she had had enough of living this day, and she was going to sleep.

Now, the sun is just coming up when I open my eyes. The light in my bedroom is thick and gray. For a quick moment, I'm not sure if yesterday really happened or if it had all been a nightmare. As I roll over, I see Charlie sniffing the pile of soiled black clothes that I wore yesterday. They're lying in a heap on the floor next to the bed in stark contrast to the rich cream and white rug. I shoo him away. On top of the night-stand sits my Glock serving as a powerful reminder that the events of the previous day truly happened.

Where's my phone? Suddenly wide awake, I have to call Tom and tell him about how Mackenzie left with her baby. That we have to let the Ackermans know that it will be a few more weeks until we can deliver a baby. I hope that Tom will call the Ackermans. Disposing of Jed's body and getting rid of his truck are at the top of my to-do list. Everything else is a distant second.

Slipping on my silk robe, I go downstairs in search of my phone. I must have taken it out of my pocket when I was drinking my shots at the island in the kitchen. There on the island, next to the bottle of Tito's and my shot glass are two phones—mine and Jed's. I quickly look at Jed's and see a text from Lee, *Fuck you, man*, in response to my text from yesterday saying Jed was going out of town. Good. It sounds like Lee bought the lie, buying me some time.

I pick up my phone, enter my password, and seeing no messages, I go to contacts and call Tom.

He picks up on the first ring. Maybe when this is all behind us, and we buy a house on an island in the Caribbean, Tom and I can make each other happy. Really get to know each other and devote our time to just living. Maybe have a small practice for the locals. The handsome fertility doctor and the beautiful midwife. We would be the stuff of legends.

"Good morning, Savannah. You've been hard to reach," says Tom sounding oddly perky.

"I could say the same about you. Listen, a minor complication. Our last girl has decided to keep her baby. Too bad, really, the boy was big and beautiful and healthy. Perfect for the Ackermans, but I always offer the girls one last chance to keep their babies, and this girl took me up on it." I can hear the exaggerated rasp in my voice from the tequila last night.

"But the Ackermans have been waiting." His voice has gone from perky to angry. "Savannah, we can't keep them waiting any longer."

"Well, they'll have to wait. I can't just make a baby materialize, Tom." My voice is so deep and husky, and I realize I haven't even had my coffee. Tucking the phone between my cheek and my shoulder, I put the coffee on. "I'll let you know later today when the next girl is due. Would you have time to call the Ackermans? I'm really tied up."

He explodes on me. "Let's decide who calls them when we have a better idea of when they'll get a baby."

"Tom, honey, as Hattie says, when you're buying a black-market baby, you might have to wait a little bit."

"Get me a date, Savannah." The line goes dead.

Someone is losing his cool, I think as I hang up. He better be careful because I don't react well to being screamed at. Even by Tom.

I pour myself a cup of coffee and go into the office to look at the whiteboard. There's always a two-week range for the births, especially because almost all of the girls are first-time mothers. With Kelly gone, Hattie and I will have to be more hands-on with our clients. Not something I'm looking forward to. Shit! I have a check-up at two o'clock today with Lucille, the next girl due. My chest tightens when I realize we have to move Jed out of the barn by then and make sure that the place is clean. We'll stash him in the truck until nightfall.

A wave of panic grips my intestines, and I go upstairs to wake Hattie and get dressed. As I stand up, all my muscles in my arms, thighs, and back complain. It's going to take more than a couple of Advil to get me through today. Jed was a big man and dead people are heavy.

Upstairs, I knock on Hattie's door. "It's your wake-up call. Time to move the dead!" I call out.

She opens the door wearing a black T-shirt, her underwear, and a scowl, her short, black hair sticking straight up from her head. "Where are we putting him until tonight?"

"In his truck. We have a girl coming in at two for a check-up. Are you feeling strong? He's going to be heavy."

She makes a face and starts to massage her right bicep. "I'm feeling pretty sore from yesterday to tell you the truth."

"Me, too. I'm going to get dressed." I head to my room,

take a quick shower, and search for more black clothes. I find a black T-shirt with the Rolling Stones tongue in red and jeans.

When I get downstairs, Hattie is standing by the sink in the kitchen drinking her coffee. "I'll drive his truck up to the barn door."

"Great," I say as we head out the back door.

"Savannah?" Hattie's voice is almost plaintive.

She's my last soldier. I have to make her feel the urgency I am feeling. "Yeah," I turn back to look at her.

"Do you ever really think about what we're doing? I don't mean killin' Jed. That's wrong in everybody's book, but what we're doing with these babies? Are we doing something good or are we doing something really fucked up?" Her big brown eyes are soft and serious.

At this moment, I will say just about anything to keep her with me, but I also believe in what I'm about to say. "The way I look at it, we provide a service for the girls who don't want their babies, and for the couples who want a baby with no red tape, no adoption records, no court procedures, no questions asked. You're right, I wish I hadn't had to kill Jed, but I couldn't let him blackmail us. It would have gone on forever. I just couldn't. I did it for us." My shoulders are pushed back and I'm right up in her face. I refuse to let her look away from me. "I did it for us, Hattie, you've got to believe that. I did it for both of us."

The corners of her lips are still turned down, but her eyes have softened a little. "Uh-huh," she says.

"C'mon. We have to get him in the truck and clean the place again before Lucille gets here." We leave the house. I head toward the barn and Hattie heads toward Jed's truck.

The weather is warm, and a gentle breeze blows the branches of the weeping willows near the barn. It looks like any beautiful day, but I know better. A dead body is wrapped in plastic bags in my barn. Rigor mortis has made Jed's muscles stiff and cold. He is going to be hard to move. On the far side of the barn there is an old green wheelbarrow, and I go to dig it out of the leaves that have been blown up around it for a few seasons now. It's left over from when my pa was alive.

Hattie finds me pushing away the leaves and debris from around the rusty wheelbarrow, grabs a shovel leaning against the wall of the barn, and starts digging out one side. I wipe the sweat off my brow as I rest for a minute and watch her work. Her large biceps are on display as she works on the hard dirt that has collected at the base of the wheelbarrow. We're going to need her strength to haul Jed into the truck and to dig his grave.

When we finally drag the wheelbarrow away from the side of the barn, we realize that the wheel at the front is flat but we're able to push it around to the barn door. Hattie has pulled the truck around and backed it up to the barn door.

"I figure we load him in the wheelbarrow, move it to the truck, and then it will be easier to load him in the back of the truck. He'll be stiff but heavy," I say.

"With that flat tire, maybe we should just drag him over to the truck," says Hattie.

"It'll be hard to lift him up to the truck. Let's try it my way first."

"Let's try it my way first," Hattie mimics me.

We go over to the corpse. "You take him from the shoulders, I'll get the legs. You're stronger. On three. One, two, three."

We hoist the body onto the wheelbarrow where it rocks precariously. The body is rock solid and stiff as a board. We can't even get to the handles of the wheelbarrow to try and push it over to the truck. "Okay, you win. We'll have to drag him over."

"Praise God. You know he's watching us, don't you?" Hattie's round eyes are as round as they have ever been.

I narrow my steel blue eyes, "We don't have time for this nonsense. Let's get him out of here."

Opening the two large doors to the barn, I use cinder blocks to prop them open.

When the doors are open, I look back at Hattie who is saying some silent prayer. I close my eyes to control my temper. "Come on, and help me drag him over."

She comes over slowly, shaking her head and bends down to get under Jed's shoulders. I grab his feet, but just as we're about to move him we hear tires crunching on gravel as a car comes up the drive.

60

ANABEL

The rest of the engagement party is a blur in my mind. Locked in the bathroom, I cried and Sylvia comforted me until I gained control of myself and then I joined Dennis as we moved into the dinner portion of the party. Sol and Tanya had begged off while I was in the bathroom with an excuse of another event, and so I was spared having to be polite to Tanya or even having to look at her perfect little face.

Like a Stepford Wife, I tried to laugh appropriately, smile for the camera, and nibble on a bite or two of salmon Dijonaise while Dennis answered all the awkward questions that I couldn't muster the courage to answer. We sent our tipsy guests home at the earliest possible hour.

In the following days, I could tell that Dennis thought I had overreacted even though he never came out and flatly stated it. In fact, we never talked about it. Neither one of us mentioned it. Our comments about the party were flat. *I really liked your brother. Sylvia had more than one Mary Pickford! The wait staff was very efficient.*

Visions of Tanya in her short red dress that barely covered her toned ass, hanging onto Sol's arm, flit through my brain at odd moments. Pouring coffee. Bending down to wash my feet in the shower. Chopping tomatoes for a salad, which is what I am doing when my phone rings. It's Ms. Alvarez. My pulse starts to race. What did she want?

"Hello?" I answer tentatively.

"Anabel, I'm going to go out on a limb here. I hope I can trust you," says Ms. Alvarez. "Can I trust you?"

"Of course. Yes, of course," I assure her.

"The adoption's been put on hold. I don't know why, but it's not moving forward, and I thought you would want to know. I'm not saying that you will get Goldie, I'm not saying that at all, but someone high up has stopped the process."

I make my way over to the kitchen table and slowly lower myself into a chair. My hands are shaking. "Do you think the parents have come forward? After all this time?" My voice is barely louder than a whisper.

"No explanation has been given. I've told you all I know."

"Thank you, Ms. Alvarez. Please let me know of any other developments."

She hangs up, and I look out the back window. The sun is shining and there's a gentle breeze dancing through the leaves of the maple tree. Two sparrows are bathing in the birdbath.

Should I dare to hope?

61

___

SAVANNAH

"Where the fuck have *you* been?" I say with a mixture of relief and anger as I come out of the barn and watch Vadoma get out of her car and approach us. She has a new look, blonde hair that doesn't really work with her olive skin. Kayleigh is tripping along behind her.

I'm relieved to see it's Vadoma. It could have been the cops or, maybe even worse, Lee. The sight of the car had given me and Hattie a surge of adrenaline. With our new strength, we grabbed old Jed and threw his ass into the truck. He landed with a thud and Hattie flipped up the back of the truck with a look of sheer terror on her face.

But it was only Vadoma, walking toward us like she had just gone out for milk. My hand went to my heart in relief. I could be mad later.

"Lord almighty! Vadoma!" cried Hattie.

"Look what the dog dragged in. Couldn't make it out there in the real world?" I ask her contemptuously.

I notice a flicker of anger in her eyes, but she tamps it down. "What the hell are you two doing?" she asks, jutting her chin at the truck. "Whose truck is that?"

I give her a look that says you have no right to be asking any questions, and she looks away, into the pasture. "We can tell you all the details later. Right now, we have to finish cleaning the barn. We have a girl coming in for a check-up at two. Hattie, take the girl up to the house. Vadoma can help me with the rest."

Kayleigh runs to Hattie and Hattie gives her a bear hug. "You want pancakes?"

"Yes, please." Hattie takes the little girl's hand and leads her to the house.

"C'mon," I say, noting Vadoma's white suede boots. "You have another pair of shoes handy?"

"I'll get my sneakers." She turns around and heads back to her car.

I go and jump in Jed's truck and bring it around to the back of the barn. When I return, Vadoma has changed into sneakers and a T-shirt.

I beckon her over to the barn. When we enter the foyer, I notice that it has a funky smell even though the doors have been wide open for a half-hour now.

Vadoma's nose is scrunched up as she asks, "What are we cleaning up?"

"Blood." I notice that she doesn't flinch.

"I won't ask whose, but where's Kelly?"

I wait just long enough to answer to let her think we might've killed Kelly. I look back at her, and I can tell that's what she's thinking. "She left. Why did you come back?"

"I went out to Las Vegas. Nothing there. Came back." Vadoma clears her throat self-consciously like she's waiting for me to say welcome back. Fat chance!

I walk over to the stain on the floor and stare down at it. "We've tried bleach, but the wood is old and porous."

"You have a girl coming at two?"

"Yeah."

"We'll have to put a rug over it. We can take one from one of the birthing rooms. C'mon." She heads into the clinic and I follow.

"I guess I'm glad you're back."

"Do we have a body to bury?"

"Yes, we do."

62

TOM

When I come out of my consultation, I see that Thacker and Meyer have called and that Savannah has not called. I'd love to get back to Thacker with the date of the exchange with the Ackermans. I'd also like to let the Ackermans know when to expect the baby. Sid Ackerman has a lot of connections, and he just might go and get a baby somewhere else and then the whole drop will be aborted.

I head to my office to hide from my colleagues. As soon as the arrest is made, my license to practice medicine in New York will be revoked, and I will be relieved of my duties. Thoughts of going out west, far away from Park Avenue and Dubois, Georgia, fill my sleepless nights. The trial might not be for a few months, and I will have to stay in New York until the end, but if everything goes according to plan, after the verdict is read and Savannah goes off to prison, I will be free.

Of course, I'll never be free. She's in my head and under my skin. I used to watch her sleep. Even in slumber she looked dangerous. How could such a complex brain, capable of so many crimes, exist in this sleek body under that beautiful face? She would sleep, her long seductive blonde hair splayed out on the pillow, the fringe of her perfect eyelashes forming beautiful semicircles above her lovely pug nose and then her deep red lips with the defined bow. One slim, toned leg with a capital T tattoo would be displayed wound around my brown silk sheets. The rise and fall of her hip and waist forming small hills in the soft material. Even her feet and hands were lovely to look at, long and thin with tapered fingers and regular toes with no bumps or corns. She was amazing to behold.

We had gotten the matching tattoos the night before I left for college. Hers was a T; mine an S. One inch high on the outside of our right ankles. Hid them with socks so our parents wouldn't find out, which seemed kind of silly to hide a couple of tattoos since we had already had a baby together. But after Savannah's pa took the baby, it was like it never happened.

I shake my head. Moore, man, get a grip. Don't shuffle down memory lane. Focus on her honed manipulative skills, her lies, and her greed. You're just her pawn. Even the tattoos were her idea, she had insisted. I was nothing but a necessary cog in all of her schemes. But does she love me? She says that she does. She talks about buying a house in the islands together and living there. She says we would make each other happy. I shut the door to my office and lean against the wood. Take a deep breath.

My phone pings. I look at the screen. God, it's her. I answer.

"Hey, baby," she says in her deep, raspy voice. My knees go weak, and I stumble over to my desk.

"Savannah. How have you been?" I can see her long leg wrapped in my sheet. The T a dark green in her lovely golden skin.

"I'm good, baby, listen. The next girl is about a week away. She could go at any time. She had a check-up today and everything looks good. I just wanted to let you know that I'll be up in New York soon. And that I can't wait to see you. It's been a long time, Tom."

"Well, this is good news. I'll give the Ackermans an update."

"Have you missed me, Tom?" her rasp makes it sound like she's purring.

I close my eyes. In spite of myself, I'm turned on. Her voice always drove me crazy. "I always miss you. I have to go. I have a consult."

"Bye, baby."

"Bye."

Maybe she's right. We could run away together, buy a house, sip drinks out of coconut shells, make love in the shade. There's still time. I could go to the airport now. Would she come? I'm not sure. She would want to deliver this last baby and make the drop and now that can't happen without getting caught.

63

SAVANNAH

Grave digging is hard back-breaking work. I'll take assisting in a thirty-hour labor over digging a grave any day of the week. It took the three of us four hours to dig a hole long enough, wide enough and deep enough to keep the coyotes from digging Jed up and after a hot day Jed was ripe. We couldn't waste a minute getting him into the ground.

Finally, we stagger back to the house, our legs and backs cramping with pain. "I'm going to check in on Kayleigh. Pour me a shot. I'll be right back down," says Vadoma as we enter the mudroom and she quickly pulls off her boots and gloves and heads into the kitchen.

I sit down to pull off my muddy boots. "I forgot about that kid. We have to be careful what we say around her. She's as smart as a tack," I say to Hattie.

Hattie is washing her hands in the big sink. "Where's her mother now?" she asks out of the blue.

I finish adjusting my sock before I answer. "Dead. Overdose. You know—" I stop suddenly.

"What?" She turns to look at me.

I hesitate, trying to decide if I want to tell Hattie who

Kayleigh's mother is and that she is the sister of the Golden One.

"Nothing. Where's the Fireball? I need a shot right now." I push in at the sink and start to wash my hands.

Hattie looks at me quizzically but lets it go. She walks into the kitchen, and I follow her when I'm done washing my hands. "Should we wait for Vadoma?" she asks lining up three shot glasses and getting out three Coors to chase the Fireball. We keep the liquor in the cabinet in the island, and she bends down to get the bottle.

"Nah. She can catch up when she comes down," I say.

Hattie pours two shots and we clink glasses and drink them down quick. The whiskey burns my throat, making me exhale slowly to ease the sting, and I take a long pull on my beer. Hattie does the same.

"Ah!" she says closing one eye as she absorbs the burn which tastes like cinnamon on fire.

"Fill 'em up," Vadoma says as she walks into the kitchen in clean sweats pointing to the shot glasses.

Hattie pours three shots without lifting the bottle like a skilled bartender. "Hey, where did you learn that?" Vadoma asks.

"Where'd you get the blonde hair?" Hattie answers.

"Bottoms up," I say and we all down the shots. My phone dings, and I take it out of my back pocket to see who it could possibly be at two-thirty in the morning.

Lucille, that's who.

"Fuck." I curse.

"What?" asks Hattie.

"It's Lucille. She's in labor."

"Tonight? Now?" Vadoma groans. "I've been driving all day, grave digging all night, I really need some sleep."

I take charge. "We'll take shifts. We're all tired. I'll take the first shift, but I need a shower. She's on her way over now.

Both of you, go to bed. Hattie, you'll take five to seven. Vadoma, seven to nine—"

Vadoma interrupts me. "I'll take five to seven because Kayleigh will be up by seven-thirty, and I'll have to be with her. Hattie can take seven to nine. You'll be rested by then and can go back out at nine. Okay?"

While I'm pissed that she is proposing an alternate plan and contradicting me, I'd forgotten about Kayleigh, so I agree and start to head upstairs for a five-minute shower and change into my scrubs. Grave digger to labor nurse. I stop at the door to the foyer and say, "And no more shots tonight. We have to get this right."

Hattie stops mid-pour and frowns. "Got it." Vadoma nods her head and flips her new hair.

<hr>

Lucille arrives shortly after three, and we get through the night. After daybreak, we settle into a rhythm of two-hour shifts with two of us in the barn with Lucille and the other one watching Kayleigh. As we head into the next evening, we are all dragging, closing our eyes between contractions. When Kayleigh goes to bed, we each take a turn sleeping. Lucille is making slow but steady progress, as I take my turn sleeping. Hattie is the one who delivers the six-pound twelve-ounce girl twenty-four hours into the process.

"Look who we have here," I say when I walk into the nursery the next morning and see Lucille feeding the baby with a bottle. We never used to let the girls come up to the nursery, but I guess now anything goes.

Lucille's skin is pale, and her greasy hair clings to her forehead. "Don't worry. She's all yours. I just need a day to recover, and then I'll be on my way," she says as she stands up and hands the baby to me. "Where can I shower?"

Feeling the moment is fragile and that I want to separate her from her baby so no bond can form, I take her down the hall to Kelly's old room and show her the bathroom. "I'll bring some fresh clothes," I say.

She nods and gives me a weak smile.

I take the baby back to the nursery, put her down for a nap, and then go back to Kelly's room and find a sundress that I think will fit Lucille. Kelly has left her clothes in such a mess, and I take a minute to kick them to the back of the closet, then I grab the biggest pair of underwear from Kelly's dresser drawer. Nudging open the bathroom door, I throw the clothes in.

"Thanks!" I hear Lucille shout over the running water.

I go downstairs to make her some breakfast, and by the time I get back to Kelly's room, Lucille is sound asleep in her bed. As I leave the tray on the nightstand, I glance down at the girl and am struck by how young she looks. Her raven black hair still wet, her perfect olive skin still flushed from the hot water, and her round face that has the look of a child, not a grown woman. Hopefully, with this behind her, she can go on to make a life for herself unburdened by a child that she could not support. She's not equipped to be a mother now.

I go back to the nursery to check on the baby and make sure she is healthy. I'm sorry to wake her up because I don't want to babysit her, but I want to check her heart, color, and reflexes, count her fingers and toes.

When I strip her down to her diaper my first thought is that she looks nothing like her mama. Blonde with fair skin, I wonder briefly what the father must look like. This child, that I hold in my arms now, could be my child. I think back to the day I gave birth to my child all those years ago and wonder if he or she looked like me? Did my pa see himself in the baby or was he afraid to look? My child would be eighteen years old now.

When I worked at the clinic, I realized from talking to the women that no matter if a woman gave birth to her baby, miscarried, aborted, or gave her baby up for adoption, they all tracked their babies. The women who had abortions or miscarriages would say things like: *I would have a five-year-old now. I would have a ten-year-old.* Like a relationship that could have happened but didn't. The women who gave away their babies said things like: *I have a four-year-old daughter out there somewhere. I have a nine-year-old son in Phoenix.* If they knew where the baby went.

I never shared my thoughts about my baby with anyone. I had no idea where the person the baby had become lived or what they did with their time. I had no idea if it was a boy or girl. But I did know that he or she would be eighteen years old if he or she was somewhere. That was the only fact I knew about my baby.

Lucille's baby starts to fidget in my arms, and I put her up on my shoulder to console her. All the babies that have been born in my barn float through my mind. All of them placed in good homes and given opportunities that they would never have had in rural Georgia born to a teenager with no way to support them.

The Golden One pops into my mind. She and Kayleigh both look like their mama. Tom has no idea who their mama is. I know it would hurt him to know. When I looked at the Golden One, I didn't wonder about my baby like I do now. The Golden One was meant to wear pearls when she grows up. She always had an air about her and a knowing look. She knew she was destined to get out of Dubois before I did.

Savannah, I reprimand myself, don't get crazy about these babies now. There's too much work to do in the next few days before going up to New York. I put Lucille's baby in a new pink sleeper with feet and put her back in the crib. The baby monitor is blinking so I know it's on, and I head downstairs to figure out how to dispose of Jed's truck and when to tell Tom I'm coming to New York.

For the first time, I'm seriously starting to think about shutting all of this down.

64

TOM

When life gets really hard, I like to go for a run in Central Park, so I leave work early and take the subway home to change into my running clothes. As I ride the subway up Lexington Avenue, I look at all the other people on the train reading their phones or listening to music with their earbuds and I want so desperately to be one of them. A person with everyday problems, money woes, relationship troubles, bad boss problems, daddy issues. I'd give anything to have a problem that didn't involve a possible prison sentence.

As I look around the train, I see a pretty, young woman with long dark hair and our eyes meet. She gives me a small smile. I know that if I smile back, we could strike up a conversation and this could be our meet cute, but I'm not free to exchange pleasantries with a nice woman. How could I possibly explain what my life is to anyone?

I get off the subway, walk to my apartment building and ride the elevator up. When I leave New York I want a small house in the woods—no elevators, no subways, a view of a mountain or a lake—I want a simple life, with simple problems. In my bedroom, my unmade bed with the brown silk sheets mocks me, and I quickly change into my running gear and head back into the living room.

As I pass the large mirror, a gift from Savannah, by the front door, I get a glimpse of myself and stop dead in my tracks. I used to be a very handsome man, but the man that looks back at me has deep dark circles under his bloodshot eyes. His skin is blotchy, and a few days' worth of stubble grows on his cheeks. His curly hair is greasy. I look away, shoulders hunched, and head out into the hallway.

My phone vibrates, but I can't bear to talk to anyone. I'm pretty sure I will sound desperate. The call ends and the phone dings, letting me know I have a text message from Savannah.

Baby born. I'll be up on the ninth. Set up the exchange with the Ackermans for the tenth.

My shoulders relax a little and I head to the park. Entering at Sixty-Fifth Street, I run three miles north and turn around to run two miles back and then walk the rest of the way to cool down. I crank up Freddie Mercury and find my rhythm. By the time I stop running, I'm feeling pretty good. I stop at a Sabrett truck to buy a water.

There are two women in front of me, and I can smell their shampoo and perfume. I can't wait to get home and take a shower. I feel so sweaty and dirty standing behind them, and I hope they don't turn around and look at me. As I stare at the shorter one's shiny hair, she turns around, smiling at something the other one has said. Now, they're both looking at me. They look similar but the taller one is more striking. However, it is the shorter one with her hair pulled back, wearing pearl earrings and a pearl necklace, that I lock eyes with. I can't pull my gaze away from her face. Terror seizes me, my knees start to shake. I see that she is getting nervous and I remember the deep circles under my eyes and the three days of stubble on my face as the other woman puts a protective arm around her shoulders and scowls at me.

I have to stop myself from saying her name. Anabel Leigh.

Without buying the water that I have been waiting for, I sprint away. I need to get away from her. It's like she can see right through me. I weave through the walkers and joggers on the path. There's no way she can connect me to the baby in the park, but it feels dangerous to wait and see if she can. I tear across Fifth Avenue and narrowly escape getting hit by a cab. My neighborhood isn't safe anymore. She could be my neighbor.

Ducking into my lobby, I still don't feel safe. She could live in this building! I have to get inside my apartment as quickly as I can. It's now rush hour and there's a line for the elevator. I can't chance it. My breath comes in ragged bursts, my chest is heaving, people are starting to look my way as I head for the stairwell.

I have to stop twice to recover my breath, but I finally make it to my floor and sprint down the hall to my door. Once inside, with the door locked behind me, I try to get ahold of myself. Somehow, I stumble to the kitchen and pour myself a glass of water from the fridge.

My phone starts to vibrate. It's Meyer. I take the call. He's the only one I can tell who I just saw. He'll understand.

"Meyer." I'm still breathing heavy.

"Tom, you okay?"

"Yes. I went for a run. Stopped for water. Anabel Leigh. Anabel Leigh . . ."

"What about Anabel Leigh?" Meyer's voice sounds concerned.

"She was in line at the cart. I stopped to buy a water."

"You didn't say anything to her. Did you?" His voice is raised now.

"No, I ran away, but I probably seemed like a madman."

"Tom, she has no idea who you are. You're overreacting. Calm down."

"The baby . . ." I'm clenching my jaw so hard it starts to ache.

"What about the baby?"

"It's been born. Savannah's coming to New York on the ninth. The exchange will be on the tenth."

"Okay, this is good news, Tom. Tom, you gotta get a grip, man. We're close."

"Yeah, we're close." My voice catches in my throat, and I sound like I'm croaking.

"I'm going to set up a call with Thacker for tomorrow morning. Okay?"

"Okay."

"Tom, get yourself a drink. Calm down. It's fine. There's no way she can connect the dots."

"Right." I disconnect the phone and pick up the Great Jones Bourbon and drink a few swallows from the bottle.

I've got to get a grip.

65

ANABEL

Sylvia and I hurry home from the park after the man runs away. I have gotten used to people staring at me, recognizing me from the TV or the newspaper, even asking me questions about the baby or if I am the woman in the park, but the man today was different. He acted like he knew me and it scared the shit out of him. Like I knew something about him.

"Syl, do you think he was the baby's father? Hiding in New York. Possibly following me for some reason?" I say as I fumble with the key to the townhouse.

"I'll admit there was something very creepy about that guy. He definitely acted weird, but let's not jump to any conclusions. He was wearing expensive running shoes, so I don't think he was homeless, but he looked like he needed a good, long shower," says Sylvia, dumping her purse on the new settee that I bought for the foyer.

As Sylvia starts up the steps, she stops to admire a large photograph of the mouth of the Manhattan Bridge that Dennis and I bought from a gallery in Soho. It takes up the whole wall and as you walk up the stairs you feel as if you are walking onto the actual bridge.

"This is amazing! I love it!" she exclaims.

"I've been admiring that photograph in the window of the gallery on West Broadway for years and Dennis said it would be my engagement gift. As if this ring weren't enough." I smile. "I didn't know you were supposed to give your fiancé a gift. Did you give Walter one?"

"No, I think Dennis just wanted you to have this photograph because you wanted it."

"You're probably right." We walk down the hallway into the kitchen. "I can't get the look in that man's eyes out of my head. It was like he was seeing a ghost looking at me. Like he was afraid of me. He ran away from me."

Sylvia plops down in one of the chairs at the table. "I know. It was definitely strange. I don't think you should go to the park alone. Okay, Bel? Promise me."

I put the coffee on, turn to her and try to smile. "Okay, but he could be anywhere. Anyway, before that happened, I asked you to come over and take a walk with me so that I could ask you a question."

"And what's that?"

"We set a date, and I want you to be my matron of honor."

"Of course! You know you didn't even have to ask. When? Where?"

"Well, that's the thing. It's only six weeks away and we don't have a venue. I'm looking at a few places this week. We're not having a big affair. We just want a small, intimate wedding. One without Sol and Tanya."

Sylvia rolls her eyes. "Definitely without Sol and Tanya!" Sylvia comes over and gives me a hug. "I'm so happy for you!"

I try to enjoy the moment, but that man's wild eyes are playing on a loop in my brain. Who is he? How is he involved with the baby? I know that he is.

Two hours later, Sylvia has left when I hear Dennis come in the front door. I've been going back and forth in my mind about whether or not to tell him about the man in the park. I know it will freak him out, but if I don't tell him and the man attacks me or kidnaps me tomorrow Dennis will be furious. I don't know why I think the man might hurt me. He seemed very eager to get away from me at all costs. Practically knocking people down to run away from me.

I'm curled up on the couch in the living room looking at patches of paint that I have painted on the wall to help me decide what color to choose as Dennis walks up the stairs. When he gets to the landing he turns to me with a huge smile that turns into a frown when he sees my face. "What's wrong?" he asks.

I sit up straight, putting my feet down on the floor, and pat the couch next to me. "Hi. Come sit with me."

He comes over and sits down next to me. "What's going on?"

I put my hair behind my ear, collecting my thoughts. "So, first of all, I'm fine. Nothing really happened, but something weird happened."

"Nothing happened, but something happened. Got it."

"Syl and I were walking in the park, and we stopped to get a bottle of water at the Sabrett cart when a man got in line behind us. He had been jogging, and he looked kind of dirty and disheveled, when I turned around to look at him, he totally freaked out. He looked at me like I was the scariest person he had ever seen. Like I was dangerous. He looked like he was either going to pass out or throw up from looking at me. Then, he ran away as fast as possible. Practically knocking people over as he went."

Dennis pulls on his mustache. "Was he like a homeless guy or a guy who lives around here?"

"Well, I don't know. He was a tall, white guy with curly dark hair and blue eyes. Maybe thirty-five. He needed a shower and a shave, but Syl says he had expensive sneakers on. Honestly, I have no idea what he was wearing. I'm used to people recognizing me from all the coverage, but this was different. He was afraid of me. What do you think that means?"

Dennis gets up and heads to the kitchen. "I'm getting a drink. Want some wine?"

"Sure."

Dennis comes back with a glass of white wine in one hand and a Coors beer in the other. While he's sitting down, he says, "Why would a man run away from you?"

"He knew who I was," I say slowly. "He knew and in a different way than all the people who know me from TV or the papers. He knew who I was, and it scared him. Like I could hurt him. I can't really explain it."

"What did Syl think?"

"She thought it was strange. Do you think this could be the baby's father and seeing me triggered something? Or he's connected to the woman in the park? It makes me feel like this is bigger than Goldie."

"What do you mean?"

"I don't really know what I mean. But if he is connected to the woman in the park maybe something bigger is going on here."

Dennis leans back into the couch and takes a long pull on his beer. I snuggle against him, and we sit there, thinking.

"Well, one thing is for sure," he says. "You cannot go to the park anymore alone. I couldn't stand it if anything happened to you." He hugs me to his chest.

66

TOM

Meyer tries to get a call with Special Agent Thacker, but Thacker insists on a meeting down at 26 Federal Plaza to plan for Savannah's arrival, surveillance and arrest at the Erickson Hotel. The Erickson Hotel prides itself on its rich clientele and upscale services and I know that they are not going to be happy about being the backdrop of a high-profile arrest. Doesn't really matter, though. I'm never going to book another room there again. Ever.

As soon as the reporters match Savannah and her black-market babies to the Golden One and the woman in the park, there will be an explosion of coverage. I have to prepare myself for being on the front page.

After I ran into Anabel Leigh, I realized that I was not living under a cloak of invisibility. Before I laid eyes on her, I felt anonymous in a city of more than ten million people. How could anyone know what I was doing? That I was tangentially related to the baby in the park.

When I realized my photograph would be on the cover of every paper, on every newscast, I'd headed to my barber, Frederick, to get a much-needed haircut and a good shave. Resolving to visit Frederick at least once a week until this ordeal was over, I also decided to buy a few off-the-rack suits to wear in court. I didn't want to be seen as an out-of-touch rich guy in the eyes of the jury or the public. Although, obviously, I am.

Meyer wanted to meet in the Korean deli across from 26 Federal Plaza again, but I refused, and we finally decided on pre-meeting over the phone and then going straight to the Feds. Meyer said it would be a full-court press—US Attorney Morris Ravens, Special Agent Nigel Thacker, Special Agent Jack Entenmann, and two agents who we haven't met before, Agent Olivia Fox and Agent Pat Biglin.

After we go through the metal detectors and ride up on the elevators, we are shepherded into a conference room that looks exactly like the last conference room but is on a different floor. I've dressed down a little this time in my least expensive suit, the price of which would buy all of the other clothes in the room, but for me it's dressed down. Funny, I never saw myself as such a clotheshorse until I spent time with these government workers. It's a different world down here in the Civic Center.

US Attorney Ravens sits at the head of the table with his staff lined up on the side of the table in front of the window. Meyer and I are on the other side. Like opposing armies but instead of brandishing guns we take out our notepads, pens, phones and recording devices. All skirmishes will be done by the tongue and not the sword.

I catch myself looking a bit too long at the female agents. Both young women look out of place in their dull gray suits, one blond, one dark, exuding investigator-glamour, but as one of them adjusts her suit jacket, I catch the outline of her revolver nestled under her arm.

"Good afternoon, gentlemen," US Attorney Ravens begins in his deep baritone. He introduces the two new agents.

"Let's check a few things off the list here. First, we will pick up the bags of money from your apartment tomorrow and take them into evidence. We have put a hold on your account in the Cayman Islands. Have you brought your passport as requested?"

Reluctantly, I take my passport out of my inner suit jacket and slide it across to Thacker. For some reason, I don't feel that it is appropriate to slide it down the table to Ravens. Thacker seems surprised, but happy to catch it.

"So, do we have a date yet? A solid date?" asks Ravens.

Meyer looks at me to answer. "Yes, sir, we do. Savannah said yesterday that she was coming in nine days. She told me to make the reservation at the Erickson Hotel, and I did. She'll have the penthouse suite." I look at Ravens for his approval. Last month, I would have looked at him like he was a sleazy politician. Today, I look at him as a powerful man who holds the key to my prison cell. He can either keep the door open or lock me in.

"It turns out that Child Services was just about to place the baby, the Golden One as she is called, but we have put a hold on that adoption hoping that Ms. Maas will be able to shed some light on who the biological parents of the girl are. You don't know, is that correct?" Ravens' eyes drill into my soul.

I start to pull on the hair at the base of my neck. "I don't know who the baby's parents are. Sometimes Savannah refers to the mothers by their names, but I never really pay attention." Meyer taps my thigh under the table. "That is . . . I don't keep a record, and she never tells me their last names."

Entenmann takes this moment to shine. "Is that because you never asked or because she won't tell you?" He looks over at Ravens to make sure his proactive questioning is duly noted.

Meyer breaks in before I can answer. "Let's move on. What else do you need from Dr. Moore?"

"We need her flight information, if possible, and the name of who she is traveling with. Do we know who the parents of this baby are?" Thacker asks, not to be outshone by Entenmann.

"She said the girl, the mother, was called Lucille and let's be frank here, there is never a father in the picture. She said she was coming with Hattie, one of her employees, and I don't know her flight information. I've never asked for that before and I don't think I should now. She's very smart. I don't want to tip her off," I state like this is non-negotiable.

Ravens purses his lips, makes his huge hands into a tent in front of his chest, and nods his regal head. Thacker, Entenmann, and the two female agents nod as well.

"Tell me about the couple expecting the baby. Who are they?" asks Ravens.

"Sid and Robin Ackerman. He's a partner at the Blackstone Group. Very well-connected. You've heard his name, I'm sure. They've been trying to get pregnant for two years with no luck. Robin is the second Mrs. Ackerman. He has three grown sons with the first Mrs. Ackerman. Is there any way you can *not* arrest Sid Ackerman? He will be mortified. He's a personal friend of the governor," I plead.

Ravens's eyes squint like a cat in the sun. "We'll look into Sid Ackerman. We're not really after the adoptive families. We want Maas. Want to shut her operation down." He taps the top of the table for emphasis. "It sounds like she's running a baby mill down there. Selling babies on the black market is illegal, especially when the provider is demanding large sums of money. Not to mention the makeshift clinic. What would happen if one of these girls needed a hospital? Needed a Cesarean? Bled to death?"

"They're all so young and healthy. It's never happened," I offer. Thinking of the stillborn baby, I feel a flame start in my cheeks.

Meyer knows it's time to bail. "Okay, so cash picked up tomorrow. You have Dr. Moore's passport. You'll start working with the hotel. We'll see if he can get any other details."

"We need a photograph. A photograph of Savannah Maas," says Thacker.

I look at Meyer, who gives me a quick nod. Pulling out my phone, I open my photos. Which photo do I want to see on the front of *The Times*? Savannah frolicking in the red bikini? White bikini? The black backless gown she wore in St. John? I decide on a photo I took in my apartment, view of the Hudson in the background. She's wearing a black turtleneck and looks like a beautiful businesswoman. I show the shot to Meyer, and he tips his head to the side, non-committal.

I send the file to Thacker. Eyebrows up, cheeks flushed, he passes the phone up the table on its way to Ravens. I can tell that Savannah's unquestionable beauty is surprising to them. I feel my pulse speed up when Entenmann looks up from Savannah's photo with desire in his eyes. They may have been picturing an unsophisticated-looking bumpkin with all the talk of a clinic tucked away in a barn. Her effect on the agents breaks down by gender: Her beauty and generous sex appeal softens the men and steels the women. Like a wave at a football game their eyebrows rise and fall as they pass the phone down the line until it gets to Ravens. He takes her in and a broad, knowing smile slowly forms on his face. He knows good newspaper art when he sees it.

67

SAVANNAH

The next morning, true to her word, Lucille gets up, comes down to the kitchen, and says that she's leaving. I notice that she's wearing another one of Kelly's sundresses and a pair of her cowboy boots, but I don't mention it. Kelly's gone anyhow and her clothes are just more trash for us to get rid of.

Hattie, Vadoma, Kayleigh, and I are sitting around the kitchen island sipping coffee and nibbling on muffins when she walks in.

"The baby's asleep. I just fed her," Lucille pauses and looks around sheepishly. "Can I have my money?"

"How are you feeling? Did you take those pills I gave you so your milk don't come in?" asks Hattie.

"Yeah. Thanks."

"Want a muffin?" asks Vadoma.

"Yes, please." She reaches out and takes two cranberry muffins. Hattie gets up, opens a napkin, and takes the muffins from Lucille and wraps them up. Lucille gives her a little smile.

I take a last sip of my coffee and stand up. "I'll be right back," and go to the office to get the envelope of cash for

Lucille. I grab it off my desk and quickly return to the kitchen. I just want to get this girl on her way.

Kayleigh has been staring hard at Lucille since she came into the room. As I come back from the office, I hear her say, "Did you just have a baby?"

Lucille just looks at Kayleigh, bottom lip quivering, eyes welling up.

"We took my sister and left her in a park with a lady."

"That's enough," I say harshly. Nothing can describe the sensation that rips through me at those words. Like an icy bucket over the head, so cold it freezes my nerves, numbs my reflexes. The air in the room becomes charged and the small hairs on the back of my neck stand up.

"Kayleigh," says Vadoma, reaching out and putting a protective hand around her shoulders.

"Take her upstairs," I snap.

"What?" asks Lucille. She turns to me. "What did she just say?"

Vadoma picks Kayleigh up and swiftly leaves the room.

I turn back to Lucille. "Her sister was adopted up north and we met the mother in a park before we went back to her apartment. The girl's too young to understand these things, but your baby is going to be adopted by a nice couple from Connecticut. I'm bringing her up there myself and meeting them in a hotel. She's going to have a good life, Lucille, and so are you now that this is behind you. C'mon, let me walk you out to your car." I put my hand on her shoulder and gently nudge her toward the back door. She's still clutching onto her muffins as we walk through the mudroom and out the door.

I lead her out to her car and wait for her to get inside. She opens the window after she starts the engine. "Susan," she says using my clinic name, "please be good to my baby. I do want her to have a good life." She looks up at me with her dark brown eyes, and I see her fighting back the tears.

"Lucille, you got nothing to worry about. That little girl is going to a good home with good people. You hear me? She's going to have everything she needs." I give her one of my most sincere smiles.

All she can manage is a slight nod of the head as she puts the car in reverse and swings around to head out the driveway. I watch her old RAV4 drive away slowly, and I exhale fully for the first time in ten minutes and stalk back into the house to confront Vadoma.

Hattie takes one look at me and knows that fire is burning in my chest by the way I am taking deep raspy breaths, and my fists are clenched. "One second more and that little scrap would have blurted out the whole story! And how does she know the baby was her sister? Vadoma!" I yell. "C'mon down here." Now I'm in the foyer screaming up the stairs and the baby starts to wail. Hattie rushes past me to get her.

Vadoma appears at the top of the stairs and gives me a fighter's stare. Lip curled, eyes narrowed. She starts slowly down. One step at a time.

"Vadoma! Why the fuck are you back here? Do you know how much trouble that girl can get us into?"

"That wasn't your tune the other night when you needed an extra grave digger. I'm sure you were able to smooth it over. You always do." She has about two steps to go but I can feel that she's relishing the height advantage.

"Come down here and let's go somewhere more private," I say.

Reluctantly, she gives up the two-step advantage and follows me into the living room, a large space that is rarely used. I close the door behind us. The room is done in forest green with crimson accents. Plush oriental carpets and gold lamps.

I go over to stand in front of the two wingback chairs, but I don't sit down. She stands in the middle of the room, glowering at me and I can tell by the look on her face that she will do anything to protect the girl.

I cross my arms. "Why did you show up now?"

"It's hard on the road with a four-year-old. She needs stability. Needs to sleep in the same bed every night. Needs family, such as we are. It was lonely." Vadoma's face softens. "I had nowhere else to go."

We stare each other down for a minute, but I understand what she's saying, "Well, you can stay here until Hattie and I get back from the drop with Lucille's baby, but then . . . I'm gonna . . . I'm thinking of . . . and you've got to keep that girl under wraps. She cannot be telling people about dropping the baby in the park."

"We knew she would remember that. I couldn't have done it without her. She played a vital role. Remember?"

"Yes, but she can't talk about it. Don't you get that?"

"I'll talk to her."

"And one more thing. How does she know the baby was her sister?"

Vadoma starts to look at the painting I have on the wall above the fireplace. It's a beautiful oil painting of a rowboat tied to a dock. Studying it, buying time.

"Vadoma! Answer me! As if I don't know, but I want to hear you admit it."

"I told her. Okay? She wanted to know about her real mama and since her real mama is dead, I wanted her to know that there's still someone out there that is her flesh and blood. Her kin."

"Jesus, Vadoma. She's never gonna see her sister again. There's no way she's ever gonna find that girl when they're grown."

Vadoma suddenly looks exhausted. The lines around her eyes are deep, and her skin looks sallow. I catch my own reflection in a mirror that I have on the far wall and see the dark circles under my lifeless eyes. I feel my shoulders drop as I realize the heavy toll that this life is taking on all of us.

68

ANABEL

"Word on the street is that someone very high up—like FBI high—put the adoption on hold," says Selma Stevens sitting in her dark red leather swivel chair wearing a fitted tan linen suit and turquoise silk shirt. It bothers me a little that the turquoise and the dark red clash, but I try to focus on what she's saying and what it means.

Dennis insisted on meeting with the adoption attorney with me to try and figure out if Goldie's adoption being put on hold is good or bad for us. We sit holding hands in the posh offices of Stevens, Kemp, Reinhardt & Mandell located on Madison Avenue in the seventies at eight o'clock in the morning because Dennis is on his way to Los Angeles for a week and he has a noon flight out of LaGuardia. I told him I would meet with Stevens on my own, but he said that he wanted to be there for me. I have to admit that sometimes when Stevens starts talking and using all her legal jargon that I just zone out and my eyes glaze over.

"So, do you think this means that the FBI has a lead on who her parents are?" I ask, this being the only explanation that I can come up with for the FBI to be involved.

"It's really hard for me to say, but something happened.

I've done some digging with my contacts down at 26 Federal Plaza but lips are zipped. Everything is very hush-hush, but it's clear that there has been a development of some kind. Maybe they found the woman who gave you the baby." As she talks, she swivels in her chair. You can see her mind working through scenarios.

I involuntarily utter "oh," that woman would surely know who the parents are. My heart has broken so many times over whether or not I want the parents to be found. Babies should be with their mothers, but I can't shake the feeling that Goldie and I will be together somehow.

"Even if the parents are found, they have a lot of explaining to do. Right? Like where have they been? Unless they've been gagged and bound and locked up in some crazy person's basement, why haven't they come forward? The whole thing is very mysterious," says Stevens.

"It is mysterious," says Dennis. "We also have other news. We're getting married. That should be good for us. Right? In the adoption process, I mean, if we get that far."

Stevens smiles. "Mazel Tov! That's great news. When?"

I feel myself blushing. What a cliché I've become at thirty-six. "Thanks! Five weeks and counting! So much to do." Dennis smiles at me and squeezes my hand.

"Technically, it's not supposed to matter in the adoption process, but in reality, it does. Child Services social workers usually like to see the babies in homes with two parents. I wanted to bring something else up at our meeting today. Do you want to apply to other adoption agencies? I know this baby is special to you, but maybe you should cast a larger net."

Dennis leans forward before I can react and says, "Before we apply to any other agencies we're trying to have a biological child."

"I see," says Stevens.

"We are trying," I remind him. Since the morning of the engagement party, I've stopped taking my pill.

"Yes, we are trying," echoes Dennis.

"Okay, I will do some more digging to see if I can find out why the adoption was put on hold. I'm sorry, I'm due in court in half an hour. I'll be in touch." She stands up and shakes our hands.

When we get down to the curb, Dennis has a car waiting to take him to the airport.

He turns to me and puts his hands on my shoulders. He looks me in the eye. "Anabel, I do want to adopt Goldie. I want us to be her parents. But I guess I want one of ours, too."

"And do you think you can love Goldie as much as you will love our biological baby? Have you thought about it? Because, I think I already love her, Dennis. I want her!"

He closes his eyes, he looks like he might cry. "Anabel, I love you. I will love Goldie, it's just that I don't already have feelings for her like you do. It's hard to love someone you've never even met. She's a photograph in the newspaper to me. I haven't held her or seen her smile, but I will. I know myself and I know I can, and will, love her." He bends his head down to try and make eye contact with me.

His gaze is steadfast and true, as I look deeply into his eyes to see if I believe he is telling the truth. What I see in his eyes is love, compassion, and caring, and I know in my heart that when he holds her, he will love her.

"I love you, Dennis, and I know you will be a good husband and father."

"I will. I promise. I know how important it is to you, Anabel. I love you."

He looks at his phone and I can tell by the stressed look on his face that he's running late. "It's okay. I'm okay. Go. You don't want to miss your flight."

He reaches out to the car handle but turns back. "Do you want the car to drop you back at the house?"

"No, I want some fresh air. Call me tonight when you get there." I give him the best smile I can muster.

He kisses my forehead and gets in the car. I wave as the car drives away and then turn slowly and start walking back to the townhouse.

69

———

TOM

Meyer is keeping me apprised of any conversations he has with Thacker. He tells me that now that the Feds have probable cause with my confession, and the date of the upcoming exchange between Savannah and the Ackermans, that they will go to a judge and request permission for a wiretap on Savannah's suite at the Erickson Hotel. Once the Feds have established that the wiretap will provide evidence of a felony violation under federal law the judge will approve the wiretap and they will have access to all of the conversations in the suite, including the one where the exchange will be made.

The hotel will be swarming with agents on the morning of the exchange, but none of the guests will know it. FBI agents are trained to blend into the nuance of a place. They will dress as bellhops, maids, and guests to make sure no one staying at the hotel will be alerted to their presence. As soon as the Ackermans leave the suite with the baby, Savannah and Hattie will be arrested. The Ackermans' fate still hangs in New York City politics.

Because Sid Ackerman controls the governor's campaign war chest, Meyer is pretty sure he will be questioned at a later date, probably at his home. When Meyer describes how

Savannah will be handcuffed, marched downstairs to a waiting patrol car, and taken to the Metropolitan Correctional Center on Park Row in lower Manhattan for questioning, I have to ask him to stop. Thoughts of her slender wrists, her soft skin, her steel blue eyes flashing makes me sick. When I think of the moment when she realizes that I have betrayed her, I literally have to get off the phone and go and vomit in my toilet.

Now, we are one week out. Thacker wants me to confirm that Savannah is traveling with Hattie. I'm not going to do that because I've never cared before and my asking now will only make Savannah suspicious. I know that I won't be able to stand up to her if she guesses what's going on. I know that my voice will give me away.

They have also set up agents in the rundown motel one town over from Dubois to get ready to raid the farm the minute they get the go-ahead from Thacker in New York. The minute that Savannah is in their possession, agents will go in and toss the farm.

Of course, the arrest of Savannah and her merry midwives, as Thacker has started to call them, will be national news on the day of the arrest and for the coming days. I'm sure that the FBI communications team got out their whiteboard and had a meeting to brainstorm names to suggest to the press. Meyer thinks that Ravens will leak the connection to the Golden One and hold a press conference to announce that a major break in the case of the mysterious baby handed off in the park was imminent.

I can't help but feel sorry for Anabel Leigh. She's as innocent in this whole mess as the babies we've been selling. Her terrified eyes haunt me at night. How the woman who was with her in the park felt the need to protect her from me. From me! I'm a baby doctor, for Christ's sake! I don't think of myself as a dangerous man, but maybe I am. I really don't know who I am anymore.

The state will revoke my medical license on the day of the arrest and I will be barred from practicing medicine in New York ever again. That's okay. I actually can't wait to see the Holland Tunnel in my rearview mirror. The bigger question is where am I going when this is all over? How will I ever be able to get far enough away so that visions of Savannah in prison aren't all that I see?

Pulling on what's left of the curls around my ears after my trip to Frederick's, I try to settle my nerves enough to do what I have to do next. Keeping my voice professional when I call Sid Ackerman is going to be one of the hardest parts of this ordeal. Sid eats other men for breakfast and then goes to Nobu for lunch. He makes kings, like the governor, influences policy in Washington and Albany, suggests to the Fed Chair what interest rate to set, and now I'm setting him up. Hopefully, the power structure will rise up and keep Sid Ackerman happy because I'm sure he has people who take care of people like me if I cause him any problem.

Meyer says that all I have to do is make the call and tell Ackerman what time to show up at the Erickson and he's right. That's all I have to do. Ackerman wasn't happy on our last call when I had to tell him that I didn't have a baby for him. I tried to explain that producing a baby on command was harder than setting the price of gold or the withdrawal of troops from Afghanistan, but he just said that his new wife wanted a baby, and I had indicated that I could get her one and now I needed to produce one. Pronto!

I also knew he wanted a boy, but now I had a girl to offer him. Praying that he takes it. *What man really wants a useless girl?* He had confided in me after the last IVF procedure had failed on his trophy wife and they had decided that it would just be easier to buy a baby. I couldn't decide whether or not to tell him the sex of the baby. Only if he asks. Only if he asks.

My hands are shaking as I pick up my phone, hit contacts,

of course it's right on the top—Ackerman—*Moore, you're in deep here, man. Just make the call.* I chide myself.

He picks up on the first ring. I know he's been waiting for this call. The wife has probably been on his case for weeks now. She'd already bought the christening gown the last time we talked. "Tom."

"Mr. Ackerman, hi, how are you?" Be normal. Conversational. Nothing's wrong.

"Fine. Do you have the baby?"

"Yes, I do. Ms. Maas will come up next week, Thursday, so you can meet the baby. Take her home."

"Shit, Moore, it's a girl?"

I grimace and curse myself out before answering, "So adorable. You won't believe it." I sound so smooth. Car salesman smooth. I hate myself.

The seconds tick by. "Fine. Whatever. It's for her anyway."

"So, the Erickson at ten a.m. Thursday."

"Fine." The line goes dead.

Like a hot pan, I drop the phone. I lean back on my gray velour couch and let all my muscles go slack.

70

SAVANNAH

After running five miles, checking on Jed's grave just to make sure that the coyotes and the vultures haven't dug him up for a midnight snack, I go into the barn to shut it down while I'm up in New York City. Vadoma has no reason to come out here while Hattie and I are up north. We only have one girl scheduled to come in for a check-up in the next few weeks, and I sent her a text with the phone number of the clinic that I used to work at and told her to start seeing the doctor there, that I wouldn't be able to help her birth her baby.

As I make sure that everything is clean and orderly after Lucille's labor, a noise outside the barn door stops me in my tracks. I assume that it's Vadoma and Kayleigh walking Charlie, but I don't hear the dog barking or Kayleigh's little high-pitched shrieks. Reaching for my fanny pack that holds my Glock, I pull her out and keep her in my hand, down low, as I go out into the center hallway. Usually I don't keep my Glock with me while I'm on my land, but since I was checking on Jed's grave, I brought her along.

A footstep, door creak. I move into the shadows of the ultrasound room. Light from the door opening creates an ever-expanding triangle into which steps a boot, size twelve or thirteen, scuffed with transmission oil spots. The triangle of light starts to shrink. I can see both legs, scruffy jeans, but the top half of whoever this is remains in darkness. Once he steps into the center hallway, I see a tall baby-faced man with very broad shoulders and a slender waist, thick sandy hair, and a bit of a blank look around the eyes.

"Kelly?" he calls.

Oh, this must be Mr. Gas Station, I think. I can see what Kelly liked about him. He's the kind of man who's good to keep around if all you want to do is ride him like a horse. I can see his appeal. Tucking the Glock in my back waistband, I pray to God that I don't have to kill another member of this annoying family.

"Can I help you?" I give him a big smile.

He looks me and up and down with an aw-shucks but lusty eye. "You must be the midwife. Kelly never mentioned you were a looker."

"Why would she?"

"Where's Kelly? And where's my brother?" He asks the last question with a bit of a snarl.

"You the guy that pumps gas down at the Exxon?"

"I'm the head mechanic there. Yeah," he says with pride.

"Of course you are." I try to tamp down the condescension in my voice. "Well, I thought Kelly was with you. Haven't seen her in days."

"She ain't with me. And where's my brother?"

"You mean after he came here with his little blackmail scheme?" I start to walk toward the door of the barn. Better to get this over with and him on his way. "C'mon, I was just closing up in here. He told me he was heading south. Didn't say where."

"Why would he tell you where he's going?"

"Just small talk after he robbed me blind."

He takes a long look down the center hallway of the barn like he's looking for Kelly or Jed. I'm trying to remember if

Jed's truck is sticking out from behind the barn. Sure am glad Hattie and I bought industrial carpet for the foyer to hide Jed's blood in the old floorboards. It gives me some kind of perverse pleasure to know that Lee is now standing right where I blew his good-for-nothing brother's brains out.

"Let's go, sweetheart. Nobody's here but me," I say opening the door to the barn, sweat running down my back. I'm afraid the Glock will slip out with the tide.

"Neither of them are answering my texts or my calls," he complains, almost a whine, as he walks out into the bright sunshine.

I close the door behind him, fighting the urge to check that Jed's truck is fully hidden behind the barn.

"You must have a momma or somebody else to complain to. Now, I got work to do. I'll tell her to call you if she comes back."

He stands there like the sexy hulk that he is and pouts. I start to walk to the house hoping he'll take the hint.

"How many babies you brought in that barn?"

I'm seriously losing patience now. "Listen, I have to get on with my day, and I want you off my property. Now!"

He takes a few steps toward his truck. "Jed said you were making bank out here selling babies." He turns around to look me in the eye. "He better show up soon."

I return his stare but don't say a word.

"Lonely out here," he looks up at the house.

"Yeah, nice and quiet," I say as I turn toward the house. "See you around."

"Yeah, see you around." He gets in his truck, kicks up some dust in a three-point turn and hightails it down my drive.

I make it a practice to never second-guess myself, but as I walk to the back door, I can't help but wonder if he's not as stupid as he looks.

71

—————

TOM

Everything's in place and my nerves are raw, frayed. I shake, tremble, whimper unexpectedly. I flinch at the tiniest noise, followed by moments of numbness, exhaustion, the sensation of things moving too slowly followed by things moving too fast. Sweat on my forehead, eyes dry. I am obviously, physically, not up to this. Why did I approach Meyer? Everything was okay. Wasn't it?

Pressing the button on my office phone, I call Mara, my assistant, into my office. She's been shy around me lately, and I don't blame her. I've been secretive, evasive, hypersensitive. I look bad, unkempt. I probably smell bad existing in this clammy state of exhaustion. It's like I've started this giant government operation. Everyone is working overtime based on my confession. Responsible but not in charge. This multi-state machine moving toward the arrest of the woman I love. All because I know I could never control her.

Do I love her? Is this love?

There's a knock on the door, and Mara sticks her head in.

"Tom, are you okay?" she asks with concern in her round hazel eyes.

I clear my throat. "Actually, I'm feeling under the

weather." I force a cough. "I think I need a few days off. Please cancel all of my appointments for the rest of the week." I know full-well that by next week my privileges will have been revoked and this sordid tale will be on every newscaster's newly plumped lips.

"Oh, okay. Is there anything I can do for you?" She doesn't quite enter the room. She's leaving herself the option of running and slamming the door to get away from me.

"Mara, I, um, I just want to say that, um, you are very good at your job, and I want to thank you for all you do."

Mara's freckled face turns pink between the tan spots, and I can see that she doesn't know what to say. Her sad eyes look concerned.

I chuckle to relieve the tension. "That's all. I'm not dying. Just wanted to say that."

She smiles weakly. "Thank you," she says as she slowly steps out of the office and closes the door.

Shutting my eyes, I inhale through my nose and force the air out my mouth. When I feel a little steadier, I start to throw some personal effects in an old Duane Reade bag that I find in the bottom drawer of my desk. This will be my last day in the office. The plan had been to work until Thursday —D-day—but I can't. I can't keep up the charade one more day.

Officially, I'll tell them I have the flu this week. As I finalize my lies, my phone vibrates in my pocket. I look at the lock screen—Savannah. I know she wants to talk about the night before the exchange. Probably booked some expensive restaurant and a couples massage. I gag.

Keep up the façade! You're so close. Deep cleansing breath.
"Hey."

"Hey, baby," Savannah's signature rasp fills my senses.

"How's everything?" Act natural. Sound like yourself.

"Good. Good, the baby's coming along nicely. Gained a pound. Angelic head of fine blonde hair, eyes-a-blue. Tom, I want to have a long conversation when I come up about our future."

"Let's talk after the baby's delivered to the Ackermans," I say to put off the conversation until she's behind bars. I wince at the thought.

"Yes, let's go away. After, I mean."

"So, you arrive Wednesday?"

"Yes, I'll make a reservation for dinner. Seven o'clock?"

"Yes, seven o'clock."

A pause. "I can't wait to see you, Tom."

"Yeah, me too." I hang up before she can tell me she loves me.

72

ANABEL

Sylvia thinks I've lost my mind. She told me this outright. "Sweetie," she said in that tone that lets me know she thinks I've gone over the deep end, "I'm not sure you have enough evidence to draw that conclusion."

"Syl, the man was looking at me like he knew me. He knew who I was, and he was freaked out. Tell me he didn't look freaked out when he looked at me!"

"Sweetie, everyone knows who you are from the news."

"But not everyone is freaked out by it." I know I sound shrill, near hysterical.

I've been up most of the night listening with rapt attention to my own inner voice weave a tale that somehow connects the man in the park to the fact that the baby's adoption was put on hold. Now, I know that most well-informed people in the city might recognize me from all of the coverage about the baby in the park. People have been asking me about it for months now, but this guy was different. He wasn't just mildly interested in me as a passing oddity, like seeing a celebrity on the street. No, he was terrified. His eyes bulged, his nostrils flared, his body shook, and then he ran away from me. He literally couldn't stand the sight of me. Why?

"Bel, I think you're losing it. I wish Dennis were home, instead of going off to Los Angeles. Why don't you come over? I have to take Paul to his fencing lesson. You can come along. Kids are great for taking your mind off things."

I don't think I could stand to be with all my sister's kids right now. She's got great kids, who I love very much, but I can't focus on being a great aunt right now.

"Listen, I think I just want to lie down and try to take a nap. I'm fine. Just tired," I say.

"Are you sure? It might do you good to be with other people," says Sylvia, clearly worried about me.

When I don't answer she says, "Well, okay. Get some rest. Bel, everything's going to be okay."

After we hang up, I get up from the comfortable over-stuffed chair that was delivered yesterday for the new master suite, and I walk over to the window. Dennis's house faces north, but if I crane my neck a bit to the left, I can just see the stone wall that runs around the perimeter of Central Park on Fifth Avenue in between the taxis and buses clogging the avenue. Like a magnet drawing me to it, I decide to go to the park.

It's late in the day, so I throw my lavender wrap around my shoulders, pat my hair down in the mirror in the foyer, and head out into the cool air. I'm aware of where I'm going and what I'm doing, but it's like an intuition driving me, a force I choose not to override by common sense and rational thought.

I head west on Eightieth Street to Fifth Avenue walking in the usual New York way. Fast and determined, never strolling. New Yorkers never stroll. Heading in the direction of the Sabrett hot dog cart where I saw the man the other day, I tell myself I'm crazy to expect that he might be there. I cross Fifth Avenue to the park side and walk down to Sixty-Fifth Street to enter the park.

Rush hour is just starting and the path is filling up. Young men with their ties thrown back over a shoulder, businesswomen in suits and designer sneakers, nannies and babies heading home from the playground, everyone has some place to go. Homes. Restaurants. Gyms. Shops. I reach the Sabrett cart and there's a group of teenage boys ordering two hot dogs each on their way home to dinner.

There's an empty bench across from the cart and I go and sit on one end. Even if he came and sat down next to me, I have no idea if I would say anything to him. What would I say? *What do you know about Goldie? The baby left in my lap? Why has the adoption been put on hold? Am I going to get the baby?* He would surely back away from me, saying something like, *I'm sorry, what are you talking about?* But he knew me. He couldn't ask what I was talking about because he would know what I was talking about. I'm certain of this.

I sit there for an hour. The temperature of the air drops and I pull my wrap more closely around my shoulders. I pretend to look at my phone, but I study each man coming and going on the path. He might not be in sweats. He might be in a suit or casual clothes. I try to imagine his face on top of different clothes, so that I don't miss him. I try to picture him cleaned up or with a hat on. What would he look like? I think I would recognize him, and I know he would recognize me.

As the sun begins to set, I begin to feel foolish. What am I doing here? If Dennis knew where I was right now, he would freak out. I force myself to my feet, take a last look at the people coming and going on the path, and seeing no one who resembles the man, I slowly start to walk back to the townhouse.

73

———

SAVANNAH

As soon as Vadoma puts Kayleigh to bed, I tell her and Hattie that we need to meet in the family room to discuss the matter at hand. Namely, how to get rid of Jed's truck. Hattie and I can't go off to Manhattan and leave Vadoma here alone with that truck out back. I'm pretty sure we haven't seen the last of Mr. Gas Station and if he finds his brother's truck on my property there will be hell to pay. We have got to get rid of it, plain and simple, but how does one dispose of a truck?

We usually hang out in the kitchen, but we're all tired and the family room has big, soft, comfortable chairs, so we pile into the room and sink down into the cushions. The baby is killing us. She demands a feeding every four hours and screeches like a cat when she's hungry. While I admire her spirit, I've taken to sleeping with earplugs when it's not my turn to mind her.

Vadoma and I are splitting a bottle of Sauvignon Blanc, but Hattie prefers shots of WhistlePig with Miller High Life chasers. We've all grown accustomed to the finer things in life. We settle in and take a few minutes to relax. We're all feeling the stress of what happened with Jed. Even though I pulled the trigger, Hattie was with me and Vadoma helped to bury him, so our fate is sealed together, and we all know it. In some respects, it's comforting to know that if I go down they go down with me, but my heart starts to race when I think about taking a life. As a midwife I've been trained to bring life into the world and protect it once it's here. Jed was a problem without another solution.

And he had Kelly. I miss Kelly. She was like a bratty little sister who you don't miss until they're gone.

"Hey, either of you hear from Kelly?" I ask.

Both Hattie and Vadoma shake their heads, staring into their drinks.

Hattie is sitting in an oversized recliner, a shot glass and bottle of beer on the small table beside her. She takes a sip of beer and studies the label on the bottle. "She's a good kid. I hope she leaves this place in the rearview mirror and don't come back. She's young. Could have a life," she says.

Vadoma has her bare feet up on the ottoman and she's studying her deep red toenails. "Think I need a pedicure."

"Well, right after we get rid of Jed's truck you can go get one. So, how can we get rid of it?" I ask.

"I think we should burn it," offers Vadoma.

"Burn it?" I ask with a frown. "Where are we going to burn a truck and not attract attention? Even out in the middle of my property, I'm pretty sure the smoke could be seen for miles."

"And the smell," adds Hattie. "No, we need a chop shop, and I think I know a guy. Haven't seen him in years, but he used to strip cars down and sell them for parts. He's in Huntsville, Alabama."

Vadoma pipes up. "Where's that?"

"About two hours west of here," replies Hattie.

I get up and pour myself another glass of wine. After taking a sip, I say, "That might work. Chop it up. Disperse the parts." I start to pace, envisioning the doors coming off the truck, tires gone, seats torn out. This could work. "Hattie, maybe this is the solution. See if you can get in touch with your guy. If he's still in business, you can drive the truck and Vadoma can follow you to bring you back here. Today's Monday. You'll have to go tomorrow. See what you can do."

"We'll have to travel at night so we can get the truck out of Dubois without any problems," says Hattie.

"Yeah, there are a few people who probably have an eye out for Jed's truck," I agree. I open my mouth to tell them that this will be our last baby drop, but something tells me to keep this to myself until the baby upstairs is safely with her new parents.

Vadoma catches the look on my face. "What?" she asks.

Thinking quick, I say, "After you sell the truck, you'll have to head directly back so Hattie and I can make our flight. We're leaving Wednesday on the noon flight."

"Let me see if I can track Rob Roy down." Hattie pours herself one last shot, raises the glass to Vadoma, then me, downs it, let's out a long "ahhh" and heads upstairs.

I finish my wine and stand up to go upstairs myself.

"You should be glad I came back," says Vadoma, eyeing me with a steady gaze.

"Yes, it's good to have another pair of hands."

"Hattie told me about her new deal with you. I want a third of the cut. It's only fair to split the pie three ways." She stands up to face me.

We lock eyes for a minute or two. An active silence grows up between us. "You know what, Vadoma? This one's on me. You and Hattie split the cut in half."

Her black eyes narrow. "What's going on?"

"Nothing's going on. Don't question the biggest paycheck of your life. Good night." I walk out of the room feeling that I've moved one step closer to the end of running this operation. Turning off the lights in the rooms as I go, I make my way to my room and plop down on the bed. The house is quiet, and I think back to going to bed in this very room before I got pregnant in high school and how I used to feel safe going to sleep with my parents down the hall.

I want that feeling back. The innocent feeling that everything is all right. I'm tired of it all. I need to convince Tom to start a new life with me in a new house on the beach, far away from Dubois and New York City. Far away from the stress of the pregnant girls and the desperate families and the trips to New York and the bags of money.

I want to shut this all down. My path feels clear. No more laboring teenagers looking at me with big, scared eyes. No more explaining to them how to protect themselves from getting pregnant again. No more threats of blackmail from the likes of Jed. No more leading this band of desperate women, because that is what we are. Me, Hattie, Vadoma, Kelly, we're all women searching for peace from our inner demons. As sleep closes in on me, I see me and Tom with the sun and the sand and maybe a baby.

74

ANABEL

I should be planning my wedding, but instead I am in the park. Sylvia's admonitions have caused me to stop confiding in her, and of course, I'm not going to tell Dennis that I am desperately trying to track down the crazed man who ran away from me in the park. Yesterday I went to the spot where he saw me three times—morning, noon, and night—with no luck. This morning, no luck.

Checking my phone for the time, I'm now on my way back to the park. Like a criminal obsessively revisiting the scene of a crime, I am drawn back to the Sabrett cart. The hot dog man now says hello to me, and I have eaten two hot dogs and a pretzel in the last few days leaving me feeling bloated and constipated.

The days are getting cooler, a few gold and red leaves are starting to appear among the green of the trees. I rummaged around in my closet to find my blue Patagonia fleece from last fall, and I tell myself that I am not going to the park to find the man but I am walking through the park to check out a venue for the wedding on Central Park West.

The thought of another hot dog makes me gag as I follow the now familiar path to the Sabrett cart. Embarrassment makes me avert my eyes from the hot dog vendor. What does he think I'm doing? I can only imagine. Eyes looking down, I head farther along the path to a bench set slightly back, nestled between two lush bushes. I take a seat and try to make myself as small as possible, pretending that I can see the world walk by without being seen.

My appointment at the venue is for two o'clock and I've already decided that I will book it so that I don't have to look at any other places. The Tiller Mansion looks beautiful on the internet and unless it is rundown and moldy that is where we will be married. We have less than five weeks to pull it all together and as I sit on the bench thinking of all the things I should be doing I start to sweat. I pull open the zipper on my fleece and push the sides back to give myself some air. Closing my eyes, I see the list that I purposely left on the kitchen counter—dress, invitations, finalize guest list, flowers, cake—I realize I'm hyperventilating and try to catch my breath.

This is absurd. Forget this man, I yell in my head and then, as I look to my left. There he is.

My entire body goes cold, and I instinctively re-zip my fleece. He's jogging toward me wearing a gray sweat suit and a Yale baseball cap. He looks cleaner than the last time I saw him, and he may have gotten a haircut. He's approaching me. I panic. I can't let him run away this time. Staggering to my feet, I go and stand in the middle of the path. He has to either knock me over or jog around me.

"Stop!" I yell, waving my arms at him. He stops and stares down at me, reaching to take the earbuds out of his ears. His breath is jagged, coming in fits and starts from his run and maybe from the sight of me. "Who are you?" I ask him. It comes out as a whisper. "What do you know about me?"

He hesitates, like he's trying to figure out where to start. Finally, all he says is, "Anabel Leigh."

"Do you know the baby in the park? Is that what this is

about? Are you . . . are you her father?" My voice is unsteady. The park is a blur around us.

"No! No!" He shakes his head.

"Please, tell me what you know about her." I reach out to touch his arm, but he pulls away. His lips are pressed together in an ugly grimace that distorts his handsome face. He reaches up and takes the cap off his head and pulls at the curls behind his ear. I try to get him to look at me, but he avoids direct eye contact. I'm so afraid that he will run away.

"I'll answer your questions on Friday. Meet me here at noon. Come alone." And with that he replaces the cap on his head and jogs quickly away.

"No! Wait!" I scream after him, but he is running fast now, and he blurs into the crowd as the path takes a turn behind the trees.

75

SAVANNAH

Hattie's friend, Rob Roy, was more than happy to take Jed's truck for fifty bucks. That's what we decided to charge him knowing that he could sell the parts for thousands. At this point, money is no object for us.

Now that they're home, I turn over the babysitting responsibilities to Vadoma and Hattie and I get ready to go to New York. I am so excited to see Tom and to tell him that I'm ready to put this all behind us that I catch myself humming. I am not the kind of woman who hums.

I look in the mirror to make sure that I haven't completely lost my mind and the woman who looks back at me is positively glowing. My eyes are sparkling, my hair looks sleek and thick, my cheeks are pink, and there's an energy bubbling out of my pores. I feel the adrenaline rushing through my veins. People have always told me I am beautiful and today I have to agree with them.

We have a noon flight, so all five of us—Hattie, Vadoma, Kayleigh, the baby, and I—load into my Audi SUV and Vadoma drives us to the airport.

Hattie eyes me suspiciously as we toss our suitcases in the

back. "Uh-huh, somebody's excited. Somebody's gettin' some tonight." She smiles at me and usually that kind of comment would piss me off, but not today.

"Well, tonight you have to babysit, but tomorrow night you can get some yourself," I say with a wink.

She shakes her head. "I don't like those soft Yankee boys. I'm gonna wait till we're home and have me a southern man. A real man," says Hattie.

"Suit yourself," I say jumping into the passenger seat. "Let's go!"

Hattie squeezes into the back with Kayleigh and the baby in their car seats. "When can we take this child out of a car seat?" she asks, obviously annoyed.

"When she's forty pounds," says Vadoma.

We get on the highway and it's a ten-minute ride to the airport. We're all lost in our own thoughts when Kayleigh asks, "Where are we going, Mommy?"

"Mommy? She calls you *Mommy* now?" I ask with contempt.

Vadoma, one of the hardest women I know, sends a sweet smile my way. "Yeah, Mommy." Then, to Kayleigh, "We're just dropping them at the airport and then you and me, we're going for ice cream."

"Yah! Can I have two scoops?"

"Yes, darlin' you can have anything you want."

"I think I'm going to gag and throw up soon," I say as we arrive at the airport.

By the time we land at LaGuardia, drive into the city, and get to the Erickson Hotel, I am bubbling over with excitement. Tom has booked us the penthouse—a two-bedroom, two-bath suite with kitchen, dining room, and living room. The décor is a little traditional for me—a lot of Queen Anne legs on the chairs and striped fabric like the White House—but it's spacious and well-stocked with the wines I like, whiskey and beer for Hattie, and Similac for the baby. Hattie's room has a crib and changing table.

As I unpack, I think about seeing Tom tonight. I rarely wear red, I feel it's a little flamboyant, but tonight I am wearing a tight red Celine sheath with spaghetti straps and a plunging neckline that leaves little to the imagination. I put my hair back in a low chignon and put an extra coating of mascara on my thick lashes. We have a reservation at seven-thirty at Eleven Madison Park, the most expensive restaurant in Manhattan.

As I continue getting ready to go out, I hope that Tom is in a good mood. He has been so nervous and skittish lately. I just know that he will be so happy when I tell him we're through with the barn and the girls. I'm going to do everything I can to help him relax, I think to myself as I apply another layer of bright red lipstick and sink my lips into a tissue to blot it.

I get to Eleven Madison Park early, but Tom is uncharacteristically late. The maître d' seats me at our table, and I order a bottle of Dom Perignon. When it comes, the waiter pours me a glass and as he walks away, I take a sip and feel the tiny bubbles tickle my throat. I check my phone to see if Tom has texted me, and I send him a text asking where he is.

As the minutes tick by, my mood swings from concerned to furious and back again. Of course, I'm free to get up and leave at any time but I feel trapped in my seat. Exposed. Oddly vulnerable. Not that anyone here cares that I'm being stood up, but I see the eyes of a few men linger as they glance in my direction.

As the minutes tick by and I've drained my glass, I'm sorry that I ordered the champagne. Now I have to ask for a check and pay. Tom has not responded to my texts, and I keep telling myself that he's stuck in traffic and will be here momentarily, but after forty-five minutes it becomes clear to

me that he is not coming. As I throw my debit card on top of
the little black leather portfolio that the check arrives in, I seriously hope that Tom is dead somewhere. There's simply no
other excuse for not being here.

TOM

"Thacker said his men saw her board the plane with an African American woman and the infant and then land at LaGuardia. She checked into the Erickson. Tom, you've got to go meet her and act like nothing is going on," Meyer had told me when he called at four o'clock, but now it's seven-fifteen and I know that she is waiting for me. She'll be all dressed up, looking gorgeous, sitting all by herself at a table at Eleven Madison Park wondering where I am.

I cannot act like nothing is going on. Meyer doesn't really understand Savannah's hold on me. My hands are shaking. I can't think straight. Haven't eaten today. There's no way I can sit in that fancy restaurant and make conversation with Savannah for a long dinner and then take her back to my apartment for a night of sweaty sex. I'm pretty sure I couldn't even get it up. And there's something sick about making love to the woman who you are turning over to the Feds in the morning. She will see right through me the very minute she lays eyes on me.

I can't go. I just can't see her and that's the way it has to be. I have to get out of the apartment, because knowing Savannah, she will storm in here when I don't show. She will talk her way past my doorman, and then like a hurricane, she will blow in here, her anger will rattle the walls, drenching me with accusations I won't be able to deny, until she gets to the truth.

I go into my bedroom and pull on jeans, an old blue sweatshirt, and my Yale baseball cap. I've got to get out of here. The island of Manhattan has shrunk to just her and me. She could be on her way to my apartment right now or on her way up in the elevator. A chill goes up my spine. I've got to run. I'll check into some small hotel in Times Square, some seedy little place that she would never go. I take my sunglasses, keys, phone, and wallet and head out the door. As soon as I leave the building, I see the unmarked car across the street. Of course, Thacker has eyes on me.

I jog over to Park Avenue and hail a cab. The chase is on. The unmarked car is right behind us as we drive south on Park Avenue. My phone rings. It's Thacker, and I decline the call. The phone lights up again and it's Meyer. I pick up.

"What the hell is going on?" he explodes into the phone.

"I'm running from her, not them," I say.

"They're going to bring you in after everything we've done to keep you out of jail," he screams into the phone.

"I'd rather be in jail than have to face her."

"Well, pull over and give yourself up before this gets any worse. I'll meet you downtown. Get Thacker to tell me where they're taking you." He ends the call.

I tell the driver to make a right on Forty-Second Street and keep driving west. Now, we're in the heart of Times Square, which has been turned into Disneyland, with huge billboards of *Aladdin* and *The Lion King*, but on the westside near Tenth and Eleventh Avenues there are still some shady rundown hotels and that's where I'm headed. The sidewalks are packed with tourists near Broadway, but as the cab crawls toward the Hudson River the crowds thin out and I tell the driver to pull over. I know running is futile. As soon as I get out of the cab the Feds will grab me. I swing open the door, giving the cabbie a fifty, and immediately the unmarked car pulls over behind us and two huge men bound out of the car ready for a chase.

I'm not sure if they are disappointed or relieved that I simply stand there and wait for them to rough me up.

"Thomas Moore?" asks the bigger of the two.

"Yes."

"FBI. Agents Felcher and Sloan. We're taking you in," says Agent Felcher, flashing his badge.

We walk toward their vehicle, Agent Sloan's massive hand wrapped around my bicep, Agent Felcher opens the back door, and I get in. I feel a slight shove from one of them and I know that this is the beginning of a new life. One that I know nothing about. I wince as he slams the door shut. It sounds final.

77

ANABEL

I decide not to tell Dennis about seeing the man again and that he told me to meet him on Friday at the park. While I should be thinking of flowers and canapés, the man in the park is always on my mind. What is he going to tell me on Friday that he couldn't tell me yesterday? What is happening between now and Friday that would allow him to tell me what's going on? Will Goldie's parents be revealed? Why was the adoption put on hold? Are they looking for relatives who might show up?

I'm supposed to be making Dennis breakfast, but I have been standing in front of the open door of the refrigerator, staring blindly at the shelves. Unable to reach for the eggs. I hear the shower turn off and that motivates me to pick up the carton. Eggs and toast. That's all I can manage.

Dennis comes into the kitchen just as I am spooning slightly burned scrambled eggs onto a plate, and I notice the thin line of smoke coming from the toaster. He hurries over and pops the lever to release the toast, grabs a fork to pull one of the pieces of burnt toast out of the toaster, and stares at it.

"Geez, sweetie, I might have to reconsider this marriage

based on this toast." He laughs and chucks the toast into the garbage can.

"I'm sorry. I think I have a case of the jitters. I can't seem to keep my mind on what I'm doing." I look at him with big, sad eyes and he takes me in his arms.

"What do you have the jitters about?"

Of course, I can't tell him it's the handsome man in the park in a Yale baseball cap that I have been stalking for a week now. "Just making sure everything's perfect for our big day." I say instead.

"What can I help you with?" he asks. He leans down, kisses my nose, and then gets two more pieces of whole wheat bread out of the bag and sticks them in the toaster. "I've been thinking of taking Friday off to help."

I feel myself start to sweat and sweep a shaky hand across my forehead as I quickly search for a reason why he shouldn't take Friday off. "Friday?" I stammer. "Friday is my next fitting for my dress. At noon. We can get everything done on Saturday."

The toast pops. Dennis grabs it and throws it on the plate of now cold eggs and takes it over to the table to butter it. "Are you eating?"

I look around and grab a banana from the bowl on the counter, walk over to the table, and sit across from him. "I'll be fine. I just have to make a to-do list and start checking things off. Then I'll feel like I'm accomplishing something." I manage a weak smile. When I look up Dennis has his head tilted to one side and is staring at me.

"Is that all it is? You're not having second thoughts or anything, are you?"

"No! Are you kidding? Give up this townhouse? No way!" My lips curved into a mischievous smile.

He laughs. "Okay. Well, please make me a to-do list too, so that everything isn't falling on you. Okay?"

"Got it! His and her to-do lists. You'll be sorry, but that will help. You know that's why I love you. You are so considerate." I get up and go to hug him. He nestles his face in my T-shirt, and I kiss the top of his head. But, as I stare out the back window, all I can think about is meeting the man in the park on Friday.

78

SAVANNAH

Hattie is asleep when I get back to the suite. All is quiet. I take a moment to go over to the large window in the living room with the view of the Hudson River to decide what to do. As I look out at the silent boats floating by below, the anger is roiling in my chest, and I realize there is absolutely no way that I can just go to bed. The thought of the baby waking up and screeching the way she does makes a new wave of rage course through my veins. Kicking off my Louboutins in the living room, I try—to no avail—to get the zipper in the back of my dress down as I go to my bedroom. After a few attempts, my cheeks are hot with frustration and fury. I can't believe that Tom had the audacity to stand me up. The bastard will pay for this. I finally rip the low-cut dress enough to wriggle out of it.

Standing there in my black lace underwear that I bought for him, I am sick of it all. Donning my black silk robe, I go back out to the living area and get myself a glass of white wine from the mini fridge. I had nothing but Dom Perignon for dinner so the wine goes immediately to my head. I can't fucking believe it. I check my phone, and seeing no messages, hurl it at the wall.

"Shit!" I say to the room. I really don't want to wake the baby. I hope Hattie brought some Benadryl because if that child starts to cry, I will be forced to drug her.

Going back into my room, I get dressed. The only nice outfit I have is the one I was planning on wearing tomorrow to meet the Ackermans. I pull on the high-waisted tan pants and white painter's blouse. Cinch my waist with a vintage beaded belt. Grabbing the matching jacket and my purse, I head out to the bar downstairs. I need some dinner.

It's now nine-thirty as I wait for the elevator—I don't know exactly because I've left my phone on the floor in the suite—and I notice that there's a maid cleaning a room down the hall. She's digging in her cart for something as I wait for the elevator.

Pretty late to be cleaning rooms, I think to myself.

The elevator dings and I get on.

When I get downstairs to the lobby, I scan the room looking for the entrance to the bar. I can't help but hope that Tom is there waiting for me. There's a man staring at his phone on a burgundy velvet couch near the fireplace and two young women wearing severe suits. I hope this isn't a meeting place for lesbians. I don't want to have to rebuff an advance. Across the room, which is carpeted with expensive oriental rugs, is a wood-paneled door. Ah, that must be the bar. The bar turns out to be just what I'm looking for—dark, with stuffed-leather banquettes and wood dividers between the tables for privacy. A place where businessmen make deals and adulterous lovers meet for a surreptitious drink.

The maître d' shows me to a table in the back of the bar and I scooch into the corner of the banquette so that I can watch the bar. The waiter comes over, and I order a chicken dish and a double Crown Royal. I don't really have much of an appetite, but I haven't eaten since noon and I'm in the mood for a whiskey or two.

If Tom is going to treat me like this, he's not getting his

share of the take. I've already promised Hattie and Vadoma my half so this will be my reward for showing up. Actually, Tom probably won't care but it might make me feel a little better.

Then, back to the farm tomorrow to shut it down and I will be on a flight to somewhere in a few days. I sink back into the soft leather and the waiter brings my drink. I take a long pull and shut my eyes as the liquor burns my throat. When I open them a man is standing in front of me—a very handsome man—with a glass in his hand.

"Would you like company?" he asks, raising one rakish eyebrow. I take him in. Six two, thick dark brown hair, smoldering brown eyes that look black in the bar's dim light, clean-shaven but with a fine amount of stubble. I think of the burn his cheeks would leave on mine.

"Love some," I say, flashing my most seductive smile. We both know how this will end. Now, how do we get there?

"Here on business?" he asks as he slides his well-built frame into the banquette.

I have the urge to run my hand up his thigh. "Yes, I have an important meeting in the morning," I say. "You?"

"Just flew in from Paris. I start a new gig tomorrow." Our eyes meet over our drinks as we take a sip.

"Staying here?" I ask.

"Yes. You?"

"In the penthouse."

He laughs.

"What?"

"It's just that I tried to book the penthouse and was told it was taken."

I smile. "I always stay in the penthouse. Have never seen one of the smaller suites."

He stares at my mouth before moving his gaze back to my eyes. "Mine is quite nice. Care to check it out?"

"I believe I would."

He gets up and offers me his hand just as the waiter arrives with my dinner.

"Put the charge on the penthouse tab. I've changed my mind. I'm no longer hungry for chicken," I say. The waiter bows his head as if he's seen this before.

As we walk out of the bar, the man puts his hand on the small of my back and we both feel the electricity from the touch.

We make our way to the elevator. His large hand is now under my jacket. *Fuck you, Tom!* I think to myself as we enter the elevator. I'm furious when the two women in the severe suits quickly squeeze into the elevator behind us.

The man has moved his hand down and is now caressing my ass. I try to look straight ahead and wish these women would get off the elevator. He presses floor number fifteen. The floor under the penthouse. One of the women gives a dry laugh and says that they too are going to fifteen. I give them the barest hint of a smile as the man continues to stroke me and it's hard to breathe.

We let them off first and they slowly make their way down the hall as the man takes my hand and leads me to the suite at the other end.

Once inside, he picks me up and carries me into the bedroom and throws me, rather roughly, on the bed. He stands in front of me and takes off all of his clothes. His body is beautiful, and I think I will pass out if he doesn't get on top of me soon. Starting with my shoes, he takes all my clothes off very slowly until we are both naked. Then he slowly gets on top of me and holds me down with his full weight as he kisses me deeply.

Starting from my neck he kisses me, moving down my body. I've never felt such desire. So forbidden. I think I might pass out. I pull on his shoulders to bring his mouth back to mine and before I realize it, he is thrusting himself into me with such force that I gasp and a few minutes later I am falling over the edge losing all sense of where I am and who I'm with.

When he sees that I am spent, he uses me to pleasure himself until I feel him shudder and his full weight bears down on me. After, he rolls off me, we both stare at the ceiling for a minute. Slowly, I get up and go over to the pile that he has made of my clothes. I notice that they are all together, not scattered around the room and as I pull on my panties I wonder if that was by design. He lays there watching me.

When I'm all dressed, I run my fingers through my hair.

"Goodbye, Paris," I say on my way out without looking back.

The next morning when I wake up, I remember carefully hanging up my suit in hopes that the wrinkles incurred by lying in a heap on Paris's floor for fifteen minutes would shake out. I'm sure the hotel can get me a steamer. I check my phone and a thunderbolt of anger courses through my chest when I see that Tom has not called or texted with a profuse apology for standing me up last night.

I jump out of bed, breathing heavy from the excess of emotion pumping adrenaline through my veins when the baby starts to screech. I know that if I go to her, I might throw her against the wall, so I start the shower in an effort to drown her out. It's Hattie's job to take care of her.

Deep breaths. In through the nose. Out through the mouth. In. Out. I get into the shower, leaving the water a little too hot in an effort to take my mind off my anger at Tom. Fifteen minutes later, I actually do feel a little better. Crushing all thoughts of Tom as soon as they enter my head, I focus on the matter at hand. Getting rid of this baby so that I can think ahead and plan exactly what I am going to do about shutting down the barn when I get back to Dubois.

I realize that the baby has stopped screeching—so glad I have a no return policy—and go about my morning routine. I only have about a half hour before the Ackermans arrive. When I go out into the living room of the suite, Hattie is the picture of serenity. Feeding the baby her bottle and singing some hymn or another to her.

She looks up as I come in. "How was your night?" She asks, giving me a conspiratorial smile.

Since I've already made the decision not to share Tom's failure to show up with her, I shoot her a lusty smile with raised eyebrows. "Let's just say we didn't do much talking."

"Nice!" She nods her head. "I will be so happy to pass this little girl onto her forever home. You better get a new phone with a new number. Once she starts to cry, they are going to be calling you. Asking for an exchange," she says with a hearty laugh.

"Should we give her one drop of Benadryl? Just to make sure she doesn't start howling?" I ask, taking a cup of coffee from the pot that Hattie has brewed.

"No, that might make her sleepy. She might appear dull or stupid. She should be okay when they get here now that she's been fed."

"Okay. You're the expert on this baby. She better not screech. I have to go dry my hair," I say walking to the bedroom.

"We're leaving straightaway? Right after they take her?" Hattie yells to my retreating back.

"Yes. Pack up while I'm with them. I hope it goes quickly. Without a hitch," I yell back.

I'm just finishing drying my hair when I hear Hattie rap twice on my door. "Yeah?" I yell.

Opening the door to my room, she says, "They're on their way up."

I smile, pulling on my blazer, giving myself a once-over in the mirror. "It's showtime," I say to my reflection.

79

TOM

I think I nodded off because my head snaps back, causing a sharp pain in my neck. The first thing I become aware of is the stench—sweat, human excrement, misery—I know that I have been taken to the Metropolitan Correctional Center in lower Manhattan. Meyer told me that was where they would take me. He said he would come down and see what he could do but he said he felt pretty sure that I would spend some time locked up as a punishment for running.

As I look around my ten-foot cell and watch the cockroaches scurry in and out of the cracks between the cinder blocks, I realize that I have joined the ranks of the infamous—John Gotti, Bernie Madoff, and Jeffrey Epstein have all sat here before me. Most people would say I was crazy. I could have spent last night making love to a beautiful woman, after dining at one of the finest restaurants in the world, but instead I chose to end up here. In hell. How did I allow my life to sink into the depths of a living hell?

Holding my head in my hands, I close my eyes and clear my head. It's cold and eerily quiet. They've taken my phone so I have no idea what time it is. Wait. I hear footsteps. Is that a key in a lock down the hall? I feel a tremor of panic rip through my chest and my blood pressure soars. I can hear the blood coursing through my veins. A steady thud in my ears. *Thrum. Thrum. Thrum.* Blocking out any real sounds.

I see two guards approaching—big, beefy guys with biceps ripping at the short sleeves of their uniforms and necks as thick as a normal man's thigh. Their faces are set but I think I detect a small smile on the face of the shorter one. I can only guess that they love roughing up soft, Uptown guys like me who might look down on them if we were to meet somewhere else. Like in line at the DMV or Target. But here, in this building, they have all the power.

They stop in front of my cell and unlock the door. The bigger one says, "Your lawyer's here. Let's go."

I breathe a loud sigh of relief and get shakily to my feet.

"Turn around," says the shorter one. "We have to cuff ya."

I do as I'm told and feel the cold metal on my wrists. I am acutely aware of the large billy club that both guards have hanging from their belts. The shorter one gives me a little shove and we exit the cell and start to walk down the long, narrow hallway. I notice that some of the bulbs overhead are out and that most of the cells are empty. I know these are holding cells, so I guess it was a slow night.

We turn a corner, and I can hear voices coming from one of the rooms up ahead. I hear Meyer and at least two others, arguing. The thought of seeing my lawyer makes me tear up. If anyone can get me out of here, he can.

We stop in front of an interrogation room, and I see Special Agents Thacker and Entenmann pointing fingers at Meyer. Shorty shoves me forward. "Here he is."

"Take the cuffs off." Meyer yells at the guards as they start back down the hallway.

The bigger guard looks at Thacker who nods his head, his lips drawn in a thin line. After the cuffs are removed, we all take a seat around the table. Thacker is the first to speak. "Well, well, well, it's the good doctor, who tonight, fucked up his own life. Everything was settled. Everything was in place. You had about the best deal that I've ever seen, ever heard of in my thirty-one years as an agent. What the fuck, man?"

"I wasn't running from you. I was running from . . ."

Thacker cuts me off with a scowl. "Yes, yes. Your lawyer here has explained that you couldn't possibly see your girlfriend. Even though your whole meaningless life rested on it. Your freedom. You couldn't trust yourself not to spill the beans. To cry on her shoulder and confess that you betrayed her. Well, the good news is we've been watching her at the Erickson, and I will tell you that she did not spend her night crying in her soup over you. No, she picked up a boy-toy at the bar downstairs and right now is probably fucking the shit out of him." Thacker's voice has been increasing in volume, and as he tells me of Savannah's betrayal he is standing over me screaming into my ear.

"That's enough, Thacker," Meyer yells. "Now you're harassing my client."

"I just couldn't see her. What's the difference? In a few hours, you'll have her and the other women. I might have blown it. You should be happy that I ran."

Thacker walks back toward his seat. "Oh, I am happy that you ran"—his laugh is sinister—"because now I don't have to honor our agreement. Now, you'll go to trial alongside your girlfriend, and you can both rot in prison." His voice escalating as he speaks.

Meyer's face is red, eyes bulging. He knows it is his turn to bluster, and I pray that he is quick on his feet. "My client turned himself in. He didn't run. He stood there on the street and let you take him in. I've tried to explain this all to you, Thacker. This all became too much for him. He didn't want to jeopardize the arrest tomorrow morning."

Thacker glowers, pats his hair down, breathes in through his nose. "Dr. Moore, did you try to contact Ms. Maas to warn her?"

"No! No! Why, does she know?" My heart is thumping so hard I think I might pass out. I quickly remind myself that Savannah will not be able to find me if she ran and has been caught by the Feds.

Thacker's cell beeps and he puts up his hand to shut me up and slowly reads the text and nods to Entenmann.

"She's in her room?" asks Meyer.

"Yes," says Thacker. "Tucked in for the night." Thacker takes a seat.

The four of us take a minute to breathe a sigh of relief, each for our own reasons. Thacker is the first to move. He looks at Entenmann and nods his head toward the door. "We'll be back," he says as he and Entenmann get up and leave the room.

Meyer lets his back rest on his chair. "What the hell, Tom? Our deal was beautiful! One for the books." He shakes his head.

At first, I want to apologize to him, but then I remember that I am paying him seven hundred dollars an hour and if I need to fuck up the plan he can rack up billable hours trying to fix it. So, instead, I say, "What do we do now? Can I leave?"

Meyer's bloodshot eyes are bulging out of his face. "No, Tom, you cannot leave. We have to try to work a new deal if we can, and I'm not sure we can. The Feds don't like to let criminals go scot-free. They were making an exception for you because they wanted Savannah. Wanted to solve the case of the Golden One that's been on the front pages for so long."

I listen to him while chewing on the inside of my cheek. "But nothing's changed. They'll have Savannah and Hattie and Vadoma and Kelly by mid-morning and they can hold a big news conference. Be the heroes. They don't even have to mention me. They can have all the credit."

"I can see that Thacker wants his pound of flesh. I'm going to offer house arrest with an ankle bracelet."

For some reason, when Meyer says "house arrest," my first

thought is of the woman in the park. Anabel Leigh and how I told her I'd meet her on Friday at noon. I open my mouth to object to house arrest but realize that Meyer will tell them to lock me up for good if I tell him that I was going to meet with Anabel. Instead, I put my head in my hands and say okay.

A few minutes later, Thacker and Entenmann re-enter the room. Entenmann takes the seat across from me, but Thacker stands at the front of the room. "We're holding you until we have the women in custody and then we'll take it from there. Hear what Savannah Maas has to say about your arrangement."

"We've only heard your side, now we'll hear hers," says Entenmann.

"My client came to you in good faith and gave you Savannah and the entire operation. That has to count for something. You wouldn't be any closer to solving this case if it weren't for him. We want house arrest with an ankle bracelet starting tonight," says Meyer authoritatively.

Thacker smirks. "He's staying here tonight." And without waiting for a reply, he leaves the room with Entenmann right behind him.

Meyer looks at me and shrugs, "I tried."

80

SAVANNAH

The thought crosses my mind that for a bigwig, mayor-controlling hotshot, Sid Ackerman seems very nervous. As opposed to his blonde, buxom, puffy-lipped trophy wife who is totally engaged with the baby, seemingly without a care in the world. The baby is playing her part beautifully. She is cooing and staring up at the woman as if to say that she is the perfect baby, one who will not scream between the hours of ten at night and six in the morning.

I'm getting a little antsy, but I know that I have to let the bonding happen so that Ackerman will wire the money.

"Do you want to feed her?" I ask sweetly.

The wife's perfect lips form a tight smile, and she nods her head.

"Of course! It's actually time for her feeding," I say as I get up and go over to the counter and take a premixed bottle of formula, give it a shake and put a nipple on it. As I walk back toward the couple, Mr. Ackerman looks up and gives me a very strange look. I try to interpret it as I hand the wife the bottle. It's part conspiratorial, part fearful, part apprehensive. In another setting, and without the wife, I'd simply ask him what the problem is but my gut tells me to tread carefully. I decide to move this meeting forward and get on my way to my new life.

"So, Mr. Ackerman, while your wife feeds the baby, maybe you and I can work out the business details," I say in a purely professional tone.

He says nothing but gets up and walks over to the desk where I have a folder. He points to the folder and raises his eyebrows as if to ask, "Are these the documents?"

I nod. My stomach involuntarily clenches, and my gut is screaming beware. Ackerman picks up the folder and scans the forged birth certificates. I try to make eye contact with him, but he won't look at me. He takes out his phone and I see that he is making the wire transfer. I look over at the wife to make sure that everything is going okay on that side of the room. The baby is sucking noisily on her bottle and staring into the eyes of her new mother.

When I turn back to Ackerman, he nods at me to tell me the money has been sent. I go to my phone and call up my account. It usually takes a few minutes. I look at Ackerman and see that he is clenching and unclenching his jaw. I start to sweat, and my mouth is so dry that even if I wanted to make small talk I don't think I could.

Thank God! My phone pings, and when I check the wire transfer is complete. Five hundred thousand dollars in my offshore account. I've taken all the money because Tom didn't show up last night.

Ackerman goes over to his wife and says, "Let's go."

She looks up at him to protest, but when she sees the dark look on his face, she simply puts the bottle down on the coffee table, adjusts the receiving blanket around the baby, stands to go and follows her husband to the door. Without a word, they exit the suite.

Staring at the door I exclaim, "You're welcome!"

What just happened? That was the strangest exchange yet. I don't think either of them said a word. The fear in my gut starts to turn to panic, and I have to get out of the hotel and on my way to the airport.

"Hattie!" I yell. "Let's go!" As I start to go back to my room, and Hattie comes out of hers, there is a loud knock on the door. I have no choice but to open it.

As the door swings open, I see bulletproof vests and drawn guns. Hattie screams and starts to pray.

The first man to walk through the door now thrusts a badge in my face and says, "Special Agent Thacker, Federal Bureau of Investigation. Savannah Maas? Hattie Jones?"

I catch my breath as Hattie wails behind me.

Agent Thacker motions for me to turn around so that he can cuff me as another agent walks over to Hattie.

"Hattie Jones? I'm Special Agent Entenmann, FBI. Please turn around."

"What is this all about?" I stammer.

"Savannah Maas and Hattie Jones, you are both being arrested for operating an illegal adoption ring. Our agents are also arresting Vadoma Krivko and Kelly Parker at your farm in Dubois, Georgia as we speak. We'll explain more down at the Metropolitan Correctional Center," says Thacker as I hear a decisive click as the handcuffs shut on my slim wrists.

"What will happen to Kayleigh?" Hattie cries. "The girl at the farm?"

"Hattie, shut up!" I explode.

"She'll be placed in foster care," says Thacker. "Now, no more questions. Let's go."

Once Hattie is cuffed, they take us out in the hallway where I see the two young women in severe suits that I saw in the lobby last night and who rode up in the elevator with me and Paris. I realize in that instant that I have been set up. The Feds have been watching my every move.

One name comes to mind—Tom. Tom has set me up.

81

———

ANABEL

As I walk into the kitchen the next morning, I find Dennis sitting at the table hunched over *The New York Times* looking glum. He is completely absorbed in whatever he is reading.

"Did the stock market tank?" I ask, trying to make a joke.

"Worse," he looks up at me with what I can only call fear in his eyes. "You're on the front page again."

"What?" I ask hurrying over to see the article. Three large photos are splashed across the front page. The baby, the man from the park and a beautiful blonde woman. Underneath are mug shots of an African American woman and another woman who looks familiar to me. The headline reads, *Fertility Doctor and Midwife Arrested in Black-Market Adoption Scheme*. The subhead, *Black-Market Baby Left in Park*. My photo runs next to a recap of how the baby was left with me in the park.

I clutch my chest and gasp. "That's the man I told you about who was jogging in the park and ran away from me," I exclaim, pointing to the photo of Thomas Moore. "And, I think, that might be the woman who put Goldie in my lap," I say pointing to the photo of Vadoma Krivko.

My finger is shaking as I point to the photos. Feeling faint,

I fall into the chair next to Dennis who puts his arm tenderly around my shoulders. "Read it to me," I whisper.

Dennis clears his throat. "Four members of an elite black-market adoption ring were arrested on federal charges, including adoption fraud, child endangerment, wire fraud, human smuggling, and forgery.

"'These arrests are the culmination of months of work by our agents. The Justice Department has no tolerance for crimes that endanger minors, and we will continue to use every tool we have to stop this black-market child trafficking,' said US Attorney Phillip Ravens.

"Midwife, Savannah Maas of Dubois, Georgia, and fertility doctor, Thomas Moore of Manhattan, are alleged to have orchestrated an illegal scheme in which dozens of young women were recruited to give up their babies who were then sold to adoptive parents for as much as five hundred thousand dollars."

I zone out while Dennis reads about the other women involved, trying to figure out what Thomas Moore was going to tell me when he met me in the park today. As I am pondering this, I hear Dennis say my name.

"Prosecutors believe that the baby left in the park with Anabel Leigh is one of the babies connected to the illegal adoption scheme. Prosecutors now believe that it was Vadoma Krivko who left the baby with Leigh in the park."

"Oh my God," I say, starting to hyperventilate. "Stop. I can't take anymore." I start to sob. "It's all so horrible. Goldie's mother is out there. She's a young woman who will probably come forward now."

Dennis pulls me in for a hug. "We don't know what will happen. She probably never wanted Goldie. I doubt she's going to come forward now. Wow, this is a lot to take in. I'm going to take the day off to be with you."

Now that I'm not meeting Thomas Moore in the park

because he must be in jail, I agree that Dennis should stay home. I feel guilty about not telling Dennis that Moore told me to meet him in the park. Keeping secrets from Dennis is not how I want to start our life together.

Wiping my eyes on a napkin, I take a deep breath and decide to come clean. "Dennis, I need to tell you something."

His face tells me that he suspects it isn't good. "Okay, what?"

"Well, you know that I saw this man, this Thomas Moore, in the park and he ran away from me."

"Yes."

"So, I saw him again."

Dennis explodes. "You saw him again? Where? And you didn't tell me?"

"I know. I'm sorry. I'm not even sure why I didn't tell you, but anyway he told me to meet him in the park, today at noon. I guess he's not coming now."

"And you were going to meet him?" Dennis stands up and walks to the sink. "You weren't going to tell me?"

I get up and go to him, but he won't look at me. "I was afraid that you wouldn't want me to go, and I thought he was going to tell me something about Goldie. I had to go." I reach out and put my hand on his arm, but he just keeps looking out the window.

"Dennis, I'm sorry."

He turns to me and gives me a hard stare. "Do you trust me, Anabel? Because if you don't, why are we getting married? I can't live a life of lies. I want to be the one you run to, not the one you're afraid to go to when life gets hard. Otherwise, what are we doing? What are we building our future on?"

"I do trust you. I love you."

"But not enough to come to me and discuss something so important. I don't know what to say."

"Please forgive me. I made a mistake. Please."

He runs his hand through his hair, one hand on his hip. I see that he is conflicted and my heart breaks that I have made him doubt me. I reach out to touch his cheek, but he turns his face away.

"Dennis, I'll never do it again. I promise. I'll always come to you. I didn't have to admit this to you now. I could have just kept it to myself, but I want us to be honest with each other. I messed up. Can you forgive me?" My voice sounds like a whine.

"Do you even have a fitting today? Or was that a lie?"

I look down. "I told you that so you wouldn't take the day off."

His lips turn down in a frown. "I want to believe you. Is there anything else you've kept from me?"

"No."

"Where did you see him again?"

"At the park."

"After we agreed that you shouldn't go back to the park?" Dennis is now raising his voice.

"No, after you told me not to go back to the park," I yell back at him.

"Oh, I see."

"What do you see?"

"That it's my fault."

We're both standing in the middle of the room now with our hands on our hips. Finally, I say, "It's both our faults. You can't forbid me to do something, and I should tell you I'm going to do something even if you don't want me to."

Dennis pushes the hair off his forehead as I realize this is our first real fight. He looks depleted and that's exactly how I feel.

"Dennis, I'm so sorry. I'll always tell you everything from now on even if I think you won't like it."

"And I won't tell you what to do. We'll talk it through. Anabel, please don't be afraid of me. Ever."

I nod, not sure what to do, but he opens his arms, and I walk into his embrace glad that I told him the truth.

82

SAVANNAH

The thing about living under the radar is that you don't have normal relationships with people. I have no family, no sisters or brothers to call for help. Hell, I don't even have any friends. All of the people I spend my time with have been arrested. Another thing, I don't have a family or business attorney to call on now that I really need one. I try to remember the name of the lawyer who helped me when my parents died but he was a small-town lawyer, and I need a big city powerhouse.

As I sit in my cell, I am seething over Tom's betrayal. He really had me fooled. I thought he was in love with me. Ha!

Savannah, you have been played.

He probably got immunity for giving me up. That bastard! Well, two can play that game. We were partners. I never had a hold on him. I never twisted his arm. Okay. He does come across as weaker than I am, but it's not like I blackmailed him. I came up with the babies, and he came up with the rich couples. We had a fifty-fifty partnership.

Knowing that they will come to interrogate me, my mind goes back to figuring out how to get a lawyer. Shit! I'm sure the Feds have ransacked the house and taken all my cash. They probably know about my offshore account. How will I even pay for an attorney? The house and the property are mine. I don't think they can take the house I inherited, but maybe they can.

Think, Savannah, think. You must know a lawyer.

Wait. What was his name? I briefly dated a lawyer before I decided that I wanted to have a real relationship with Tom. Jon. Hadn't he moved to New York and gone to some white shoe firm? Jon Wade. That was his name. I'll call Jon. He was a publicity-seeker. Too big for Atlanta where I met him. I must be all over the papers and the TV by now and being my lawyer will give him unprecedented airtime.

I wish I could huddle with Hattie and Vadoma to concoct a story and get them to turn on Tom, but I know that the Feds will never let that happen. I wonder if they got Kelly too. She could run but she can't hide from the government. My mind goes over all that has happened, and I have to admit that I am fucked. I don't think I can talk my way out of this and then I remember Jed.

Murder.

I start to tremble for the first time, and I feel a fear that starts in my stomach and moves up to my chest making it hard to breathe. I'm sure they've searched the entire farm, but have they found the grave? Have they found the stillborn baby?

I hear a commotion and see two guards dragging a woman down the hallway. From the way she's dressed, I think she must be a hooker. Stilettos, green satin hot pants, tube top. As much as fashion changes, hooker fashion stays the same.

She stops and looks at me. "You an escort?"

I laugh.

"Keep going. The cell at the end," says the bigger guard as she shoves the hooker down the hallway.

Once they lock her up, they come over to my cell and unlock the door, "C'mon. The big boss has come to see you."

"Oh yeah, who's that?" I ask.

"You'll see," says one of the guards as she puts the cuffs on me.

I'm led down the hall and into an interrogation room with four chairs around a table.

"Take a seat," says the other guard. As soon as I do, they exit the room and lock it from the outside.

The room is cold and there is absolutely nothing in it except the chairs and table. The walls are bare. I wait for what seems like an eternity before the door opens and a man enters. He is a large African American man with broad shoulders and short salt and pepper hair. He stands in front of me searching my face. I stare back at him.

"Well, well, well, here she is, the Merry Midwife herself," he finally says, and I notice that one of his front teeth is chipped.

"I want a lawyer," I say.

He puts back his impressive head and laughs.

83

ANABEL

As the weeks fly by leading up to the wedding, I eagerly scan the news every day for updates on the case of the "Merry Midwife," as Savannah Maas has been nicknamed by the press.

"I'll bet she's not merry anymore," Dennis had said one morning when *The Times* ran a long piece on her and Thomas Moore. How they had dated in high school and then reunited years later when she was a midwife and he was a fertility doctor.

The day after the news broke, I had called Ms. Alvarez and asked about Goldie. She had confirmed that the Feds had put the adoption on hold, and she had told me in confidence that the other family had decided to move forward with a different baby. I was so happy when I heard her say that, but she followed it up by saying that the Feds were trying to determine who the baby's biological mother was and if she wanted to be reunited with her baby. My heart had surged when she said Goldie was not going with the other family and plummeted when she said they were looking for the biological mother.

"In my experience, many mothers do not want to be found." She said sensing my disappointment.

I had asked her, again, if I could see Goldie and after waiting for a week to hear back, she had said I could. I was so excited that I had cried and then ran out to the toy store to search for gifts for the girl. It was a tough choice between the book and the stuffed cat, so I bought them both. I also bought apple juice boxes and animal crackers. I wanted to bring the same thing I brought last time so that there would be a pattern to my visits. Dennis was also coming to meet her for the first time, and I was nervous but happy that he wanted to come.

On the day of the visit, I hurry Dennis through breakfast and can't conceal my excitement as we take the subway downtown.

"I'll bet she's grown so much. I haven't seen her in two full months," I say as the subway rumbles, and we sway with the motion of the stops and starts.

"I'm just so happy to finally meet her. Do you think she'll let me hold her?" Dennis asks. He looks a bit nervous, chewing on the inside of his cheek.

I smile at him. "Of course, she will. I'd let her settle in. See if she remembers me and then gradually work up to it. You can give her the cookies."

"She likes animal crackers?"

"She did last time."

We get off at the City Hall stop and find our way up to the street. Ms. Alvarez is letting us meet with Goldie in the room near her office like I did last time. I am so excited to see her that I can't stop smiling.

"I haven't seen you so happy in a long time." Dennis squeezes my hand as we wait in line to go through the metal detectors at the Family Court Building.

"You are going to love her," I say, squeezing his hand back.

Dennis goes first and empties his pockets into a bin. I put my jacket, the bag with the gifts, and my purse in another bin, and we go through security. I greet the guard who nods at me sullenly, and we quickly grab our belongings and ride the elevator up to Ms. Alvarez's floor.

She is waiting for us as we come off the elevators. "Hello, Anabel. Hello, Dennis," she greets us with a smile.

"Hi, Ms. Alvarez. How are you?" I ask.

"I'm good, Anabel, I'm good. Goldie is here waiting for you. She's gotten so big, but I wanted to meet you here to share some news."

My heart starts to pound against my ribcage, and I search her face to determine if the news is good or bad.

It's Dennis who answers her. "What news, Ms. Alvarez?"

She hesitates and I fear for the worst. "They have identified Goldie's mother."

My knees feel weak, and I grab onto Dennis's arm.

"The mother was young. She was a drug addict, and she died of an overdose a year after Goldie was born."

My mind is swirling. A young woman is dead. This is so sad. But Goldie is free to be adopted. I feel sad and overwhelmingly happy at the same time.

"There's more," says Ms. Alvarez. "The other girl in the park the day Goldie was given to you?"

"Yes. The older girl who got out of the stroller and ran into the crowd?" I ask.

"Yes, she's Goldie's sister. They have been reunited, and we'd like to place them together."

"Is she here? Is the older girl here?" I ask.

"Yes, she's in the room with Goldie. Her name is Kayleigh. She's four years old and very precocious. Very smart."

I look up at Dennis who smiles and says, "Well, let's go and meet them."

As we walk into the room, the girls are sitting close together on the couch. Kayleigh has a picture book open on her lap and she is reading the words to Goldie who is staring at the pictures.

"Cat," reads Kayleigh.

Goldie laughs.

"Girls," says Ms. Alvarez. "This is Ms. Leigh and Mr. Wells. They've come to spend a little time with you. Is that okay?"

"Animal crackers," says Goldie, pointing to the bag in my hand.

I laugh. "Yes, I brought you both some animal crackers and some juice," I say, happy that I've brought enough for both girls.

I start to walk over to the girls with a bright smile on my face. "Hi, Goldie. How have you been? You've gotten so big. And Kayleigh, I'm so happy to meet you," I say as I sit down on the couch next to Goldie.

"Why do you call her Goldie?" asks Kayleigh.

"Because of her gold hair," I say. "What do you call her?"

"At the farm we called her Baby."

"You lived on a farm?"

"Yes, a big farm. We both did until we left Baby in the park."

For some reason I start to tear up when she says this.

Dennis comes over to the couch. "Hi, Goldie. Hi, Kayleigh. I'm so happy to meet both of you. Would you like those animal crackers?"

Both girls smile and nod. I silently whisper *thank you* to Dennis and open the bag. Dennis takes the boxes of animal crackers out, opens each box, and hands one to each little girl. I give them each a juice box.

"I also brought you each a present." I say handing the book to Kayleigh and the stuffed cat to Goldie.

Kayleigh looks at the book. "I used to have *Goodnight Moon*. Vadoma, my mother, used to read it to me and Kelly did sometimes."

I know from the papers that Vadoma is the woman who dropped Goldie in my lap in the park and Kelly is the one woman that they haven't found yet.

"Your mother?" I ask.

"She said she was my mother, but she wasn't my real mother. She was really nice to me. Nicer than Savannah. She was mean." Kayleigh looks like she might cry.

Dennis gets up and moves across the room to where a toybox sits on the floor and pulls out two small balls. "Hey, do you know what I can do?"

Goldie is sucking on the straw in her juice box but looks up at Dennis and shakes her head.

"I can juggle!" he says, with a big grin. "Would you like to see me, Kayleigh?"

"Yes!"

Dennis starts to juggle the two balls.

"Such hidden talents, Mr. Wells!" I laugh.

"I have many of them!" he replies with a mischievous smile.

Both little girls are pointing at Dennis and laughing when Ms. Alvarez opens the door.

"Well, don't you all make a nice family?" she said.

Dennis catches the balls one last time.

"That was so much fun!" says Kayleigh as Goldie climbs into my lap.

"Don't go," says Goldie, looking up at me with sad eyes.

"I'll see you again real soon," I say, looking imploringly at Ms. Alvarez.

"Yes, I have to talk to Ms. Leigh and Mr. Wells and maybe we can set up another time for you to get together. Patty, your foster mom, is waiting in the hall and has to take you home now. Kayleigh, help your sister get her things together," says Ms. Alvarez.

Goldie puts her arms around my neck, and I pull Kayleigh in for a group hug.

"We'll see you soon, girls," I say, my voice cracking.

"I'll show you some other tricks I know," says Dennis.

Ms. Alvarez lets Patty in to help the girls get ready to leave and after another goodbye we follow her down the hall to her office, each taking a chair in front of her desk.

"Oh my God," I say. "I was not expecting that. They are so adorable together."

Ms. Alvarez is staring at Dennis. "What do you think, Mr. Wells?"

"They are beautiful little girls. I can see how important it would be to keep them together."

"I'm glad to hear you say that, because we always try to keep siblings together if we can. There will be no adoptions of either girl until the end of the trial, but what I'd like to suggest is that we expedite the process for both of you to become foster parents. The girls will go to live with you and then when the trial is over—barring an unforeseen outcome—you can adopt the girls. I know it's a lot to take in. I would suggest you go home, discuss it, and let me know. When's the wedding?" asked Ms. Alvarez.

"In two weeks," said Dennis.

"Honeymoon?"

Dennis and I look at each other and then I say, "We're still discussing our plans."

"Okay. Go home. Talk. Do pros and cons. Two little girls is a lot. Be sure you both want to jump in. Let me know by Friday. I'm sorry to rush you, but there will be other parents who are interested."

"We will definitely let you know as soon as we make a decision." I smile at Dennis. I suspect he already knows what I want to do, but he needs to want both of them as well.

84

TOM

When Meyer tells me what the Feds have found at the farm, I can feel the hair on the back of my neck bristle.

"Did you know about this, Tom?" Meyer asks, his eyes like needles boring into mine.

I am speechless. My mouth opens but no sound comes out. A body. A man's body has been found buried out in the pasture on Savannah's land. Shot in the head. Most of the head is gone, blown away by the bullet. His name was Jed Pineman, and he was the brother of Kelly's boyfriend. The Feds supposedly got that information from questioning Hattie.

We're sitting in my living room. After two weeks in prison, the Feds agreed to house arrest with an ankle bracelet. I cried when Meyer told me I could go home. I could see in his eyes that I was a huge disappointment to him. So weak. It is clear that he has little to no respect for me and what's worse is that I agree with him.

While I know absolutely nothing about Jed Pineman or why he was shot or who shot him, there is something that is gnawing at the back of my brain. Something that is making my stomach roil. What is it? What's wrong? It's more than this dead man.

I feel my shirt become damp. I feel faint. Meyer looks over at me.

"Tom? What do you know about this man? I hope nothing. I hope you know nothing about who this guy is or who shot him in the head. Because if you even know a little something about this guy, we're dead. Do you hear me? Dead?"

I stand up and walk to the window, momentarily toying with the idea of opening it and throwing myself out.

"It's not the man," I say as I turn to face Meyer.

Now it's Meyer's turn to look sick.

His face is ghostly white as he says, "What are you saying, Tom?"

I decide it's just easier to tell him fast. "One of the babies. Was born . . ."

"Yeah?" He's off the couch, standing beside me with an angry look in his eyes.

"Was stillborn."

"Yeah?"

"And I don't know what they did with it. What if it's also buried out in the pasture?"

Meyer paces back and forth, tearing at his hair. "Okay, so she calls and tells you the baby is stillborn. That's her side of the business. Without giving me any details, and hopefully there are no details, what else did she say?"

I turn back from the window, pulling on the hair at my collar.

"Take your time," says Meyer, plopping into my navy leather Eames chair.

"She didn't give me any details about the baby. She talked about needing to push back the date that we delivered Sid Ackerman's baby."

"That *she* delivered the baby."

Meyer is back on his feet. "We've got to separate her responsibilities from yours." He starts ticking off Savannah's responsibilities on the fingers of one hand. "She was responsible for the young women, birthing the babies, for maintaining the clinic, managing her staff, obtaining the documents, and you supplied names. That's all you did." He holds up one finger on the other hand. "Supplied names and contact info of couples who couldn't get pregnant. You had tried to solve their problem, physically it couldn't be done, so you passed them along to Savannah. Minimal involvement."

"But, morally speaking, shouldn't I have been concerned about a dead baby?" I put my arms out, palms up, imploring him to answer me.

Meyer pulls his pants up and looks up at me. "Morally, smorally. We're talking legally."

I take another look out the window and wonder if I'm high enough to ensure that I die if I jump.

85

SAVANNAH

Following yourself in the news is a strange pastime. Even though I am locked up in prison, there's a little thrill that comes from seeing your photo on the front page of *The Times* or as the first story on the six o'clock news. Tom has been very generous with the number of photos of me on our various vacations that he has shared with the media. No one knows that I spend most of my time at the farm, either in scrubs or jeans. No, there are photos of me in a red bikini—which made the cover of *The Post* and *The Daily News*—in a black Dior sheath dress, traveling in Gucci, lunching in Versace. I always look stunning. I always look rich. I'm sure his lawyer is responsible for the gallery of photos and the branding. Tom always preferred me in Levi's and my University of Atlanta sweatshirt.

They're obviously positioning me as carefree and material-istic. Making millions so that I can live a life of island-hopping luxury. But really, who have I hurt? The girls who got knocked up and couldn't wait to get rid of their babies? I gave them a new start in life, a second chance. I even gave them a little nest egg to get started. Or, the rich couples, drowning in their money, praying for a baby? I gave these rich snobs a family.

That's what I did. Where's the harm in what I've done? Sure, sure, I got a little greedy. Not even greedy so much, but I wanted to see how far they would go. There was power in pushing the limits. Still, everyone walked away with what they wanted.

I actually worry now what will become of the babies. Is the government going to yank them out of their families and put them in foster care? The thought of it makes me cringe. I really hope they are left where they are in families who have the means to provide for them.

The only real crime I've committed in my own eyes is killing Jed. Not that he didn't deserve it. We're going to say it was self-defense and that's no lie. Under Georgia's *Stand Your Ground* law you can use deadly force if you're threatened on your own property. He was trying to blackmail me, and his being on my property threatened me. And he had Kelly tied up. I had to save her. I didn't see any other way out. In hindsight, I should have shot him and called the police and pleaded self-defense right away, but I didn't want to invite the cops to come sniffing around the farm.

Jon Wade has taken my case. I knew he would. He loves the limelight. I would say that I'm number one with the press, Goldie is number two, and Jon has been able to make himself number three. The press loves a bombshell—me—they love a baby—Goldie—and they love the tall, handsome lawyer in the tight four-thousand-dollar suit who has stepped in—pro bono—to defend the bombshell. The reporters live for stories like this. Tom's lawyer has somehow been able to make Tom less glamorous. Less hedonistic. Less a part of my business as he calls it. Jon has not been pushing photos of Tom on the press either, probably because he'd rather push photos of himself. Oh well, as long as he gets me out of here, I don't care.

Hattie and Vadoma have both turned against me, which I thought would happen. Since I was the ringleader, their story is that they were just doing as they were told. Of course, in actuality, they were both free to leave whenever they wanted. I wasn't holding a gun to their heads. Vadoma did leave—and she came back! Worst decision she ever made. Ha! We haven't been able to talk to each other, so I only know what my lawyer tells me. They haven't found Kelly yet, but they're still looking. I have a soft spot for Kelly, and I hope she is somewhere far away. South America or Morocco or South Africa. Somewhere she can hide.

Jon is coming in an hour. We only dated for a few months, but he had wanted more. I gave him up for Tom. When I think of Tom the bile in my stomach acts up. Why did he do this to me? To us? We could be lying on a beach right now, sipping mojitos, and holding hands. Instead, we have been arrested and are facing trial. It also makes me furious that he is under house arrest eating order-in sushi while I am here in a cinder block cell eating shit and watching my back in the shower.

Finally, the guard arrives to take me to the private room to meet with Jon. Some of the guards are as mean as hungry dogs but this guard, Flo, is mellow. She confided to me that she thought what I had been doing was not a bad thing. That maybe I should have charged less money but, all in all, nobody was hurt. I had thanked her for bothering to tell me what she thought and now we smile at each other like we have a secret.

She leaves me locked in a small brown room. Brown walls, brown carpet, fake brown wood table and chairs. The room feels like a grave. Like I am alive but dead and buried in this brown box. Jon arrives a few minutes later, and I can tell that something is wrong. He usually enters the room with a roguish smile and windswept blonde curls but today he comes in like a storm cloud.

"What's wrong?" I ask.

"They found the dead baby. Brought dogs out to the farm and sniffed him four feet deep. Savannah, I want you to be straight with me, how many bodies are buried on your property?" Jon's blue eyes show fear. Like he has just discovered that I routinely murdered people and buried them in the pasture.

I laughed. "Jon, baby, you are funny. Sit down. Let me explain," I say and wait for him to sit down.

He remains standing, glaring down at me.

"Okay, have it your way. The baby was stillborn. It happens. And that is the last body buried on my farm. Now, please sit down. You're making me nervous."

He reluctantly pulls out the chair across from me and drops down into it with a sigh. "Are you telling me the truth?"

"Yes."

He stares hard at me, trying to gauge if I am telling the truth. This is the first time he seems to not believe in me. I stare back at him with nothing to hide. He breathes in deep through his nose. "Okay. So, I called one of my sources at Ravens' shop, and she tells me that they are very close to bringing Kelly in. Is that good for us or bad?"

I smooth my hair and think about his question. "You know, Kelly is the reason I got into this business."

"What do you mean?"

"Well, I was working as a midwife at the local clinic and one night I go into my barn because I hear something and it's Kelly giving birth. She's fifteen years old and desperate to have the baby and not be late for supper. I help her birth the baby, and she asks me to take it and get rid of it. So, I call Tom and that's how this all started."

Jon closes his eyes and rubs them with his hand. I know that he is trying to figure out if this helps me or hurts me.

"They say she's with another girl and a baby. Who's that?" he asks.

"That would be Mackenzie. Had the baby at the farm and wouldn't give him up. I always asked the girls one last time if they wanted their baby and every other girl said no but Mackenzie, she said yes. And I'll tell you something else, it's

Kelly that seduced Calvin Banks, the clerk at the Department of Vital Records, who falsified all the birth certificates. I've never even been in the Department of Vital Records, and she recruited the girls. She was integral to the business."

Jon reaches for his leather satchel and takes out a pad of white paper and takes some notes. "So, after Kelly left who went to see Calvin?"

"I sent Hattie in."

"That's good. Will Kelly corroborate your account of her giving birth in the barn?"

I shrug. "It's the truth, and Kelly's not manipulative. She's young and she'll be scared. She owes me, though. Because of me, she got away from her abusive father, I took care of her problem, and she has more money than she could ever imagine."

"Why'd she leave?"

"She left when I shot Jed. She was dating Jed's brother, Lee, who, by the way, has been looking for his brother. Jed was the father of the stillborn baby or so he said. Jed didn't know that the baby had died, but it turned out that he suspected it. I didn't tell the girl that her baby had died. I just told her that we had given it to a family up north. I thought it was easier on her that way. By the time Kelly left, everything was going to shit. It had all become too much. Even for me." I look down at my nails that haven't been filed since I got here. Just cut really short. They don't even look like my hands. "I had decided to shut down the barn. The night that Tom stood me up I was going to tell him this was the end. That we were done with the business. But he had gone to the Feds before I could tell him I wanted out. If he had waited, well, we'd both have gotten out." I shake my head.

"I guess when Tom said he wanted out, he meant it. No going back now, so let's figure out how to portray Kelly's run," Jon says.

I feel defeated. My head feels too heavy for my neck. I'm a

fighter, but it seems that everyone is against me. It's funny how facts viewed from different perspectives look so different, but I guess if I think back to some of the things we've done it will look pretty bad. Like Kelly seducing Calvin. Yes, I sent her over there specifically to manipulate him but if he had been an honest, upstanding public servant would her seduction have failed? Everyone we worked with was complicit. I didn't hold a gun to anyone's head.

Except Jed, of course.

"Okay," I say to Jon. "How do we spin Kelly's escape?"

Jon puts his hair behind his ears. "Well, we start by never saying the word escape. We just say that she left the farm. It was time. She had worked with you for how many years?"

"Five."

"Five years and she felt it was time to move on. You are not responsible for why she left. They can ask her and they will."

"And she'll say I shot Jed. Although, he arrived that morning with Kelly. He had kidnapped her or she had gone to him, I don't know, but he used her to shield himself when we went in the barn. You might even say that I was defending her. He had his arm around her neck and it's a good thing I'm a damn good shot because I took off his head while he was holding onto her."

Jon sits and stares at me. "You are one interesting woman. When we had our little fling, I thought you were just a gorgeous nurse."

"Midwife."

"Right, whatever, but you are something else." He smiles at me with his shit-eating grin.

I can't help but smile back. "I do have many skills."

"I remember," he says as the guard tells us that our time is up.

86

ANABEL

We've been married for one month, and I wake up every morning thinking that I will get the call today. We decided to postpone our honeymoon so that we can stay in New York to be available to bring the girls home. Yesterday we went to Macy's and bought out the children's department. I chose mostly T-shirts, sweaters, jeans and leggings, but I couldn't resist throwing in a few sundresses and even one or two fancy dresses with smocking in pink and lavender. I'm not sure if Kayleigh will like them but Goldie isn't old enough to protest. I better put them on her fast before she is.

Dennis is at work, so to pass the time and not sit and stare at my phone, I go up to Kayleigh's room. We have the nursery set up and ready to go for Goldie, but we are still working on Kayleigh's room. We decided to put a daybed in the nursery just in case the girls feel more comfortable in the same room at the beginning. I have to keep pinching myself to make sure I'm not just dreaming. Soon, we will be a family of four. It just doesn't seem possible.

I open the package of the Little Mermaid sheets that I bought for her bed. The mattress is still wrapped in plastic, so I grab a pair of scissors from the toolbox that Dennis left up here so that he can hang the wooden sign that we bought that has Kayleigh spelled out in rainbow colors, and start to cut away the plastic.

Just as I finish slicing it down the middle, my phone rings. It's in my back pocket and I answer it eagerly when I see Ms. Alvarez's name.

"Hello."

"Hello, Anabel! I am calling with great news! You and Dennis have been approved as foster parents so the girls can come home with you. I'm so happy for you."

I am overcome with emotion and can't speak.

"Anabel?"

"I'm here," I croak, as the tears flow down my cheeks. "When can we come and pick them up?"

"This afternoon. At my office. Three o'clock."

"We'll be there. And, Ms. Alvarez? Thank you. Thank you for everything."

"You're welcome, Anabel. I can't wait to see you."

As soon as she hangs up, I call Dennis. He picks up on the first ring.

"We've been approved!" I yell into the phone. "We can pick them up today! At three o'clock."

Now it's his turn to cry. "Oh, Anabel. I'm so happy."

"Me, too! I can't believe this is really happening."

87

SAVANNAH

We are now in the second week of my trial. Each of us will be tried separately, and I have the honor of going first. I am accused of manslaughter, wire fraud, endangerment of minors, improper financial gain, and tax evasion. Everyone is being called to testify against me—Vadoma, Hattie, Tom, Kelly, who was finally picked up in San Diego last week—will each get an opportunity to blame everything on me. They even subpoenaed Lee Pineman to answer questions about his brother.

For the trial, Jon bought me two shapeless suits from Banana Republic, one black and one dark gray, and one man-tailored white shirt and one blue. He told me to pull my hair back in a messy bun and would only give me a Maybelline mascara and blush to do my makeup. As I look at myself in the mirror, I look dowdy for the first time in my life with tired eyes and lackluster skin. I guess that's how he wants me to look. I think sadly of my walk-in closet at the farm filled with chic dresses, designer trousers, silk blouses, and every conceivable type of shoe. Jon is making me wear loafers! Ugh! I'm sure they have all been confiscated, boxed, and labeled as evidence of my extravagance.

Tom will be on the stand today, and I can't wait to see that scheming bastard. What I wouldn't give for ten minutes alone with him—five minutes to yell and curse at him and then five minutes to hear why he did this to me, to us. I know already that he will not have the courage to look at me, but if he does, I am going to muster all the hate and anger I feel into my eyes and burn a hole in his face. I look at myself again in the mirror and thoughts of Tom betraying me have put a healthy glow in my cheeks. I unbutton another button of this hideous cotton shirt and steel myself for what is about to happen.

In the courtroom, as I predicted he would, Tom looks straight ahead at all times during his testimony, never looking at me sitting at the defendant's table. I suppress a chuckle when I realize that his lawyer has also dressed him in a hideous, off-the-rack navy suit. He talks at length about all my responsibilities and very little about his own. He makes it seem like the only thing he did was give me names and contact information for the couples who couldn't conceive a child of their own. He goes into extreme detail about the extensive work he did with each couple to help them conceive and how he only passed them along to me as a last resort.

On cross, Jon adds a few things to Tom's responsibilities, namely that he was the one who chose the couples we worked with based on their ability to pay us five hundred thousand dollars per child. He gets Tom to admit that he researched the couples and if he felt that they couldn't pay he didn't work with them. Jon grills him about setting up the reservations for the suite at the Erickson for me each time I came to New York and also about the vacations that the two of us took with the money we got from the couples. No matter that all of the trips were planned by me. Tom got on the plane with a first-class ticket and met me more than fifteen times.

Jon's last question is, "Is it true that you went to the FBI and gave them your partner Savannah Maas because you were afraid that you would be caught?"

"No, I finally realized that I wanted to do the right thing. I told Savannah I wanted to stop. She knew I wanted to stop."

Jon chuckles and repeats, "The right thing. You wanted to do the right thing. Is it true that because you gave the FBI Savannah Maas and the other women on trial that you will walk away with no jail time, free as a bird?"

I watch Tom's face fall. He pulls at the hair touching his collar. It looks like he's going to cry. He disgusts me. I can't believe that he used to turn me on. I look away as he says, "I have been granted immunity."

A wave of nausea washes over me, and I can't breathe.

88

TOM

As soon as I testified against Savannah, giving the prosecutor all he needed to make sure she did time, the house arrest was lifted. Meyer was able to convince Ravens not to revoke my immunity because I ran. I owe Meyer my life and will be forever grateful to him for fighting for me when I kept making it hard for him.

I'm thinking of going west, maybe to Montana or Idaho, to a town big enough to get lost in but small by New York City standards. Maybe work with my hands. The Feds took every cent that I earned from the black-market baby business, but I was also earning two million a year from the clinic, and I got to keep the money I saved from my earnings.

Several networks have approached me about selling my story, but I don't really have the interesting details about the farm, the clinic, the young women, or the babies. My story is really about my obsession with Savannah and, frankly, that is not a story I want to tell. Being obsessed with someone makes you weak and vulnerable and these are feelings that I never want to feel again. Netflix offered me two million to tell my side but I'm not proud of what we did and I'm also not desperate for money, so I told them no.

Even though I have been ordered to stay in New York until all of the trials end, I have already met with a real estate agent. She'll take care of selling my apartment when I leave. All the furniture is staying. The beautiful leather sofas. The antique glass tables. The artwork. It all reminds me of her. Savannah picked most of it out and it all needs to go.

There's only one thing that I really want to do before I go to the airport and pick a place to fly to. I want to talk to Anabel Leigh. I had Meyer do a little investigating for me. He learned that Anabel is fostering the two girls. I need to talk to her about them before I leave.

I just have to figure out how to do it.

89

SAVANNAH

It's so nice doing business with people in high places. After I was sentenced to twenty years for my combined crimes, Jon Wade met with Sid Ackerman, out of the public eye and after-hours, and in exchange for never uttering his name, my sentence was reduced from twenty years to two with a promise of parole in eight months. Of course, it will be a surprise to everyone following the trial, when I walk out of prison in eight months. Jon's working on them to count the month I've already served toward the eight.

There are other surprises that only I know about. There are two trunks of cash stored beneath the large, immovable ultrasound machine that I had installed five months ago. The one that was positioned in concrete in one of the examination rooms after I stored the cash under it. Waiting for me is approximately four million dollars. I also still own my house and the land it sits on because I inherited them. I didn't buy them with the money from the sale of the babies. However, I was told that the Feds took my furniture and personal items. My designer clothes, my jewelry, my artwork, the equipment in the clinic. Oh well, easy come, easy go.

I'll do eight months in the country club of prisons in Westchester, courtesy of Ackerman, who is scared shitless that it will come out that he was one of my clients. If Martha Stewart can do five months, I can do eight. I'm younger.

I'm being transferred tomorrow. Turns out that Kelly, Vadoma, and Hattie have no interest in calling me as a witness in their cases. They know me too well. They weren't there for me, and now I'll be damned if I'm going to be there for them. Let them all rot. None of them have the balls to help themselves. Truth be told, I was hoping that Kelly would reach out to me through her lawyer. Kelly is like the little sister that I never had. Her betrayal is the only one that stings. Don't know why. Bitch ran out on me after I saved her ass, but whatever, I'm moving on.

Once I'm out of here, I am moving permanently to Seychelles. I will spend my days on the beach. Maybe open a little café. The judge ordered me to spend my time in prison thinking about what I did, to feel remorse. But see, here's the deal, I'm not sorry, even a little bit, for what I've done. I helped lots of girls out of a tight spot, and I've given the chance of a good life to their babies. If there was any moment that I would have hoped worked out differently it was the night that Caroline's baby died. It's the only baby we lost.

Some would ask if I am sorry for shooting Jed in the face. I would laugh. If he came back to life, I would shoot him again. How dare he try to blackmail me? Seriously, who did he think he was?

As for Tom, he turned out to be a weak, scared little man who I can't believe I ever wanted. What woman wants a man who can't live up to her expectations? Who is so much weaker than her? I don't know if I will ever fall in love again, because I did love him, but if I do, I want a man who is my equal. Frankly, Tom is not that man.

So now, I have eight months, or seven if Jon can do his

magic, to figure out what I want to do with the rest of my life. I'll be thirty-five, beautiful and rich when I get out. A whole life ahead of me. The only thing I know I won't be doing is birthing babies. No, I have birthed my last baby. Let someone else feel the power of bringing life into this world.

90

ANABEL

I'm still basking in the glow of being a mom when I wake up. Getting Goldie was a dream come true, but there are no words for having both Goldie and Kayleigh. It makes my heart melt that they are together. Two little girls who lost their mother but whose story kept them with each other. It is the plot of a Shakespearean story. And Dennis is so happy. It's too much. I get out of bed, stretch and pad down to the kitchen for a cup of coffee.

There on the table sits *The New York Times*. I glance over and the words leap out at me. I literally can feel them land on my chest and I have to take a step backward. Picking up the paper, I feel my hands shaking as I sit down. The headline is in all caps across six columns. The entire front page, above the fold screams: *Merry Midwife Gets Twenty Years*.

For playing God, moving children around like they're a commodity, forging birth certificates, killing that guy, making millions of tax-free dollars, Savannah Maas gets twenty years. I don't know how I feel about the sentence. Somehow, I feel safer with her in prison than roaming free.

Her lawyer is quoted as saying that, "Savannah Maas was justified in using deadly force against Jed Pineman when she reasonably believed that such force was necessary to defend herself and one of her staff members against his imminent use of unlawful force against her while on her property." He went on to talk at length about the *Stand Your Ground* law, how Jed had threatened her outside her barn, on her land, which justified her shooting him in the head.

I scan the rest of the article, stopping to read a paragraph way down in the story that says that all the children would stay in their adoptive homes pending a full background check and home study of the families who had adopted them. No charges were likely to be brought against the adoptive parents.

It had taken the jury just three hours to agree to drop the manslaughter charges. The time she was doing was really for wire fraud and having the payments sent to offshore bank accounts. The Feds don't like it when you get money without paying your taxes and fees.

It had already been reported earlier in the week that Thomas Moore was granted full immunity for his role in securing the families because he had reached out to the FBI when his conscience couldn't take it anymore.

What had Thomas Moore wanted to tell me? Like a hamster running in a wheel, my mind just keeps going over and over him telling me to meet him in the park. Why was talking to me important to him? He obviously wanted to tell me something, or he wouldn't have told me to meet him. I think about going over to his apartment building and asking the doorman to announce me, but I know that I can't do that without talking it over with Dennis. Should I risk having a fight with Dennis? Maybe. I know my relationship with Dennis is more important than hearing whatever it is that Tom wants to tell me, but my curiosity keeps my mind whirring. What if there is something I need to know about Goldie and Kayleigh? I consider approaching Dennis about going over to Moore's apartment.

Coffee. I need coffee to settle my nerves. Dennis has left a pot of coffee for me, and I pour a cup and go back to the newspaper. The trials for the other women will start on Monday and run concurrently. The young one, Kelly Parker, has the most charges against her because it was her job to recruit the young pregnant women and she was the one who seduced the clerk at the Department of Vital Records and had him forge all the birth certificates. I look at her face in the photo and she looks so young. I shake my head and decide to go upstairs to get dressed.

I know that the girls will be up any minute, so I take a five-minute shower and throw on a sundress. Gone are the days of pondering what I should wear and trying new ways to curl my hair. Dennis and I have agreed that I will stay with the girls for the next year and then we will decide if I should go back to work or not. If I had to decide today there is literally nothing that would make me leave Goldie and Kayleigh. Being with them and Dennis is the best thing that has ever happened to me.

I've brushed only half of my hair when I hear their voices. I drop the brush on the counter and rush out of my room and down the hall. Goldie is standing in her crib, and Kayleigh is doing forward rolls to amuse her. With every roll they both crack up.

"Look, Baby, look!" Kayleigh calls out before she tumbles over. I make a mental note to ask her if she wants to take gymnastics at the Y.

"Good morning!" I say. "Wow! That's amazing, Kayleigh!"

"Baby likes it," she says with a smile.

I pick up Goldie and give her a kiss. "Soon, you'll be tumbling, too," I tell her. "Let's go get some breakfast. Let's go down to the kitchen."

"I'm hungry," says Kayleigh and heads out of the room and down the stairs.

"Nana," says Goldie.

"You want a banana?"

"Nana," she says nodding.

When we get down to the kitchen Kayleigh already has two bowls, two spoons, the Cheerios, and two bananas on the table.

"Look at this," I say, putting Goldie in her highchair. "What a good girl. Getting everything out for breakfast. I'm going to have some too, though, so we need three bowls."

"Oh, I'm sorry. I didn't know. Vadoma didn't like Cheerios."

"Well, I love them!" I say, going to the cupboard to get another bowl.

"Tell me when to stop pouring, Baby," says Kayleigh, as she pours the cereal into Goldie's bowl.

"Stop," says Goldie.

"Kayleigh, you should call your sister Goldie now. That's her name."

Kayleigh sits down and looks down at her hands and her little mouth turns down in a frown. I think my heart is going to break.

Finally, she looks up at me and says, "It's just at the farm I wasn't allowed to give her a name. I was only allowed to call her Baby."

"Why was that? Do you know?"

"Savannah told me that if we gave her a name she would belong to us, and she didn't want Baby to belong to us."

Tears gush from my eyes as I look at Kayleigh. "Well, you know what? You and Goldie both belong here with me and Daddy. This is your home now, you and Goldie. You belong to us, and we belong to you and Goldie, and that's forever. We are your mom and dad now and we'll always be together. Okay?"

Her voice is muffled from crying, but I hear a soft, "Okay."

"I'd like you to call me Mom. Can you do that?" I ask.

"Okay. I'll try to remember," she says.

"Kayleigh?"

She looks up at me like she might be getting in trouble. "Yes?"

"I'm glad you're here," I tell her with a big grin.

She grins back. "I'm glad I'm here, and I'm glad Goldie's here, too."

Goldie laughs when she hears her name, and we all look at each other and smile.

91

TOM

Writing a letter is sometimes easier than telling someone what you want them to know, therefore, I have been writing Anabel Leigh a letter for two days now. After every draft that I delete from my laptop I tell myself to go get my duffel bag, that is already packed, and head to the airport, but ten minutes later I am back at it.

What do I want her to know? And why do I want her to know it? To establish a connection with her? I haven't had time to analyze how I feel but here goes another draft:

Dear Anabel,

By the time you read this letter, I will be gone. I'm not sure where I'm going but probably somewhere out west.

My lawyer did some investigating for me, and I know that you and your husband are in the process of adopting the two girls. There is something I want you to know about them. They are my nieces. My younger sister, Debbie, was their mother. I do not know who their father was or if they have the same father. Debbie was a drug addict and died a year after the younger one was born. She was thirty-two years old. Savannah didn't know that I knew that Debbie was their mother. Debbie called me and told me right before she died from an overdose of heroin.

It is my biggest regret in this whole mess that I didn't take care of the girls. I knew that Savannah had trouble placing them when they were infants and that leaving the younger one in your lap in the park was a desperate act to find her a home. Savannah knew that she would be adopted in New York and she was right. It must have been an act of God that Vadoma put her in your arms that day. He must have known that you wanted her.

I was especially happy to learn that you have opened your heart and your home to both of them. I will forever be grateful to you and your husband. Thank you for raising them and loving them.

I am wondering if, in the future, you might find it in your heart to share a photo of them once in a while with me. I will completely understand if you don't want to have anything to do with me, but now that this is all over I long for some kind of connection to them. My parents, their grandparents, are gone and Debbie is gone. I do have a brother, Chad, but I haven't seen him in years, so they are the only family I have left.

Since there is no record of their births, I would like to let you know that the older one was born on November 5, 2021 and the younger one on July 24, 2024.

When I am settled, I will send you my cell phone number and you can decide if you want to share a photo or any news of them with me. I will understand whatever decision you make, and I will never make a problem for you or them in any way.

If you ever have any questions about my family, my sister, my parents, our medical history, or our heritage, please let me know.

Again, I wish that I had done more, done anything, to help the girls. Thank you.

Sincerely,
Thomas Moore

I am crying so hard that I can't even type my name. This will be the letter I give to Anabel. I will hand deliver it to her home late at night, and she will get it the next day when I am thirty thousand miles in the air headed to a state currently unknown although Montana keeps coming to my mind.

Hitting print, I go and retrieve the hard copy of the letter and sign my name. I should probably have Meyer read it over, but I don't care. Savannah's trial is over, and I was happy to see she got twenty years. I just hope she doesn't come looking for me, but I am going to be very hard to find. I'll make sure of it.

92

ANABEL

I wake up to the sound of the girls giggling down the hall. I can tell by Goldie's belly laughs that Kayleigh is engaging in some shenanigans that is cracking her little sister up. What a sweet sound—little girls laughing. I turn my head to see if Dennis is awake, and he is turned on his side staring at me.

"What?" I laugh when I see his smile.

"Nothing. Just the way you wake up with a smile on your face now that the girls are ours."

Yesterday we had all gone to the lawyer's office and signed the official adoption papers and afterward we went out for ice cream. Both girls had been allowed to choose two different flavors and get two large scoops with any color sprinkles they wanted. The waitress had taken our photo—our first official photo as a family.

"Let's make pancakes with chocolate chips," I say.

"We are going to have very fat children if you keep feeding them this way," Dennis tickles me and I giggle.

"I know, I just want to spoil them a little bit."

"Okay, peas and carrots for dinner."

I make a face and head into the bathroom to get ready to go and get the girls. As I think about making the pancakes my stomach starts to protest. I suddenly feel nauseous. My stomach had also been upset yesterday morning on the way to the lawyer but I wrote it off as excitement. It's probably nothing, but as I flip my head over to collect my hair and put it back in a ponytail to wash my face, I gag.

I couldn't be. Could I? I pull out the neck of my T-shirt and look down at my breasts. Were they always that full? Oh my God! I stoop down and rummage around until I find the brown bag with the tests that I bought just in case. I go through the familiar ritual.

While I wait for the results, I think back to reading Tom's letter yesterday. I'm so glad he sent it for a number of reasons. One, I can stop wondering why he was so eager to talk to me. Two, we now know the girls' real birthdays and exactly how old they are. And three, we know that no one is going to come and try to take them away from us. I don't know how I feel about Tom. They are his flesh and blood, and he did nothing to help them. How does someone do that? But I haven't completely ruled out sending him a photo once in a while. We'll see.

Snapping back from my reverie, I pick up the wand. Positive. I cannot believe it! I stare at myself in the mirror and a smile so wide that it hurts my cheeks shines back at me.

I wrap the wand in a towel and bring it downstairs where Dennis and the girls are stirring pancake batter. Each girl is standing on a kitchen chair on either side of Dennis and already there is batter on each girl's face and Dennis's cheek.

I leave the towel by Dennis's place at the table and walk over to the group. "I'll take over stirring," I say to Dennis. "Go look in that towel," I say pointing to the table.

Dennis gives me a quizzical look but goes over and unwraps the wand. We've taken a lot of these tests, so he knows immediately that it is positive. He stands there and tears come to his eyes making me tear up.

He comes over and joins the group putting his arms around me from behind and giving me a squeeze.

"I love you," he whispers in my ear.

"I love you, too," I say.

"Love you," says Goldie in her tiny baby voice.

"I love you," says Kayleigh.

Sometimes dreams do come true.

EPILOGUE

Power. Everyone thinks they want it, but few of us would know what to do with it once we had it. Sid Ackerman has power and uses it to protect himself and his family. After the trials of all the Merry Midwives, he used his influence over the judges and the women involved to make sure that the story died a quick death.

Even though Kelly, Vadoma, and Hattie had no idea who Sid Ackerman was, he negotiated lighter sentences on the condition that they agree to never sell their stories. Through their individual lawyers, he had them sign away their rights to talk about the farm, Savannah, Tom, the young mothers, the babies, or the families who received the babies. If they did, he could sue them. All of the judges trying the cases owed him favors, and he called them in to make sure that the women were given short sentences and encouraged to leave the state of New York.

The pattern established with Savannah was followed for each woman. Each was convicted of multiple crimes for which they were given twenty years, which was reduced to two years after the story ran in the news. Then, they were all paroled after eight months. Only Savannah's lawyer was able to knock it down to seven months.

So, where are they all five years later?

Hattie married her parole officer and is pregnant with her second child.

Vadoma moved back to Florida where she waits tables for minimum wage and tips. She thinks about Kayleigh every day and wonders if the girl misses her.

Tom moved to Bozeman, Montana and works for the Indian Health Service as an obstetrician. There are very few fertility problems on the reservation, and he enjoys birthing babies and having them go home with their rightful mothers. His first purchase at the airport upon arrival was a leather cowboy hat.

A year after he settles in, he sends Anabel a card telling her he is in Montana and gives her his phone number if she is interested in sharing a photo of the girls.

A week later, he receives the most beautiful photo of Goldie and Kayleigh at the Central Park Zoo watching the penguins play. Anabel tells him that she and Dennis have agreed to send him one picture a year. He responds with the prayer hands emoji.

Savannah sells the farm in Dubois, Georgia and moves to Seychelles where she marries a fisherman and has two gorgeous babies. When *The New York Times* first nicknamed her the Merry Midwife she laughed, but now that is exactly what she is at the island's free clinic.

Kelly studies for and passes the exam for her GED while in prison. When she's released, her first call is to Mackenzie who has been living and working in San Diego and waiting for Kelly to come back.

When Kelly realized that she was the focus of a national woman hunt, she left the apartment she was sharing with Mackenzie and traveled up to Seattle where she was finally caught trying to cross into Canada. The Feds raided their apartment and took all of her money, but she can't wait to get back to California, get a job, and start college. She plans to become a midwife. She feels that she never did anyone any harm, except maybe poor Calvin who lost his job for falsifying all the birth certificates, and she wants to help women give birth to healthy babies. Legally.

ACKNOWLEDGMENTS AND AUTHOR'S NOTE

I have always explored themes of family, motherhood, choice, and caregiving in my writing. One related topic that I have not written about before is miscarriage. Having suffered four miscarriages, I wanted to write about that experience through fiction. While I was thinking of a new storyline for my new book, I was also watching the documentary *Taken at Birth* about Dr. Thomas Hicks, an obstetrician, who birthed the babies of young girls and sold them to couples who wanted to adopt. Out of my own experience with miscarriage and Dr. Hick's story I created my two main characters.

After the fun work of creating the story, the characters, and writing the book comes the hard work of publishing it. The writing itself is a solitary pursuit. Authors spend hours and hours alone with their characters. Feeling our character's emotions sometimes makes us feel like we have multiple personalities! But, at some point we ask others for help. These are the people who helped me bring Anabel and Savannah to life.

First, I want to thank my beta readers. Lois, my best friend since second grade and my biggest supporter; Jane who always offers the best advice on character development; Laurie for her encouragement and feedback; and Mary for her wise comments. Also, thank you to my first blurb readers Lisa, April and Liz.

I owe a huge debt of gratitude to Shawn, a retired FBI agent, for the fascinating discussions about the inner workings of the FBI. I knew nothing about FBI investigations and Shawn was kind enough to educate me about what the FBI really cares about (the money!).

A huge shout-out to the team at Acorn Publishing who provided invaluable guidance and feedback. Thank you to Holly, Jessica T., Jessica H. and Zala for holding my hand through the publishing process and pushing me to find the best title for the book. It only took us a month on the title alone! To my editor, Marci, who helped me fine tune the book, adding emotion to my characters, and weeding out inconsistencies. And, of course, the folks at Damonza for the wonderful cover.

I also want to thank Lisa, the owner of the Town Book Store, for her enthusiasm and support of my writing, for carrying my books in the store, and for hosting an event for me to celebrate publication. It was also a chance meeting with Barbara Mannino at the bookstore that gave me the final push I needed to actually move forward with publication. Thanks, Barbara, for inspiring me and being excited by my story.

Before I close, I want to say that I did take some liberties with the timeline of the trial but I felt it was in the best interest of the story.

And finally, a special thanks to my sons, William and Charles. William and I share an artistic spirit. He and I have spent many hours discussing the title, how best to convey emotion in writing and acting, storytelling, and creating art in general. And, although he is a tech guy, Charles has keen insights into marketing and how important the packaging, the blurb, and cover art is for sales. I don't want to brag, but I do have the best sons a mother could possibly wish for!!

Please check out my updated website, designed by Chris Cadalzo, and follow me on Facebook and Instagram. Thank you for taking your time to read my book!

ABOUT THE AUTHOR

Photo Credit: Susan Cook

Ann Ormsby earned a master's degree in journalism from NYU and has worked in marketing communications for nonprofit and government organizations. When she left full-time employment to raise her boys, she started writing short stories and novels that dig deep into family relationships. Her op-eds have appeared in the *New York Daily News*, *The Star-Ledger*, and *The Huffington Post*.

Invested in her small New Jersey town, Ann serves as co-vice president of the Westfield Service League, a nonprofit that raises money for local charities. As a bookseller at The Town Book Store, she loves helping people find their next good read.

Secrets of the Midwife is her third novel.

Visit Ann online at:
annormsby.com

instagram.com/annormsby
facebook.com/ann.ormsby.1

ALSO BY ANN ORMSBY

The Recovery Room

Living in the Rain